I0676024

FORTS:
FATHERS & SONS

Steven Novak

First published in the United States of America by Parallel Worlds. An Imprint of Canonbridge LLC, 409 Main Street, Silver City, Iowa 5157

Subsequent publishing in the United States of America by Quiet Corner Press in cooperation with The Literary Underground, Yucaipa, California 92399. www.litunderground.com

Cover design and interior illustrations by Steven Novak

www.novakillustration.com

ISBN: 0615466826
ISBN-13: 978-0615466828 (Quiet Corner Press)

FOR MY WIFE, MY MOTHER AND MY BROTHER

There are none more important.

ACKNOWLEDGMENTS

First and foremost I want to thank my family and friends for standing by me through the highs, lows and then more of the lows. With them I'm more than I ever thought myself capable. Without them I'm nothing.

I also want to thank my friends at The Literary Underground who helped me turn the bucket of lemons that was tossed into our lap into an absolutely massive vat of lemonade.

Lastly to each and every single person who plunked down their hard earned money to hold this book in their hands, we're pals now, you and I. If I see you on the street I'm giving you an awkward high five. If you call me on the weekend I won't even use the caller ID to screen it – most of the time. Hopefully right about now you aren't having buyer's remorse.

-Steven

1. STRANGERS IN A STRANGE LAND

A thousand years of peace had come to an abrupt and violent end. Off in the distance, trees that had stood eons longer than there have been inhabitants in this quiet, peaceful world collapsed to the ground. The thunderous boom resulting from the massive structures meeting their untimely demise echoed throughout the red forest. The creatures that called this very old, very simple place home felt tremors for miles in every direction. In response to the commotion, frightened groups of these thin, pale-skinned beings took to the treetops, hoping to learn the cause of the disturbance. Making use of limbs longer than the whole of their bodies, they scurried up the sides of the massive growths. One by one large, egg-shaped heads containing grotesquely large eyes parted the densely covered foliage, breaking the crest of the afternoon sky. Like a flock of birds, their heads moved in silent unison, focusing on the ruckus in the distance. Less than a mile away, patches of trees toppled to the ground as great plumes of

1

dust and smoke rose toward the sky to take their place. The monstrous wall of debris began to spread across the forest, blocking out the light of the three sister suns.

For the very first time in its history, this place was slowly being enveloped by a darkness brought on, not by night, but something else entirely - something evil, angry, and aggressive – something that would change it forever.

Overcome with fear, most of the tiny creatures rapidly left their lofty perches, turned tail and scurried away in the opposite direction as quickly as their spindly legs would carry them. They saw what they had needed to see; it was instinct now that compelled the flock to get as far away from the situation as possible. An extraordinarily inquisitive, meek looking creature, however, ignored his primal instincts, choosing instead to do the exact opposite. While the others fled, this tiny thing moved toward the inconceivable force tearing its home to pieces. Sliding down the treetop, the awkward, lanky little creature headed toward the massive dirt cloud with curious caution. Within a matter of minutes, the wall of debris swallowed it completely. In the belly of the great dusty beast, sight beyond a few feet suddenly became impossible, forcing the little creature to rely on its oversized ears to guide it. With every step forward, the volume of the brutality rose significantly. With every step forward, the heart hidden behind the hollow bones in its chest beat faster - the thumping making its way upward into the creature's head, pressing painfully against the folds of brain tucked safely inside its skull.

Through the haze of dust particles came something resembling a voice. Still too far off for the little creature to fully understand, it continued to stumble forward into the smoky abyss while listening carefully.

During a brief lull between the splintering of wood and the banishment of history, the tiny creature heard the voice once again.

This time it was deeper, louder, carrying with it a frighteningly stern seriousness, "Put your backs into it, you mutts! The area needs to be cleared by nightfall!"

With each step forward, the once-thick cloud of dirt began to clear; fuzzy images slowly twisted into focus. For a brief moment the terrified creature halted his forward progress in order to fully consider the logic behind its actions. Despite its choices to this point, this tiny being was not stupid. The feeling of danger coursing through its body was undeniable, thick and palpable, and very real. Since it was a child, the little thing had been much too inquisitive for its own good. A large portion of its youth was spent going to places and doing things that it had been repeatedly instructed not to do. Its parents had warned it on more than one occasion that curiosity would one day get it in trouble. It seems that on this point they were painfully correct.

Taking a deep breath in order to muster a bit of courage and just barely managing to halt the shaking of its thin hands, the creature made the decision to resume its journey toward the disaster area, now a little less than fifty or sixty feet away. When at last the debris cloud dissipated, the tiny, inquisitive thing realized for the first time that it should have heeded the warnings of its parents. A massive area where a lush, thriving forest once stood in beautiful elegance for generations had been almost obliterated. Thick trees covered in grayish-brown bark, once reaching proudly into the sky, lay scattered haphazardly across the forest floor. Upright walking, green-skinned, monsters adorned in layer upon layer of heavy coal black armor strolled defiantly among the wreckage surveying their progress, while others seated upon great snarling four-legged beasts continued the task of tearing down yet more ancient trees.

For the little creature, the sight was so unreal and resembled something plucked directly from a nightmare.

Every centimeter of its wiry body quivered with uncontrollable fear. The little creature slowly backed away from the madness, filling the full of its vision. It wanted to be somewhere else. It wanted to be anywhere but here. It wanted to run and continue running until its feet were covered in sores and it could run no more. In this single moment the tiny creature understood all too well that it should never had come to this place. It should have fled with the others. It should have sprinted home to its parents and curled up into the safety of their arms. Indeed, this was a sight the tiny thing would not soon forget. Some things, having been seen, could never be unseen.

The terrified creature's backward movement came to an abrupt stop when it bumped into something large, was grasped tightly around the neck and lifted into the air. Now firmly in the clutches of a hulking armored figure, the creature began to flail its limbs wildly, searching for any possible means of escape, but finding none. The massive bodied, green skinned monster drew the squirming, wailing body of the pathetic little thing to within inches of his face, quizzically taking in its comically overstated features.

"Disgusting," the monster muttered more to itself than to anyone in particular.

The dark eyes of the muscled figure focused coldly on those of the meek, squirming thing being tossed back and forth between its gloved fingers, "I am your new master, little one. Your home is now my home. Your family is now my family. Your food is my food. Most important of all, your life is now my life. Do you understand what I'm saying? Are you even capable of processing ideas such as these with your tiny brain?"

The grip around the skinny creature's throat was slowly draining the life from its body. Its long limbs hung low and loose, flapping back and forth in the breeze created by the collapsing forest. With its throat crushed, it was unable to form anything resembling a word; the meek thing instead mumbled a sad, breathy, completely unrecognizable response; while tears streamed down the curves of its face.

"What a pity. You're hardly worth the strength it will take to strangle you," the green-skinned monster remarked, a slight chuckle in his deep voice.

As the thick cloud of dirt continued its ascent into the once crystal-clear mid-day sky, the sound of the collapsing trees drowned out the final pained cry of the little creature.

A thousand years of peace had been brought to a conclusion in a matter of minutes.

As had been the case since the dawn of time itself, the end of one story heralded the beginning of another.

2. WEIRD LITTLE TOMMY JARVIS

The playground was quiet. Empty chain swings softly swayed back and forth in the summer breeze as the sun began its slow descent over a row of houses off in the distance. On his way home from an hour-long detention after school, Tommy Jarvis kicked at the sporadic patches of grass sticking through the concrete of the sidewalk beneath his feet. For the third time in as many weeks he had not turned in his homework on time. This was becoming a consistent problem with Tommy, so much so that his math teacher, Mrs. Hickenbottom, had decided that it warranted sixty minutes of quiet time at the end of the day. It made Tommy miss the bus home. Missing the bus meant that he would have to walk. Walking home was a solid six miles of exercise. Most would consider this a fairly annoying situation. Quite surprisingly, Tommy Jarvis was not all that upset.

In fact, the strange, sour-faced little boy was in no rush to get home.

In many ways, the monotonous drowning silence that accompanied the act of laying his head down on the desk for an hour provided a welcome break from the norm. The lack of students resulted in endless empty hallways leading to emptier rooms filled with vacant, cold desks. The school was quiet, and quiet was a luxury that Tommy had not experienced in quite some time.

He had almost forgotten just how wonderful quiet could really be.

Passing by the Johnson's house, Tommy pulled his heavy backpack off his right shoulder and moved it to the left. The right was sore. It was time to make the left do a little work. Ideally he would have preferred to strap the heavy sack over both shoulders and let the weight distribute itself evenly across his back. The problem with this was that one of the straps was broken. As was generally the case with all things in his life, Tommy never once whined, moaned or complained about the one-strapped bag situation. For him, one strap would always do just fine. One strap was more than enough to make do, and when that one strap eventually snapped due to the incredible amount of stress it was now forced to bear, he would use the tiny loop attached to the top of the bag to lug it around school.

After all, what was the use of complaining about the strap on a backpack?

Tommy Jarvis had more important things to worry about. A broken backpack was small potatoes. It was smaller than small potatoes and maybe even smaller than small tomatoes. It was tinier than the tiniest of teeny-tiny – which was pretty teensy-tiny.

Past the Wilson's house, then the Peterson's and over the chain link fence, Tommy strolled through old Mr. McGregor's backyard. He went around the drugstore on the corner of Jefferson and Hollowood Road and walked past the office of the weird old dentist whose name he could not remember. He was making good time. Sure, his shoulders and lower back were sore and burning, and the switching of his backpack from shoulder to shoulder was coming at much quicker intervals, but he was making good time. In fact, he was making such good time that he decided to slow down a bit. What was the point in making good time when your destination was somewhere you ultimately did not want to be?

"Hey, Tommy!" The voice came from somewhere behind him, off in the distance. Tommy recognized it in an instant. Low, yet strangely high pitched at the same time, laced with a decided undertone of smarminess, it had to be him. "Hey! Weirdo! I'm talking to you, freak!" Donald Rondage - it had to be Donald Rondage.

Tommy lowered his head, dug his chin into his chest, and walked as fast as his already tired legs could manage.

"Where do you think you're going, weirdo!?"

Despite the fact that Tommy was nearly running, Donald Rondage must have been moving faster. His voice was rapidly getting closer and louder.

A moment later Donald stopped directly in front of Tommy, the tires of his bike skidding across the sidewalk, leaving black streaks along the top of the cement, "I said...where do you think you're going, weirdo?"

Tommy turned to run in the opposite direction but three more bicycles skidded into his path. Perched atop each of them sat a member of Donald's goon squad, everyone the caricature of a lumbering, mindless oaf. Each burly boy looked a good deal older than his actual thirteen or fourteen years. Tommy was caught, blocked in on both sides by walls of mean, nasty, sweaty, pimply-faced youth.

Donald's voice rose from behind once again, "What'cha gonna do now, weirdo? Got nowhere to run, do ya?"

Tommy took a deep breath, lowered his head, and looked toward the ground. He knew he could not fight them. Not only was he outnumbered, he was outsized as well. Fighting back would only make things worse – would only make them madder. Fighting back would serve only to stretch out his suffering.

He heard Donald's bicycle drop to the ground and a pair of knuckles crack. "Answer me, loser!"

Two hands shoved him in the back, sending him toppling forward into the row of bikes. Three more pair of hands pushed him in the opposite direction. Tommy's backpack tumbled to the ground. His feet tripped over themselves which sent him spiraling toward the concrete. He landed with a heavy thud on his side.

"Next time I ask you where you're going, maybe you won't ignore me!" Donald roared as he towered above him.

The tip of the massive bully's foot collided with Tommy's stomach, forcing him to bend his legs. From behind, the foot of another goon crashed into his spine, while another cracked against his leg. In stereo, the four boys yelled expletives that would have prompted any of their parents to wash their mouths out with soap. Tommy closed his eyes tightly, trying his best to keep his breathing steady, absorbing each of their blows with a calmness that only someone who had been in this situation before could manage. No matter what they did - no matter how many times they did it - Tommy knew beyond a shadow of a doubt that they could not hurt him.

They were big and mean and remarkably strong for their age. In the grand scheme of things however, they were amateurs.

There was nothing they could do to him that he had not already felt a million times before.

By the time the kicking and shouting stopped, Donald Rondage was breathing heavily, giggling between deep breaths. One of his henchmen ripped open Tommy's backpack and dumped its contents on the ground. Loose papers caught the wind, floating away in all directions. In response, a roar of laughter rose from the group of boys as they exchanged high fives, low fives and the occasional knuckle bump above Tommy's fallen body, proud of what they had accomplished.

Donald leaned close to Tommy's face - so close that Tommy could feel the warmth of the boy's breath on his cheek as he spoke, "See you tomorrow, weirdo."

His words were less of a warning than a promise. It was a promise the oversized fourteen-year-old would certainly keep and a promise Tommy had all but learned to accept at this point in his young life. It was a promise so commonplace that it did not frighten him as it had years ago. This was his life now; it was the way things were, and the way they would continue to be.

When something has become commonplace, commonplace is no longer frightening.

As quickly as they had arrived, Donald and his goons were gone. The world was quiet again. A soft breeze caused the loose papers to dance across the ground. Gritting his teeth, Tommy forced himself to stand despite the painful welts that were already forming on his legs. He gathered his scattered homework and stuffed the papers into his backpack. As he started to toss the sack over his right shoulder he noticed that the one functional strap was torn, rendering it useless. He stared at it for a moment, allowing himself to fully absorb the stinging pockets of pain sprouting up on various parts of his body like the glow of lightning bugs against a pitch black night.

Across the street, an old woman with widen eyes watched him through a crack in the vertical blinds on her bay window. Tommy recognized the look on her face instantly – pity mixed with confusion. He had seen this expression before. The moment she noticed him gazing back at her, she retreated into the shadows of her house, the blinds swinging back and forth in her wake. Tommy grabbed the little strap on the top of his backpack and resumed his walk home. His pace was slow and plodding, not only because of the stinging pain in his legs, but because he still was not in any sort of hurry.

Often times when one has nowhere to go, one finds themselves in no hurry to get there.

3. CARING LITTLE STACI ALEXANDER

While on her way to retrieve the day's mail, Staci Alexander noticed her neighbor Tommy Jarvis making his way across the street toward his house. His pants were dirty, his hair a ruffled mess. He attempted to hide his face by staring at the ground, but it was painfully obvious that it was red and bruised. This was not the first time she had seen Tommy this way and something inside told her that it would not likely be the last. Staci's family had lived next to the Jarvis' all of her life. She remembered how she and Tommy would jump through the sprinkler in her backyard while their parents sat on the patio, laughing and talking about things she did not understand. She and Tommy had been good friends in grade school. In fact, she would go so far as to say they had best friends. She had even let him hold her hand on the school bus one morning. At first it had seemed weird to hold a boy's hand. The weirdness, however, had slowly morphed into something indescribably pleasant, oddly warm and strangely sweet. Tommy had been different back then. He was so funny, always smiling and making her laugh with a stupid joke only the two of them ever fully understood. In the summer before middle school though, Tommy's mother had died, and with her death everything changed. When his smile disappeared, so did the jokes. He did not want to make her laugh anymore. Laughter became stupid. It felt like he did not even want to be around her. Tommy's face twisted into something unrecognizable – something dark and sad and lonely. Once after his mother's death, Staci had attempted to hold his hand. As quickly as she had extended it, he rejected the offer. Tommy had retreated into himself and in doing so he pushed everyone and everything away, including her.

"Hi, Tommy!" Staci cautiously called. She lifted her hand into the air, waving for him to see.

The boy stopped briefly, glancing toward her with his sad eyes. He said nothing and lowered his head while opening his front door.

Staci slowly dropped her arm. She could not help but feel sorry for both Tommy and his little brother. Sometimes, if she left her bedroom window open at night, she could hear yelling coming from their house. The yelling, the breaking and the screaming sometimes got too loud, forcing her to close the window again in order to fall asleep.

Every single time she closed the window she felt bad, like she was turning her back on Tommy. In the end though, Staci understood that there was nothing she could do, and even if there was, she was not entirely sure Tommy would want it.

Once inside the house, Staci dropped the mail on the kitchen counter before she walked upstairs into her mother's office. Janet

13

Alexander was on the phone with a client talking about loans, mortgages and other things which held no real interest for Staci. Plopping herself into a chair, she patiently waited, absent-mindedly thumbing through a book on a nearby bookshelf.

Her mother finished the conversation moments later, hung up the phone and turned to her daughter with a smile. "And what can I do for you today, lovely Miss Staci?"

"Nothing...just bored."

"How about the mail?"

"It's downstairs on the counter."

"What about your homework, all done?"

"Ya...I did not have much."

Staci kicked at the new hardwood floor in her mother's recently remodeled office, staring down with a faraway look on her face. This was not a look that Janet Alexander often saw from her daughter. "What's wrong baby? Everything alright?"

Staci thought about the question for a moment, attempting to formulate an appropriate response in her head, but failed. Though their lives had moved in vastly different directions over the last few years, the truth of the matter was that sometimes she still found herself daydreaming about Tommy.

To put it plainly, she often missed her friend.

With a deep sigh, Staci turned her head and gazed out of the office window; she glanced at Tommy's house but almost immediately looked away. Janet noticed the glance, instantly understanding exactly what weighed so heavily on her daughter's mind. Briefly her eyes wandered in the direction of her neighbor's home. It was no mystery to anyone in the neighborhood as to what was going on over there, though no one truly understood to what extent.

After Megan's death, Chris Jarvis had turned to drinking to help him make it through the day. More often than not, the drinking led to poor judgment. Poor judgment usually leads to bad things.

It was amazing what the bottle could do to an otherwise good man.

The awful things that Chris Jarvis put his sons through were just plain wrong. On more than one occasion, when the sounds coming from next door became almost too much to bear, Janet had found herself moments away from calling the police. Had it not been for a nearly twenty-year friendship and an understanding of how rough his wife's death must have been on Chris, she might have done just that.

Looking at her sweet, innocent little fourteen-year old daughter, with her light brown hair pulled back into a tight ponytail, and her sad green eyes, Janet felt compelled to rescue her in the way only a mother could. She wanted to make her forget about the Jarvis boys and fill her head with all the wonderful, non-threatening, non-adult things that she believed should stuff a little girl's head.

"Hey, I've got an idea. Your dad won't be home until late…so howzabout' the two of us going out to dinner? It'll be fun…you know, girls night out!"

Staci looked up and half-heartedly shrugged her shoulders.

"Come on Staci…tell you what, after dinner we'll go to that store you've been bugging me to take you to…do a little shopping!"

Staci glanced up again, this time with a little smile. Her mother's ploy had worked, at least momentarily. She was willing to forget about Tommy Jarvis and continue on with her life - mostly because she really did not have any other choice. Standing up, Staci rushed to her mother's side, wrapping her arms around her tightly. Dinner would be fun. They would laugh, talk and order something

15

she had never tasted before. They would go out afterward. New shoes, maybe a purse - her mother would get her anything she wanted. As Staci hugged her close, she could feel the heat of her mother's body against the side of her face. The feeling warmed her cheeks, traveled down into her chest and wrapped itself tightly around her heart. Her mother made her feel safe, secure, and loved. The very big heart of the very little girl that was Staci Alexander wished beyond all hope that the day would never come when she was forced to let go.

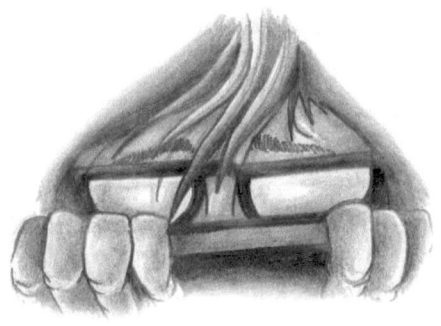

4. NOSEY LITTLE OWEN LITTLE

From the bay window, Owen Little watched intently as the situation in his neighbor's front yard played out like a scene from a television show. Donald Rondage, Nathan Gallagher and the Williams brothers had surrounded Tommy Jarvis. They were taking turns kicking him as he lay curled up on the sidewalk. Owen found it strange, watching this happen to someone. Part of him wanted to help, and yet another, more dominant part, was filled with the fear of what might happen if he did. The last thing he wanted was to end up writhing around on the ground in Tommy's place. By the time the foursome had stopped kicking and had spilled the contents of Tommy's backpack onto the grass, Owen had slid behind the couch, completely out of sight. Only the top of his head and his eyes, hidden behind his thick glasses, peeked out, as he tried to slow his breathing and keep his hands from shaking. Even from as far away as forty feet and behind a thick pane of glass, Donald Rondage looked enormous. He was huge, hulkish, and very scary.

17

In the sixth grade Donald had become the first kid to sprout something that resembled facial hair above his upper lip; ever since then the rest of the children had been terrified of him. How could you not fear a twelve-year-old with a mustache after all?

It was not until Donald and his thugs had left Tommy and headed down the street that Owen began to slowly relax.

"Owen, what the hell are you looking at?"

Owen's heart skipped a beat; spinning around like a top he hopped up from his hiding place behind the couch. His father was standing on the other side of the room with a confused, not to mention more than slightly annoyed, look on his face.

"Oh, um, hi Dad...nothing. I was not looking at anything. Just dropped something behind the table...and I was um, you know, looking for it."

Resting his hands on his hips, Mack Little stared into his son's eyes. It was painfully obvious that the boy was lying. He was shaking like a leaf on a breezy day and seemed moments away from having an asthma attack. He also noted that the table Owen claimed to be looking under sat on the opposite end of the living room, a good thirty feet from the spot where his son now stood jittery behind the couch.

"Then what are you doing behind the couch, Owen? Last I checked the table was over there."

A million responses danced around in Owen's brain, all moving toward his mouth as fast as they could, like a terrified crowd with the end of the world hot on their tail, "I um, I don't, um...it rolled...I think...maybe." Owen knew his excuse made no sense whatsoever, but under the circumstances it was the best that he could do.

Mack sighed deeply, turned his head and rolled his eyes. He loved his son but had never been able to relate to the boy. Owen was gangly and uncoordinated – little more than a giant head bobbing back and forth on top of a fragile, twig-like body. The boy had started wearing glasses before the age of seven, often got bloody noses and spent the vast majority of the day tripping over his own feet. When Owen was eight, Mack took him to the park and had attempted to teach him how to catch a baseball. After twenty minutes of the ball smacking his forehead and eventually breaking the lenses on his glasses, Mack had realized it was a lost cause and called it a day. Owen was destined to be a scientist, or a biologist, or a chemist, or something else that ended in an "-ist." Mack had long since come to terms with that. His son was smart. Too often he used words that Mack did not understand. He read books Mack had never heard of and sometimes had trouble pronouncing the titles. It was very possible that Owen was smarter than Mack would ever be and for the most part he was fine with that because he loved him – for the most part. Looking past his son, Mack glanced at the window and saw Tommy Jarvis walk past his house, heading toward the end of the block. The Jarvis boys - now there was a sad little tale - depressing little anecdote in which Mack did not want his son involved.

"Don't you have some homework to finish, Owen?"

"All done with it."

"Then how about you come outside and give your old man a hand with the hot rod? There's a lot of work that needs to be done before the car show in a couple of weeks."

Hot rod? Owen wanted nothing to do with the hot rod. "You know what? Maybe I should get a jump on the paper that's due next week." Unlike his last pathetic excuse, Owen's mind did not stumble for a second finding this one.

Working with his dad in the garage was not exactly high on the list of things that he wanted to do. In fact, it was not on the list at all. He loved his father, but not quite as much as he hated cars, and grease, and working under hot cars while covered in grease. Quickly moving past Mack's burly form, Owen headed down the hallway which led to his bedroom at the other end of the house. He was very nearly there when he heard his father's voice, "Owen."

Turning around, he noticed his father staring at him with a stern, serious look on his face.

Mack Little took a deep breath. "Stay away from Tommy Jarvis."

"Okay, Dad."

"I'm serious, Owen. I don't want you hanging around either of the Jarvis boys. Do you understand me?"

"Sure...I understand."

"Good." Mack Little exhaled.

Owen turned to walk away, but was stopped once more by his father's deep voice. "Owen."

"What?"

"I love you."

"I love you too, Dad."

Turning to leave, Owen finally made it to his bedroom. He closed the door, opened a book and started to read. As wonderful information and beautiful knowledge started to fill his eager brain, thoughts of Tommy Jarvis' sidewalk beating were patiently pushed out of sight – which was, after all, exactly where they belonged.

Just ask his father.

5. QUIET LITTLE NICKY JARVIS

Nicky Jarvis was planted in front of the television on the living room floor when he heard his older brother come in the front door. Immediately after entering, Tommy stopped briefly to drop his backpack on the hardwood floor just inside the doorway, then glanced in Nicky's direction. Instantly, Nicky recognized that his brother was in bad shape. His hair was a mess, his head hanging low, his expression tired and forlorn. The look on his face vaguely resembled the looks Nicky had seen on the animals at the zoo a week earlier when he class had been on a school field trip - sad, lost, and hopeless, as if they were meant to be somewhere else, to see something more but yet had been completely and totally unable to do so.

A crooked, pathetic smile formed on Tommy's lips, "Hey, bro." His voice was distant and dreamy.

Nicky immediately returned the smile, lifting his right hand slowly and waving at his brother. Tommy half-heartedly waved back and headed up the stairs and toward his bedroom without saying another word. Nicky watched him walk the entire way until he turned left at the top of the stairs. He could hear him make his way toward the bedroom at the end of the hall and was soon out of sight. The sound of the door closing came a moment later. With a deep sigh, Nicky turned his attention back to the television. Every day after school the action was the same. Moments after stepping into the house, Nicky plopped himself onto the living room floor and turned on his cartoons. He loved cartoons. The bright colors, the characters with their funny little smiles drawn onto their even funnier faces - cartoons made him feel good. They made him smile; it was not often that Nicky had been given a reason to smile. There was also the fact that many of the characters had reminded him of the things that Tommy would sometimes draw. He loved to watch his older brother draw. To see his fingers moving so quickly while creating entire worlds by simply dragging a pencil across a sheet of paper was amazing. When they had been younger, the brothers would often lie on the porch where Nicky would have Tommy draw pictures for him. He would name an animal, like "cow" for example, and Tommy had drawn a cow. He would say "cat" and moments later Tommy would have drawn a cat. Sometimes Nicky would feel adventurous and offer up a more difficult suggestion like "Superman" or "police officer" and Tommy would have thrown him a dirty look.

People were so difficult to draw.

The pair would spend hours outside in the sun, laughing and talking and enjoying their time together. Back then, as far as Nicky had been concerned, there were few things better in the world than simply having a brother.

Now though, all of that fun seemed a long time ago, and very far away.

Staring into the glow of the television screen, lost in the wonderfully safe world of cartoons, Nicky had lost track of time until he noticed, from the corner of his eye, that the front door opened slowly. His father was home from work.

The instant Chris Jarvis stepped through the doorway and into his home, after a rather long and extremely frustrating day at work, his foot caught on Tommy's book bag, causing him to twist and stumble. With his arms flailing wildly, he just barely caught the railing on the stairs and managed to stay on his feet. Had he not been able to grab the railing, he would have been lying face down on the floor. Regaining his balance, a frustrated and confused Chris Jarvis looked down to see what he had tripped over. Sitting exactly where it should not be - exactly where he had told Tommy to never leave it - was Tommy's ripped, dirty book bag. Every last ounce of blood in Chris Jarvis' body quickly rushed to his head, slamming into the underside of his brain like a train smashing into a car left on the railroad tracks.

The pressure in his skull quickly built up, pushing its way back down, escaping through his open mouth in a fiery rage. "TOMMY! GET YOUR ASS DOWN HERE!"

In the opposite room, Nicky sat perfectly still with his legs crossed, staring with a blank expression at the enraged red-faced man he had once believed was his father. The light of the television screen flashed wondrous colors off the contours of his face.

"TOMMY! TOMMY, I SAID GET THE HELL DOWN HERE!"

Picking up the broken and dirty book bag, Chris threw it violently into the living room. The bag skidded across the table past Nicky, who had rolled onto his side, burying his head in his hands.

23

It crashed onto the floor, ripped open and scattered loose papers and heavy books in every direction.

"GOD DAMN IT, TOMMY! GET DOWN HERE RIGHT THIS MINUTE!" Chris screamed again, even louder than before.

Hesitantly, Nicky peeked at his father between his fingers. This was an all-too-common scene for the eleven year-old. He was both tired of it and accustomed to it at the same time.

When Tommy still did not respond to his father's screams, the large, angry red, huffing and puffing shape of Chris Jarvis turned his attention to his other son. "Nicky, where the hell is your brother? Is he upstairs? Did you see him come home? Is he upstairs? IF YOU'RE UP THERE, TOMMY, YOU BETTER GET YOUR SCRAWNY LITTLE ASS DOWN HERE RIGHT NOW!"

Slowly Nicky removed his hands from his eyes, remaining silent. His breath quickened its pace and his limbs shook back and forth in small, jittery motions.

"Well, is he up there or not, Nicky? I'm asking you a question. You should answer your father when he asks you a question."

Nicky felt his heart beating rapidly in his chest. It pressed against his ribs, making the undersides ache as if trying to punch its way out. Sitting straight up, he leaned back on his arms, very slowly scooting across the floor.

With every backward movement, Chris Jarvis took one forward. Ever since his wife died, Nicky had not said a single solitary word. Not a peep, not a mutter, nothing. It would be the understatement of the century to say that Chris had found this frustrating to deal with, frustrating to live with, frustrating to be around. Every unanswered question, every silent non-response, and every blank faraway stare - the annoyance of having to deal with an eleven-year-old who would not talk on top of everything else in his pathetic excuse for a life was quickly wearing on him. It not only tested his patience, but tested his resolve as well.

With his father still moving toward him, Nicky continued to slide back on his rear end. Thick, salty beads of sweat formed on his forehead and dribbled down his face.

"Answer me, Nicky. Answer your father. Just open up your mouth and answer me. Say something...say anything! Is your brother home or isn't he? Just one word...just one measly little word...a yes or a no. Answer me, Nicky. ANSWER ME RIGHT NOW!"

Having scooted back as far as he could go, Nicky found himself pressed against the wall with the snarling, beastly thing wearing his father's skin just a few steps away.

"Leave him alone."

The soft, determined voice came from the stairs. It was Tommy.

The very second the sound of his eldest son's voice worked its way into his ears, Chris Jarvis turned to face him, immediately forgetting about the younger boy. Tommy was, after all, the one who had started this entire debacle. It was his bag he had tripped over. It was all Tommy's fault. It was Tommy who did not know how to put his things away, Tommy whose grades were slipping in school, Tommy with the weird little drawings and the even weirder grown-up thoughts.

Tommy – who looked so unbearably similar to his mother.

"Oh, there you are. When I tell you to come downstairs, you had better get your ass downstairs, young man. Do you understand me?"

Glancing briefly to the side of his father's legs, Tommy spotted his little brother against the wall underneath the bay window. Quiet little Nicky - he looked so small - so pure. Hidden behind his green eyes and unmoving mouth there was innocence and possibility and the promise of things that were good and fresh and new.

"ANSWER ME, TOMMY! DO WE UNDERSTAND EACH OTHER?"

Tommy had decided some time ago that he would do whatever it took to make sure his brother did not have to go through everything he went through. At least one of them would come out of their youth unscathed. At least one of them would move into adulthood somewhat clean.

Staring into the eyes of the man that he once called his father, Tommy saw nothing remaining of the man that he remembered from a few years ago. That man was dead and gone, replaced by the huffing, lumbering shape with the acid, alcohol smell pouring disgustingly from its breath.

Gazing directly into the eyes of this creature now hovering like an angry old oak tree high above his head, he said the words that he had to say in order to fulfill his promise to Nicky, "Yes."

"Yes what?"

"Yes we understand each other."

Chris Jarvis stared back into his son's eyes, his brain awash with the wonderful pain-numbing haze that melts over you like a finely woven blanket of butter, those moments when you realize that you have reached the bottom of the bottle. A quick stop at the local bar on his way home from work helped him clear his mind, helped him to see things straight. It helped him see though the lies of his eldest and the almost mocking silence of his youngest. It helped him deal with the pressures of his life and made some semblance of sense in a world that he no longer controlled.

"Guess what, Tommy...I don't believe you."

In one quick motion, his hand reached out and snatched Tommy by the wrist. With his eldest firmly in his grasp, he immediately started toward the stairs, dragging the boy behind him, whipping him violently as he went.

"I don't believe a God damn word you've said to me, Tommy. You're lying to me, and I can't stand liars. I'm gonna teach you not to lie to me, Tommy. I'm gonna show you what happens to little boys who lie to their fathers."

Up the stairs went the mad pair of wildly flailing bodies; up the stairs and into the bedroom at the end of the hall; the terrifying noise muffled by the heavy slamming of the door.

With his every limb shivering, Nicky Jarvis crawled back in front of the television, grabbed the remote and turned the volume up high. It was not that he did not want to hear the sounds that came from upstairs, but rather that he somehow instinctively understood that his brother did not want him to hear.

6. THE FORT

As the day often does, it chose to turn into night, which then folded once again into a brand new day. By the time Tommy Jarvis rolled his sore, aching body out of bed the sun had just begun its long trek into the sky. Putting on a fresh shirt, he pulled on his shoes and crept slowly into his little brother's bedroom. After shaking Nicky awake and helping him get dressed, the brothers made their way downstairs, out the front door and into the yard. It was Saturday morning and their father would not be up for hours. When he finally would wake, no doubt with a pounding headache, aching knuckles, and a somewhat fuzzy memory of the night before, Tommy did not want either of them to be home. The pair managed to make it as far as the sidewalk when they heard a voice coming from behind. "Tommy! Hey, Tommy!"

The brothers turned their heads in unison, just in time to see Staci Alexander jogging toward them, her ponytail bouncing back and forth with each step.

Tommy instantly grabbed his little brother's arm, pulling his waif-like form across the street in the opposite direction.

"Hey! Wait a minute! Wait up!" Staci yelled as she tried to catch up. "Where are you guys going?" She had not talked to either of the Jarvis brothers in years and was not entirely sure why she wanted to so badly now.

Something in the back of her mind was telling her that she needed to, though. It was deep and far away, but surprisingly loud, something she could not ignore, even if she did not fully understand it. Maybe it was the talk with her mother last night, maybe it was simply because she missed talking to her friend Tommy. Whatever the reason, she found herself running after them, and no part of her wanted to turn around and go home.

Dragging his little brother by the arm slowed Tommy down so Staci easily caught up to the pair.

Slowing to a walking pace as she caught her breath, she looked at Tommy with a cautious smile. "Hey Tommy. Where are you guys going?"

Instead of answering her, Tommy walked between the Parker and Thompson houses, stepping through the adjoining tree line in their backyards. He believed that Staci might turn around and head home the minute they entered the wooded area, but she remained hot on their tails, still trying to get Tommy's attention. "Come on, Tommy...just tell me where you're going."

"Nowhere. We're not going anywhere."

"You're obviously going somewhere, Tommy. You're not just walking through the woods for no reason at all. You've got to be going somewhere."

"Nope, nowhere...now leave us alone."

Staci lightly tapped Nicky on his shoulder. "Where are you guys going, Nicky?" She was fairly positive that Nicky would not answer but thought that it might get the attention of his overly protective big brother, which was exactly what it did.

Tommy immediately stopped in his tracks, spinning around to face her. "Don't...touch...him."

The look on his face caught Staci by surprise and for an instant she began to rethink her decision to follow the Jarvis brothers. Maybe her mother was right. Maybe she should just stay away from them. Maybe it was not her problem. Maybe he was not the same Tommy that she grew up with. Maybe she should just turn around and go home.

After recognizing the expression of fear in her delicate eyes, Tommy looked away, lowering his head in shame. In his heart of hearts he knew that she did not mean any harm. He should not have snapped at her, "Look, I'm sorry Staci, it's just...what do you want?"

"Nothing, really. I just want to know where you're going. Maybe, I dunno...can go with you?"

"Why?"

"Why not? We used to do stuff together all the time."

Earlier images of Staci crawled out from their hiding places inside Tommy's brain, once again making their presence known. He remembered the summer nights when they had managed to catch fireflies. They had been able to fill a glass jar which they then set on the windowsill, making their bedrooms visible without ever having to turn on the lights. He remembered the caring, sad, vaguely apologetic look on her eyes at his mother's funeral, almost as if her mother had died as well. He could not be mean to her - not Staci. No matter how badly he thought that she was better off just leaving him and his brother alone, no matter how much he wanted her to turn around, go home and never speak to him again, he could not be mean to Staci.

"Fine...you can come if you want to...just keep quiet."

When he glanced at his little brother, he saw a slightly mischievous smile slowly creeping across the young boy's face. Looking again at Staci, he saw the very same smile.

Maybe he was making a mistake.

After grabbing hold of his brother's wrist, the trio continued moving through the trees. They had not been walking for more than three minutes before Staci chimed in once again. "So where are we going?"

"You'll see when we get there," Tommy answered with a deep, obviously annoyed sigh.

"How far is it?"

"Do you want to come or not, Staci?"

"Yes."

"Then stop asking questions."

Five minutes later the group exited the trees, making their way up and over a large grassy field. They went down the other side, toward another thin line of trees which extended as far as the eye could see in either direction. They walked through the woods and came across a stream which blocked their path. Staci, who found the walk tiresome asked, "How much further Tommy?"

Tommy stopped. Letting go of his little brother's wrist, he turned to face her. "We're here," he said, pointing up with his index finger.

Staci's head craned back as her eyes followed his finger into the air. Above her, built into the branches of a large, very old looking tree sat a rather large fort. It seemed to be constructed of rusty old nails and sheets of wood that had been more than likely left on the side of the street, or pulled out of the dumpsters at a construction site.

It was impressive in size, considering it had been built by a fourteen-year-old not known for being handy with a hammer and his somewhat scrawny eleven-year-old mute brother.

Nicky quickly left his older brother's side and started climbing up the planks of wood that had been nailed into the side of the thick, brownish-gray trunk. From the instant he began climbing, a grin almost too big for his face burst into existence. Staci could not recall ever having seen the boy move so quickly or look so happy. She chuckled to herself at his exuberance.

Still staring at the massive structure, she added with no small amount of surprise in her voice. "Wow...did you build this, Tommy?"

"Yea...quite a while ago...it took me an entire summer."

"I didn't know you could build stuff."

"Neither did I."

By this time Nicky was up the ladder and was stomping around happily on the rickety wooden floor high above their heads. His head peeked through a window, down toward Staci, motioning wildly with his right hand for her to join him.

Smiling at him softly, she then turned back to Tommy, "Is it okay?"

He rolled his eyes, sighed deeply and nodded yes. He turned and walked toward the stream. Staci giggled at him under her breath. She found something cute about his annoyance, something she could not quite put her finger on – something she was happy to see again. Once Tommy moved away from her, she turned back toward the fort and began to cautiously make her way up the wobbly half-rotted steps. When Tommy was sure she was not looking, he turned around and watched as she awkwardly tried to get her footing on the ladder's rickety rungs, while his younger brother happily peeked through a hole in the fort's floor. For a brief instant Tommy nearly smiled, but quickly caught himself and looked away.

When Staci reached the top of the ladder, Nicky grabbed her arm with both hands as he helped her into the fort. Once inside she stood up, dusted the dirt off of her knees and looked around. Strangely the fort seemed even bigger from the inside than it did from the outside. In one corner sat two dirty old lawn chairs placed around two large tree trunks with a piece of wood resting on top of them, forming a makeshift table. On the table rested a couple of empty soda cans, a few discarded Twinkie wrappers, a rusty old tool box with a hammer and a bunch of bent nails, a deck of playing cards and a stack of comic books that had seen better days. What really caught her eye were the hundreds of drawings taped on every wall - – there were drawings of trees, drawings of people, drawings of strange landscapes, faraway places and animals both fictional and real. Each and every single one was distinctly different from the last. While taking in the magnitude of them all, her eyes glanced at the far wall where one drawing in particular caught her attention. Very slowly she walked across the creaky floor to get a closer look.

It was a house – not just any house though – it was her house.

Through a window on the second floor she saw herself on the bed, lying on her stomach with her legs dangling in the air behind her, while she read a book. Above that drawing was another one which featured a profile of her head with her hair drawn back into a ponytail and a soft smile on her face. Not far away from that one, yet another. This one showed her standing at the bus stop with her backpack flung over her shoulder. Standing next to her were rough, half-finished outline sketches of her friends. As she took in the drawings around her Staci felt her chest getting warm. The warmth slowly traveled up her face and settled somewhere in the area around her cheeks, which turned hot and red. The drawings were beautiful, each lovingly rendered and incredibly detailed. She reached for the closest drawing and slowly ran her index finger across the contours of her face. She could feel the slight indention in the paper where the graphite had been pressed into it. All at once she was flattered, embarrassed and confused. Why had Tommy drawn so many pictures of her? Why did he put them up on the walls of his tree fort? What would she say to him now that she had seen them?

The questions flew in her brain like a hundred birds crammed in a cage much too small; they came to an abrupt stop when she heard a booming, unfamiliar voice coming from outside.

"I TOLD YOU I'D SEE YOU TOMORROW, WEIRDO!"

Quickly running to the opposite window, she looked out across the trees. Teetering perilously close to the stream was Tommy. Heading in his direction, like a group of enormous fleshy armored tanks, were Donald Rondage and three of his goons.

Donald stopped, put his hands on his beefy hips and looked around. His gazed at the tree fort and at Staci who was now leaning halfway out the window with a surprised, scared look on her face.

"HA! Who's that loser, your girlfriend? Is your stupid little mute brother up there too?" Donald slowly turned back toward

Tommy, a sloppy grin cutting across the lower half of his face. "No offense, but aren't you a little old for tree houses, weirdo?"

Tommy did not answer back. He dug his heels into the ground, preparing himself for Donald's inevitable attack.

"Tell me something, weirdo…how good of a swimmer are you?"

Moments after finishing his sentence, Donald lunged at Tommy with all the strength his oversized fourteen-year-old body could muster, slamming into his stomach with full force. The collision knocked the wind out of Tommy as the pair tumbled back, splashing into the stream behind them.

7. WELCOME TO FILLAGROU

The slow moving, extremely muddy stream water engulfed the tumbling boys, folding them into the darkest recesses of its depths. With no up, down, left or right, and unable to see beyond a few inches, both Tommy and Donald grabbed hold of anything within their narrow reach. Hair, skin, clothes, whatever they could wrap their hands around and clutch tightly was fair game. The boys tugged, pulled, and punched in the general direction of each other, all the while trying to hold their breath and see through the dark brown nothingness of the chilly water. Realizing that he was not going to be able to hold his breath much longer, Donald began swimming frantically towards the direction he thought might possibly be up. The moment Tommy felt the boy's bulky form start to move away, he grabbed a handful of Donald's pants, instinctively following in the same direction, air bubbles escaping from the side of his lips. The instant Donald's head popped out of the water he opened his mouth and inhaled a lungful of much needed air. His vision was clouded, his head dizzy, and his breathing labored. Reaching forward with his eyes closed, he grabbed a handful of grass and dirt, using it to pull himself onto land. Tommy popped out of the water soon after, struggling to catch his breath as well. He opened his eyes and noticed Donald lying in the grass with his eyes shut tight. The big oaf was having great difficulty catching his breath, wheezing and gasping as if caught in the midst of an asthma attack, his oversized belly rising and heaving.

A half smile curled its way across Tommy's lips, but quickly dissipated when he noticed that something about the scene was not quite right.

The grass crushed underneath Donald's rear was more red than green, and not a normal looking red, at that. No, this was a darker, more saturated and strangely vibrant red. Tommy looked at the surrounding trees, but they were not trees like any he had ever seen. Every leaf hanging from their strangely gray branches was the same rich crimson. He looked down, fully expecting to see the muddy stream that Donald had knocked him into. Tommy saw little more than a puddle. The tiny patch of cloudy water was no more than four feet across at its widest point. Frantically, Tommy spun in the puddle, his outstretched arms pushing off the reddish green grass which surrounded him. Where was his brother? Where was Staci? Where was the stream? Where were his tree fort and Donald's goon squad? Where was he – and how did he get here?

Crawling onto land, he quickly made his way to his feet, raised his hands in front of his mouth and started screaming at the top of his lungs, "NICKY! NICKY!"

Each yell echoed through the endless red forest surrounding him, repeating itself at least fifteen times before it was swallowed up by the emptiness and the trees. While Tommy was in the middle of screaming, Donald sat up after managing to catch his breath.

He looked at the yelling, spinning, frantic Tommy and laughed to himself. "Stop screaming, loser…it was just a little water. It's not gonna kill you."

Tommy turned toward him angrily, moving quickly in the direction of the bully. When he was within inches of Donald's burly face, he opened his mouth and wailed angrily, "LOOK AROUND YOU, YOU MORON!"

Surprised by Tommy's forcefulness, and more than a bit confused by it as well, Donald did just that. His eyes drank in the red trees, the red grass, the lack of a stream, the absence of a fort, and of course his missing cohorts. Once his brain had properly registered the reality of what his eyes were seeing, it sent a message to his legs telling them that he needed to stand up. By this time Tommy had moved away from him and resumed his high-pitched screaming. Donald lumbered toward him, grabbed his shirt and tugged the blond-haired boy violently toward his chest, "WHAT THE HELL DID YOU DO, WEIRDO?! WHERE ARE WE?!"

"How I am supposed to know?" Tommy fired back, shoving Donald in the chest and pushing him away.

The violent reaction enraged Donald, who ran toward Tommy, pushing him even harder in retaliation, making good use of the full force of his weight. The blow caused Tommy to fall in the grass.

Angry, confused and more scared than he was willing to admit, Donald yelped, "I KNOW I DIDN'T DO THIS, WEIRDO, SO IT MUST HAVE BEEN YOU, FREAK!" The burly bodied boy moved in close to Tommy, poking his index finger against his forehead, pushing forward with a fair amount of force. "You better tell me what you did right now, freak, or I swear to God, I'll make you pay. Do you understand me? FIX THIS RIGHT NOW! Fix this right now and put us back where we belong! DO IT NOW, OR I SWEAR TO GOD I'LL BEAT YOU WITHIN AN INCH OF YOUR LIFE!"

Chunks of whatever Donald had eaten for lunch flew from his mouth with every word, smacking Tommy in the face as the booming sound of his deep voice bounced off the walls of his inner ear. Tommy had just turned his head to the side in order to avoid the onslaught of food bits and spittle when he felt the ground move. It was not a shake, or a shimmy, or a jerk, but a quick rolling vibration. Only moments afterward he felt yet another movement, this one just a bit more violent. He tried his best to focus on the vibrations and get a feeling of exactly where they were coming from, but Donald's insistent screaming was making the task difficult.

"Donald, shut up for a minute."

He tried harder to ignore Donald and focus, as yet another vibration - this one smaller but more violent than the previous two - shook its way across the tips of his fingers.

"SHUT UP!? WHO THE HELL DO YOU THINK YOU ARE, TELLING ME TO SHUT UP!?"

Underneath the growl of Donald's voice, Tommy heard a soft, yet extremely deep boom coinciding with yet another, slightly stronger vibration. "Just be quiet for one second, Donald!"

"YOU'RE DEAD, WEIRDO! DO YOU HEAR ME? DEAD! ONCE WE GET O..."

Finally Tommy could not take it anymore. "JUST FOR ONE SECOND WILL YOU PLEASE SHUT UP AND LISTEN!"

The look on Tommy's face and the tone of his voice caught Donald off guard, quieting him long enough to hear the deep rumble for himself. It was coming from somewhere in the forest – somewhere far away – though getting closer. Donald felt the sensation of a vibration travel from the ground up into his legs.

Confused, he looked off into the sea of enormous red trees, but saw nothing. "What was that?"

Standing up, Tommy moved next to him, staring blankly in the same general direction, "I don't know."

The silence between the rumbles was getting shorter and shorter. The vibrations at their feet were getting more and more prominent, now traveling all the way up into their heads. From behind came the rustling of leaves and snapping of branches. The boys turned in unison just as something large and white ran out of the dense red bushes not more than a few feet away, colliding with their bodies at full force. All three forms crashed to the ground in a wild, sloppy heap.

Tommy was lying face down in the red grass when he opened his eyes. His entire right side hurt. Something heavy was pressed against his shoulder, pinning him to the dirt. Pushing himself out from underneath the weight, he managed to roll onto his back. Propping himself on his elbows, he reached across his chest and massaged his right shoulder. To his left Donald was sitting with his back toward him, tenderly rubbing what was most likely a large knot on the top of his head. When he turned toward his right, he found himself staring at a pair of oversized bright red eyeballs. The frighteningly red eyes were set in deep sockets taking up almost half of the space on a thin, very pale, nearly translucent wide white face.

Tommy's body froze.

For an instant, while staring into the massive eyes of something clearly not human, he seemed to have lost the ability to breathe. After slowly managing to get control over his bodily functions, he inhaled quickly before scooting across the grass, bumping into Donald. Annoyed, Donald turned, spotted the odd looking creature and moved back in fear, alongside Tommy.

The bony white creature, with its uncomfortably long limbs sat motionless - staring at the frightened boys with a look of shock and confusion on its strange face. A clump of its long, sporadically placed, stringy white hair dropped in front of its eyes. The odd creature brushed it away before extending one of its long fingers at the children.

With half a whisper, it muttered, "You...you...y...y...you can't be...can you?"

Tommy saw the creature's bony arm shaking and realized that the monster seemed to be just as scared of them as they were of it. Before he had time to figure out what this could mean exactly, another large and much closer booming sound filled the air, jolting all three of the confused figures back to reality. The white creature's head jerked to the right, staring off through the trees and into the forest. The large apple-sized red pupils in its eyes shrunk down to the size of a grape as it focused on something so far off in the distance that the boys could not hope to see it. Another enormous boom echoed through the trees, followed by a violent vibration that forced both boys to steady themselves so that they stayed seated. The creature turned and looked at them. An expression of total and all encompassing fear stretched across its tight, dusty white skin.

As its dry, cracked lips parted, its squeaky voice muttered only one simple word, "Run."

41

8. HELP IS ON THE WAY

"TOMMY! TOMMY!"

It had been almost five minutes since both Donald and Tommy went spiraling into the stream. Five long minutes and neither of them had come up for a breath of air. The moment after the boys had collided and plunged into in the murky water, Staci hurriedly made her way down the fort's rickety ladder. She stood on the edge of the grass, frantically screaming in the direction of the filthy, barely moving stream, "TOMMY! TOMMY!"

She turned toward the motionless group of kids that made up Donald's goon squad. They look just as scared, if not more so than she. "DON'T JUST STAND THERE, GO GET HELP!" She screamed.

For the first minute or so after Donald and Tommy had splashed into the murky water, the three boys were laughing their heads off. They pointed, cackled, and seemed to thoroughly enjoy the craziness brought on by their faithful leader. As time continued to pass, the laughter was replaced by genuine fear when Tommy and Donald had failed to emerge from the water. They had just wanted to mess around with Tommy, smack him a few times and remind him of his place in the complicated hierarchy of middle school and possibly make themselves feel a bit better about their own lives in the process. The last thing they wanted, or even had imagined was anyone drowning, or the possibility they faced now – that someone might be dead.

The reality of the current situation did not sit well with any of them.

"GO GET SOME HELP, YOU IDIOTS!" Staci yelled again from the bank of the stream.

The boys looked at each other briefly; then, almost as if they had shared a single brain, they turned and ran in the opposite direction. Not a one of them had any intention of getting help. Fear had overtaken them and they simply wanted to get away. They wanted to run and hide and pretend that they had never heard of Tommy Jarvis' fort in the woods. If anyone asked about Donald or the weirdo or the tiny stream in the middle of nowhere, they would simply look confused and say they had no idea what anyone was talking about.

Looking confused and stupid was something these three did well.

After seeing the three boys run away and believing that they were on their way to get help, Staci turned her attention again to the muddy water, "TOMMY!"

Reaching between her legs, she snatched a long branch from the ground and poked at the top. Maybe it was a stupid thing to do, and maybe it did not make an ounce of sense, but Staci was more scared than she had ever been in her life, and in that moment very little seemed to make sense. So many thoughts were bouncing around inside her skull. She could not organize any of them, let alone begin to use them to formulate something resembling a plan.

"TOMMY! TOMMY! Please, where are you, Tommy!"

Her eyes were hot and wet, tears rolling from underneath her eyelashes and down her cheeks. Her legs felt shaky – strangely similar to cold, wobbly spaghetti. She found it difficult to remain upright.

"Please, Tommy…please…where are you…" She mumbled in between breaths, the salty tears now trickling into her mouth.

Just as her legs gave way and her body tumbled in the grass, little Nicky Jarvis wedged his own body underneath her, slowing her descent. It had taken him a long time to navigate his way back down the ladder. The rungs had always been too far apart for his short legs so he was forced to move slowly to keep from falling and breaking his neck. Staci had lost all control over her emotions; she tightly wrapped her arms around the spindly body of the eleven-year-old boy. Squeezing his arms and pulling at his shirt, she mumbled something incoherent into the fabric of his sleeve. Very slowly Nicky pushed her off him. Once she let go of his shirt and was mumbling in the soft grass beneath her knees, Nicky stood and made his way timidly toward the water's edge. He sat on the bank and slowly lowered himself into the murky water while trying to control the fear building in his chest. Even the very simple task of breathing required much concentration.

Nicky had no idea how to swim, but it did not matter. The water looked like a great green monster ready and willing to swallow him whole. Even that did not matter. Despite common sense, despite the better judgment of his eleven-year-old brain, Nicky knew that he needed to get into the water and he needed to do it as quickly as he could.

Tommy had always been there when he needed him and now he would do the same, no matter the cost.

Staci pulled her head out of the grass. Through a pair of hazy, tear-filled eyes, she spotted Nicky lowering himself into the drink. She was keenly aware of the boy's inability to swim. It was a problem they both shared. All through her youth her father had attempted over and over again to teach her to swim, even to doggie paddle, but the instant she came into contact with the strange weightlessness water created, her body froze. With her limbs useless and her heart racing, more often than not she would sink like a rock. She hated swimming and hated water and there was no way she was going to let Nicky Jarvis get anywhere near it.

Spastically crawling across the grass toward the boy, she screamed so loud that it caused her vocal chords to ache. "Nicky! NO! Nicky, don't go in there!"

Staci had just seen one Jarvis boy go under and not come up; she could not let the same thing happen to another.

Nicky was chest deep in the murky liquid when Staci leaned over and wrapped her arms underneath his arms. She tried to pull him back toward land. "No! Nicky! Get out! GET OUT!"

Twisting his body to face her, he did his best to push her arms away, but each time he removed one, she clawed at him with the other. Staci was determined to get her arms around the sopping wet boy, who turned out to be surprisingly strong for his diminutive size. Despite her determination, Staci was losing the battle. With each attempt to grab a flailing arm or a piece of fabric she found herself slowly moving closer and closer to the stream's edge. She managed to grab one of Nicky's arms briefly, but the boy's defiant, wild flailing caused her to lose her footing completely; she flipped forward and splashed down on top of him. As the entire weight of her body collided with the top of Nicky's head, both children began to sink. The dark abyss immediately engulfed them. It folded itself around them, pulled them downward and refused to let go. Like the dark green, hungry monster Nicky had imagined it to be, the water gobbled them up and swallowed them whole. Tugging their thrashing, oxygen-deprived bodies into itself without an ounce of sympathy or remorse, it drew them down furiously and spit them out toward a fate already determined and a world that would change them forever.

9. RUN, RUN AS FAST AS YOU CAN

For a creature that seemed so awkward and lanky at first sight, the skinny, pasty-white, red-eyed thing now ran through the forest with incredible speed. It leaped over fallen trees and around bushes with no problem whatsoever and looked shockingly graceful while doing so. It cut through thick underbrush with the speed and accuracy of a housefly slicing through the air. The creature's surprising speed and mobility was making it difficult for Tommy and Donald to keep up. With every passing second it was getting further and further from their line of sight. Adding to their worries was the fact that whatever was chasing them through the dense foliage was getting perilously close. Behind them the boys could hear the sound of trees being knocked over; bushes, logs and wood snapped to cinders under the pressure of an immense weight. Donald's body was not exactly made for long distance running. His legs were on fire and the ever-expanding pain in his chest was making it more and more difficult to catch his breath. He could no longer see the strange white creature as Tommy had managed put a fair amount of distance between it as well. When an enormous tree came crashing to the ground not more than fifteen feet away, he leaped to the side in fear, tripping over something buried in the dirt of the forest floor. Tumbling head over heels forward, he crashed headfirst into the ground, the weight of his body sending loose red leaves spiraling like tops in every direction. For a brief second consciousness escaped him.

Almost as if the forest floor had swallowed it whole, the white creature suddenly dropped out of Tommy's view. As his feet skidded across the dirt, Tommy came to a stop, using the opportunity to catch his breath. He glanced over his shoulder and spotted Donald lying flat on his face, partially covered by a blanket of red leaves. Behind his burly tormentor, the forest seemed to be exploding in the distance. Trees were tipping over in every direction as an enormous dirt cloud expanded across the entire forest like a thick brown fog. The dusty haze parted only for an instant, cut in half by a gigantically thick and dark gray leg as it stepped through the trees and slammed into the ground. In a strange way, the enormous appendage reminded Tommy of an elephant's foot, only a hundred times larger. The ground beneath Tommy shook violently as another massive foot crashed to the ground not far from Donald, who by this time had managed to pick himself up. Donald was quite shaken and somewhat disoriented. Tommy looked back toward the area where the white creature had disappeared, then again at Donald and the insanely massive amount of destruction that surrounded him.

Despite his reservations, he knew that he could not let Donald get squashed, no matter how much he hated him. There had been times when he would lie in bed at night wishing for the burly boy's death; but now, with the reality of that moment upon him, no matter how much he despised the pudgy annoyance named Donald Rondage, he could not just leave him.

He was better than that - even if he did not want to be.

Donald had hit his head hard on something when he tripped as it was throbbing and sore. His vision had gone from crystal clear to fuzzy and blurred. When something heavy, huge and gray crashed to the ground not far behind him, the boy, only half-aware, suddenly found himself engulfed in a cloud of dirty smoke that leaked into his mouth and nose and quickly made its way into his lungs. There was so much happening that he was unable to process any specific part of it with even a modicum of success. Sounds, smells and pain were hitting him from all sides at once, each more confusing than the last. The thick layer of dirt that had entered his mouth and nose was now coating his lungs, sending him into a wild coughing fit.

Stumbling forward blindly, he tripped over another branch, but this time he was saved from falling on his face by Tommy, "Come on, Donald! Get up!" Tommy was pulling him in a direction that seemed to be heading away from the noise. Donald did his best to follow, despite the still expanding pain in his head.

Together the boys scurried through the forest with Tommy leading the way as best he could, while navigating the escalating carnage around them. He did not know exactly where he was going, but he kept his eyes on the spot where the white creature had disappeared. He really had no other choice. A monstrous, frightening growl emanated from high above the trees, traveled downward into the forest and rattled the trees around them. An

49

instant after another tree tumbled to the ground, an even thicker brown cloud of dirt enveloped the boys entirely, causing Tommy to lose sight of where he was headed. Now the boys were stumbling blindly, their hands waving out in front of them. Another massive monster's enormous gray foot slammed to the ground not more than a few feet from where they stood. The sheer size of the beast's appendage and the force with which it was delivered turned the boys upside down, sending their bodies spinning into the air. Momentarily weightless in the hideous earthen colored fog, their arms flailed wildly in a vain attempt to grab something to stop them from falling. Strangely, instead of hitting the forest floor as one might expect, they fell through it. A thick patch of leaves covering a hidden trap door opened; the pair passed through it and into a dark hole. Their bodies finally came to a stop after splashing down into three feet of muddy water. Tommy lifted his head out of the foul smelling liquid just in time to see the trap door quickly shut, blocking out not only the dirt cloud, but what little sunlight had been able to make its way through, bathing both boys in total darkness.

Still a bit foggy and not quite sure exactly what was going on, Donald noticed the door close above their heads. As the thick blackness enveloped him he attempted to yell something but was stopped when a bony hand, attached to even longer, bonier fingers covered his mouth. He felt the hot, stinky breath of the pale white creature against the side of his face and immediately froze.

"Shhh...don't speak."

Both Tommy and Donald went quiet even though their hearts were still racing and their hands were shaking uncontrollably. From above the sounds of falling trees, enormous stomping feet, and the ungodly roar of the oversized creatures continued. With each second the sounds were getting further away. Whatever was chasing them only moments ago, was now passing directly over their heads. With time, the rumbling slowly became less noticeable and Tommy got the distinct impression that somehow they had escaped.

Once the sounds disappeared completely, Donald felt the bony hand being removed from his mouth. In the darkness he heard the creature splash through the cold water that he and Tommy knelt in, the murky liquid covering their stomachs. The blackness surrounding him was stuffy and humid, but at least he was not inhaling copious amounts of dirt - so he saw this as a positive thing.

The light of a torch suddenly bathed the area surrounding the boys in a warm brightness, which led them to believe that they were in some kind of underground tunnel. The dirt walls looked uneven and handmade, as if a hundred hurried hands with no real plan had dug them out. A few feet away, in the low ceilinged tunnel, the strange white creature was holding a torch. The reflection of the fire in its red eyes glowed brightly as it stared at the ground above them, listening intently with its huge ears, making sure that whatever had been chasing them was completely gone. One thin finger remained pressed against its lips, indicating to the boys that they needed to remain quiet.

Both boys took its advice.

When the creature seemed sufficiently sure that the danger had passed, it turned toward their still shaking forms, half submerged in the puddle. Cocking its head to the side slowly, it examined every single solitary inch of their bodies. A thick pink tongue poked its way out of its mouth, running gently across its dry lips, moistening them. Putting one long leg into the water the creature awkwardly moved closer to the boys, using the torch to light up different parts of their faces as it inspected them closer still.

Both Tommy and Donald moved away from the creature, but were stopped by the dirt wall.

Neither had any idea what to say, and even if they did, it was unlikely they could formulate the words.

None of this made any sense. What was one supposed to say while being examined by skinny monsters in dark tunnels after being chased through a red forest by gigantic elephant feet?

Silence seemed the only option.

The creature stopped scanning them. Lowering its torch, it stepped back out of the puddle. Reaching up with one hand, much the same way that a monkey might, it scratched the top of its stringy haired head with a set of four rapidly moving fingers.

"You know what ...you two don't look anything like I expected."

10. THE FINAL PIECE OF THE PUZZLE

From behind a row of sparse bushes on top of the hill, Owen Little watched with growing interest as Donald Rondage's friends came running out of the trees they had just entered not more than five minutes before. Immediately after clearing the tree line, the group of boys scattered in every direction, like a flock of birds after hearing a loud noise. As they moved further up the hill, Owen ducked down to keep from being seen. The frantic group of boys seemed to be too scared to have noticed him anyway, even if he were standing right in their path, waving his hands in the air and screaming at the top of his lungs. Once the wild yelping ruffians had moved past him, Owen again peeked out from behind his hiding place, gazing toward the tree line at the bottom of the hill. What on earth could have scared Donald's goon squad like that? He had seen every one of them get mouthy with teachers, parents and other adults on more than one occasion. He had witnessed them beating up just about everyone in school at one point or another. Occasionally a few of them smoked in the bathroom, and though he was not one-hundred percent positive, he was pretty sure they had been responsible for spray painting an enormous male reproductive organ on the front doors of city hall last summer. These were the absolute toughest, meanest fourteen-year-olds in Baxter County. Nothing could scare them – nothing. One part of Owen's brain told him that the smart thing to do was to turn around and run in the very same direction they had gone, and not stop running until he got home. Whatever was in those trees, whatever could scare Donald's brawny henchmen was not something he wanted any part of. Yet another part of his brain told him that this was a mystery worth investigating. It convinced him that this was a situation that could not simply be left un-checked. This was the same inquisitive and slightly nosey part that made him watch Tommy Jarvis get beat up in front of his house just the day before. This was the same part that tricked him into believing that sneaking around and following Donald and his friends into the woods this morning was a smart idea as well.

This was the part of Owen's brain that had often gotten him into trouble, because it was the part of his brain that, try as he might, he could not ignore.

Timidly, Owen made his way out from behind the bushes and started moving cautiously down the hill. As he got closer to the tree line he heard voices. Someone was crying, then yelling, though he could not quite make out what was being said. Moving closer still, he could tell that it was a girl's voice.

"No! Nicky! Get out! GET OUT!"

She sounded hurried, wild and hysterical. Owen stopped for a moment to rethink what he was doing. Who was Nicky? He could not think of anyone named Nicky, and whoever Nicky was, he was still down there with a hysterical girl and Donald Rondage. Just what did he think he was doing? What was the point of looking? What if something bad was happening? Or worse yet, what if something really bad was happening - something he was not supposed to see? What would he do then? What could he do? As was more often than not the case with Owen, despite common sense, the nosey investigative side of his brain had once again won out. It tackled the common sense side to the ground, rubbed dirt in its mouth, gave it a wedgie, and instructed Owen to keep moving.

Which was exactly what he did.

Reaching the trees at the bottom of the hill, Owen crept up behind one of them, peeking out just in time to see a brown-haired girl go splashing into a stream headfirst. Quickly Owen ducked back behind the tree, his heart pounding harder, his chest rising and falling in double-time. After much deliberation, he again peered out from behind the tree, staring at the predominantly still stream waters, with just a few air bubbles sporadically breaking their surface. Swiftly he pulled his head out of sight, his mind racing. Why was she not coming up for air? She really should have come up for air by now. How long had the brown-haired girl been underwater? Looking down at his watch he hoped to do some quick calculations but realized that he did not know exactly when she had fallen in. The watch would be of no help. He started to think that he should do something – but what? Could he just do nothing and let her drown? Where was Donald Rondage? Was he in the water too? Who was Nicky? Why was she yelling for Nicky? Owen found it impossible to focus on just one question and even more impossible to formulate a plan of action. Peeking out from behind the tree yet again, he noticed that the waters were completely still, still and silent, and dark, and foreboding, and other words meant to express an incredible level of fear.

Despite the panic trouncing though his insides like a giant dinosaur through a major metropolitan city, Owen knew that at the very least he needed to look. He needed to go down to the water's edge and at least look. Diving in and rescuing the brown-haired girl was well beyond his level of courage - more like something his father would do - but he at least needed to look. Looking was something he could handle. He was good at looking.

Besides, if he did not, could he live with himself?

After taking three deep breaths to muster up the courage, Owen bolted out from behind the tree. He ran in the direction of the water as fast as he could with his eyes shut tight. He did not know why he was running, and running with his eyes closed made even less sense. Yet, despite the pointlessness of his actions, this was exactly what he was doing.

Moving at full speed, like someone with an IQ much lower than his, he screamed at the top of his lungs, "ARE YOU OKAY!? I'M COMING TO HELP YOU!"

His foot tripped over a rather large rock, which caused him to tumble forward, smash onto the ground near the bank of the stream and awkwardly roll into its murky waters. As the darkness grabbed him and pulled him down, Owen quietly cursed himself for having been born, not only with his brain, but with his two left feet as well.

The entire situation really would have been quite sad and pathetic, if it were not at the same time so comical.

11. FIVE TO SAVE US ALL

The boys followed the strange white creature in complete silence for at least ten minutes. The only sounds in the dank tunnel were the flicker of the fire on the creature's torch and the sound of their feet digging into the damp dirt as they walked. The bizarre creature led them deeper and deeper underground through the sloppily hand carved tunnels, while using the torch to guide the way. It walked slightly hunched over, its stride long and graceful, while at the same time looking herky-jerky and awkward. Its movements reminded Tommy of an ostrich, or at the very least some type of oversized bird. From behind him, Tommy felt Donald poke his shoulder with one finger. He turned to look in his direction. Donald silently made a gesture with his hands indicating that he thought Tommy should ask the weird white-skinned thing where it was taking them. As much as it made complete sense to ask the creature exactly where they were going instead of blindly following, Tommy had trouble mustering up the courage. Every time that he had opened his mouth nothing seemed to come out. Donald pushed him harder in the back, whispering into Tommy's ear with some urgency, "Ask him where he's taking us, loser…come on…do it."

Annoyed, Tommy turned to Donald, moving in close to him, "I'm not going to ask him, you ask him. Maybe you should stop calling me 'loser', as well. In case you forgot already, you wouldn't even be alive right now if it wasn't for me."

"Whatever, dork, just ask the thing where we're going. What if he's leading us to a giant pot of human stew or something?"

"He's not going to make us into stew."

"How do you know? Maybe he only saved us because he's hungry…look how skinny he is. You don't know. Dude looks like he eats human stew to me."

"Look, if you really want to know where we're going, then ask. I mean, unless you're scared?"

"Shut the hell up, I'm aint' scared of nothin'."

"Then ask."

"Don't think that just because you helped me out we're suddenly buddies or that you're a tough guy or something…cause we're not…and you aren't. I would have gotten away from that thing whether you helped or not. The minute we get out of here I swear I'm gonna kick your as…"

Before Donald could finish his sentence he bumped into Tommy, who had just backed into the creature. Both Donald and Tommy quickly moved away, nearly tripping over each other in the process.

Images of the two of them floating around in a pot of human stew next to strange alien vegetables flashed through Donald's brain while Tommy found himself immediately overcome with a strong desire to apologize, "We were ju...we were, I'm sorry, we jus..."

"I'm taking you both to Tipoloo," the creature interrupted in a squeaky voice. The light of the torch cast long shadows across his face.

Not knowing what to say in response, both Donald and Tommy stared, waiting for the creature to continue "It's the last safe place in all of Fillagrou. It's there that you'll meet the Elder. He'll know if the two of you are...who I think you are."

Both boys were confused, but at the same time too terrified to answer back, unsure if the pale, white-faced creature had finished talking. Obviously forced, incredibly awkward smiles crept slowly across their faces.

From over Tommy's shoulder Donald chirped , "Umm, okay...sure. Sounds great...can't wait. Off to Tripagoo it is, then, buddy."

The creature stared at them for a moment, looking confused and a bit disappointed. Rolling its eyes, it sighed deeply before it started walking.

After another minute of silence, a question dancing around in Tommy's brain became too irresistible not to ask, "Excuse me, mister, guy...sir..."

"My name is Pleebo."

"Well, umm...Pleebo, can I umm, ask you something?"

"Sure, just keep up, it's not much further." Pleebo responded. When they came to a spot where the tunnel veered off in two directions, Pleebo picked the one on the left.

Tommy and Donald followed him into the tunnel, which descended down at such an angle that the boys had to put their hands against the walls in order to stay upright, "Listen, I appreciate everything you've done for us, I do…really…but I can't go with you to, Tipaglue or whatever. I have to get home. I have to go back. My brother is waiting for me…I can't just leave him alone…I have to go back."

Pleebo turned toward Tommy, "You can't go back. Not now, anyway. The Dark Guards will be patrolling that area all night looking for me. If you go back there, you'll just get caught. Besides, if you are who I think you might be…I can't afford to let you get caught."

Tommy thought of his brother. The last thing that Nicky had seen were the two of them going underwater and never coming back up. Did he think they were dead? No matter what this weird, white tunnel ostrich had done for them, he had to get back to his brother. There was simply no way he could stay here. He had to go back and he had to do it now - before it was too late.

Coming to a sudden stop, Tommy turned around, pushing Donald aside. "I'm sorry, but I have to go back."

From behind, Pleebo's slender fingers reached out and grabbed him by the arm. The grip was surprisingly strong for something with such spindly arms. "You can't go back, not that way. I promise I will get you exactly where you want to be, but you have to trust me, you most definitely cannot go back that way. You won't make it. You're too important."

Confused, annoyed, and with a bit of anger growing in his stomach, Tommy growled back, "Who exactly is it that you think we are?"

"Well, I'm not completely sure…but I think you might just be two of The Five."

Pleebo's response was cryptic at best, and did not satisfy Tommy's need for answers, "Two of the five what?"

"Two of The Five to save us all. Who knows though…you might not be. Maybe you're just a couple of kids who ended up in the wrong place at the wrong time. You might turn out to be nothing more than just a pair of lost, useless outlanders…" Pleebo's face tightened as he leaned in close to both boys, staring them down with his enormous red pupils, "…in which case I will in fact have to eat you."

All the air in the boys' lungs disappeared, their mouths fell agape, their hearts no longer pumped precious life-giving blood.

They stared back at Pleebo, whose face looked stone serious, while they tried to stop shaking uncontrollably. After what seemed like an hour, but was more than likely five seconds, a thin smile stretched across Pleebo's long face, and his squeaky voice chuckled softly, "Relax, I'm just kidding."

Still laughing to himself Pleebo turned around and continued walking.

The boys looked at each other confused, affording themselves a moment to start breathing again.

Glancing past Donald, Tommy gazed at the dark tunnel behind him, the tunnel that led back to the forest and to his brother. He turned again, watching as Pleebo moved ahead, giggling to himself in response to his little joke. For some reason he had decided to trust the creature – for the time being, anyway. What other choice did he have? Moving past the motionless Donald, he caught up to Pleebo. Before Donald followed, he put his arm behind his back, poking questioningly at the seat of his jeans. After confirming that he had not pooped his pants, he quickly caught up with the two.

Less than two minutes later the trio came to what seemed to be a dead end and stopped. Pleebo set his torch in the dirt near his feet and brushed away a spot of dry brown clay on the wall in front

61

of him with his bony white hand, exposing a very ancient looking stone panel underneath. Carved into the panel were four triangles all pointing toward an ornately- decorated circle. Pleebo pulled a cone shaped stone from a necklace which dangled on his slender neck and inserted it point first into the circle. The tunnel around them started to vibrate back and forth softly. A deep rumbling sound emanating from far inside the dirt walls echoed through the darkness. Digging his hands into the clay on either side of him, Donald steadied himself as small clumps of stone began to shake loose from above, falling on his head. The dirt covering the remainder of the door fell to the ground as the door began to roll sideways into the wall.

When the rumbling had stopped and the doorway opened, Pleebo turned to the boys, who were still brushing loose sand off of their faces, and said with a glimmer of pride, "Welcome to Tipoloo."

12. CAPTURED

The instant Staci's body emerged from the cold dark water, she breathed in some much needed oxygen, spitting small amounts of the dirty liquid from her mouth at the same time. She slowly opened her eyes and started to take in the out-of-focus world around her. For a moment she had trouble remembering where she was and what she was doing. Her lungs were on fire, her head pounded, and her thoughts seemed as fuzzy as everything around her looked. Rolling onto her stomach, her vision started to clear and she was able to make out Nicky Jarvis standing not more than five feet away. The boy was staring into the sky with a wide-eyed look on his face. Like a sudden, unexpected tidal wave, the memories of what had happened suddenly came rushing back. Tommy, Donald, Nicky, the stream, falling in and drowning, recollections of everything that had occurred up to that moment smacked into her all at once. She found herself choking back not only the filthy water lodged in her gullet, but her tears as well.

Despite her every joint feeling almost too sore to move, Staci managed to awkwardly prop herself onto one knee.

Biting down hard on her emotions she spoke to Nicky with her sore, grave voice. "Nicky...Nicky, are you okay? What happened?"

The young boy turned to her briefly, acknowledged her presence, but of course did not answer.

When she tried to stand, a sudden jolt of pain flickered in her head. She quickly lowered herself onto one knee to keep from tipping over. "Did you pull me out of the stream? What happened?"

Once again Nicky did not answer. He pointed frantically at the forest around him, trying desperately to get the attention of his still woozy companion. Moving over to Staci, Nicky did his best to help her onto her feet. Once she stood fully erect without leaning on him for support, he let her go and moved away. His eyes never left the strange new world around them.

When Nicky left, Staci willed her aching limbs to follow. "Nicky, wait! Where are you going? Come back!"

The pain in her head pounded away at the interior of her skull; she used her right hand to massage her temple in an attempt to alleviate the pain. As she rubbed the side of her face, she noticed the oddly colored grass and the even more oddly colored grayish wood splinters beneath her feet. She lifted her weary head and looked at her surroundings for the first time since coming out of the water; what she saw was something resembling a war zone. In every direction trees were tipped over and shattered. Clumps of dirt and grass were strewn as if the earth had been lifted up and tossed into the air with no regard for where it might land. A thin cloud of brown dust and dirt permeated the air, blanketing everything for miles in every direction. Vision beyond short distances was almost impossible.

Where in the world was she? What was going on?

Frantically, she turned and looked behind her. There was no stream or fort, nothing remotely familiar. She saw only a disaster area and a small puddle of water from which her footprints led.

A great sense of dread sank into the pit of her belly, resting heavily. It weighed her down, making it once again hard to stand. Wherever she was, she was positive she did not want to be there, and most likely was not supposed to be.

"NICKY! Nicky come on, we're getting out of here!" Staci yelled urgently, as she ran in the direction of the youngest Jarvis brother. Her sore limbs and the pain in her head quickly became little more than an afterthought to getting away, even if she was not exactly sure how she was going to accomplish such a feat.

Catching up with the boy she grabbed him by his arm and spun him around, "NICKY STOP! Come on, we're getting out of here!" She had no idea where "here" was, how she was going to get out of it, or even what was going on, but she knew that allowing the boy to wander around aimlessly in what appeared to be a freshly-made disaster area was not likely the best course of action.

Nicky pushed her away, fighting the best he could. Whatever had happened to the two of them had more than likely happened to his brother and Donald. Tommy was here and he was not going to just leave him behind. Managing to wiggle his arm free

65

from Staci's grip, he hurriedly put some distance between them with a sudden burst of speed.

Staci matched his energy though, catching up to him quickly. This time she wrapped both arms around his waist, using all her might to pull him in the opposite direction, "NICKY! NO! STOP IT!"

The two wrestled for position, pushing, pulling and grunting with every ounce of strength that they could muster. The pair stumbled backward and crashed into an enormously thick gray tree. Staci managed to pin the boy's hands above his head against the trunk. She was out of breath, sore, frustrated and more scared than she had ever been in her life. Everything was spinning out of control and she felt the need to have control over one thing. At the moment, that thing happened to be Nicky Jarvis.

"STOP IT NICKY! Where are you going!? Where are you running to!? You don't even know where we are! You don't even..." Staci's voice slowly trailed off when a strange sound sneaked its way into her ear.

She cocked her head to the side, still pinning Nicky to the tree. She saw nothing. With wide eyes, she turned back to Nicky to see if he had heard the sound. "Did you hear that?"

Nicky stopped struggling and looked around nervously, as if he had heard it as well. Again the strange sound filled the air like a dog panting, but worlds deeper and a universe louder. Staci let go of Nicky's wrists and slowly moved him away from the trunk. Something about it caught her attention. Something was strange. It looked soft, spongy, and maybe even a bit moist. Glancing down at its base, she noticed something else quite strange. Were those toes?

With one finger she poked the thick trunk. It was malleable, smooth and leathery, unlike any tree she had ever touched. Almost immediately after she poked the strange tree, the forest around them began to rumble. From high above a monstrously sized head connected to a neck as long as half a football field swooped down through the cloud of dirt. Coiled like a snake in midair, it came to a stop inches from the children. Staci froze in place. Much like when her father had tried to take her swimming as a little girl, every limb in her body locked. She was unable to make even the slightest movement. In fact, the only thing she was still able to do with any amount of success was to scream.

And she screamed very loudly.

Both children backed against the massive tree, that they now understood to be a massive leg, until they could go no further. The monster's gargantuan head was the size of a truck. Its long snout was wrapped with huge strips of leather, most likely cut from the hide of an equally enormous creature, which seemed to work as a muzzle, keeping the incredible beast from fully opening its massive jaws. The monster sniffed the air around it with nostrils so large that she or Nicky could climb inside and get lost forever. The great gray-skinned creature apparently did not like the smell of the children and growled its displeasure through the constraints of the tight muzzle; its breath blew Staci's hair wildly in every direction. It shook its enormous skull violently from side to side and quickly floated back into the sky from whence it came.

From somewhere above the trees came the sound of sliding metal against thick cable as ropes were being dropped. Instinctively Staci grabbed Nicky and pulled him closer. At least fifteen human-like figures dressed in elaborately decorated armor jumped off the creature's back. Just before hitting the ground, they came to an abrupt and jerky stop, unhooked themselves from the harnesses around their waists and landed on the forest floor. Their movements were quick and precise, making it obvious that this was something they had done many times before. One of the large men pulled a long broadsword from a sheath on his back as he approached the children who were by now crouching at the foot of the great beast. In one quick, dangerous motion the figure extended his sword toward their trembling bodies.

From behind a large almost black helmet covering the whole of his head, he spoke in a deep, rocky voice, "Who are you?"

Staci immediately began to sob while mumbling to herself. She reached across Nicky's chest, pulling his bony body closer to her.

The soldier moved his sword within inches of her teary face, letting the tip of the blade rest threateningly against her forehead. With the smallest amount of pressure, he pushed it forward just enough to draw the smallest amount of blood as his voice barked from behind his helmet, "SPEAK!"

Staci could feel a tiny drop of blood trickling down, traveling over the bridge of her nose. In this moment, all she could think about was her mom and dad, and the fact that she would most likely never see either of them again. Faced with what could be the end of her life, these images filled her entire young brain; these thoughts only succeeded in making her cry more.

"SHEATH YOUR WEAPON, LIEUTENANT!" Another voice called out.

An even larger figure, in even more elaborately decorated armor, strolled up beside the first, and stared down at the children through a thin black slit cut into the front of his helmet. The first soldier reluctantly sheathed his sword and stepped back. The larger soldier, who obviously outranked him, knelt in front of Staci and Nicky. He paused, taking a moment to fully look them over. He examined every inch of their minuscule bodies with great interest.

Extending his gloved finger to the blood trickling from Staci's head, he smeared some of it onto its tip.

Quietly under his breath, with just the slightest hint of shock in his deep voice, he whispered more to himself than anyone else, "It's red."

Seeming to be revolted by the very idea, he grabbed a handful of leaves from the ground, using the wad to wipe the blood from his glove in utter disgust. He stood up, lifted a finger into the air, and made a slight gesture that immediately brought two other helmeted soldiers to his side. "Strap them in. We're taking them with us." His voice was thick with his distaste over the pair of tiny, crying, red-blooded creatures in front of him.

One of the soldiers snatched Nicky, who tried his best to wiggle from the bulky figure's grasp. The other soldier reached down and grabbed the still sobbing Staci. One by one each of the helmeted soldiers locked themselves back into the harnesses that had dropped them from the sky. One by one they disappeared back into the dust cloud. Somewhere within the dirt and the disaster area, the gigantic creature let out a muzzle-mouthed roar. Moments later it moved in the direction its master had ordered, smashing to cinders what was left of the forest with each step.

13. SO SAYS THE ELDER

A soft warm light came from above which forced Tommy to squint after entering the doorway leading to the underground city, Tipoloo. Once his eyes had adjusted to the radical change in lighting he noticed that it was generated by hundreds of lanterns dangling from a dirt ceiling at least twenty feet above the street. Much like the tunnels Pleebo had led them through, the city of Tipoloo looked as if it had been dug out by hand. At twenty or so feet high, and maybe twenty-five feet across it seemed to be little more than a larger, more elaborate tunnel. Cut further into the earth on either side were small alcoves that the residents of the city most likely called "home". Enormous stone slabs, each one a different size and shape, stood in front of every dwelling, creating a privacy wall. Each stone had a poorly made wooden door, tied together with forest vines. No two were alike; each seemed constructed specifically to fit whatever shape the enormous slab happened to be. Everything in the city looked rushed, handmade and moments away from falling apart.

As the boys followed Pleebo through the streets, heads of creatures shyly peeked out of holes in the stones or cracks in the wooden doors. Each individual was wildly different from the last. Some were bird-like things covered in dirty multi-colored feathers with long egg-colored beaks that curled like a roll of tape at the end. Others were enormously horned beasts with snouts like dogs; the thick fur heavily covering their eyes had to be constantly brushed away. Still others were long nosed, big eared stumpy trolls no more than three feet tall – one in particular proudly sporting a cracked monocle attached to the front pocket of his dusty brown jacket. There were blue women with heads like hammerhead sharks, more than a few holding babies that did not look to be of the same species, wrapped in tattered blankets. Despite the enormity of differences, there were a few things they seemed share.

Each and every one of them looked hungry, tired and sad.

In fact, an undeniable air of hopelessness cascaded across the rickety old city like a thick fog, creeping and crawling into every single crack of every single doorway, resting heavily on the hearts of those living inside.

The further Pleebo led the boys down the street, the more creatures came out of their homes to stare at both Tommy and Donald with questioning eyes.

Pleebo turned to speak to the boys as they walked. "Don't worry about them. They just aren't sure what to make of you. You're the first of your kind down here. Plus, don't take this the wrong way...but you are a little weird looking." His thin lips coiled into a smile, chuckling to himself at yet another of his little jokes.

A legless orange-green creature with a perfectly round head and the very tiniest patch of stringy gray hair wheeled himself out of a nearby dwelling on what looked to be a slightly modified wheelbarrow. Coming to a stop four feet away from the boys, he looked them over from top to bottom. The scars on his face told the tale of a long and hard life much better than any words.

"What happened to them?" Tommy asked, as a round little thing, no more than two feet tall, peeked out from behind a large boulder. It had an enormous head taking up one of the two feet and tiny facial features resting dead in the center.

Lifting his skinny arm, Pleebo waved gently in the strange little thing's direction. The tiny-faced man raised his arm, barely eight inches long, and waved back.

Pleebo then turned and answered Tommy. "The same thing that happened to all of us...the Dark Army."

An even tinier man with a barely noticeable, yet strangely thick brown mustache and bright red skin, whizzed past Donald's ears on wings moving too fast for the human eye to capture. The buzzing sound created by his wings scared Donald, causing him to jump to the side; he very nearly fell over. The tiny mustached man then zoomed past Tommy, finally hovering in the air directly in front of Pleebo.

"Pleebs, please don't tell me that you think these two little poops belong to The Five." He grumbled annoyingly, his voice surprisingly gruff considering his rather minuscule stature.

Pleebo chuckled slightly at the forwardness of his friend's comment. "I don't know if they are or they aren't...but they sure do look the part."

In a blink, the tiny man whizzed over Pleebo's shoulder and came to a still-airborne stop a few inches from Tommy's face. He quickly flew from one side to the other like a little hummingbird, examining every inch of the boy while roughly stroking his shaggy mustache.

He zipped back to the space in front of Pleebo, put his hands on his hips, rolled his little red eyes and said, "If these two are part of The Five, then we better hope the other three are a little more intimidating. Otherwise, we're all doomed."

"Let's just wait and see what the Elder has to say, Roustaf." Pleebo responded, trying to keep from bursting into a fit of laughter.

Annoyed by the little man's comments, Donald tapped Tommy on the shoulder. "Who's he calling a poop?"

After about five more minutes of walking and eliciting odd stares from every creature they passed, Pleebo came to a stop outside a very large stone house.

Pleebo pushed open an oval shaped door and motioned for the boys to enter. "Time to meet the Elder."

Both Tommy and Donald hesitated. The boys were fairly sure that no one in the town meant them any harm. If they had, they would have been bobbing up and down in a boiling pot of stew by now. This knowledge, however, did not make the situation less worrisome. Donald made no attempt to move forward, so Tommy took the initiative, cautiously stepping through the doorway.

The room was dark, and dank, and somehow more humid than the amazingly stuffy city street. A single candle giving off an odd blue flame flickered in the corner on top of a poorly constructed table. Putting his hand in the center of Donald's back, Pleebo gently pushed the boy into the room after Tommy. He followed them both inside and closed the creaky door .

Once all three were inside, the large crowd of creatures that had followed them through the streets rushed toward the door, fighting for position, hoping to hear the discussion about to take place inside. Tiny, mustached Roustaf wedged himself into a six-inch wide crack in the rock wall. He sat down and stared impatiently into the dark room while he absent-mindedly twiddled the corner of his bushy mustache.

Inside the dark dwelling Tommy noticed movement in the corner. From underneath a tattered blanket on a barely standing bed, a frail, ghost-like figure pulled itself up. The creature looked like an extremely old version of Pleebo, though somehow even thinner. With even the slightest of movements the old creature's bones cracked and ground together, vehemently voicing their disapproval of their changed position. From its pale, nearly translucent face, hung a long, stringy white beard filled with knots and matted gray hairs. Almost as if moving in slow motion, the creature lifted its head and glanced in the direction of the boys with its washed out, faded red pupils.

Achingly lifting one of its waif-like hands, it gestured in Tommy's direction. "Come here my boy...come here."

Tommy looked briefly at Pleebo, who silently nodded his approval.

"Come now, boy...don't be frightened."

With much trepidation, Tommy moved toward the frail figure seated on the edge of the bed. When he got close enough, the ancient creature leaned forward and reached out its arm, tenderly touching the side of his face. It pulled him close to his eyes and examined him, running its bony fingers through his hair then turning him to the side in order to look at the boy's profile.

With a tired voice, it whispered more to itself than to anyone in particular, "So very...very young. For the life of me, I will never understand why they would send us one so very young."

Removing his hand from Tommy's face, the Elder gently patted the boy on the cheek and shifted back on his bed, leaning awkwardly against the dirt wall.

From the shadows on the other side of the darkened room came Pleebo's voice, "Is it them? Are they a part of The Five?"

The Elder chuckled softly in his faraway voice, which triggered a small fit of coughs. Once his coughing was under control, he stared back at Pleebo with his head cocked to the side.

"So impatient, Pleebo...always so impatient...just like your mother." He turned his faraway gaze to Tommy and Donald. "Have a seat, young ones...I have quite a story to tell you."

14. THE UNAVOIDABLE FALL OF FILLAGROU

In a time before the concept of time had been given shape, the land of Fillagrou was among the most beautiful and peaceful in all of reality. Its inhabitants had lived in relative peace and happiness for generations, making their home among the dense trees of the red forest. After years spent nurturing a relationship that had been beneficial to both parties, they slowly, through patience, hard work and caring, became a culture at one with nature. Life for them was good and perfect and wonderful.

As was generally the case with all things, when a plateau had been reached, there was nowhere else to go but down. History had shown that the denizens of fate had little patience for perfection, preferring an existence that could not be so easily classified, quantified or understood. For the Fillagrou people, the end to the perfection that had been their lives came in the form of a King, the evil King Kragamel of the dark war world known as Ocha.

In the time before King Kragamel had risen to become the tyrant ruler over not only the world of Ocha, but the whole of the universe, he was a simple, unassuming Prince, the son of a King who held sway over a small but powerful piece of land near the vast eastern sea. The control of trade routes across this sea had given the King great power, despite the somewhat diminutive size of his empire. As the only son and single heir to the throne, the life of the young Prince had been harsh. By no means whatsoever had the King treated his son with kid gloves. In fact, it had been his firm belief that the only way to prepare the boy to one day reign over his empire was to take him to his breaking point, and then just a bit further. Cruel, unnecessarily harsh punishments had hardened the boy, teaching him the dark truths about existence that few had ever been able, or willing to recognize. The King had firmly believed that the greatest of rulers were not so much born, as they were bred. The young Prince would be made into a King, whether he liked it or not.

Not many years later the King would die rather unceremoniously in his bed with only his son at his side. No less than an hour later, the young Prince became the young King. It was by sheer accident that the newly crowned King happened upon a discovery that would change his life from that point forward and allow him to extend the reach of his family's empire far beyond what his father could ever had imagined.

During the construction of a massive, elaborately decorated mausoleum meant to house the ashes of his father, the new King had ventured into a newly exposed hidden passageway buried deep in the earth which exited into another world. This was a world unlike anything he had ever seen. It was a world covered almost exclusively by an enormous red forest seemingly without end.

77

Calling the forest home and taking up residence atop the trees were a simple, harmless race of stark white beings known as the Fillagrou. These simple creatures knew nothing of war or hatred, or empires. The young King had recognized that this new world would easily fall under the might of his army.

An entire world brimming with endless untapped resources was ripe for the picking. Like a helpless flower growing out of the soft grass it waited to be plucked, and pluck it he would.

King Kragamel had returned to Ocha and immediately ordered that the passageway be widen so that it was large enough for the entire army to pass through. The very moment the digging had finished, the invasion began.

The actual takeover of Fillagrou had taken little time at all. The Fillagrou people were unaccustomed to violence of any kind and because of this had been completely unprepared to defend their homes. Like cattle, millions had been slaughtered as the King's armies killed anything and everything within reach of their blades. Enormous sections of the vast forest were reduced to little more than ash, leaving those who had managed to survive the army's onslaught homeless, forcing them underground. Those unable to escape to the safety of the new world below had been sold into slavery. Some had become the King's servants, while others had been used for hard labor and were worked to the point of near death.

Every square inch of the red forest had been laid to waste but in the process the King's men stumbled onto yet another doorway, leading to yet another world. Soon after that, another had been discovered, after that, another still. Each new world had presented the tyrant King with a new opportunity to further expand his empire. More importantly, each conquered world had provided new slaves, new soldiers, new beasts of burden, new weapons and an endless number of exotic riches. Sooner than you might think possible, the King's dark army had smothered the whole of reality like a great pestilence, choking it to near extinction and bending it to his will.

Ninety-nine worlds had been discovered, ninety-nine worlds had been conquered and more dead than numbers dare count.

Many refugees from the other fallen worlds had fled to Fillagrou, seeking to join its people in the safety of their hidden underground cities. Their existence would be a meager one - harsh, unforgiving and miserable – but it would be existence nonetheless.

Tired of hiding in haphazardly constructed underground tunnels, and pushed to the point of insanity by the atrocities against his people, a great Fillagrou prophet Elder by the name of Nelvo had ventured into the King's newly constructed castle in western Fillagrou and demanded an audience. After having first been beaten to within an inch of his life by the guards, he was dragged into King Kragamel's chambers and tossed at the tyrant's boots. Despite having more limbs broken than remained unbroken, Nelvo had forced himself to his feet, stared directly into the eyes of the King and made a prophecy though the mass of busted flesh and shattered bone that was his face.

"When all hope is lost and only one of the one hundred worlds remains to be discovered, five who bleed the color of the forest itself will arrive. The grounds will shake, the clouds will open, and a great war will commence. The Five will lead an army to the fortress walls in the land of darkness and send the evil back to where it belongs. Five will arrive but four will return...The Five to save us all."

The enraged King rose from his throne and had strangled the life from Nelvo with his bare hands. At first he had seen no reason to take the Elder's words as anything other than the ravings of a lunatic, but at the very same time he had never been able to forget them.

With his vast army at its absolute strongest, King Kragamel left the land of Fillagrou in the hands of his only son, Prince Valkea, and returned to Ocha where his now unstoppable army made short work of each and every remaining family enemy. Had his father lived to see this moment, he would no doubt have been filled with great pride. The tyrant King Kragamel had accomplished more than his father dreamt possible. His family's name was feared throughout not only Ocha, but ninety-nine other worlds as well. He had accomplished everything he had set out to do and now found himself holding the fate of the universe in the palm of his hand.

For King Kragamel everything was good and perfect and wonderful, but as fate has shown us time and time again, it has little patience for such things.

15. THE GREAT KING WALCOTT SHELLAMENNES

Owen Little grabbed a handful of grass and dirt and used it to tug himself out of the muddy water. Lying on his stomach he took a moment to catch his breath and spit the remaining liquid from his lungs. Still feeling a bit woozy, he was unsure exactly what had happened prior to waking with lungs full of dark, muddy water. In fact, the last thing he could remember was running toward the stream in an attempt to find out what happened to the brown-haired girl who had fallen in only moments ago. After that, nothing. When he next opened his eyes he was underwater and drowning. Common sense told him that he must have slipped, fallen, bonked his head and rolled into the stream. The very idea - while plausible considering his complete lack of coordination - sounded so embarrassing and stupid that he found it difficult to even entertain the possibility.

With his face smeared against the dirty forest floor, Owen was jolted back to reality after hearing the sound of a girl screaming somewhere off in the distance. Looking toward his left, he noticed the very same brown haired girl that had fallen into the stream. Sitting next to her, wrapped up tightly in her arms was a little boy. The two were pressed up against the leg of a dark gray beast so enormous in size that the top of its body disappeared into the dust clouds high above the trees. The creature's massive head was only inches from the girl's screaming face, sniffing at her soaking wet body.

A sudden jolt of fear traveled to the very tips of Owen's limbs and he quickly, yet silently lowered himself down into the water. Only his eyes were visible as he watched the bizarre situation play out before him. It was like something from a science fiction film rather than reality. The moment the giant creature's head retreated back into the clouds, Owen got his first good look at the two terrified figures and instantly recognized them both.

The girl with the brown hair was Staci Andrews. Owen had known Staci since kindergarten, though it was unlikely that she ever noticed him. Staci was pretty and popular, more often than not surrounded by a wealth of friends at school, while Owen could count the people he considered friends with one hand and still have enough fingers left over to hold a pencil. He had never seen Staci with anything but a smile on her face and a hop in her step. She seemed to live the kind of life he quietly envied, though he would vehemently deny it if ever asked. Now, with a torrential rain of tears cascading down her cheeks, she barely resembled the girl Owen had watched with a strange fascination from afar for so long.

The small boy sitting next to her was Nicky Jarvis. He did not know Nicky quite as well as he knew his older brother Tommy, but he had seen the boy around school several times when they were younger. Nicky Jarvis was known mostly for the fact that he never spoke a word, and was often spotted getting picked on in the schoolyard because of it. Despite being in different grades, and never having been formally introduced, Owen believed he had some things in common with the boy.

Raising his mouth ever so slightly out of the water to take another breath, he quickly lowered himself back down to avoid being noticed. A large group of armored men floated down from atop the gigantic monster with all the precision of a swat team invading an enemy bunker. Owen was completely submerged when he started to swim.

None of what he had seen made any sense. Things like this did not exist – things like this could not exist.

He had to be dreaming or imagining it or something. If he was not dreaming, and everything that he saw was actually happening, he wanted to get as far away as possible. Staci was a pretty girl, but pretty girl or not, she was going to have to fend for herself. His idea was to swim back to where he came from and get the help of someone more capable – which was just about anyone.

The water was pitch-black. It was nearly impossible to tell in which direction he was swimming. Down quickly became up, and up became down when moving wildly through the murky drink. Left and right were concepts that no longer had meaning. Spotting something resembling light, he kicked his legs with all his might and started swimming toward it. When he lifted his head out of the water again, he realized almost instantly that he was right back where he had started.

Off in the distance, two beefy armored men held both Nicky and Staci while they attached themselves to cables dangling from the back of the monstrous creature; they quickly disappeared into the sky - taking the screaming children with them. His heart raced and his brain did back flips inside his skull as Owen dove once again into the puddle.

A moment later his drenched head emerged in the exact same spot.

The giant creature and the armored solders were gone. Somewhere off in the distance he could hear the thunderous feet of the gigantic monster shattering trees with every step. As he pulled himself out of the water, he struggled to fight back an onslaught of tears. Not only was he stuck in this weird red forest, but he had not done anything to help Staci or Nicky. He was useless, pathetic, alone and ashamed.

"Now, now, my boy. Don't get too down on yourself."

The voice came from somewhere behind him but Owen was not sure exactly from which direction. Without thinking, he sat up, rolled back toward the water and started to lower himself once again into the puddle - still praying beyond all logic that it might prove a viable means of escape.

"Wait, wait, where are you running to, boy? There's no need to be scared."

Half-submerged, the terrified boy frantically looked in every direction, but saw nothing.

"You're not the only one here who sat idly by and did nothing, my boy." About fifteen feet away from the puddle, a large green rock began to move; it twisted ever so slightly as two stumpy, three- fingered arms popped out of either side. Once it was standing on its end, a pair of equally stumpy legs extended from its base just as a dirty greenish-brown head popped from the top. Fully erect, the creature resembled a turtle, though it was roughly the size of a grown man. The massive thing seemed to move in slow motion, weighed down by its thick, heavy shell. It moved so slowly that it looked almost painful. The eyes on either side of its wrinkly face opened, staring solemnly at Owen.

"I remember a time when I would have made every last one of those fiends taste the steely resolve of my blade," the creature muttered in a slow, almost shameful voice. "But ah…that seems so long ago now."

From a very old looking leather belt around its exceptionally wide waistline, the turtle man pulled a small knife out of its sheath. Moving it close to his face, he stared sadly at it. Owen stared at the creature with a look of utter horror on his face, not quite believing what he was seeing.

Returning the knife to its place, the lumbering turtle man moved in his direction. "Pleased to make your acquaintance boy, I am King Walcott Shellamennes, the son of former King Waldorf Shellamennes, the current King of the Tycarian people, the holder of the sacred cup of Peladrov and the keeper of the great Mud Chalice." Having finished naming his accomplishments, King Walcott slowly extended his three-fingered paw to Owen, a crooked smile on his wrinkled face. "And who might you be?"

Owen hesitated as he looked at the flat wide hand dripping with a layer of thick dirty slime.

"My boy, if you choose not to greet me properly, I will be forced to take it as an insult to the very throne of Tycaria and strike you down where you float."

Though Owen believed he could easily outrun the bizarre turtle man if he had to, he figured it best not to tempt fate and carefully shook the creature's goop-covered paw.

Half confused, half terrified, he managed to mutter, "Hi, umm…I'm Owen Little…son of …umm…Mack…and the keeper of…I don't know, books, and stuff…I guess."

85

King Walcott gripped the boy's hand tightly, shaking it up and down. "Pleased to make your acquaintance, Mr. Owen. You have a grip worthy of a warrior."

"Thanks...I think." Owen responded, his teeth clattering as he tried to hide his obvious discomfort.

Grabbing hold of Owen's hand with both of his, King Walcott pulled the boy's soaked form from the water. "Here, let me help you out of that puddle, my boy. A dirty old puddle is no place for one with a handshake such as yours. You know, now that I've had the opportunity to see you close up, I don't believe I've ever come across one of your race in my travels. Tell me...what world do you call home?"

Owen shivered as a cold breeze sailed in from above the trees, sending a chill down the back of his neck. He replied with some confusion, "I dunno...Earth, I guess."

"Earth, you say? Hmm, never heard of it. Ah well, I suppose it matters not where either of us once called home, Owen Little. We're all brothers now, are we not? We are all orphans as a result of the evil deeds carried out by the nefarious King Kragamel and his wicked offspring."

Owen had no idea what the strange turtle man was babbling about, but it did not matter. He was barely listening anyway. The bizarreness of the situation had pushed him into a state of silent unbelieving. One minute he had witnessed Staci Alexander drown, and the next he was talking to a nearly seven foot tall turtle with something vaguely resembling an English accent.

Nothing he could say would ever quite do any of it justice.

Tired of watching the strange pink child stare blankly into space, King Walcott turned to walk away, "I suppose that you're heading for Tipoloo same as I, Owen Little. You're quite welcome to join me on the journey. We'll have to move quickly though, as the Dark Guard's patrols will no doubt return post-haste. It would be advisable to be far from here when such a thing occurs."

King Walcott motioned for Owen to follow him as he broke into an extremely slow, plodding run. It was a full on sprint for him, but little more than a brisk walk for Owen.

"Tally-ho! I challenge you to keep up with me, Owen Little! Long before I was King of Tycaria, I was a medalist at the Tycarian games!"

16. THE FORTRESS OF PRINCE VALKEA

Staci and Nicky were tossed into a ten-foot by ten-foot steel cage on the enormous flat back of the great lumbering beast, alongside fourteen or fifteen strange looking creatures. They spent the next ten hours packed in with the sad, malnourished, incredibly odd-looking things.

For the vast majority of the trip, Staci had sat quietly with her shirt pulled over her head, trying to catch her breath in between violent fits of tears. She was having incredible difficulty coping with everything that had happened to her since she had decided to follow Tommy and Nicky Jarvis to the tree fort in the woods. The only way she could think to cope at all was to curl up inside and lock the door tight. A scarily thin woman with pink skin and ears growing up the sides of her head, attaching at the top like a pair of earmuffs, noticed her fragile emotional state.

Sitting beside Staci, the pink skinned woman wrapped the shivering girl in her equally shaking, frail arms.

Her voice was soft, soothing and understanding. "Its okay, my dear…it'll be alright," she repeated over and over in a warm, comforting tone meant not only for Staci, but for herself as well.

In a strange way Staci reminded the woman of the daughter she had lost years ago when the King's armies laid waste to her world. When she saw the faraway look in the young girl's eyes, the pink woman instinctively felt the need to comfort her as she would have comforted her own child.

The instinct of a mother was one of the few things that all races seemed to share.

Opposite Staci, Nicky leaned against the thick bars. His eyes drank in the strange world around him. From the forest floor, he had not seen the sky, but now, while rocking gently back and forth on the back of the huge gray dinosaur, the whole of this strange world came into plain view. It was covered in dark clouds with a subtle reddish hint that allowed the light of what seemed to be three suns peek through sporadically, something that the boy found to be both frightening and strangely beautiful. At some points, the clouds became so dark that Nicky could swear they almost looked black.

"It once looked very different you know…the sky I mean."

Nicky turned to his left and spotted a lanky, pale white creature hunched over at a frightening angle with his back to the cage. The creature's entire upper body was covered in scars and welts. Some of them leaked a dark purple substance that he assumed was blood. The frail white thing looked as if it had not eaten in weeks. Its skin drew so tightly against the bones underneath that it was almost unnoticeable – almost like a living skeleton.

With a faraway look on its face, the white thing gazed wearily at Nicky out of a pair of enormous soft red eyes, "Fillagrou was once the most beautiful place in all of reality, you know. Ah...would that you could have seen it then, my boy...would that you could have seen it then." Almost in slow motion, the creature turned its wobbly head away from Nicky and stared at the dark red sky though the bars above him. "They took everything from us, everything my father and his father before him had worked so hard to build. My family...my friends...my son...my dear son...Jakka...and why? We did nothing to them. Jakka was such good boy...so kind...always with a smile. He never hurt a living thing in his life, he never even entertained the idea. It doesn't make any sense... " The creature's voice began to trail off.

For an instant, the weary old Fillagrou swore that he could see his son's face in the clouds above and bit his thin lower lip to keep from screaming. The creature closed his eyes slowly, burying his massive head in his long, bony fingers. He would remain in this position, sobbing silently for the next five hours.

The long trek finally came to a stop outside a fortress with spires so high that they dwarfed even the great beast. The fortress walls extended for miles in all directions. Standing on top of them at perfectly measured intervals were more soldiers armed with massive bows. The giant gray beast lowered itself into a sitting position as guards stood at its hindquarters, tugging angrily at thick leather straps wrapped around its legs. Moments later, a huge crane latched onto the top of the cage holding Nicky, Staci and the rest of the prisoners and dropped it softly inside the fortress walls. A nearby soldier unlocked it, ordered the tired group out and sent them in different directions. When the disoriented creatures became confused or walked in the wrong direction, the soldiers did not hesitate to whip, punch, or crack them in the face with the handles of their weapons. The large commanding officer that had earlier in the day examined Staci's blood pulled her and Nicky aside.

"NO! Wait! Where are you taking her!?" The skinny pink woman asked as she clutched the fabric of the little girl's shirt, refusing to let go. A thick-shouldered guard wrapped his arms around her waist and attempted to tug her in the opposite direction, but was unable to pull Staci from the hysterical female's grasp. Even after whipping her violently, she still held Staci tight. Annoyed with the difficulty his soldier was having, the commanding officer walked over to the woman, lifted his boot and kicked her in the chest. The force of the blow sent the pink woman tumbling into the dirt. She immediately grabbed her chest, rolling around and screaming in pain. Pleased with his ability to gain control of the situation, the commanding officer snatched Staci by the wrist, lifted her violently into the air and threw her over his shoulder. He grabbed Nicky's arm with equal force and carried both screaming children across the courtyard and into the castle through an enormous door. The interior of the fortress was dark, dank and dusty. The air smelled of stagnant sweat. From the darkened hallways outlining the room, ungodly screams could be heard echoing off the thick stone walls, eventually disappearing into one of the endless maze of hallways. The trio passed a group of guards, ascended a massive staircase, passed even more guards, headed down a long elegantly decorated corridor containing yet more guards before reaching another monstrously-sized door which opened into a long, cold sparsely lit room.

A single silent figure stood forty feet away with his back to them, staring out a window overlooking the courtyard of the monstrous structure. Unlike the dark gray armor adorned by every other soldier Nicky had seen up to that point, the coverings worn by this enormous creature seemed to be made of pure gold. Around his waist hung a deep purple sash covered in finely detailed gold stitching. His head remained hidden in the shadows and because of this Nicky could not make out what the figure looked like above the shoulders. He could tell, however, that unlike every other soldier, this silent creature wore no helmet.

Without turning, the figure spoke in a deep voice, "I hope you have good reason for bothering me at this time of day, General Gragor. You know how I appreciate the way the sky looks in this awful place just before nightfall. In fact, it is the only time I can stand the miserable warmth of this world."

The guard carrying Staci lifted her off of his shoulder and dropped her with a heavy thud onto the ground beside him. Pulling Nicky in front of him, he shoved the boy to his knees, "I do indeed, Sire, but, in fact, this is news of some importance."

Still hidden in the shadows, unmoved, and staring out the window, the figure dressed in gold sighed deeply, clearly annoyed.

"Do you now? Let me guess, a few slaves giving you problems? Some of the more troublesome guards are complaining about wanting to return to Ocha again? Or wait, no…let me guess, my father would like me to give more detailed progress reports than the ones I am currently required to send to him on a daily basis? Please…tell me what painfully boring bit of important information you feel the need to bother me with that I haven't already heard a million times before?"

"It involves the prophecy of the pale ones, Your Majesty."

Immediately the figure spun around, gazing with some surprise in the direction of his underling. For a moment the entire room was steeped in heavy silence. The only audible sound was the soft whimper of Staci, who had yet to look up from the floor and the hurried breathing of an intimidated Nicky.

The figure dressed in gold raised a gloved finger in the direction of the children. "This? You speak of prophecies and this is what you lay before me? Whimpering little children, one of them a female? Have you gone completely mad, Gragor?"

Trying his best to disguise his frustration, General Gragor wrapped his hand around a clump of Staci's hair, pulling her to her feet. With his other finger he pointed at the cut on her forehead. "She bleeds red, my Prince."

Once again the creature dressed in gold stood eerily still as he decided how to respond to the situation unfolding before him. For years his father had warned him of the idiotic prophecy made by the Fillagrou Elder. Though he would never have said it to his father's face, he silently thought the old fool stupid, chuckling at how seriously he took the ramblings of an ancient, decrepit tree-dwelling freak.

After several minutes he finally broke the silence. "Release the poor dear children, Gragor. Where are your manners?"

General Gragor instantly let Staci slip from his enormous gloved hand. She dropped back to the floor where she immediately curled into a ball, tucking her head between her knees. As the creature dressed in gold took a step forward, General Gragor took one back and away from the children.

"It makes sense, doesn't it, Gragor? Seeing them now in front of me…these, prophecies coming to life…it makes complete and total sense, somehow. Only a people as pathetic as the Fillagrou would send avenging angels even more useless than they."

He laughed loudly at his own joke. The sound echoed though the room, out the window and across the entire courtyard, eliciting awkward stares from each and every one of the soldiers below. Moving closer to Staci and Nicky, he at last stepped into the light, making his face visible. Covered in dark green scales, his skin had a lizard-like quality to it. His eyes were deep set, his pupils a black so dark they seemed almost to go on forever into nothingness. Raising his gloved hand, he rubbed it across his bald, thickly scaled head. Through a mouth that extended from ear to ear, housing nearly endless rows of sharp, jagged, ivory-colored teeth, he smiled at the children. When Staci looked up, she caught her first glimpse of his monstrous face. It took everything in her power to keep from screaming. His was a race built for war, bred for evil through generation after generation of natural selection.

This was indeed the face of fear.

Standing no more than three feet from the children, he knelt down, putting himself face to face with them. "Hello, little children. My name is Prince Valkea, and I must admit...I am *extremely pleased* to finally meet you."

17. A HERO'S WELCOME

After the Elder had finished regaling Tommy and Donald with the long history of the invasion of Fillagrou, the prophecy, the doorways to other worlds and the general destruction caused by the armies of King Kragamel, he informed them that he needed to rest and would speak to them again in the morning. Pleebo helped him into a comfortable position and escorted both boys out of the modest dwelling. When Tommy and Donald stepped into the street they were greeted with wide smiles by all the creatures that were patiently waiting outside. The wise, ancient Elder had confirmed that the boys were two of The Five, sent to save them all. This fact instantly brought a renewed spirit to their shattered lives. There remained a few looks of worry here and there, concern about the young age and diminutive size of the boys, but for the most part, smiles seemed the norm. Each and every creature in the crowd had been terribly affected by the King's armies. They were prepared to grab onto whatever glimmer of hope they were given, even if it came in the very unlikely form of two unassuming human children.

Pleebo led the boys through the crowd to his dwelling which was not far from the Elder's. He offered them a humble meal consisting mostly of what he called boiled Fluto root. The above-ground foliage roots grew deep in the soil and could be easily plucked from the dirt ceilings of every home in the city. The fear of capture had kept them from searching for food in the forest, so the root had become the inhabitants' primary source of nourishment. It did not taste like much, sort of like chewing on hot leather, but neither Donald nor Tommy had eaten in some time. This made it easier to ignore the bland taste and somewhat foul smell. Halfway though dinner, the threesome were joined by Pleebo's younger sister, Zanell. Zanell resembled Pleebo quite a bit, only slightly shorter and with softer, more delicate features. Throughout the course of the meal, Pleebo had asked the boys many questions about where they came from. While Donald did his best to answer, Tommy had remained silent. When dinner concluded, Tommy had excused himself. Leaving Pleebo's dwelling, he headed out into the city streets. Ever since the boys had spoken with the Elder, Pleebo noticed that the seriousness of the situation weighed heavily on the young boy's mind. While Donald seemed to relish the idea of being a savior to an entire world – or at least doing a better job of pretending – Tommy struggled with the enormity of it all.

Sitting across from Donald, Zanell stared at the boy with a broad smile. Her large red eyes were wide, attentive and dreamy, with an almost star struck quality to them. "It's strange…to see you in person. I mean…you don't look anything like I thought you would," she said in a soft, squeaky voice.

"Oh, no? What did you think we would look like?" Donald responded with a crooked grin. Despite the fact that he was more creeped out by Zanell's unique appearance, he enjoyed the attention she gave him all the same. Girls – any girls - had never looked at him like this. He found himself liking it on some weird, unexplainable level, even if the girl in question was a waif thin, six foot tall, nearly transparent, root eating, freaky underground monster with fingers as long as his forearm and ears the size of his entire head.

"Beggars can't be choosers, right?"

Zanell reached across the poorly constructed table and grabbed Donald's hand, turning it upside down.

With a wide smile, she stared longingly at the strange patterns on his palm. "I don't know. I guess I always thought you would be bigger...older maybe...and a whole lot uglier."

Donald choked on the Fluto root. "You...you...don't think I'm ugly?" He muttered while coughing up bits of the tasteless, half-eaten weed.

"Not exactly, no. You're unique...I guess. Is it true that your blood is the same color as the forest?"

Donald swallowed deep, "Umm...sure...I guess...ya."

"I love the color of the forest. I've only actually seen it once. Most of my life has been spent here in Tipoloo, hiding. I remember it though...I remember it well...don't think I could ever forget it."

Pleebo was watching them from the other side of the table with a concerned look. He had noticed Zanell's infatuation by the way she stared at Donald, and while he found it a little funny, it worried him at the same time. Fillagrou was no longer a world for love or happiness or childish flights of fancy. It existed now only for pain, suffering, and disappointment. The smile on his sister's face, though was something he had not seen in a long time - something he missed very much. How could he take that away from her?

His finger tapped the top of the table lightly to get their attention. "Excuse me..."

Donald jumped slightly, turning toward Pleebo while trying to act innocent.

"Before this goes any further, Donald, I feel like I need to ask you exactly what your intentions are concerning my little sister."

Taken aback, Donald tripped over his words, as if he were trying to break into a full sprint after spinning in circles for five minutes, "Intentions? Huh? Wha...I don't kno...I mean, I'm not sure exactly what...I don't really have any intentions, I was ju..."

Pleebo interrupted Donald's sentence when he laughed a little under his breath, as he had done a number of times before.

"It's okay Donald...I'm just kidding. You know...for saviors, you kids are really gullible."

Donald relaxed a bit. Once again Pleebo was making fun of him again with the jokes. Donald was quickly starting to dislike the jokes.

Still chuckling to himself, Pleebo exited through the front door of his dwelling and glanced up and down the street. He spotted Tommy Jarvis sitting in a corner at the end of the block, absentmindedly scratching something into the dirt wall with his index finger.

The air inside Pleebo's home had been too stuffy. In fact, the air in the entire city of Tipoloo felt as thick as paint, sticky and convoluted. Tommy felt hot and heavy, and tired. Nothing seemed to make sense anymore. If he had not pinched himself at least fifty times without any effect whatsoever, he would have thought he was dreaming. On top of it all, try as he might, he could not stop thinking about his little brother. *"Was he okay? Was he scared, or worried?"* He would not be safe alone at home with their father, and because of that, Tommy had to get home quickly.

From behind him came Pleebo's now familiar voice. "Hey kiddo...how are you feeling?"

Tommy turned briefly to look at him, but could not think of the words to formulate a proper response.

"Do you mind if I sit?"

Once again Tommy did not answer. He hung his head low and stared at the dirty ground. He could not bring himself to look Pleebo in the face for too long. Pleebo's life had made his look like heaven in comparison. His entire family had been murdered, his home overrun, his friends struck down. The occasional beating Tommy's dad had thrown his way seemed like small potatoes compared to that. When he got right down to it, in his heart of hearts Tommy firmly believed that Pleebo and the Elder had the wrong person. He did not feel like the savior of an entire world. He was just a kid. To do the things that they expected of him seemed unbelievable, not to mention impossible.

He was not who these people needed. He never would be, and things would only get worse for them.

"Listen, Tommy, I know it seems like a lot..."

Tommy quickly interrupted. "I'm not who you think I am."

"What do you mean?"

"What do you mean, what do I mean? Look at me. I'm just a kid. I get beat up on the way home from school. My own father, more times than I even care to remember, has smacked me around. I can't save anybody...I can't even save myself. You have the wrong person. It's not that I don't want to help, but what is it that you think I can do? I'm just...I'm not the person you need...I'm sorry."

99

Pleebo watched the boys fingers move gracefully across the wall. Each line dug into the soft dirt brought whatever he was sketching closer to life. Creating images in this fashion was not a skill his people shared and to see it this closely fascinated him. Turning his head away from the boy, he gazed down the nearly empty street. Most of the city's inhabitants had returned to their dwellings to rest for the evening – those that required sleep anyway. On a very real level, he more than anyone, understood exactly what the young boy felt. Tommy was wrestling with ideas that he had been forced to face many years ago.

"Tommy, I was not much older than you when one of the King's armies swept into our underground hiding place and tore it to pieces. It was a lot smaller than Tipoloo – maybe fifty feet long – housing only a few families. Though my parents had known war for some time, they did not understand it at all…could not understand it. We had been a beautiful race once. Maybe the most beautiful and honest in all of reality, but at the same time we had been like children. Our greatest achievement was also our greatest failing. Violence had not been a part of our lives, let alone violence on the scale that the Ochans brought to us. It was not something we understood or even acknowledged. My father was a simple, thoughtful, and extremely proud child of Fillagrou. He had no idea how to react to violence. He had tried to reason with one of the Ochan soldiers because, quite simply, it was all that he knew how to do."

Tommy looked at Pleebo. As Pleebo talked, he seemed almost lost in his story. The remembrances of the moments of which he had spoken obviously still affected him deeply as he replayed them in his mind.

"The soldier had laughed at him as he pled for mercy…begging for the lives of his family. He laughed at him… then struck him down in cold blood…right in front of my eyes. Not knowing what to do, I ran. I ran as fast as I could, grabbed my baby sister, my mother, and then ran some more. A few years later, I joined the resistance. My mother was not happy. She tried to convince me that I was throwing away every ideal the Fillagrou had spent eons building."

Pleebo slowly and mournfully raised his hands to his face, forming fists. The bones in his knuckles cracked and popped. "With these hands, I helped build Tipoloo. I dug until my fingers bled, until the flesh peeled away and I was digging with little more than bone. I was nobody, Tommy…I was just a dumb kid. Never once in my life did I imagine that I would be called on to save the life of anyone else. Heck, I did not even think I was capable of such a thing. I don't imagine any of us knows what we can do until we're face to face with a situation and forced to react. That's the secret, Tommy. Maybe it's something you won't fully understand until the moment arrives…that instant when action becomes reaction. Let me tell you this, though…it's not the tests themselves that define us…it's how we react to them. When I first saw you, I have to admit…I doubted that you were who I thought you might be, but now…"

Pleebo stopped in mid-sentence. The pupils in his enormous red eyes grew twice as large as he stared at Tommy.

"What?" Tommy asked, worried by the look on the creature's face, unsure of what was going on.

Pleebo raised his arm and pointed one of his long fingers at him. Tommy's entire hand had lit up with a soft, bright white light which extended halfway up his forearm. Not only that, but the light seemed to be growing brighter. The heat coming off of it warmed

101

the side of his face. The ominous glow seemed to originate from the tips of his fingers, growing brighter still, inching its way further up his arm. Although not fully aware of what he was doing, Pleebo backed away slowly. His mouth dropped open, his thin lips moved up and down as if he wanted to speak, though no words escaped. The dirt wall that Tommy's hand had been pressed against began to evaporate inward as the light emanating from him engulfed it, erasing it much the same way the sun might evaporate water. Overcome with fear, Tommy also slowly backed away. The incredible energy pouring from his hand, however, followed him, cascading across the large dirt wall, covering it like a blanket.

Terrified, he managed to mumble pleadingly, "Pleebo...I..."

The glowing light now fully engulfed his arm and inched its way up his neck. Tommy turned to Pleebo, his wide eyes begging for help. Pleebo had continued to back away, amazed and alarmed at what he was witnessing.

Tommy felt the tickle of light inching its way up the side of his face. He heard its energy crackle in his ear. He closed his eyes tight, bit down as hard as he could, and prayed that whatever was happening to him would stop. He wanted to cry or scream or shout, but was unable to do so. He thought of his father and his brother. He thought of Pleebo and what had happened to Fillagrou. He thought of everything that he had seen here, and everything his father had put him though over the last two years. He thought of his mother and her smile, and the very last thing she had said to him before she died. He remembered the feel of her fragile hand, the sound of her labored breathing, the look on her faraway eyes as she smiled at him for the very last time. He thought of everything – and somehow, he made the strange sensation stop.

When he opened his eyes again, the light was gone and his arm had returned to normal. In front of him, a massive empty tunnel had replaced the dirt wall. He turned to look at Pleebo, only to find the street filled with a wild assortment of creatures, each with their mouths open wide in surprise. Donald stood with a look of shock, awe and fear. Tommy never imagined he would see such a look on the boy who had made his school days such a living hell. Next to him stood Pleebo and Zanell, next to them, a six-foot tall turtle with a tiny knife in his oversized paw, and next to him…Owen Little.

Tiny red Roustaf buzzed past Tommy's ear, hovering for a moment at the opening of the newly-formed tunnel. He turned around with a look of shock on his face, his hands high on his hips.

Rubbing one hand up and over his head, the little man sighed deeply as he twiddled his tiny mustache.

Slightly grinning in Tommy's direction, he screamed as loudly as a man of his minuscule size could possibly muster, "Hot damn, kid! Them's some magic fingers you've got there!"

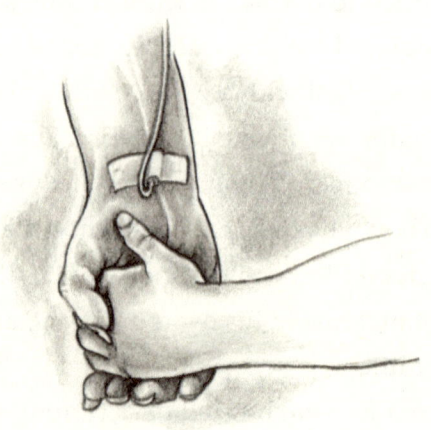

18. THE PROMISE

The long white hallway on the fourth floor of the Fairchild Medical Center was mostly empty and rather quiet. Occasionally a nurse or a doctor walked by with their head buried in a set of papers on a clipboard, their shoes clicking against the tile floor with every step. It was night, and with visiting hours coming to an end, most everyone, patients and family alike, had either drifted off to sleep or returned home. On an empty bench near the end of the hallway sat ten-year-old Tommy Jarvis. Too short to reach the floor, his legs swung back and forth over its edge. His hands rested softly on his lap as he twiddled his fingers quietly, trying his hardest to think about anything other than this place. His mother and father were just behind the door on his right.

For almost a year now his mother had become progressively sicker. At first the trips to the doctor had been for small things like high fevers or sore throats or pain in her joints. In the last few months, the trips had become more frequent. She had been admitted to the hospital three weeks ago, and it was here that she remained. Every night like clockwork his father left him and Nicky with Auntie Carol so that he could visit her. On the weekends – like today – he would bring them along. Nicky might be too young to really, truly understand every nuance of what was going on, but Tommy believed the young boy understood the basics of the situation. Their mother was sick and she was not going to get better.

She was dying.

No doubt Nicky could not make total sense out of the concept of death, but he knew that a time would come very soon when he would never see his mother again.

Tommy looked up as the door to his mother's room opened; his father stepped out with a sleepy-sad Nicky pressed tightly against his chest. He looked in Tommy's direction. "Hey buddy...how are you feeling?"

Tommy did not know quite how to respond. The idea of summing up everything going on in his head seemed like a task more impossible than anything he had encountered in his young life. He saw no point in trying.

Chris Jarvis gently laid the half-awake Nicky on the bench next to his older brother, softly brushing the hair from the boy's eyes. When Chris looked down he noticed that his hand was shaking. He could feel a torrent of emotions building up inside him, but he forced himself to ignore them. Chris needed to be strong, even if he wanted to cry and scream, and denounce his faith in God, the universe, and whatever unseen force was putting his family through this. He wanted to yell at the doctors for not doing more, or curse the nurses for their pointless pitying looks, or simply run away and leave all the sadness and the stress behind, but he could not. Chris could not do any of these things or a number of others. Not in front of his boys, and not now. These were things better left to the nights alone, shrouded within the darkness of his room, while lying on the marital bed with soaking wet eyes. He had to be bigger than that; he had to be better than that, for them – even if it hurt more than he could stand.

After taking a deep breath and wiping away a single tear from the corner of his eye, Chris knelt down in front of Tommy, gazing into the soft blue eyes of his eldest son. "Hey big man, your mom…your mom wants to see you alone for a minute. Would you like to do that? Are you going to be okay, or do you want your ol' dad to go with you?"

Tommy noticed as well his father's shaking hands. He spotted the very faint glimmer of wetness, catching the pale glow of the fluorescent lights in the corner of his father's eye.

Despite trying so hard, Chris Jarvis could not hide his emotions well.

Tommy wanted badly to see his mother - to hug her and kiss her and hear her tell him that she loved him…and that she would always be there for him…but he knew that was not going to happen. Maybe it was the look on his father's face or the eerie, bordering on downright frightening, silence coming from his mother's room, but something inside the boy told him that if he went through that door, it would be for the last time. After today he was never going to see her again.

"Well buddy, is that something you think you might want to do? I know your mom would really like to see you."

Despite his brain telling him to say "no", Tommy nodded yes. He carefully slid off of the bench and moved toward her room.

Gently his father patted him on top of his head, mussing his hair a bit, whispering in a shaky voice, "It's okay, buddy...everything will be all right."

Despite his best efforts, Chris Jarvis was not convincing anyone – least of all, himself.

Once he put some distance between his father and himself, Tommy heard his father's voice crack silently as he struggled to keep from breaking down right there on the spot. It was this very tiny, yet extremely telling moment that would stick with Tommy for years afterward, because his father's voice would never sound the same again. Not only did Chris Jarvis' voice crack on that day, but his soul did, as well – a crack so deep that it could never be repaired – spreading slowly, until the dam of his emotions shattered completely, devouring everything in its path.

The hospital room was dark, barely lit by the glow of a television set hanging high in the corner, the volume turned all the way down. As Tommy approached his mother's bed he noticed how small and frail her body looked. The light blue sheet hung over her as if it were resting on a skeleton. Her breathing was labored, her face gaunt, her eyes sleepy, distant and dreamy. She looked far away, almost as if her mind were off somewhere floating above, just barely clinging onto the motionless form that had been left behind and propped upon pillows. Tommy saw her left eye move slowly to the side, independent of her face, as she spotted him standing next to the bed gazing at her. A weary smile shaped her worn face, but even the act of smiling seemed to be a painful experience for her. Her mouth opened as if she wished to speak, but only a puff of air and a gentle hum, just barely a sound, escaped.

Somewhat ashamed at her inability to form sentences, she squinted, focused her mind and tried again, "T...Tommy...ho...how is Mommy's...s...special little...guy?"

Her hand crawled across the bed sheets like a pale white spider moving toward him. When it arrived at the end of the bed Tommy reached up and held onto it gently. He wanted to squeeze it as tightly as he could, but did not for fear that it might someway cause her pain.

"Mommy...is...g...going to go away for a while...bu...I don't want you...to...ever forget how...much I...I love you...okay, baby?"

The tidal wave of emotions Tommy had been doing his best to keep inside started to make their way out of him in the form of hot liquid now streaming from his eyes. His face instantly grew balmy and tepid, his lip started to quiver uncontrollably and his neck felt wobbly, unable to properly hold the weight of his head. While trying to catch his breath and failing, Tommy looked up at the motionless form that only slightly resembled his mother.

In between deep breaths he did his best to form a sentence, "Bu...but I don't want you to go." It was not much, but was the best that he could manage before breaking down completely.

Megan Jarvis started instantly to weep uncontrollably, as she saw the tears pour from her little boy's eyes.

She had cried so much over the past year that she found it amazing that she had any tears left, "No...no...don't cry, baby...you need to be strong for Mommy...you...you need to be st...strong." Using every last ounce of strength buried within her, Megan leaned over the side of the bed, ignoring the incredible pain shooting throughout her body. Reaching down with one hand, she pulled her son toward her.

Tommy moved closer, his face now sobbing into the thin, flower-patterned fabric of her hospital gown.

"This is just part of life To…Tommy. Ju…just another part…" Megan stuttered softly, pulling her first-born's head away from her shoulder so that she could look him directly in the eyes, "All of life is beautiful…all of it. Even…the parts we hate, and even…when it reaches its end."

Tommy was not completely sure what she meant, but he absorbed her every word like a plant absorbing the life-giving energy of the sun, promising himself that he would never forget even a single one.

"You're a very special…boy…Tommy Jarvis. I…I…knew from the moment I saw…your tiny little…face. Promise me…promise Mommy that you'll enjoy life. Promise…me…that you'll look for its beauty. Promise me, that…you'll be happy. Promise me…that you'll do…do…everything that…"

She stopped for a moment, her lips slowly opening as if she were thirsty before she continued, "Promise me that you'll…that you'll do everything you think…you can't…" Her voice trailed off. Her eyes slowly looked away from him toward something she could see that he could not. The hot air softly blowing from her mouth and nose became shorter and colder against Tommy's skin. Her neck grew looser and her head heavier. Her hand slid off his face, floating downward, weightless, and landed softly on the sheet covering her body.

Tommy climbed onto her bed, wrapped his arms around her, and buried his face in her shoulder. Deeply he breathed in the smell of her hair, relishing it as it floated into his brain.

In between fits of tears, he whispered softly into her ear, "I Promise."

19. **INTO THE DUNGEON**

As ordered by the Prince, General Gragor lugged Staci and Nicky from his chambers, across the castle, down an enormously long set of winding stairs and through a humongous steel door leading to the fortress dungeon. The light inside was almost non-existent, the air cold, stiff, and stuffy. Built into either side of a long, dark hallway were extremely small, dank, rancid smelling cells, each with a malnourished prisoner or two locked behind a thick set of crisscrossing steel bars. From deep within the darkness of the cells, Nicky could hear soft moans, painful and tired, each laced with a sense of hopelessness. The sounds frightened him. His breath shortened and his heart raced as he slowed his rapidly moving feet to a drag.

Stiffly, General Gragor shoved the boy in his back, nudging him forward and prompting him to pick up the pace.

Halfway down the hall, General Gragor instructed the children to stop in front of an empty cell. With a closed fist, he motioned in the direction of a guard standing twenty feet away, who pulled a lever on a nearby wall. The cell door opened with a very deep, ancient sounding roll.

"Get in." General Gragor mumbled with some annoyance, this time poking Staci in the spine and shoving her inside.

Once both she and Nicky were within its walls, General Gragor motioned to the guard again and the cell door closed behind them. Before turning to walk away the massive creature leaned close to the bars, slowly removing his helmet. His face was as hideous as that of Prince Valkea. General Gragor seemed much older, though, his green scales showing the wear and tear of years spent in the trenches of war. The stern, serious look in his eyes indicated beyond a shadow of a doubt that he had seen horrors the children could scarcely imagine.

He took a moment to silently look over the children, before he gruffly spoke, "If it were up to me, the both of you would be dead already. The Prince may not believe in the prophecy…and I can't say that I blame him, but the way I see it …why bother taking a chance? Let me tell you this…at the very first sign of trouble, whether I'm ordered to or not, I will put an end to your lives without hesitation or regret. I've killed things smaller and more pathetic than you in the name of my King, and I will gladly do it again. This is my promise to you." He growled menacingly underneath his breath, put on his helmet and headed through the door at the end of the hall.

"KEEP A CLOSE EYE ON THESE TWO!" He commanded sternly before he vanished from sight. Nicky and Staci sat with their knees pulled into their chests, their backs against the cold stone of the cell wall. Staci had stopped crying, silently rocking back and forth, her eyes closed tight. Whispering under her breath she prayed that she would wake up and discover that his had been a horrible dream. She imagined she would go downstairs and find her mother making her breakfast and hug her longer and tighter than she had ever hugged anyone before. Nicky Jarvis felt as lost, confused, and scared as she looked, though on the outside he tried to remain relatively composed, succeeding only a little. He scooted closer to Staci and rested his arm around her, pulling her close; the gesture was as much for him as it was for her. Just having someone – anyone – near felt good – felt reassuring.

Underneath her breath, Staci quietly mumbled, "I'm so sorry Nicky…I'm so sorry."

She was overcome with a feeling of uselessness. She was ashamed of the way she had reacted to everything, but at the same was not sure how to stop it. She regretted not having had the strength to pull Nicky out of the water, as if their being here was in some way her fault. She missed her parents – her father, her mother – she missed them so much that simply thinking of them made her heart ache. She wondered if she would ever see them again and became significantly more frightened when she realized that she did not have an answer.

Looking around the cell, Nicky took note of the absence of beds. In fact, there was not anything at all in the tiny cell. Not more than ten feet lengthwise and five feet across, this place seemed less like a cell and more like a large closet. Everything was dark. The only light came from a few dimly lit, sporadically placed, lamps running along the ceiling. Every shadow cast seemed perilously deep, dark and black, obscuring the poor souls hidden within them.

"You're the youngest I've ever seen in here."

The voice came from a darkened cell on the other side of the hall. Nicky looked toward the sound, but saw only shadows.

"I've been locked up down here for weeks...I'm not sure exactly how many. It's remarkably easy to lose track of time in this place. Most don't seem to last more than a week, so I guess I should consider myself lucky...if being left alive, only to suffer from starvation and infection due to untreated wounds can in fact be considered lucky. I guess, maybe not."

Staci gazed wearily in the direction of the voice. Whoever was speaking to them from inside the shadows seemed to be one of the few people in this entire place that did not want to hurt either her or Nicky. Just like the children and the pink woman in the transport, the owner of the voice was a prisoner too.

"I noticed that General Gragor himself led you two down here. We are not generally given the honor of seeing the Prince's top military advisor. You're a lot tougher than you look, or you simply made him really, really angry. Either way, you're okay in my book." The creature behind the voice stepped slowly out of the shadows and pressed himself against the bars, using them to remain upright. His appearance was very fish-like. The entire, unclothed upper half of his body was covered in greenish-blue scales that looked worn, dirty, and beaten. A large patch of them on his right arm appeared to have been peeled away in a violent, slow and very painful manner. Light green blood seeped from various cuts scattered randomly across his flesh. The front of his face was flat, with two nostrils dug directly into the center. His eyes were pushed off to either side of his head; one of them was welted shut and puffed out at least an inch, as if it had received a heavy blow not too long ago.

Turning his head to the side, the fish man looked at the children with his one good eye. "My name is Fellow by the way…Fellow Undergotten of the city Chintaran." Fellow waited for a response from either of the children and received none.

No matter how unassuming this new creature seemed, the children were too shell-shocked to make friends with anyone, let alone a strange one-eyed fish prisoner they had met only moments prior.

Sensing that he was not going to get a response, Fellow continued, "It's okay…you don't have to answer. Believe me, I know what it's like…especially when you first find yourself locked up down here. I did not say anything to anyone for at least four days after they threw me into this hole. The creature that had occupied your cell before you…his name was Milosh. Interesting guy…a Horcalax…I think that's what he called himself. His body was pretty much a pile of living, breathing, gelatinous goop…you know, if a pile of glop could live, breathe, and regale long, drawn out stories of its home world... In any case, he was the one and only of his kind that I had ever met. One day, completely out of the blue…the guards scooped him up, plopped him into a bucket then hauled him away and did God knows what with him after that. I haven't seen him since. The reason I tell you this is, while I understand your reason for silence, your time down here may be perilously short, my little friends…endeavor to make the best of it while you can." Fellow's eyes closed. His sad grin turned into an even sadder frown. "Milosh…I hope that somehow he's alive…though I doubt it."

Staci watched the strange fish man intently. He looked beaten and tired, as if the weight of the entire world was resting on his weary shoulders, dragging him down. His every movement was labored; his body was no doubt wracked with indescribable pain. While one part of her felt sad for him, another was struck to the core with the idea that his situation might just be her future.

The guard at the end of the hall angrily turned his head toward Fellow, and for a few moments everything was silent.

When Fellow spoke again, it was in a soft whisper. "I was just a simple builder before this all started. I kept to myself… never bothered anyone…all I ever wanted was a piece of land to call my own…maybe some clear blue waters nearby to swim in. Immediately after the war started, I went from building homes to making weapons. Now, I'm no pacifist mind you, but let me tell you, little ones…making items meant to kill…this was something that never sat well with me."

The children remained huddled together in the corner, staring at Fellow with a mixture of fear, confusion, and pity in their eyes. They seemed to have no interest in talking and it was because of this that Fellow began to wonder if it might be better to simply leave them alone for the time being and give them time to come to terms with their situation.

"Ah, but I'm bothering you…I'm rambling again. I apologize, children…I'll leave you be."

Staci quickly jumped up, moving toward the bars with surprising urgency. It had been too long since she had someone to talk to, and something inside her told her that she could not let the opportunity slip away, "NO! WAIT!"

Fellow turned toward her again, "Yes?"

"Wait, don't go…I'm sorry…we want to talk…we want to talk…please don't go. Please don't go, please. Don't leave us." She began to sob slightly; her hands gripped the cell bars so tightly they almost hurt.

115

Fellow's voice was soft and comforting. "It's okay, child, it's okay…just relax…I'm not going anywhere. There's no need to cry. Besides…," he chuckled, "…even if I wanted to go, I'm not sure the rather burley Ochan at the end of the hall, with the sharp weapon strapped to his back, would be willing to go along with the idea."

Through her tears and shortened breath, Staci laughed a little at his joke. It was badly delivered and came at the most inappropriate time, but it was a joke. It had been so long since she had heard a joke. Fellow took note of her slight amusement and smiled. Walking next to Staci, Nicky meekly wrapped his hands around the bars. Both children stared at the injured, broken-bodied fish man with a renewed warmth and openness in their eyes.

"My God…you're just children." Fellow whispered under his breath in disbelief. "What kind of monsters would do this to children?" He sighed deeply and feigned a smile at their tiny, frail forms. He hoped to keep them from crying. His functioning eye focused on the top of Staci's forehead and almost instantly his smile turned to an open-mouthed look of surprise. Across the top of her head - dried, caked, yet still noticeable - was red blood.

Fellow's mind traveled back to weeks ago to when he had first been thrown into the dungeon. The cell occupied by the children had been the temporary home of a Fillagrou farmer who often sat awake at night, muttering to himself the story of the Elder, the prophecy, and The Five who would come and save them all. Of course, Fellow had believed that it was little more than an ancient, somewhat corny sounding superstition. It appeared to be the hopeful deluded ramblings of a people who had lost everything and because of that they had created something in their minds to help them through the darkest of days.

Now, though, with a little girl bleeding red right in front of his face, he could not seem to shake the memories of the crazy old creature's words. Even if it were a mere coincidence, the fact that General Gragor had escorted the children down to the dungeon proved that they had met the Prince himself. If they had been given an audience with the Prince, this implied that on some very tiny level at least, he took something about them very seriously.

Even the slightest amount of fear or discomfort in the Prince's day brought a mischievous smile to Fellow's sore face.

Leaning in close to the bars, Fellow said, with just the slightest twinge of happiness in his voice, "Now I see why the Prince has such an interest in you two."

It seemed that surviving all those weeks in this hellish dungeon really had been a blessing.

20. THE MAGNIFICENT SEVEN

The crowd of people that filled the small street in the city of Tipoloo was quite immense in size; they stared at Tommy Jarvis with shock on their faces. Packed together tightly, they seemed like one enormous, multi-colored life form, folding and melting and spreading across the city's streets like water. The chatter emanating from the crowd grew louder with every new body that joined it.

"It's him."

"The prophecy is true."

"The Five to save us all!"

"They've arrived!"

"We're saved!"

The electricity of one, spread to another, and to another until a hurried excitement could be felt moving throughout the entire crowd. Those who had witnessed Tommy's incredible feat firsthand rushed to wake their neighbors and relate the news. The neighbors rushed to tell their neighbors, those neighbors rushed to tell their neighbors, and so on and so forth. Within a matter of minutes the entire city was alive with excitement, filled with a sense of hope that everyone who called it home had not experienced since the onset of the Great War.

Through it all, Tommy stood in stunned silence, still unsure of what exactly had happened.

The crowd of spectators circled the young boy. Pleebo rushed to his aid, putting himself between the manic horde and the baffled child. "WAIT! WAIT! Everyone quiet down and back away! Give the boy some room!"

As the mass of creatures continued to move forward to get a closer look at Tommy and his amazing powers, Zanell positioned herself at her brother's side, trying in vain to calm them. When he saw Zanell move, Donald reluctantly did the same. He had no idea what was going on and did not particularly want to get anywhere near Tommy with his glowing fire hand, but he did not want to look like an uncaring jerk in front of Zanell.

Standing beside Tommy, Donald glanced at him and whispered. "How in the hell did you do that, loser?"

Even if he had wanted to, Tommy could not answer. Instead he stared back at Donald with a look of complete confusion spread across his face.

Little Roustaf darted in and out of the crowd, trying to calm their growingly violent excitement. "PIPE DOWN, YA CRAZY MIXED UP BUMS! GIVE THE KID SOME SPACE!"

119

Annoyed at the crowd's reaction and fearing for the young boy's safety, King Walcott Shellamennes pushed his way through the sea of multi-colored alien flesh and fur to come to the boy's aid.

Reaching beside him, he snatched Owen by the arm, tugging the boy alongside for safety's sake, "Sally-forth, Owen Little! That young man is in need of assistance!"

Pleebo, Zanell, Donald, Owen, King Walcott and Roustaf formed a protective circle around the boy. Tommy was just beginning to come down from the initial shock of what had just happened. He stared at his hands. He still felt a tingling sensation crackling and popping somewhere under his skin, similar to what he felt when he had slept on them the wrong way.

The inhabitants of Tipoloo were not trying to get their hands on Tommy with bad intentions, in fact quite the opposite. For most of their lives they had lived in squalor, had watched their families die and their worlds burn. The creatures spent more days than they had cared to count hungry, beaten, aching and praying for something to save them.

Until this moment, they had all but given up on life.

They had seen the promise of Tommy's power with their very own eyes. Instantaneously, they had been filled with hope, with the promise of a new day – with the possibility of a future. Their somewhat overzealous reaction to Tommy's amazing powers was little more than unbridled, unchecked happiness at its most pure and honest. Unable to fully process the emotions that had been brought to light by the concept of a world without suffering, their emotions were, instead, erupting in an unorganized, dangerous manner.

"PLEASE! EVERYONE! STOP! THIS ISN'T THE WAY TO HANDLE THE SITUATION!" Pleebo screamed, as hands and paws and tentacles attempted to push him aside, hoping to touch the wonderful savior that he and the others encircled protectively.

As determined as the group was to protect Tommy, the crowd was growing larger by the second, and they were only seven. Outnumbered nearly thirty to one, they realized that they would not be able to hold back the mass much longer.

The hairy arm of a large walrus looking creature with two gigantic tusks hanging from his mouth shoved Donald to the side, knocking the boy to the ground violently. Donald landed hard on his rear end. Anger boiled up in the pit of his stomach and traveled to his brain, clouding his better judgment in a red, smoky haze. Gritting his teeth, the furious boy formed his hands into fists, quickly rising to his feet. He grabbed a handful of hair on the creature's chest and lifted it straight into the air as if it were as light as a feather.

"I'LL TEACH YOU TO SHOVE ME, JERK!" Donald screamed at the enormous, now airborne beast.

Seeing the young boy perform such a feat of impossible strength, and quickly recognizing the intense look of anger on his face, the crowd immediately quieted down. Slowly the great mass of bodies retreated, fearful of what the angry young boy might do next.

An equally stunned Pleebo had noticed the unbridled rage on Donald's face and realized the situation was getting even more out of hand.

Trying to stay calm, Pleebo moved toward Donald slowly and softly said, "Donald, put him down. He didn't mean anything. It was an accident. He was just exited...go ahead and put him down."

"NO! ACCIDENT, MY ASS! He shoved me to the ground! Who the hell does he think he is, shoving me!? No one shoves me!"

The creature dangling in Donald's grip let out a scared yelp as the boy thrashed him from side to side. Donald was shaking the nearly four hundred pound beast with frightening ease.

Standing behind Donald, Zanell cautiously rested her hand on his shoulder, pleading, "Please put him down, Donald...he didn't me..."

"NO! HE SHOULDN'T HAVE PUSHED ME! No one pushes me! Who does he think I am!? I didn't do anything to him! Pushing me like I was not even there! No one ignores me! Not my MOM, not my BROTHERS, NO ONE!"

The anger coursing throughout Donald's body was growing larger every moment. It was a dark rage that had been brought on as a result of very old, very deep wounds. The day his father walked out on him and the fact that his mother could not possibly care less about him, and the way that his older brothers treated him like dirt on a daily basis, were the things that had directly caused the anger to erupt, like scorching hot magma. Adjusting his grip on the creature's fur, Donald pulled it back, as if he intended to throw the terrified beast across the city street.

From behind him came the cold assured voice of Tommy Jarvis, "Put him down, Donald!"

"SHUT UP, FREAK! I'M NOT PUTTING ANYONE DOWN!"

"I said...put him down. Donald."

"OR WHAT, LOSER!?"

Still holding the large creature without a single ounce of strain on his muscles, Donald turned and looked at Tommy. Tommy's right arm lit up like the sun itself, much as it had before. The unearthly light slowly moved up his arm, over his shoulder and into his ears, lighting up his eyes from the inside like a jack-o-lantern on Halloween.

Every time Tommy's lips parted, the ominous glow escaped from his mouth.

In a deadly serious tone, Tommy looked at Donald and insisted, "Put...him...down."

The bizarre and terrifying sight erased the rage boiling up in Donald's belly and brought him back to reality. He looked up and saw the terrified creature that he held in his hand. Its eyes were shut tightly as it mumbled what sounded like a prayer. Unsure of exactly what he was doing or how he was doing it, Donald lowered the creature gently back onto the dirt and backed away, trying to make sense of what had just happened.

Pleebo watched as the glow emanating from Tommy's arm faded and noticed that Donald was also calming down. The crowd had settled into a hushed silence, and Pleebo afforded himself the luxury of breathing freely again.

Wiping the sweat off his brow, he turned his attention to his shocked sister. "Zanell, go and wake up grandfather. We need to speak to him right now."

Zanell nodded and pushed her way through the crowd, doing exactly as her brother instructed.

Standing next to King Walcott, Owen Little was shaking like a leaf, still in shock over what he had just seen. In less than twenty-four hours he had gone from doing his science homework and avoiding work on his father's hot rod, to this – to complete and utter madness.

With a shaky hand he tapped Pleebo on the arm, "Umm...I know I'm going to regret asking this, but who's your grandfather?"

Pleebo gazed at the scared little boy with the very old looking Tycarian hovering behind him like a protective father. He then glanced at Tommy, Donald and Roustaf, who were now standing next to him. .

He turned his back on the still silent crowd and spoke in a dumbfounded whisper, "All of you...follow me."

Slowly the crowd parted, letting the group through with expressions of shock and awe sprayed across their faces as they watched the boys pass by. Pleebo led the group back down the street and headed towards the dwelling of the Elder. He let everyone into the small quarters before closing the door behind him.

Zanell was at the other end of the dark room, helping the ancient creature out of bed for the second time that evening. He looked tired and frail and seemed to be in immense pain, having to move again without sufficient time to properly rest his tender joints.

Pleebo moved toward him, aiding his sister in her attempts to sit the old creature upright. "I'm sorry grandfather...I know you wanted to wait until tomorrow, bu..."

"It's all right, my boy, it's all right. I fully understand that there are more important things than the suffering of an old wreck such as me, especially in this day and age."

As soon as he was sitting, the Elder lovingly tapped Pleebo on the side of his face, smiling at him. "Besides, how could I stay mad at you when you look so much like your mother?"

He gazed dreamily upon Pleebo before he directed his attention to the people that now packed his tiny dwelling. The Elder signed deeply as he glanced about the room. His eyes stopped roaming when he noticed Owen, "Ah...it would seem that the third has arrived...good. Welcome, young man, I've been quite anxious to meet you."

"Grandfather," Pleebo said shyly since he was not sure if he should interrupt, "Outside, in the street, Tommy's hand..."

The Elder lifted his bony finger and nodded to Pleebo, indicating to his grandson that an explanation was unnecessary. After letting a stiff and very painful ache in his back run its course, he sighed deeply once again before he turned his attention back to the group.

"You are now three, but you must be five before we stand any chance at all. The other two are currently being held captive by the Prince in his fortress at the end of the red forest."

Owen had no idea what was going on, but immediately realized who the strange looking old creature was talking about. Quietly, he mumbled to himself, "Staci and Nicky."

Tommy, who was standing at the far side of the room, instantly chimed in , "What did you just say, Owen?"

"Nothing...I mean...I just said...Staci Alexander and your brother..."

"What about my brother?" Tommy asked, pushing his way past King Walcott and moving to within inches of Owen's face. Though Tommy and Owen had never been friends, he had known of his existence since kindergarten. In many ways, Owen was a lot like him, shy, quiet, choosing to keep to himself – whether by choice or not. Upon hearing the mention of his little brother's name, something inside Tommy came to life. In that instant, nothing else mattered - not the Elder, not Fillagrou, not the war or the weird thing happening to him. All that mattered was his little brother and whether or not he was safe.

"Y...your brother..." Owen continued, slightly stuttering, "...and Staci...I saw them...a bunch of guys in armor took them..."

"TOOK THEM!? WHO TOOK THEM!? HOW LONG AGO!?"

"I...I...I don't...know..."

From his bed, the tired voice of the Elder interrupted, "Calm yourself, Tommy Jarvis. You will be given the opportunity to find and rescue both your brother and the young girl. In fact, you may find this difficult to fathom, but from my vantage point, it has already occurred."

Tommy moved briskly toward the Elder with a purpose and intent long beyond his years. Looking the tired old creature directly in the eyes, he said two words, "When? How?"

The Elder smiled.

For years he had made the prophecy a part of his life. After Nelvo's passing some years ago, he had taken over the mantle of Elder of the Fillagrou. With the position came the power of sight beyond sight. It was the sight that Nelvo had possessed for so many years. It was the sight that had allowed him to make the prophecy in the first place. Since then, the Elder had experienced the prophecy firsthand; he studied it, repeated it, lived it, and became one with it in ways he could have hardly imagined beforehand. Yet, over the years, while the suffering continued and the promise of anything different became less and less likely, there had been times when even he doubted the truth of the images associated with it. Now though, staring directly into the face of a determined little boy from a land unlike his own, he found his faith justified.

Reaching up, he touched the side of Tommy's face the same way he had touched Pleebo's only minutes ago. "I can see now why they sent you...I should never have doubted."

The Elder was quite serious when he spoke to everyone in the room. "Seven of you will go to rescue them. Not a single more and not a single less. You will take only what you carry on your person, and nothing else. Tommy, Donald, Owen, The Tycarian

126

King, Roustaf, my grandson, and one you will meet when you've reached your destination. It is you that will strike the first blow...it is you who will at last set into motion Nelvo's words."

Not hearing her name mentioned, Zanell quickly interjected, "But grandfather, what about me?"

"You will be needed here, Zanell."

"But grandfath..."

"Please Zanell...have faith in the prophecy...have faith in me."

Zanell nodded, lowering her head quietly. A small part of her wanted to continue pleading her case, but what more could she say? As much as she wanted to go, she had been raised to believe in the prophecy. She was raised even more so to believe in her grandfather. When her mother had died some years ago, it was her grandfather that raised her and kept her safe. She owed him her life and she was not about to lose faith in him now.

The Elder sighed deeply, trying to ignore the growing pain throughout his tired body. He did not need the sight beyond sight to tell him that his time in this world was quickly growing short. Such things were obvious, even to the blind. Soon everything that he was, everything Nelvo had given him upon his death, would be passed on to another. Most likely this would be his last act as the Fillagrou Elder and he was not about to let the pains of his useless old body keep him from performing it.

"On the road to reunite The Five, the seven will face grave danger at every turn. But through friendship and teamwork they will survive. If the prophecy is to come to fruition, The Five must be reunited...at any cost. Five will arrive, four will return. All of reality walks beside you on this journey my friends; failure will mean the end of all things. Go now...take with you the knowledge of the importance of the situation facing you and fight accordingly. You are the last hope…you are the only hope."

21. COUNSEL WITH THE CONJURER

As Prince Valkea marched through one of the many corridors in his immense fortress, he noticed that the air around him felt stuffier, heavier somehow. Outside the massive walls, the land of Fillagrou had begun the patient darkening that came with dusk. For the Prince, the nights were over much too quickly. In Ocha, night could last upwards of three months, while in Fillagrou it seemed barely twelve hours. This was just one of the many reasons why he missed his home world so greatly. The place where he now resided was too stuffy, too hot, and much too bright for far too long. It was filled with forests and plants and other such things for which he held no patience or interest. Over the years, he had grown to despise the color red. It haunted his dreams; even while awake, he could see it whenever he closed his eyes, making the very act of blinking almost unbearable. Where he wanted there to be only black, he saw red - annoying, frustrating, disgusting red.

The Prince had taken this position because his father had demanded it. He often cursed the King's decision behind his back. A very large part of him wished that the old creature would die. His father's death would allow him to take the mantle of King. Before returning to Ocha, he would leave this wretched little place and all its disgusting little creatures in the hands of another unfortunate soul. Those were, of course, thoughts that he kept to himself. Prince or not, he could be put to death for even thinking such things.

Prince Valkea finally came to a stop in front of a thick, fifteen-foot-high wooden door at the end of the corridor. Two guards on either side immediately stepped in front of him to unlatch an endless number of heavy iron locks. The sound of each heavy lock as it clicked open echoed throughout the empty fortress, bouncing off its endless stone walls, carrying on forever. When the guards were finished, they stepped aside and lowered their heads as the Prince passed through. Prince Valkea slowly pushed open the enormous door and strode confidently into the room. Once inside, the guards quickly closed and locked the door behind him.

The room was very nearly pitch-black, somewhat cold, very damp, and eerily silent. It smelled heavy and pungent and thick, as if something had died within its walls and was decaying in a darkened corner. The light of a blue flame crackled and burned on the far side. Next to the fire a very old creature adorned in a thick black cloak rested on its hands and knees, its forehead pressing against the floor. The robe seemed ancient – covered in a thin layer of dust that could only have built up from years of inactivity. Despite the Prince's arrival, the creature remained motionless, lost in some sort of prayer. Prince Valkea moved slowly toward the blue fire and the hunched figure.

The Prince rolled his eyes deeply; in a voice heavy with annoyance muttered, "Conjurer...I seek counsel."

The dusty figure did not respond. The only sound heard in the room was the crackle created by the strange blue flame and the labored wheeze of the tired old figure underneath the cloak.

In a more serious tone the Prince again stated, "Conjurer...your Prince has informed you that he requires your counsel."

Never moving, the cloaked figure responded from his hunched position. "Your request has been heard and understood, oh, great Prince."

Every single part of Prince Valkea hated the conjurers. Mystics, prophets, magicians, it all seemed like such nonsense to him – and the conjurers were all three combined. To the young Prince the entire race was little more than a holdover from days long since forgotten – relics of a time better left in the past. If it had not been for his father and the ancient traditions of his race, he never would have allowed one of the creatures inside the walls of his fortress. In fact, if it had not been for his father's insane belief in the Fillagrou Elder's nonsensical ramblings, he would not have troubled himself with coming into the conjurer's disgusting chamber at all.

The Prince was annoyed that the conjurer seemed intent on ignoring him and moved toward the fire. He grabbed the creature by the back of its cloak and angrily lifted it into the air. "FOUL CREATURE! I SAY THIS TO YOU ONE MORE TIME! YOUR PRINCE REQUIRES COUNSEL!"

With one hand he spun the conjurer around to face him. , As a direct result of the Prince's anger, the blue flame shot upward as if stoked by a handful of gasoline. Prince Valkea pulled the conjurer close to his face and ripped the cloak from its head, staring into its milky white eyes.

"Ugly things, these conjurers — foul, ugly, deplorable things."

The conjurer race was an offshoot of the Ochan people, but the similarities ended with their appearance. While the Prince's face was covered in healthy looking green scales, the conjurer's were much more yellow in tint - dirty, light yellow, with just a hint of brown - the color of dirty sugar. Unlike the Ochan people, the conjurer race was completely blind. It was because of this very ailment that they were believed to have evolved their other senses to terrifying heights. Through hearing, taste, and touch, the conjurers were believed to be conscious of things in the world around them on a level that the average Ochan could never imagine – including the world of magic. Of course, that was if one believed in such things, which the Prince most certainly did not.

In fact, Prince Valkea thought that the powers of the conjurers were little more than pathetic, ancient legends, parlor tricks at best. To him, the entire race was nothing more than a great band of freaks - worthless old relics that had long since outlived their usefulness to the world of Ocha.

He moved the conjurer closer to his face. "Next time your Prince speaks to you, I suggest that you acknowledge his presence. Do we understand each other, creature?"

Almost sarcastically, the conjurer answered, "Indeed we do, mighty Prince. Indeed we do."

"Good." Prince Valkea let go of the creature's robe and stepped away "Do you know why I'm here, old fool?"

"Indeed I do, great Prince, indeed I do."

"Tell me, then, what nonsense does your blue flame have to offer on the pink-skinned children that arrived in my chamber earlier this day?"

The conjurer turned back to the flame. The blue light reflected in his clear, milky eyes.

A long, thin tongue snaked its way out of its toothless, wrinkled mouth and over his lips. "You take the danger these things present too lightly, young Prince. There are ancient powers at work...some light, yes...but some quite dark indeed. To stand in arrogant defiance of them is a grand mistake."

The Prince chuckled quietly under his breath at the old creature's words. "Great powers? They are but children. Tiny, pathetic, useless children...I see no proof of these powers that you speak of, old fool."

"Your words say one thing, but your heart says another, glorious Prince. Be warned, failure to heed these warnings could prove to be your undoing. It is a mistake that the great King Kragamel would never make."

When he was compared to his father in such a manner, the Prince overflowed with rage. He lunged toward the conjurer and grabbed him again by the cloak, whipping him violently from side to side, "DON'T YOU DARE SPEAK OF MY FATHER, YOU DISGUSTING CREATURE!"

"I...apologize glorious Prince...I...I meant n..."

"I KNOW WHAT YOU MEANT! Do you think me stupid, conjurer? Do not believe even for one second that your condescending tone has gone unnoticed. Were it not for my father and his idiotic beliefs in all things unreal and foolish, I would kill you where you stand!"

Tugging the conjurer mere inches from his face, Prince Valkea smiled at him with his endless row of sharp teeth, "Tell me, old fool...do you think your magic could save you from the steel of my blade?"

With a blank expression, the conjurer answered after a long pause. "Do you know how your father came to power, mighty Prince? Do you know the circumstances surrounding the death of your grandfather? You wait for power like a scavenger waiting to pick at the remains of a carcass caught by another mightier beast. Your words do not scare me, great Prince, because they are just that...words. The words of a child lost in the very long shadow of one much greater than he and nothing more."

Prince Valkea's smile quickly faded. He had heard enough.

The defiant words of the old creature angered him beyond the point of reason. Every part of his body trembled with the frustration of a lifetime spent as his father's son. In one smooth motion he reached to his side, removed the dagger from his belt and plunged it into the conjurer's stomach. Behind them both, the blue flame once again sparked violently upward. An unholy noise vaguely reminiscent of a scream shot up from its center, echoing across the darkened room.

With his jaw clenched tight, Prince Valkea growled at the conjurer through a half-smile, "DO YOU FEAR THIS YOU, OLD FOOL!? DO YOU FEAR THIS!?" Spittle shot from his massive, toothed jaw, splashing on the face of the quickly dying creature.

The Prince then twisted the blade back and forth, grinding it further and further into the soft flesh of the conjurer's belly. Each time the old creature tried to mutter a word, Prince Valkea pressed his dagger deeper, preventing it from accomplishing the task.

"As I told you it would, your magic does nothing for you now, does it foul beast? My first action as sovereign leader of Ocha will be to wipe your entire race from our land. I will see to each and every one of your kind's deaths personally…and I will do this…in your name." With one last push, the Prince drove the remainder of the dagger into the conjurer's stomach. "Take this knowledge with you into the hereafter."

In one quick motion he removed the dagger and shoved the lifeless body into the fire. The strange blue flames engulfed the conjurer's body, its wicked crackles screaming in agony as it reluctantly devoured the flesh tossed upon it. Wiping the blood from his blade, Prince Valkea placed it back on his belt and left the conjurer's chambers, still smelling the searing of its flesh.

Once back in the corridor, the Prince turned to one of the guards and spoke with a patient, self-satisfied tone. "You there…tell General Gragor that I need to speak to him immediately. Tell him I want the doorway that leads to the world of these meddlesome little children found as soon as possible. There is no more time to delay. I feel very much like conquering a world."

22. CHRIS JARVIS AND THE ALEXANDER FAMILY

When Chris Jarvis awoke, he was staring at the ceiling in his bedroom through a pair of blurry eyes. His body was covered in a very old, very sticky, dirty sweat. What day was it? What time was it? What had happened the night before? Chris found himself with many questions and absolutely no answers to any of them – unfortunately, this was a very familiar feeling.

Taking a deep breath, he rolled over onto his stomach, sliding awkwardly onto the floor. He took a moment to clear his head and let the pain pulsing behind his eyes fade a bit. He stood up slowly and walked into the bathroom to take a much needed cold shower. While letting the water cascade across his sore body, he tried to remember what had happened the previous afternoon.

Vague memories of sparse instances bounced around in his brain, but everything was in pieces, random and jumbled. He recalled moments – going to the bar after work, coming home, tripping over Tommy's backpack and nearly breaking his neck, but everything was choppy, unedited and out of order. Fragments of images were unable to come together, like two positively charged magnets pushing against one another. Slowly Chris pulled his hands to his face, and for some reason he made a fist. The knuckles on the right hand hurt a good deal more than any other part of his body. They looked red, and every time he moved his fingers even the slightest, he could hear the bones crack and pop softly, like old wood on a campfire.

Tommy – book bag – fists – tears.

The images continued their sadistic dance inside his skull, mocking his inability to piece them together. Tommy – fists – tears. For some reason it was these brief remembrances in particular that kept forcing their way to the front of the line. Something deep inside him – maybe fear, possibly good sense – hinted to him that he might be better served to stop searching for an answer.

Chris heeded the words of this deep, dark part of his soul and shut off the water, giving up the search. This was not the first time in his life that Chris Jarvis had chosen to simply forget something, rather than to deal with the shame that came with remembering, and more than likely, it would not be the last.

After dressing, Chris made his way downstairs to the kitchen. There was no sign of Tommy or Nicky. The house was quiet, almost too quiet. Chris had grown to hate this house in the past few years. It was the first home he and Megan had purchased. It was the place where their children had been born. It was the place where they had spent Christmases, and New Years, and Thanksgivings. It was also the place where Megan had gotten sick.

It was the place where he had watched the cancer eat away at her like a hungry, soul-starved reaper, slowly taking her away from him. With every creak of its floorboards or chip of paint peeling from its walls, he was reminded of her, and with every reminder came the hurt. If he ever came into money or found the strength, he would pack up the boys and move away in a heartbeat.

With strength he could do a lot of things.

He made a couple pieces of toast, grabbed a beer from the refrigerator and plopped himself into the recliner in the living room. This was not exactly the Breakfast of Champions, but, then again, Chris Jarvis was hardly a champion. Clicking on the television he noticed that a Sunday morning newscaster was giving the weather forecast for the upcoming week. Was it Sunday already? How could it be Sunday already? He vaguely remembered getting home Friday night and now it was Sunday? Had he really somehow lost an entire day? How could that be possible?

A knock at the front door jolted Chris back to reality. Wearily, he pulled himself off the recliner, walked across the room and opened it. Standing on his front porch with a hurried, angry-lost look on her face was his neighbor, Janet Alexander. The bags under her eyes were deep and blue, giving the impression that she had been crying non-stop for hours.

"Chris, I'm sorry…but I was wondering if I could speak to your boys?"

Janet had not come to his house in years. When Megan had been alive, she and her husband Dale were over all the time for drinks or barbeques, or simply to just shoot the breeze. They were friends, the four of them, and had enjoyed each other's company. The first couple months after Megan's death the couple had sporadically stopped by to see how he was doing, or had made an occasional phone call just to say hello. Chris had been unreceptive to their attempts at communication. One evening, after a long day of drowning his problems in a bottle, Chris had marched over to their house, knocked on the front door, proceeded to call Janet a few choice names and then tried to punch Dale in the mouth. He pretty much put a period on the sentence that had been their friendship.

At least he thought that was what he had done. He found it difficult to remember the details.

"Chris? Are you listening to me? I need to speak to your boys about Staci. Are they here?"

Chris was still woozy, his mind was cloudy and his legs felt wobbly. He put one hand on the inside of the door to keep from falling. "No, I don't think...no, they're not here...I...don't think..."

"Where are they Chris? I need to ask them if they've seen Staci."

"Why...what...what's wrong with Staci?"

"She didn't come home last night. We called the police, but they haven't found anything. I know the kids don't really see each other anymore, but I...I...I don't know...I just want to know if they know anything."

Chris tried to straighten up, breathing in deeply while puffing out his chest, praying that Janet would not notice the state that he was in. "I'm not exactly sure where they are...when they get home I'll...umm...I'll send them over to your house."

Janet Alexander felt sorry for Chris Jarvis but she also hated him just as much. Now, with her little girl missing, she found herself more disgusted with the man than usual. To be blessed with two healthy children and treat them the way he did was beyond wrong. She could barely wrap her mind around it. What if Staci were gone? What if she were gone forever? What would she do without her little girl? Chris had been given two boys and did nothing but let it go to waste. As she stared at him in his doorway – half-dressed with a beer in his hand – she felt ashamed that she had ever called him a friend.

Choking back her tears Janet turned and walked away without saying another word.

"I'll call you if I hear anything, Janet!" Chris called out, waving awkwardly in her direction.

Without turning around, she lifted her hand into the air to acknowledge his comment, then buried her head into her other hand and began to cry for the sixth time in half as many hours.

Chris closed the door and stumbled to his recliner. For the first few minutes he could not get Staci Alexander off his mind. She was such a sweet girl. Megan used to often joke about the fact that she thought Tommy had a crush on her, which made the boy's face turn bright red.

They were so cute together, the two of them when they had been kids - so cute, and so innocent.

The idea of sweet little Staci Alexander gone forever was a concept Chris did not want to think about. He could not deal with it. He finished the beer in his hand, then went to the refrigerator and grabbed another, then another. Before long the cool bubbly liquid all but washed away thoughts of the Alexander's daughter. Chris drifted off into the peaceful, problem-free slumber that he knew so well. Things were safer here, safer, easier and quieter. Chris loved the quiet.

23. THE LONG TREK BEGINS

The group had been walking in a single file line through the dimly lit, incredibly stuffy tunnels hidden underneath the red forest for a good part of the day. Stuck in the back of the line, Donald had spent the last two hours complaining. His legs were sore, he was finding it more and more difficult to catch his breath and he was in desperate need of a break that the group could not afford to take. Time was not on their side. Every minute counted, every second precious, if they hoped to rescue Nicky and Staci. King Walcott's enormous rocky shell bobbed back and forth in front of Donald. It blocked out the light of Pleebo's torch and forced him to carefully walk in the near dark. This only added to the young boy's frustration.

A few hours into their journey, the group of travelers came across an exceptionally narrow section of tunnel. King Walcott's sizeable girth was wedged in-between the walls. The Tycarian King waved his stubby limbs wildly in a vain attempt to shake himself loose. When his shaking had proved to be ineffective, Donald was forced to push him from behind while everyone else tugged from the front. After some grunts, groans, strained muscles and good old-fashioned hard work, King Walcott was pulled loose. The situation could have gone a lot smoother if Donald had been able to replicate the immense strength he had shown on the previous day in Tipoloo, but neither he nor Tommy had managed to repeat their miraculous feats, despite several attempts.

At the front of the line, with a torch gripped tightly between his fingers, Pleebo came to an abrupt stop, reaching a dead end.

He turned to the group and sighed. "This is far as we can take the tunnels. The rest of the trip will have to be made above ground."

Roustaf whizzed past Owen and Tommy, hovering next to Pleebo's head, "Are you nuts, Pleebs? We won't last an hour out there before a patrol snatches us up!"

From somewhere behind King Walcott's massive body came Donald's voice, " Ya...especially not with King SLOW-amennes over here."

Annoyed and surprised at the rather snarky comment from the pudgy, pimple-faced boy, King Walcott glanced angrily over his shoulder . "Now there, that was quite uncalled for, child! Have your parents ever instructed you that you should respect your elders? If all children from your world are as frustrating as you, I believe it might be a blessing that the doorway leading to it has never been found!"

"Aww, come on, leave the kid alone you big oaf, he didn't mean nothing," Roustaf chimed in from the other end of the tunnel.

142

"Stay your mouth, my little red friend. This does not involve you!" King Walcott quickly shot back.

"LITTLE!? Why I oughta…! Who are you calling LITTLE!?" Rolling up the tiny sleeves on his even tinier arms, Roustaf gritted his teeth and zoomed in the direction of the giant turtle-man. His progress came to a halt when Pleebo grabbed him.

Roustaf still attempted to fly forward, his arms swinging wildly. He screamed through his teeth, "You better hold me back, Pleebs! You better hold me back before I teach this guy a thing or two about just who's little! You're lucky he's holding me back, you giant slow jerk, because if he wasn't you'd be in a world of hurt right about now!"

"Everybody calm down! Save your energy for the Prince and the Dark Guard…we're going to need it." Pleebo yelled, in an attempt to get the two to settle down.

The heat in the tunnels was stifling and the air thick and heavy, weighing on the flesh of everyone in the group. This no doubt caused each one of them to be a little on edge. Pleebo found himself annoyed and frustrated with the entire situation. Every single ounce of his good judgment told him that Roustaf was right. Continuing the journey above ground was a bad idea.

Despite this fact, there did not seem to be any other option, "Look Roustaf, as far as moving above ground goes, we really don't have any other choice. The tunnels don't go all the way to the castle, and even if they did, we're going to need food and provisions. We can't get to the Prince's fortress using the tunnels alone. We're going to have to go up eventually. If Tommy could blast us some new openings it might be a different story, but it doesn't look that that's going to happen. What we need to do now is be productive and figure out the safest way of getting to the fortress once we're above ground."

Everyone in the tunnel momentarily grew silent. The only audible sounds came from the soft crackle of the flame on Pleebo's torch and the rumble from Donald's hungry stomach. It had been days since he had eaten anything substantial and the image of a cheese and pepperoni pizza kept popping up in his head, taunting him with its deliciously greasy goodness. If there was food above ground like Pleebo said, then he had no problems whatsoever with going topside – Dark Guard be damned.

King Walcott at last broke the deafening silence, "By George , I've got it!"

Everyone turned to look at him, including Roustaf who sighed deeply, with a sarcastic *"oh this ought to be good"* look on his minuscule face.

"As is the way with most things, the answer to our problems lies in the land of Tycaria."

Unsure of where King Walcott was going with this, Pleebo asked, "What do you mean, King Walcott?"

"The second doorway, my dear boy...the second doorway."

Both Pleebo and Roustaf realized at exactly the same time what the Tycarian King was talking about. A few years prior, the Prince had discovered what he believed to be the hundredth doorway, only to find that it was nothing more than a second doorway to the already conquered land of Tycaria. This enraged Prince Valkea who had been quite excited about the possibility of unearthing a new land to conquer and make his father proud. He had immediately ordered his men to close and seal the doorway the best way possible. Frustrated and wishing to move on, he had soon forgotten about its very existence. The people of Tycaria managed to open up the doorway after the guards had been sent away and for a short time used it to sneak refugees out of their war-torn world into the relative safety of Tipoloo.

"If we were to enter through the second doorway into Tycaria, we could then make our way across the Villadhor Mountains to the original doorway, which if memory serves, exits not too far from the Prince's fortress."

Pleebo thought it sounded like a decent plan. Besides, they did not seem to have another one. He had been to Tycaria once years ago when he helped to sneak slaves into the tunnels. The mountains were treacherous and barely habitable, yet it was this very treacherousness that had kept the King's Dark Guard from patrolling them as often as they did the larger cities. They posed a very different kind of danger than the group would likely face if they attempted to make their way to the Prince's fortress going through the red forest; it seemed like the lesser of two evils and might be their only chance.

Roustaf pried himself loose from Pleebo's fingers and glided over to King Walcott, landing softly on his shell-covered shoulder, "You know what? That's not really all that bad a plan, old timer. Are you sure that you can get us through those mountains though?"

A slight smile crept its way across King Walcott's wrinkled old face. He confidently replied, "My days on the front line may be little more than an old man's memory at this point. I remain however as formidable a tactician as you are likely to ever encounter, my dear Mr. Roustaf. Besides, who better to lead you through the Tycarian Mountains than the current King of the Tycarian people, the holder of the sacred cup of Peladrov, and the keeper of the great Mud Chalice?"

Pleebo looked in the direction of the children, amused at the idea of something called a "Mud Chalice" heralded as an achievement.

145

He smiled coyly at Tommy and Owen. "Well kiddos...what do you think?"

The boys had no idea what to say. They did not know anything about Tycaria or the layout of the red forest or the scheduled patrols of the Dark Guard. It was because of this lack of knowledge that they found it impossible to have an opinion.

Donald's voice came from behind King Walcott's massive body. "Do you think we could find some food in the mountains?"

"Indeed, Sir Donald," King Walcott answered sharply, "There are a few pockets of Tycarian survivors hidden throughout, former soldiers from the glorious Fifth regiment who would likely jump at the chance to join us in our most noble cause."

"Sounds good to me. I'm so hungry I would even settle for one of those crappy dirt roots again."

From the front of the line Tommy tapped Pleebo on the shoulder, looking directly into his enormous red pupils, "Which one is quicker?"

"If we can keep a good pace through the mountains, it would definitely shave some time off our journey."

"Then we should take the mountains. The sooner we get to my brother, the better."

Tommy had not been able to stop thinking about his brother ever since they started their journey. He was so small, so innocent, and without Tommy there to protect him, anything could happen. He had made a promise to himself years ago that he would not let anything happen to his little brother and he intended to keep it.

Then there was Staci – if anything happened to Staci – he was not sure if he could forgive himself.

As far as he was concerned, whatever route could get him to the castle quicker was the route that they needed to take.

Pleebo took a long, hard look at the sad group of misfits crammed into the tunnel behind him. In all honesty, they were a pathetic looking bunch. As a child, his grandfather had told him the story of the prophecy every night before he went to bed. This motley crew was a far cry from what he had imagined the saviors of his world would look like. Not a single one of them seemed like they could stand up physically to even one of the King's Dark Guard, let alone invade a fortress full of them. Yet, for some reason he could not fully explain, Pleebo felt confident about their chances.

Maybe it was his firm faith in the prophecy, maybe it was the amazing feat of magic Tommy had performed the day before or maybe it was simply because he wanted very badly to believe in something – anything – once again. Whatever the reason, despite his common sense and better judgment, he foolishly thought their chances were good.

Well, maybe not good exactly, but at the very least fifty-fifty and fifty-fifty was good enough for him.

"Then I guess it's decided, we're taking the mountains."

24. ANSWERS TO QUESTIONS

Staci had not slept in a very long time. Every inch of her body felt tired – so tired that even the slightest movement seemed a chore; her eyes were constantly begging her brain to shut down and recharge. The noises in the dungeon never seemed to relent. Everything from soft, pain-filled moans, to outright screams of agony relentlessly moved throughout the darkened hallways and blackened cells. Every sound assaulted her senses like fingernails against a blackboard. It was impossible to relax for even the briefest of moments. If the sounds were not enough, the dirty stone floor and the mucky air stinking of sweat and death succeeded in compounding the issue. Little Nicky Jarvis, lying not three feet from her, did not seem to have the same problem. The young boy had been curled up against the wall, sleeping soundly for the past three hours. A part of her was jealous that he had found a way to sleep despite everything that was going on, while a part was happy that at least one of them had been able to rest peacefully. Inspired by the relaxed look on Nicky's face, Staci shifted her position against the hard stone and attempted once more to get some rest. Her eyes had been shut for less than ten seconds when a familiar voice jolted her back to the waking world..

"Wake up, little girl."

Forcing open her tired eyes, she spotted Prince Valkea standing outside her cell. The dark shadows cascading eerily across his face somehow made him appear even more heinous than she had remembered – if such a thing were possible.

"How are you enjoying your stay in my fortress, little one? While we may not offer the best amenities, you have to admit that there is a certain...undeniable atmosphere, no?" Staci's sat straight as a board against the wall, her heartbeat slowly picking up in pace.

"You are no doubt asking yourself why one as regal as myself would ever consider stepping foot in a place such as this dungeon? Don't be mistaken, my dear. I love each and every corridor in my fortress as if I, myself, had designed it. In all honesty though, the dungeon is hardly befitting of one with royal blood coursing through his veins such as I. Maybe it's the dirt, maybe it's the lighting, or maybe it's simply the fact that it houses the absolute most disgusting, foul creatures ninety-nine worlds have managed to produce. Whatever the reason...I try to avoid this dreadful place whenever I can."

Wrapping his hands around the bars, Prince Valkea pushed his face through a slit.

With a mouthful of endless, jagged, razor sharp teeth he grinned sadistically at Staci. "For you my dear, foul creature that you are, I have made an exception. You see, there's a question I need answered and I believe you might be just the creature to answer it."

In the cell across from Staci, Fellow Undergotten was slowly waking up from a sleep that had been forced upon a weary body that simply could not bear to be awake any longer. The moment his ears had caught the voice of Prince Valkea his attention was immediately piqued. In all the time that he had spent locked up in this terrible place, not once had he heard that awful voice through its dark halls. With his single functioning eye he spotted the back of the Prince standing outside of the children's cell. Not wanting to alert Prince Valkea to his current state, Fellow remained motionless, listening intently.

"The doorway that brought you to this awful world that the pale skins so annoyingly refer to as Fillagrou...tell me where it is, little girl."

Staci did not answer. It was not because she did not want to, or was defiant in the face of the tyrant Prince, it was because she had no answer to give. In fact, she did not completely understand what he was asking. Everything that had happened thus far was a blur - one long, painful, extremely confusing blur of images fading into each other with no beginning, middle or end, and none of it made an ounce of sense.

"Don't you dare sit in silence, little girl. Do not attempt to pretend, for even a second that you don't understand what I'm asking you. I need to know where to find the doorway that led you here. I need this information quite badly and I can promise you that I will do anything and everything in my power to ensure that I get it."

Staci's jaw quivered uncontrollably and her hand started to shake. The familiar hotness once again crept across her face as her heart kicked into overdrive.

She managed to mutter out a sad excuse for an answer, "I...I...I don't kno..."

"DO NOT PLAY GAMES WITH ME, YOU VILE LITTLE CREATURE! The more you insist on lying to me the more I will ensure that you suffer! Now tell me where the doorway is before I lop your head from your shoulders in an excruciatingly slow manner!"

Prince Valkea's booming voice woke Nicky; he immediately pressed his back against the wall, scooting as close to Staci as possible.

Prince Valkea took note of the little boy, "On second thought, maybe I won't hurt you, little girl. Maybe I'll hurt...that one instead. Yes, that's exactly what I'll do. It will be the boy who suffers because of your idiotic defiance. In his case though, I won't make death as simple as a beheading. No, for that one it will be long...and painful...and drawn out. I will ensure that he feels each and every terrifying second of it. There are scientists and scholars in Ocha who would welcome the chance to open up a strange little alien boy and examine what I would imagine are his very unique insides."

Frightened beyond reason and unable to answer the Prince's question even if she wanted to, Staci once again muttered, "I...I...don't...I...don..."

"STUTTERING BUFFOON! YOU HAVE PUSHED ME TO THE VERY LIMITS OF MY PATIENCE! You have forced my hand, little girl! With each mind bogglingly frustrating stutter you dare me to prove the truth of my resolve and that is exactly what I intend to do!"

151

With one hand the Prince motioned toward the guard at the end of the hall. The enormous, beefy helmeted figure quickly made his way to the Prince's side, bowed, and hit his chest with his dark gloved hand in a show of respect, strength and loyalty.

"Guard, take the young boy out back and teach him what happens to those who refuse to answer even the most basic of questions."

The guard nodded and motioned to another guard at the other end of the hall, telling him to open the cell door. Before the other guard could pull the lever that would do just that, the voice of Fellow Undergotten screamed, "NO! LEAVE HIM ALONE!"

Prince Valkea turned toward the injured fish-man with a quizzical, angry expression on his face.

When he saw the weakened, near death form of Fellow Undergotten, he chuckled softly to himself, "You dare speak to me in such a manner, slave? You? You who can barely stand of your own volition? Were it not for the bars that you're locked behind to keep you erect, you would no doubt be sprawled across my floor like the sad thing you are."

Fellow took a deep breath, gritted what remained of his teeth, and used the bars to pull himself up. Ignoring the pain coursing through his body, he removed his hands and forced himself to stand as tall as he possibly could without toppling over. Every centimeter of his body was wracked with pain, every muscle straining and shaking. Puffing out his chest, he lifted his jaw and stared at the Prince though his one working eye.

In a shaky, yet surprisingly strong voice he muttered, "I said...leave them alone."

Prince Valkea lowered his head, his eyes locked on those of the fish-man behind the bars. His upper lip twitched. *The gall of this creature - the unmitigated gall"*, he thought. *"Just whom exactly does he think he's speaking to?"* His muscles grew tight with anger, his breathing deepened.

Prince Valkea's gaze never turned away from Fellow when he spoke to the terrified children in the cell behind him. "I want you to watch this next moment closely little girl. I want you to remember what happened here this day. Remember it and keep it with you until the next time I come to your cell and ask you the very same question I had asked only moments ago."

With a movement remarkably similar to the one that he used to strike down the conjurer, Prince Valkea reached to his side, snatched the dagger from his belt, thrust it through the bars and sank it into the stomach of the wobbly, barely erect form of Fellow Undergotten. The blue skinned fish-man instantly let out a high-pitched squeal. The dagger in his belly pushed his already injured body past its limit. His legs went limp and crumpled underneath him as he toppled forward, crashing to the ground with a heavy thump. Staci shoved her arm between the bars, attempting to reach Fellows' wilting body.

A fresh batch of tears welled up in her eyes when she screamed with every ounce of her strength, "NO!"

Feeling the life draining from him, Fellow crawled toward the bars and reached for her hand. He was not completely aware of where he was or what had happened. The world around him was fuzzy and white and eerily silent. Sounds began to pop out of existence like bubbles on the surface of water. Some unseen force compelled him to crawl toward the bawling form of Staci Alexander. The blood in his body that escaped thought the hole in his stomach pushed its way up and out of his mouth, dripping onto the stone floor.

Through a wall of hot, sticky insides, he gurgled in Staci's direction, "It...it's...okay..."

Prince Valkea watched the two attempting to reach each other and chuckled smugly underneath his breath. The soft chuckle quickly grew to a more boisterous, full-on laugh.

After wiping the blood from his hands, Prince Valkea turned to walk away. "Remember this moment, little girl. Watch this creature's death and remember it. I will return tomorrow, and if you still choose not to have the answers, the little boy will share his fate."

With tears in her eyes, Staci stretched her arm to its very limits. When she felt as if she could not possibly stretch her arm any further, she willed it to go just a bit more. She did not know exactly why she was reaching for him. After all, there was nothing she could do to help, and yet something deep inside told her that this was exactly what she needed to do.

Fellow stretched his arm as far as he could, to the point where his very existence began to fold in on itself, smothered by a thick, blurry gray expanding over everything. One final time he took a deep breath - this time he did not exhale. His body went limp and the gray was replaced by black.

At the exact moment when Fellow's arm went limp, the tip of Staci's finger came into contact with it, and something magical, unpredictable, and quite unbelievable happened.

Prince Valkea had just stepped through the doorway that led out from the dungeon when a bright white light cascaded across his back, lighting up every bit of the empty space around him.

He turned around, saw where the strange light was coming from and muttered unbelievingly to himself, "What sort of magic...?"

The light that filled the small hallway seemed to emanate from Staci's hand. The unearthly glow grew from the right side of her chest, traveled across her arm, and into her slender finger. As if it were a living, breathing thing of spirit and conscience and mind, it moved from her body into that of Fellow Undergotten. The incredible glow crawled underneath his skin, lighting him from the inside out. Like water seeping through a crack, the light pushed through his open wounds.

Somehow, beyond the laws of reason and logic and science, the bizarre light healed every sore, cut and bruise. It filled his motionless form with life and gave birth to that which had been dead only seconds before.

When the light finished its work, it vanished just as quickly as it had arrived, retreating back into Staci's chest. Because she was not quite sure about what had just happened, Staci pulled away from the bars, feeling empty, staring blankly at her hands through her still damp eyes. Because her legs felt weak, she dropped to her knees onto the dirty stone floor. In the cell across from her, Fellow Undergotten breathed in air once again, cautiously opening his two perfectly functioning eyes.

25. THE TINY RED DIVERSION

From the crouched position behind a particularly thick patch of red bushes, a frustrated Donald Rondage turned to Pleebo, who was crouched next to him and whispered with a bit of sarcasm, "*Now* what are we supposed to do?"

Not more than a hundred and fifty feet away sat two helmeted members of the King's Dark Guard, watching over the entrance to the second doorway which lead to the land of Tycaria. They sat perched atop massive creatures resembling an ostrich, only these ostriches had legs as thick as large men, dark feathered bodies as thick as horses and six-foot long beaks that curled underneath into a very sharp, very dangerous looking hook. The guards seated stoically on top of the large creatures paced back and forth in front of the doorway. The massive glistening eyes on either side of the creatures' head moved back and forth with amazing speed, scanning the forest for any kind of movement.

Once again, Donald interjected, "How in the hell are we supposed to get past those guys?"

Pleebo looked away from the guards and the huge, angry looking beasts, and ran his hand across the top of his head. Frustrated, he did not have an answer to Donald's question. He wondered why everyone assumed that he had the answers to any question. He was not an Elder like his grandfather, he could not see things that no one else could. He knew *of* the prophecy, but he did not *know* the prophecy, and those were two very different things. Ever since the group started on their little journey, they had turned to him for answers for everything, no matter the importance. It was wearing on him.

Annoyed at the fact that Pleebo did not seem to have anything to offer, Donald turned to Roustaf, Tommy and Owen, who were farther down the line. "Well?" he demanded hoarsely, aware that he needed to keep his voice down.

Standing beside Donald, with his appendages pulled halfway inside his shell, King Walcott peeked out of his shell. "I believe that we'll need a distraction in order to safely enter that doorway, my friends."

"Ya, ya…a distraction," Roustaf chimed in, "One of us has to distract the guards and get them to move away from the doorway…give the others time to high tail it through. The only question is, who here is loony enough to do it?"

Tommy had been watching the guards intently through a hole in the bushes, while listening to the conversation of his travel mates. The helmeted figures were enormous in stature and appeared to be well armed. Huge lances at least twelve feet long

157

were strapped to the side of the massive beasts and those lances had frighteningly dangerous looking tips. On their backs, the guards carried thick swords. A number of smaller daggers were strapped to various places on their bodies. Behind the soldiers, the doorway to Tycaria seemed little more than a small opening between two large rocks built into the hill. Had Pleebo not told him it was a doorway, Tommy would have never guessed. He wondered if King Walcott would be able to squeeze his massive shell of a body through the skinny opening. No matter how scary the guards, or how small the doorway, Tommy understood keenly that the group needed to keep moving if he were ever going to see his brother again.

Turning his attention back to his companions he assuredly said, "I'll go."

Pleebo quickly interrupted, "No Tommy, no way…under no circumstances can we can let you, Donald, or Owen be the one to go."

Donald and Owen agreed with Pleebo on this point – mostly because neither of them were in any rush to offer up their services in the first place.

"Any one of the rest of us is expendable. The three of you, though, have to survive and make it through the doorway in order for the prophecy to be realized."

Tommy sighed deeply and rolled his eyes in protest. "Look, I'm sorry…but I don't care about your stupid prophecy. I have to get to my brother, and if no one else here is willing to do it, the…"

"I'll do it."

Everyone at once turned toward Roustaf.

"Ya, you heard me correctly…don't look at me like that, ya scrubs…I said I'll do it. It only makes sense, right? Pleebs needs to make it through…there's no way King Walcott over there could ever hope to outrun those Ochan bastards and keep em' busy long enough for anyone else to get through...the kids can't go...that only leaves me. So yea...I'll do it. No problem at all. They look like a couple of crumb-bums anyway...it'll be a snap."

Roustaf rolled up his shirt sleeves. He made sure that the buttons on the shoulder straps of his dirty blue overalls were cinched nice and tight.

Running his fingers across his bushy mustache, he turned in the direction of the guards. "I may not be as spry as I was a few years back, but I can still zip with the best of em'. There's no way those two jokers and their raggedy looking Scarbeaks will be able to catch me. Don't you guys worry about me...I'll be fine. I can handle these bums...you schmoes just worry about getting your posteriors through that door."

Pleebo stared at his minuscule friend with admiring eyes. The two had met years ago, after Roustaf's home world was taken over by the King's armies. The tiny little man had been living in the forest on his own for some time when he stumbled across Pleebo. He had been alive, though just barely. Most of his time had been spent evading capture. He had been tired, hungry, confused, alone and running out of the will to go on. Had Pleebo not come across him when he did, Roustaf would probably had not have survived. The two instantly formed a friendship and had been close ever since. Despite being from different worlds, they had lived through similar experiences. It was this that drew them to each other; it was this that made them inseparable. As much as Pleebo did not like the idea of his friend putting his life on the line, he understood that Roustaf's choice made the most sense. Out of anyone, Roustaf with his great speed, diminutive size, and amazing maneuverability, had the greatest chance of surviving unharmed.

"Are you sure about this, Roustaf?"

"Completely. Don't you go worrying about me Pleebs…I'll be fine. I'm a pretty tough nut to crack…you know that. Besides, there's no way that you're getting rid of me that easily." Roustaf winked comically at his friend, flashing him a tiny thumbs up, "Just promise me that once those goons are hot on my patoot, you turds will get your butts through that door. I'm looking in your direction, King Walcott."

King Walcott grinned appreciatively at the little winged man. "You have my solemn promise, Mr. Roustaf, that I will move these tired old legs of mine as if they belonged to a lad of one hundred and fifty years."

Roustaf stared back at him, confused. "One hundred and fif…just how old are you? You know what, never mind…just tell me when I get back. All right…let's do this."

With those words, Roustaf fluttered his wings at speeds much too quick for the naked eye and quickly zoomed forward toward the guards. Dodging in-between trees, around bushes, over rocks, through the branches of trees, he rapidly closed the distance between himself and the two helmeted figures. Like a little red hummingbird, he whizzed past the enormous snout of one of the Scarbeaks, causing it to let out a loud high-pitched squeal and shake violently back and forth. Finally, Roustaf came to an abrupt stop directly in front of one of the helmeted guards.

With his left hand he reached forward and knocked twice on the side of the metal helmet with a closed fist. "Hey, schmuck! Anyone home in there?"

The guard turned angrily in his direction, as the large beast he was seated on let out a heavy, frustrated breath through the holes on the topside of its beak.

Roustaf flashed him a hearty, sarcastic smile, clipped his nose with two fingers while he waved his other hand back and forth in front of it as if to indicate a foul smell. "I've never been this close to one of you guys. Wow! I guess what everyone has been saying is true! The absolute worst thing about the Prince's fortress has got to be the smell."

With lightning quick reflexes the guard reached behind him, removed the sword from his back and pointed it at Roustaf. From behind him, the other guard drew a dagger from a holster strapped to his chest. After angrily kicking the sides of his feathered monster, he moved toward the tiny winged red man. In one fluid movement, the burly soldier swung his dagger. Roustaf dodged the blow with ease and took off in the opposite direction at high speed. The pair of soldiers tugged back on the reins of their Scarbeaks, kicked the creatures stiffly in their muscled, feathery bodies, and set off in hot pursuit.

Roustaf was fast. His size allowed him to maneuver through spaces that the guards and their massive creatures could never hope to fit. The Scarbeaks were remarkably fast. Despite their heavily muscled forms, they moved with a graceful ease that seemed to defy the very laws of physics. In conjunction with each jump, duck or long stride the creatures let out a loud, high-pitched squeal. The volume of the squeals was precisely what had enabled Roustaf to judge just how close they were without having to look behind him. Despite his speed advantage, no matter what Roustaf tried, he could not seem to shake the creatures. Flying very fast for such a lengthy amount of time was also beginning to wear on him. Every muscle in his upper body ached. His wings were hot and sore and felt moments away from being torn from his back. He did not know how much longer he could keep up the pace.

He needed to shake the guards and he needed to do it now - before it was too late.

With both hands, he reached to his chest, grabbed the straps on his overalls, gritted his teeth, quickly shot up and headed toward the top of the trees. In response, the Scarbeaks flapped their wings, tucked their legs and lifted off the ground, flying after him. The sound of the creatures' high pitched wail got louder and louder as Roustaf realized they were catching up. He attempted to shake them, zigzagging back and forth widely. The maneuver accomplished little toward creating distance, but it did cause the guards to loosen their formation as they attempted to anticipate the next move of their miniscule prey. As Roustaf passed in front of one guard and then the other, they lunged at him with their sword and barely missed. One of the swings had almost struck the tip of his tiny wings. Had it connected, it would have sent him crashing to the ground. Looking above, Roustaf caught a glimpse of the underside of a large, bushy topped red tree - the thick foliage completely blocking out the sky.

Lowering his head, he flew into the thick leaves, weaving through the tiny openings in the branches with a speed and experience that could only have come from half a lifetime spent in the air.

Knowing that they could not follow him, the guards maneuvered their creatures around, up and over the underside of the tree. Each of them popped up at an opposite end, just as Roustaf zoomed through the middle. When they charged at him from either side, they found themselves unable to halt the forward progress of their creatures fast enough and collided in midair. The Scarbeaks let out a pair of pained screams, bucked wildly like bulls shaking off rodeo riders and threw the helmeted guards off their backs. The guards crashed through the trees, cracking and smashing branches as they fell a good hundred feet to the forest floor. Roustaf stopped, hovering in-mid air just above the tree tops. Breathing heavily, he took a moment to slow the beating of his heart. Looking down, he watched both guards hit the ground. They were far down from his vantage point, their painful crashes looking like little puffs of brown dirt and red leaves. The now riderless Scarbeaks squeaked and cawed wildly, flying aimlessly in the sky.

A crooked smile formed on Roustaf's face as he muttered to himself, "Wow...I can't believe that actually worked."

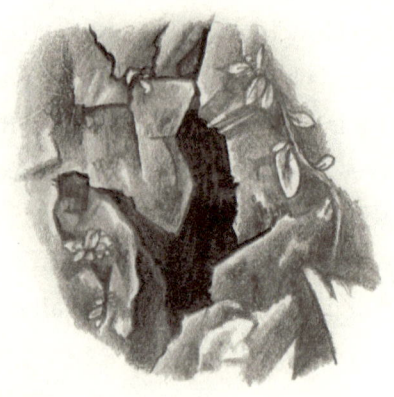

26. RACE TO THE DOORWAY

Not more than five seconds after Roustaf had darted in the direction of the guards, Donald mumbled to the group in a somewhat surprised tone, "Wow, that little dude's got some guts."

Pleebo nodded silently in agreement.

The closer Roustaf came to the soldiers, the more impossible it had been for any of the group to see him. Because of his diminutive size, by the time he had reached the pair of guards, no one among the travelers could see him at all. What they could see, though, was the rapidly growing anger of the guards. The Scarbeaks the soldiers sat upon squealed, squawked and spun wildly in circles. The massive Ochans pulled weapons from their sheaths and swung crazily at the air. From a distance, it seemed as if they were trying to swat a bothersome fly and the sight made Pleebo smile ever so slightly. A few moments later the Scarbeaks bolted quickly away from the door and ran into the forest. Their massive, beefy legs cut swiftly across the ground like a speedboat over the surface of water, no doubt in hot pursuit of the annoying little Roustaf.

Tommy immediately stood from behind the bushes, leaped over them in one determined motion and screamed, "Let's go!"

Pleebo was next, followed by Owen and Donald, with King Walcott bringing up the rear. King Walcott did not so much as jump over the bushes as plow through them, but the result was the same. Now running at full speed, Tommy kept his eyes on the doorway, his legs pumping in double time. Pleebo was much quicker than the boy and passed him, already nearing the doorway entrance.

Not more than ten feet behind Tommy, Owen Little kept a fairly decent pace. Despite the coordination of a drunken lemur, Owen's thin, wiry frame allowed for a decent amount of speed if he carefully focused on every step. The strong desire to not get captured and hauled away on a monstrous beast like he had earlier seen happen to Staci and Nicky made it a whole lot easier to concentrate.

As Tommy reached the door, Pleebo waved for him to pass through. Before Tommy stepped inside, he glanced off in the distance, noticing that the Scarbeaks were now flying at a ninety-degree angle toward the tops of the trees. He felt a somewhat hyper Owen shove past him, jump headfirst through the crack in the rocks, while screaming, "MOVE! OUTTA MY WAY! MOVE!"

Pleebo tapped Tommy on the shoulder and nudged him to follow Own through the doorway. "Get in, Tommy! Come on, no time to waste!"

165

Tommy hesitated at first, thinking briefly about Roustaf. He hoped the little man was all right. Pleebo gave him a much stiffer shove as he forcibly moved him toward the narrow opening.

Both Donald and King Walcott lagged behind. Donald was close but nearly out of breath. With every step he had found it more difficult to breathe correctly. Air was coming in, but it was not going out, and on the rare occasion that it did go out, it was not coming in. Behind him King Walcott was making terrible time. His legs were moving faster than they had moved in years – just as he had promised they would – but apparently he had not been all that fast, even at a youthful one hundred and fifty. By the time Donald, now completely out of breath, reached the doorway he was nearly spent. An abundance of thick, salty sweat poured down his face as he struggled to catch his breath. Turning sideways he shuffled his way through the darkened crack in the rocks, while Pleebo urged him to move faster. King Walcott reached the doorway a minute or so later, feeling as if he was about to pass out. His head was blurry, stuffy, and dizzy. His shell – massive to begin with – now felt twice its size and three times its weight. For the life of him, he could not remember the last time he had moved so quickly. While he felt exhilarated and excited, a very large part of him prayed that he would never have to do this again.

Gasping for air, he turned toward Pleebo and stuttered between deep and gasping pants, "Ha! I am nothing if not true to my word, eh, Mr. Pleebo? King Walcott the fleet of foot! That's what they used to call me in my youth! King Walcott the fleet of foot!"

Pleebo chuckled quietly to himself at the absurdity of the statement.

He rolled his eyes and gently pushed King Walcott into the crack within the rocks. Only half of the turtle man's large body had gone through when he became stuck. Pressing his palms against King Walcott's thick shell, Pleebo pushed with all of his strength, yet the Tycarian King would not budge. Turning around, he wedged his back against King Walcott, dug his feet into the dirt for leverage and pushed harder. Still the rotund creature would not move.

"Push harder, Mr. Pleebo! Put your back into it, my good man!"

Pleebo took a deep breath and shoved again – still nothing. Glancing behind him, he did not see any sign of the guards or Roustaf or the Scarbeaks. Was his tiny friend okay? Had he gotten away? Were the guards on their way back? The process of getting everyone though the doorway felt like it was taking much too long and he was worried. Quickly Pleebo ran twelve steps in the opposite direction from King Walcott. Lowering his shoulder he charged at the rear of the Tycarian's massive shell as fast as he could. The intent was to ram the entire weight of his body into that of the stuck former King. Pleebo did not really weigh much, but the force was enough to shake King Walcott loose, pushing him forward into the darkness as he yelped, "Success! Tally-ho, my good man! TALLY-HO!!"

Once King Walcott had been swallowed by the darkness, Pleebo glanced across the forest, looking for Roustaf. He saw nothing. Hopefully Roustaf was okay. Hopefully he was able to lose the guards and was now hiding safely in the trees somewhere, propped upon a branch. Pleebo could imagine he was chuckling to himself at a job well done, with a cocky grin on his face and stroking his mustache – hopefully. Pleebo sighed deeply. He had to keep everyone moving. He did not have any other choice as he headed toward the doorway.

In front of the doorway, hovering not more than five inches from his face, was none other than Roustaf. "What are you waitin' for, Pleebs? We ain't got all day, you know."

The cocky smile, the absent-minded stroking of the facial hair, the dirty blue overalls that had not been washed in at least a year, everything was there in full force and Pleebo could not have been any happier.

"Don't look so surprised to see me, buddy. You did not think I was going to leave you alone to lead this little group, did you? Are you kidding me? This nonsense is way too important to leave in your less than capable hands. The goal is to save the world, not make it worse, big guy"

Pleebo smiled back at his friend. "Good to see you, too."

With a sly grin on his face, Pleebo raised his hand to Roustaf and flicked him playfully in the chest with one of his bony white fingers. The force of the blow sent the little man flying into the doorway.

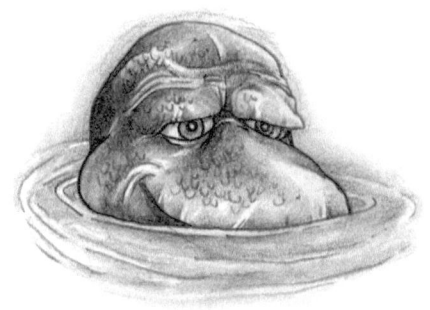

27. WELCOME TO TYCARIA

When Tommy had stepped into the blackness of the doorway, a feeling of complete weightlessness took control of his body. As he hovered in the heavy, smothering darkness, the concept of up disappeared and the idea of down folded into the nothingness as if it were a memory half forgotten from long ago. A part of him was worried that he was moving in the wrong direction, that he would somehow end up exactly where he had started. Tommy knew, though, that even if this were the case, there was absolutely nothing he could do about it.

Whatever force controlled him was controlling him completely.

Much in the way his body drifted so did his mind. Thoughts and memories of his brother, Staci, and his mother bounced off of one another like bubbles colliding under water. Some of them collapsed into each other, became one and created something new.

A cold breeze pushed its way through the all-encompassing black, cascaded across his cheek and sent a chill to the very tip of his fingers. A second breeze, from the opposite direction, fluttered the hairs on his head, making those on the back of his neck stand at attention. Before long the breeze changed into a strong, cold wind that flapped his clothes wildly from side to side, occasionally causing his shirt to smack him in the face. Piggy-backed on the tail end of the breeze was the undeniable smell of an ocean of clean, clear, fresh water. The sound of waves rolled into his ears as if crashing onto the shore. Tommy nearly stumbled when his feet came into contact with something solid, yet invisible, as the strange feeling of weightlessness slowly disappeared. A force lacking any form or shape propelled him forward and through the black on this newly discovered piece of land. A tiny speck of white light, no bigger than a grain of sand, appeared directly in front of him. It quickly grew larger and brighter, filling his vision completely. He lifted his hands to shade his eyes from the ominous glow. The light, however, was so intense that his hands did very little. It seemed almost to pass through his flesh and bones as if they had been made of glass. The light was nearly unbearable as Tommy took one more step forward. This time his feet could not find solid ground. The young boy toppled head over heels into the massive field of light. His arms flailed wildly as his hands reached for anything that could halt his rapid descent. Around him the white quickly evaporated, replaced by something new, something more real and weighty.

Blue. Now he could see only blue . Blurry, spinning, blue.

As suddenly as he fell, Tommy splashed down into the chilly water. Unable to take a breath or even close his mouth, his lungs instantly started to fill with the cold, bluish-green liquid. He spotted something resembling light above him and swam toward it.

Moments later he broke the water's surface, gasping for air while coughing liquid from his lungs. The sky was covered in a heavy blanket of thick, gray clouds. The glow of an odd sun, more orange than yellow, peeked sporadically though small holes. Not more than five feet from him, Tommy spotted Owen treading water and doing it badly. Once every few seconds the boy's head fell beneath the waters' surface, filling his mouth with the cool, salty liquid.

Struggling to stay afloat Owen called out. "Tommy…can't…swim! Help…can't…swim!"

Tommy quickly swam toward Owen, wrapping his arm around the boy's waist to keep him from drowning.

Donald's screaming voice could be heard behind them, "OH CRAP!!"

Tommy turned just in time to see Donald falling through the air, perilously close to an enormous cliff. He came to an abrupt stop when he belly-flopped into the water. Near the top of the cliff at the water's edge, Tommy saw a very small opening cut into its rocky side; he instantly understood that this must be the other side of the doorway.

Donald's head popped up from under the water as he breathed in a big gulp of fresh air.

Angrily he screamed, "What the hell!? You've got to be kidding me!" With an annoyed grimace, he looked toward the opening within the mountainous rock. "Ohh, give me a break! A cliff?! Seriously!?" As Donald bobbed up and down with the gentle waves, he turned toward Tommy and Owen, "Do you two see this!? A cliff! A CLIFF! Why didn't that idiot mention that there was a cliff!? I am going to kill that stupid turtle!"

Almost as if on cue, the enormous body of King Walcott fell from the crack and splashed into the water, his massive body sending waves in every direction. Unlike the boys before him, King

Walcott did not immediately come up for air. He thrust his limbs out of his shell and swam through the water with a speed and ease that contradicted the appearance of his incredible girth. The boys looked through the water and watched as his dark outline moved about the ocean in quick, precise circles.

As he darted between them, a smile crossed his face. King Walcott cheered happily, "Ahh! It feels good to be home, lads!"

Behind the four of them, Pleebo and Roustaf fell into the ocean. Roustaf avoided a splash-down when he caught the breeze with his extended wings and flew toward the group.

He stopped in front of Tommy and Owen and said with a self-satisfied smirk, "Eh...you kids needed a bath anyway."

Not far away, Pleebo's head popped out of the water. He noticed the group and slowly swam over to them. The large shell of King Walcott rose up out of the water as the Tycarian floated gently on its underside. His slimy green head stuck out like a turret on the front of a tank.

He slowly paddled across the water to Pleebo. "Welcome to Tycaria, gents! No time for idle chit-chat though, no time to dawdle. Everyone...follow me to shore. If we want to make it to the mountains before nightfall, our pace will have to remain brisk! Tally-ho!"

His gigantic body moved across the water like a rock skipping across the surface of a lake. For the first time since meeting the Tycarian King, the group was going to have trouble keeping up with him, rather than the other way around.

28. THE LOWEST OF LOWS AND THE HIGHEST OF HIGHS

Prince Valkea shoved his way through a row of fortress guards, pushing one of them violently to the ground. The Ochan Prince was having trouble wrapping his mind around what he had just witnessed, and more importantly, exactly what it meant.

The girl – the pathetic looking, tiny pink-skinned girl – had somehow given life to the dead.

The Prince had witnessed various forms of magic throughout the course of his life, but nothing like this. Nothing had ever come close to this. To give life to the dead was the act of a god. The idea that godlike powers could be wielded so freely by such a puny, pathetic being angered and confused him in ways that he simply was not prepared, or willing, to understand. Was his father right? Was the prophecy more than just the hopeful nonsense of an over-imaginative race on the brink of oblivion?

Was it – could it be – real?

As much as he wished that he could answer with a resounding "no" to these questions, he found it impossible to ignore what his eyes had just witnessed.

On top of it all, the fact that the little girl looked more surprised than he had been after what she had done terrified him.

When he saw the girl bring the deceased Chintaran back from the dead, Prince Valkea had instructed the guard on duty to keep an eye on her, then turned and left the dungeon without saying a word. He needed time to fully digest the reality of the situation and formulate an appropriate response. A part of him briefly considered notifying his father. Another part of him quickly pushed the idea out of his head. No, he would handle this himself. He would prove his father wrong and handle the situation on his own, if he could just figure out how.

Shoving past another row of guards, the Prince strode into his throne room, slamming the massive wooden door behind him. Across the large chamber, with its high ceilings and sparse decorations, was General Gragor, looking at the courtyard through an open window.

When he heard the Prince enter the room, General Gragor removed his helmet, and faced his ruler. "Prince, I have word on..."

Before General Gragor could finish his sentence, Prince Valkea angrily kicked over a nearby marble bust made in his own image and screamed, "WHAT!? WORD ON WHAT!? What is so very important that you saw fit to bother me with it right at this very moment, Gragor!? Tell me what you have on your pathetic excuse for a mind! Tell me now while my world is collapsing around me!"

General Gragor had seen the Prince angry many times during his years of service to the King. He had met his father years before the Prince was even born and considered himself to be as good a friend as the great King Kragamel ever allowed. He had been present when the boy was pulled from his mother, had seen him take his first steps, and had watched with mild disgust when his father left the fate of Fillagrou in the young Prince's less than capable hands. The Prince had always had a temper. Now however, as he watched the hot-headed young man pace back and forth in the throne room, hands on his hips and head sunk low, General Gragor noticed something more pronounced than the usual temper to which he had become accustomed to all these years. The Prince was scared - definitely scared and confused.

"Sire, I understand it is not my place to ask...but is something bothering you?"

Prince Valkea turned and stared into General Gragor's eyes with a cold seriousness meant to mask his true confusion. "You're right...it is not your place, underling."

General Gragor recognized the anger in the young man's voice and the false sternness on his face. "Many apologies, Prince. I have overstepped my bounds."

"Indeed you have. Were it not for your undying loyalty to my family for more years than I care count, I would surely strike you down where you stand."

"Of course, Sire."

"In the future, I suggest that you consider your words carefully before they escape your gaping maw...Understood?"

"Of course, Sire."

General Gragor's dislike for the young prince ran deep. He found the boy annoying and prone to rash emotional judgments. The Prince also relied too heavily on his subordinates, having little to no actual knowledge of how to reign over an empire or properly conduct a battle. His father, on the other hand, was a ruler that General Gragor admired deeply. The King understood the necessity for violence, and always knew where and when to properly utilize it. King Kragamel was the kind of leader that did not have to convince anyone of his power. It was obvious. It was there for all to see, and not a soul in all of Ocha would dare question it. The King's strength had been earned, rather than given to him. It was because of his oath to the great King Kragamel, and his love for the Ochan people that General Gragor stood beside the boy Prince. Were it a different time, place and situation, he imagined that he would have treated the young Prince Valkea much differently.

The Prince shuffled across the room and slumped onto his throne. The sharp nails of his fingers tapped lightly on the armrest as he took a deep breath to calm himself. "The children, Gragor...the children...they..."

As he spoke, his eyes drifted casually to a window on the opposite side of the room. His people had enslaved entire worlds. One by one they had beaten them down, had captured and killed their kin, raped the land of all it had to offer and had forced entire races to do their bidding. All of reality had become a great and glorious monument to the strength of the Ochan race.

It was beautiful – all of it so very beautiful.

Now though, the existence of one tiny girl unceremoniously brought to light the very real possibility that it could come to an end. The Prince understood that he could not tell General Gragor what the girl had done. General Gragor was a loyal servant, but his loyalty lay first with the King. If he knew that there was even a chance that prophecy could be true, General Gragor would inform his father. The Prince could not allow his father to know – not yet. No, he had to handle this himself.

"Of which children do you speak, Sire?" General Gragor questioned. "What has happened?"

"Nothing. Nothing has happened. I do have something… something very important that I need you to do for me, though, Gragor…now that you mention those children."

"Of course, Sire."

The Prince leaned forward in his seat and stared squarely into his General's eyes, "Kill them. Have them both killed immediately. In fact, while you're down there, kill every single solitary being in the dungeon, including the guards. If it breathes, I want it dead by daybreak."

General Gragor found this to be an odd request. The Prince had ordered the death of his own men before – sometimes on little more than a whim – but the urgency in his voice was different this time. Something must have happened. Something must have happened to scare the boy Prince badly. He reminded himself not to put too much thought into it though. The children were going to die, just as they should have when he had first brought them back to the fortress and that was all that mattered.

"I will take care of it myself Prince."

General Gragor wrapped his hand around the sword at his side, running his fingers along the thick, textured leather of the handle with a giddy anticipation brought on by the idea of putting an end to the bothersome, strange little creatures.

The General walked towards the door but stopped when Prince Valkea asked, "Gragor…before you leave…What was the news you wanted to relay to me?"

"Of course, Sire. I almost forgot."

The Prince slid back in his chair and sighed. "Hopefully the news is good…I'm not sure I could deal with it at the moment if it were otherwise."

"Indeed it is, Sire…extremely good."

The excitement in his voice caused the Prince to perk up just a bit. For General Gragor to show emotion of any kind was nearly unheard of. In all the years that the Prince had known him, his expression remained frozen, stoic and serious. The Prince often questioned whether or not he had emotions at all.

Sitting at the edge of his throne, he leaned toward General Gragor. "The doorway? Have your men found the doorway?"

"No, not yet, Sire…but they have discovered something nearly as important, if not more."

Prince Valkea could scarcely imagine what could possibly be better than the discovery of the hundredth doorway. His armies had won every major battle there was to win. Each and every one of their enemies had been beaten and conquered - some had been wiped from existence altogether. Every square inch of land in the known universe had been claimed in the name of Ocha. Besides the last undiscovered doorway to the last unconquered world, what was left?

Then, as if he were slapped in the face, it came to him, "Tipoloo…you've found Tipoloo."

The Prince smiled fiendishly and General Gragor grinned. "Indeed, Sire. Not only have we found it, but the invasion has already begun."

29. SLAUGHTER OF THE INNOCENTS

The pale-skinned children from the hundredth world had brought with them an infectious feeling of possibility that permeated the streets of Tipoloo. It slid under every doorway, through every crack, into every home, and filled the city's inhabitants with a wonderful, warm feeling to which they were not accustomed. This was an odd feeling, a new feeling, a beautifully strange feeling that some of the younger children, those who had been born inside the city walls, had never felt. On every corner of every street, large groups of vastly different species talked amongst themselves, hopeful smiles spreading across their tired, beaten, war-torn faces.

It appeared as if the prophecy was more than just words. It had turned to flesh and blood. It was real and could put an end to the incredible hardship they had come to know as simply being alive.

179

As Zanell turned the corner and headed toward her grandfather's dwelling, she passed a family of Huerzo Snubs, living outside a tiny opening which had been cut into a section of the city's earthen walls. In many ways, the four foot tall Huerzo Snubs resembled ladybugs. Their enormous oval-shaped bodies seemed impossibly large for their spindly legs and yet they managed to move with an inspiring gracefulness. This was mostly due to the aid of a pair of nearly transparent wings attached to their backs that constantly flapped, enabling them to maintain their balance. The mother Huerzo sat quietly on a rock, watching her two young children playfully wrestle in the street just a few feet away. Each time one of the children was knocked over, it rolled through the dirt like a marble on a sidewalk, its tiny legs flailing wildly in the air. When Zanell passed by, the mother Huerzo looked at her, smiling a timid smile in a way only a Huerzo could do justice. Zanell had not seen a smile of this nature on her face in a very long time, not since her mate had been captured above ground a few years back while searching for food with a gathering party. The tiny bit of happiness in the mother Huerzo's expression momentarily warmed Zanell on the inside. How uncommon, how truly wonderful and uncommon. This was exactly what the boys' appearance had brought to Tipoloo. This was exactly what Tipoloo needed.

Zanell had noticed similar smiles all day long. In fact, the smile of the mother Huerzo became the rule rather than the exception. She passed by a small group of four or five Ricardian children. Zanell overheard them whispering to each other about the way Tommy Jarvis had blasted a massive hole in the city's wall just a couple of days earlier.

"I heard that he blew a hole in the wall and vaporized four of the King's guards with it!"

"Shut up…that's not what happened…it was seven of the King's guards! Afterward he opened another hole in the ceiling and flew off into the forest. I think he's on his way to take on King Kragamel one-on-one!"

"Now you're the one who needs to shut up. He can't fly!"

"Can, too! I saw it with my own eyes!"

"You did not see anything, liar. You were with me when it happened!"

"Well…whatever happened, I know that crusty old King is in for a serious beating when Tommy and Pleebo get hold of him!"

The Ricardian race was well known for their wonderful storytellers and wonderful exaggerators. Ricardian children, on the other hand, were known to take exaggeration to unbelievable levels. Zanell smiled slightly, laughing a bit on the inside at the sweet, overzealous innocence in their words. At the same time she could not really blame them, because she felt it too. She believed in her grandfather, she believed in the prophecy, and because of this she believed in the possibility that Tommy, Donald and the others might be the catalyst that ushered in a bright new world. Hidden deep beneath her hopefulness, though, she was worried about her older brother. Zanell had never been away from him for more than a day and she already missed having him around. From the day their mother died, Pleebo had been more than just a brother to her. In many ways he was her parent and even more importantly her best friend. If anything happened to him – well, she simply would not have any idea what to do with herself.

If only her grandfather had let her go with them, then she could watch him. Then she could keep an eye on him and make sure that he was safe.

Zanell opened the door to her grandfather's dwelling, stepped inside and closed it gently so as not to frighten him. "Grandfather?"

She set a bowl of Fluto root that she had brought with her on a small table nearby, along with a goblet of water. The room was dark, the air stuffy and stale. It smelled of age and experience and knowledge. From his bed in the corner of the room, the Elder's tired, creaky body pushed and pulled itself slowly up, as each of the ancient creature's joints cracked and popped.

Zanell quickly made her way to his side and propped him up with pillows. "You need to eat, Grandfather. I've brought you some dinner...Fluto root...your favorite. I even mashed it up for you so you wouldn't have any problems getting it down."

"Thank you, Zanell," the old creature said.

Once she was convinced he would not tip over, Zanell turned back to the mashed Fluto root that she had placed on the table. The Elder grabbed her skinny arm and turned her towards him .

"What is it, Grandfather?"

The old creature touched the side of her face; his eyes were half closed, his lips forming a dry, dusty, ancient smile. "Don't worry about the root, Zanell. Save it for yourself. I won't need it."

"What? What are you talking about? It has been too long since you last ate grandfather...you need to keep your strength up."

With his bony hand, he gently ran his fingers through her stringy white hair. "You look so much like your mother, Zanell. Both you and your brother...you both look so very much like Lanell. I was so proud of her...so proud of the Fillagrou she grew up to be. You'll.... you'll make me...equally as proud, Zanell. In fact, you already have. I only wish…that I could be alive to see the wonderful things your future will bring…"

Zanell tried to ignore her grandfather's words. He had often complained about his age, regularly making jokes or little comments about how much time he had left to live.

She convinced herself that this was exactly what he was doing now. "Shut up, Grandfather…you're going to be around for a long time. You're as healthy as a Subertivean Ox."

The old creature sighed deeply. "Every journey comes to an end Zanell."

"What are you talking about? You look fine. You'll eat something and you'll feel much better, like always. Stop talking like that."

Reaching up slowly with both hands, the Elder placed them softly on either side of her face.

With a half sad, half-contented smile he looked directly into her enormous red eyes. "There is a wonderful beauty in endings, Zanell. Were it not for the pain of endings, we would never experience the exquisite hopefulness that can come only with a new beginning."

Suddenly Zanell no longer thought her grandfather was simply complaining for the sake of complaining. Every crease and wrinkle in his face screamed of stern seriousness. He knew something that she did not. A lone tear slipped from her eye, rolling down the side of her soft, drawn skin. Her thin lips quivered as she tried to formulate words but she heard only the sound of her increased breathing.

Pulling her closer, her grandfather kissed her gently on the forehead. "I need you to run, Zanell. I need you to run to the southern passage and keep running until you've entered the forest. I need you to do this right now, my dear."

"Grandfather…I…I don…why?"

"Have faith in my words…this one last time. Go…go and don't look back."

Almost as if on cue, the ground beneath Zanell's feet shook violently, sending her careening into a nearby wall. A few seconds later the ground shook again – this time even more aggressively. The blue burning candle in the corner tipped over and fell into the dirt, smothered into oblivion. Zanell forced herself back onto her feet and quickly rushed to her grandfather.

Wrapping her arms underneath him, she tried to lift him from his bed. "SOMETHING'S WRONG, GRANDFATHER! COME ON, WE HAVE TO GO!"

The Elder's body slumped like a heavy, useless rag doll. Even if the ancient creature had desired to move there was no way he could ever hope to run. To escape what was coming was not his fate and he knew this.

Using what little strength that remained in his tired body, he pushed her away . "No! I can't go anywhere, Zanell! This is exactly where I'm supposed to be. You have to trust me! You have to run, now!"

Zanell wiped away the torrent of tears flowing from her face as the ground rumbled yet again. This time thick chunks of dirt fell from the ceiling. "NO! I WON'T LEAVE YOU! I CAN'T!"

Again she reached for her grandfather and again the old creature pushed her back. Suddenly the city shook with such incredible force that it sent her falling. She slammed against the creaky wooden door as massive amounts of dirt and stone fell from the ceiling, a few of the larger chunks hitting the top of her head.

The entire room was covered in a thick brown mist. "GRANDFATHER!"

From somewhere inside the cloud of dirt came the Elder's far away voice. "RUN ZANELL! TO THE SOUTHERN PASSAGE! GO NOW!"

As she attempted to stand, another violent shake caused Zanell to roll through the door and into the street. Everywhere around her the inhabitants of Tipoloo were frightened and screaming, scattering in every direction without rhyme or reason. Some seemed to be looking for shelter, some for family and some for weapons. Near the end of the street the ceiling collapsed viciously, as if a bomb had been set off somewhere above. The head of an enormous gray beast blasted through the earth and slammed into the city floor, chomping away every ounce of soil in its path with its massive open mouth. It swallowed the dirt it had just torn away, shook its head from side to side wildly, pounding against either side of the street in the process. The massive cranium was close to the ground; excess dirt and sand blowing from its nose. Opening its gigantic mouth, the terrifying thing let out a growl so ear piercingly loud that the entire street vibrated. Zanell immediately covered her ears, as she backed away from the growling, monstrous beast. As quickly as the enormous head arrived, it shot back into the sky leaving a gaping hole in its wake. The city of Tipoloo looked like a war zone. Mounds of dirt and rock continued to fall from the tunnel ceiling. Clouds of grainy, thick sand enveloped Zanell, making it impossible for her to see anything that was more than three feet away. More crashes, shakes, and noise rose from inside the destructive cloud. No doubt these sounds were the result of other massive holes being opened up by equally angry beasts at various other points throughout the city. The incredible clatter drowned out the horrified voices of the city's inhabitants; communication of any kind was no longer a viable option. The sounds, the sights, and the harsh reality of what Zanell witnessed was too much for her to process. Everything was happening fast. She had seen battle before. She has seen the dead and injured, but never in Tipoloo, and never on this scale. It all seemed unreal.

She managed to get to her feet just in time as armed guards with weapons drawn, came through the incredible hole the creature's head had opened. A few of Tipoloo's inhabitants grabbed clubs or crudely made spears and attempted to engage the guards in armed combat. They were no match for the well-trained, massive bodied, angry and determined soldiers.

Everywhere around Zanell, their forms partially obscured by clouds of dirt and dust, innocents were being slaughtered.

With deadly precision, without regret or remorse, the Ochan army was doing exactly what they had been trained to do. They were killing everything. The city of Tipoloo had been the single stain on the legacy of their people for years – an embarrassment to the glory of the empire. Now, with the chance to take care of that which had eluded them for so many years, they were assuredly making the most of the opportunity.

Zanell's tears were thick with sand and soot. When she wiped them, it smeared across her already dirty face, sticking to her skin in clumps. She looked in the direction of her grandfathers dwelling. It was now totally obscured by the smoky madness that had engulfed the city.

Softly through her shivering lips she whispered, "I love you" to her grandfather before she ran toward the southern passage as fast as her shaky legs would carry her. Behind her, nearly everything she had ever known and loved - died.

30. NEW ALLIES

The trip across the westernmost part of the Nellasor Swamp to the Villadhor Mountains was, for the most part, uneventful. The group stayed low and moved quickly, taking the absolute shortest route possible, making remarkably good time thanks to King Walcott's knowledge of the area. He led them along a mostly out of the way route. It was because of this that the group had only one encounter with the Ochan military. At the foot of the mountains a regiment of about eight or ten Ochan soldiers had just finished ransacking a small village and were shackling fifteen or twenty Tycarian prisoners to the leg of a massive green lizard. The lizard's tongue was so long that it could curl around its entire body three times over if stretched to its full length. It took the combined might of the entire group to keep King Walcott from charging into what remained of the village and engage the soldiers in battle.

It was Pleebo who finally convinced the proud Tycarian King that getting to the Prince's fortress and fulfilling the prophecy was the wiser choice of action. "If we fulfill the prophecy we can save them all. If we don't, then all this was for nothing. I hate leaving them but we have to keep moving. There isn't any other choice."

Reluctantly, King Walcott agreed. Watching his people dragged off in shackles and doing absolutely nothing proved to be one of the hardest things he had ever been asked to do. If months ago his cabinet ministers had not insisted that a group of their best surviving soldiers lead him away from Tycaria and to the safety of Tipoloo, he would no doubt still be gallantly fighting for the freedom of his people alongside what remained of the resistance.

He left only because his people had demanded it – they believed it to be in the best interest of Tycaria to save their King. It was for this reason that he had forced himself to leave, no matter how much every part of his soul might have disagreed.

Owen Little took note of how remarkably different Tycaria was from Fillagrou. The land was much swampier, cooler; the air felt sticky and moist and smelled sour. The dark, heavy cloud cover seemed to extend for miles upon miles in every direction. This led the boy to believe that a very heavy rain was not only possible, but inevitable. Tycaria and Fillagrou did have one thing in common though – the results of a never-ending war could be seen everywhere. Twice the group had passed the bodies of Tycarian citizens, or at least what remained of them. They were little more than empty, hollowed out shells of all shapes and sizes, piled on top of each other. Some shells seemed to have been split open - only a thick, greenish, half-dried glop remained inside. A few of the piles were stacked so high that they very nearly reached the treetops.

Modest dwellings and large buildings had been burned to the ground and now looked like jagged, ashy stones growing awkwardly from the ground. To say that it was a grizzly sight would have been the understatement of the century. The images instantly reminded Owen of the ones he had seen in history books or occasionally on the late night news.

The very idea of war – or murder on such a massive, pointless level – confused him greatly.

Owen had prided himself on being able to discover how things worked, on being able to take things apart, dissect them and examine them from an objective point of view. He had firmly believed that he understood things better than others his age might because of this very skill. With war, the boy found this method of discovery impossible. Even deconstructed, sprawled out in pieces and examined objectively, he still could not make any sense of of it.

By the time the group reached the base of the mountains a downpour had begun. The rain felt so heavy and thick that each time a drop came into contact with one of the boys it caused a fair amount of pain. From Donald's point of view, the mountains looked massive, extending to the north and south endlessly, with sharp, jagged surfaces and huge snow-topped peaks that disappeared from sight into the cloud-covered sky.

Tapping King Walcott on the back of his shell, while trying to avoid the painful rain, Donald said sarcastically, "You've got to be kidding me. This is supposed to be the quicker way!?"

King Walcott smiled at the shocked and annoyed look on the boy's face and smiled even wider after noticing that the others looked exactly the same, "Do not fret for a moment, Mr. Donald. We won't be going over the mountains. We'll be going through." He pointed one of his flat, three fingered paws toward a cave off in the distance. "That cave will take us underneath the mountains and

189

drop us near the doorway back to Fillagrou. We must keep moving though, my friends. It will be night soon and the rain tends to get a wee bit heavy at night."

Donald could feel welts forming underneath his clothes. He found it almost impossible to imagine how the raindrops would be more violent and painful than they already were.

He stared at King Walcott, gap jawed. "Heavier than this?! Are you nuts!?"

King Walcott laughed under his breath, and lifted his paw to the sky, letting the rain pound away at the surface of his palm. His long, rough tongue snaked out the corner of his mouth, catching some of the falling moisture.

With his eyes closed and a contented smile on his face he said softly, "I know. Isn't it beautiful? It feels so wonderful to be home."

After about an hour and a half of crawling through the dark, dank, wet caves underneath the Villadhor Mountains, Owen felt tired, as did the rest of them. They had been moving non-stop for some time now and even Tommy – the most determined among them to continue onward – felt the stress of the unwavering pace.

Pleebo moved to the front of the line, alongside King Walcott. "Maybe we should stop for a while. I don't think the children can keep up this pace much longer, and for that matter, neither can I."

King Walcott glanced briefly at the tired group. Even tiny Roustaf had stopped flying and was lying half-asleep on Pleebo's shoulder. For the last half hour the pace had slowed significantly.

The group dragged; continuing on without any rest was not going to do their cause any good. "You may have a point, Mr.

Pleebo. The cave opens up not far from here. I believe it would be a safe place to stop and rest our weary joints."

A little later the small passageway turned into a much larger cavern. At the center of the enormous clearing was a crystal-clear, blue body of water near the base of a waterfall. Had Tommy not been so tired or worried about his little brother, he would have taken the time to appreciate the remarkable beauty of the place a bit more.

King Walcott stopped at the water's edge and turned to face the exhausted group of travelers. "We shall halt here and rest. The cave's exit is less than a day's travel and we will need our energy to make the trip."

Donald and Owen tumbled to the sand and curled up on their sides. Every part of their bodies ached. The minute they laid down they knew they would have trouble getting up again.

King Walcott plucked a purplish-brown mushroom from the soil under his feet. "The mushrooms all around you are quite edible." With a flick of his wrist he popped the entire thing into his mouth and swallowed. "Not to mention incredibly delicious. The water behind me is safe to drink as well. Eat, drink and sleep, my friends. We have a long journey still to come."

Tommy reluctantly crumbled onto the ground, propping himself against the cavern wall with a deep sigh. From the dirt beside him he snatched a mushroom and timidly put it to his nose, sniffing it. There was no smell. It did not look the least bit appetizing to his eyes, but to his empty stomach it seemed about as tasty as a bowl of ice cream. Shyly he nibbled at the corner of the large, light purple colored top. Surprisingly the odd looking fungus did not taste bad at all, sort of like wet, sugary bread, with a very similar texture.

With everyone reclined in various states of fatigue across the dirt floor, King Walcott took the opportunity to breathe in the air around him. As a boy he had often traversed these caves. He smelled the familiar air, heard the relaxing sounds of the crystal-clear waterfall behind him and was reminded of happier times. His heart felt warm in a way it had not felt in years. It was going to be difficult leaving Tycaria again, very difficult, but he reminded himself that what he was doing was for the sanctity of places such as this. He remembered his wife and his son and the soldiers who had given their lives helping him escape to Fillagrou He hinged his hopes on these children, not only because some part of him was beginning to believe the wild Fillagrou prophecy, but because there was really no other option.

The sad truth was that Tycaria had lost the war. There was no way around that and there was no coming back from it. Nothing he could do would ever change that. Even if these children were barely a chance, barely was significantly better than not at all.

"King Walcott Shellamennes!"

The deep voice came from the water which caused King Walcott to spin around. Though half asleep, the others jumped to their feet, glancing at the massive puddle in the center of the cavern. Peeking out of the pool of water was the green head of a Tycarian. The creature stared wide-eyed and stern, looking only at King Walcott. As the stone-faced creature moved forward, more of its body appeared from underneath the drink, revealing its knees. Lifting one of its paws into the air, the Tycarian made a subtle hand gesture. Slowly the heads of other Tycarians popped up from underneath the water's surface. One after another seven heavily armored soldiers stepped out of the pond and onto land. The group approached King Walcott, dropped to one knee and lowered their heads as a sign of respect. The soldier in the front looked young and handsome, as handsome as a man-sized turtle could possibly look, save for a large scar that ran over his right eye and down the side of his face. Scattered across his shell were telltale signs of years of battle. Cuts, scratches and large gaping chips made it obvious that he had experienced war firsthand for quite some time and had survived to tell the story.

Pulling a long broad sword from a sheath strapped to his back, the young Tycarian soldier set it in the dirt at King Walcott's feet. "King Walcott Shellamennes, son of former King, Waldorf Shellamennes, current King of the Tycarian people, holder of the sacred cup of Peladrov and keeper of the great Mud Chalice…we pledge our allegiance to you and welcome you home."

King Walcott nodded as he gently placed his hand on the top of the young soldier's head.

Happily he motioned for the soldiers to come forward, indicating that it was safe. "There's no need to be frightened, my friends. I'd like to introduce to you to the finest soldiers a King could ever hope to call his own…the glorious Fighting Fifth!"

31. THE FATE OF THE ELDER

Moments after Zanell had been tossed through the front door of her grandfather's dwelling and into the city streets, a large chunk of the ceiling directly above the Elder broke loose, collapsed and dropped a heavy load of dirt on top of him. The immense weight smashed the bed underneath him and broke most of the bones in the lower half of his body. The Elder attempted to dig his way out from underneath the heavy mixture of clay, rocks and sand, but there was simply too much of it and he was far too tired. A cloud of thick brownish-gray dust rose up from the pile of debris that covered him and filled the room. His vision had decreased a fair amount in the past couple years, but even a much younger Fillagrou, with absolutely perfect vision, would have found it nearly impossible to make out anything through the mass of thick smoke. The Elder heard a heavy crash somewhere on the opposite side of the dust cloud outside his dwelling. The crash was followed by the monstrous growl of an enormous beast that sent vibrations across the city's endless tunnels.

Everything was happening just as the Elder had seen in his visions. Moment for moment, instance for instance, the situation was playing out exactly as he knew it would. Zanell and the Fluto root, the collapse of the ceiling, the breaking of his bones, the incredible pain shooting across his back, the roar of the great unseen beast. It was perfect in its insanity. He realized he could no longer feel his legs that were buried under at least a ton of dirt, yet strangely, he smiled.

Were it not for the sight beyond sight and the knowledge it afforded him, he would have been frightened beyond comprehension at the prospect of his demise. It was the realization of his dreams, though, that filled him with a sense of wonderful, warm, indescribable peace. The madness and death outside his dwelling, and his situation inside, crystallized for him the fact that there was truth to the prophecy and reaffirmed his belief in the Fillagrou race, in the Elders that came before him, in Pleebo and Zanell, in everything he had taught the majority of his adult life and most importantly in The Five to save them all.

In the pain of his ending he found truth, and in truth discovered hope.

The door to his dwelling was violently kicked open. A heavily armored soldier stepped into the dusty, darkened room. He held a two-sided axe tightly in his hand. The weapon was massive - almost half the size of the soldier's body, both ends splattered with a rainbow of sticky, half-dried blood in various shades and colors. The mammoth Ochan spotted the weary, half-alive Elder pinned underneath a mountain of soil, lowered his ax and chuckled underneath his breath. Behind him, like a demented circus of pain, the screams of the citizens of Tipoloo bounced back and forth off the city walls.

For the Elder, the world was gradually becoming blurrier. He found it increasingly difficult to maintain a steady breathing rhythm. His inhales were longer and deeper, while at the same time, his exhales shrank dramatically in length. The numbness in the lower half of his legs inched its way up his body and hovered achingly in his chest.

The massive soldier moved slowly but deliberately in the Elder's direction, still laughing at the sad situation of the tired old creature. The kills had been easy for him on this day. The various races living underground in these dank, disgusting tunnels were malnourished, weak, and vastly undertrained. They proved to be the weakest of the weak, the most useless of the useless. Killing these pathetic creatures came easily for the Ochan, yet still very satisfying. As easy as the others had been to dispatch, the ancient Fillagrou in front of him now, half gone to the world and pinned underneath a mound of earth would prove the easiest of all.

Nearing the Elder, the guard slowly raised the enormous axe above his head.

He muttered from underneath his dark helmet, "So pathetic...the lot of you...so very pathetic. Though you may not realize it, I'm doing you a great favor by putting an end to your miserable excuse for a life."

To the Elder, the soldier was just a dark blur spread out across a dusty, smoky background. His eyes felt light and his lids heavy. Simply keeping them open was difficult. The numbness in his chest silently crept its way up into his neck. White-hot images of his wife and his children flashed in his brain, beautiful explosions like dying supernovas across the pitch-black nothingness of space. Fondly he recalled climbing the trees in the red forest while a youth in order to pick the delicious Caba fruit that grew only near the top. He remembered the exquisitely smooth, relaxing feel of the cool water in Lake Willacha on his skin when he had gone swimming with his brother during the summer months. He could feel the night he had first kissed his wife, once again amazed at the sublime softness of her skin. Fond remembrances of the birth of his daughter Lanell faded in and out of his reality; how her tiny features had fascinated him! He called to mind the exquisite feeling of transforming into more than himself when he had first experienced the unexplainable wonder of the gift of sight beyond sight. He evoked the image of Zanell's beautiful red eyes from moments ago when he last gazed upon them. In an instant the Elder could see anything and everything that happened or will happen, and it felt divine. These were the images he would take with him into the next world. They would become his pillow, his blanket and the exquisitely soft bed on which he would rest for all eternity.

With his dying breath, the Elder gazed wearily at the blurry figure of the soldier and smiled.

In the instant before the numbness traveling up his body overtook his lips, he whispered only three words, "Watch your head."

With his axe still perched high above him, the soldier stared at the dying old creature. A confused expression spread across his helmeted face. Seconds later the roof above him collapsed, burying both he and the Elder underneath a mountain of earth forever.

32. OFF WITH THEIR HEADS

It had been hours since little Staci Alexander brought Fellow Undergotten back from the dead. Since that moment, she had spent the majority of her time seated against the cold cell wall, staring blankly at her hands. Directly across from her, the face of Nicky Jarvis shared her same expression, and in the cell opposite them, the look was repeated again on the face of the recently reborn Chintaran. Not one among the three had been able to make an ounce of sense out of what had happened.

Fellow could remember very clearly his final moments and could recall the instant when he had been brought back to life with equally stunning clarity. It was the spaces in between that seemed to elude him. The girl, the sweet, innocent little girl had powers –

incredible powers – powers he could not begin to understand. As a rule, Fellow had put little faith in the prophecy of the Fillagrou people. It simply did not seem realistic, and in a world as harsh as the war torn one he lived, there was little time and patience available for things not clearly real. He had prided himself on believing in that which he could see only with his eyes, on the quantifiable, the obvious and the explainable. He had no time for the concepts of magic and fate– strange ideas better left to others. Now though, all of this had changed. Not only was magic real, it had touched him. It was something he had experienced. He was now the living embodiment of magic – and fate. Every injury he had suffered over the course of the long war with the Ochan nation was gone, wiped away as if they had never existed. The bad back he had tolerated after an accident suffered as a boy was also healed. Every muscle in his body felt alive, strong and young. It did not make sense, yet at the same time it existed. Looking past the intoxicating feeling of his rebirth, his mind wandered to the safety of the children in the cell across from him. The Prince had witnessed the little girl's powers firsthand and he no doubt understood, just as Fellow did, exactly what they implied concerning the future of the Ochan nation. While the Prince may not have taken the children seriously at first, he was forced to after this incident. Fellow understood that he had to do something, though he had no idea exactly what. He had to protect these two strange children somehow since they theoretically represented an end to the war. He also owed the little girl his very existence, a debt he could never hope to fully repay.

No matter the cost, however, he was going to try.

Crawling on his hands and knees toward the steel cell bars, Fellow's voice was hushed, but deep with seriousness. "We have to get you out of here. Prince Valkea isn't going to let you live for long, especially now that he knows what you're capable of."

Staci was still staring blankly at her hands. Raising them in front of her face, she began twiddling her fingers back and forth as if they were something completely foreign to her. Nicky Jarvis, on the other hand, listened intently to the creature in the opposite cell. Nicky crawled over to Staci and put his hands on her shoulders, trying to gently shake her out of her trance.

Every prisoner in every cell along the long hallway of the dungeon had also witnessed Staci's powers, each of them trying desperately to hear what Fellow was saying to the magical little girl. Some among them were familiar with the prophecy and had understood the magnitude of the recent happenings. Those unfamiliar with the stories, though, had been no less impressed by the strange girl's powers.

Nicky shook Staci harder, to no avail. Despite his attempts to coax her back to reality, she remained stoic, lost in the lines and contours of her palms. Realizing that the child was unable to understand a word he was saying, Fellow altered his game plan, turning his attention to the rest of the prisoners in the dungeon.

Painfully he wedged his head through the bars and screamed, "LISTEN! ALL OF YOU! WE MUST NOT LET THESE CHILDREN BE HARMED! DO YOU UNDERSTAND ME!? IF YOU REALIZE WHAT HAS JUST HAPPENED HERE, YOU KNOW THAT WE MUST NOT LET ANYTHING HAPPEN TO EITHER OF THESE CHILDREN, NO MATTER THE COST!"

The guard at the end of the hallway quickly closed the distance between his post and the screaming Chintaran.

Drawing his sword from the sheath on his back he grumbled angrily, "QUIET, PRISONER!" With his free hand he struck Fellow on the side of the head, sending the fish-man tumbling into his cell. "One more word out of you and I guarantee it'll be your last!"

The guard turned to the children's cell and stared at Staci for a moment. Strangely, he found the tiny, frail-looking female a little frightening after what he had seen earlier. Though he tried to disguise how he felt, he failed. Turning her gaze away from her hands, Staci glanced at the Ochan.

Immediately the heavily armored soldier stood in a battle-ready position, tightening the grip on his sword. "You just stay where you are, creature! Don't think even for a second that your magic frightens me, because I assure you it does not! Make even the slightest movement and I guarantee that you will taste the end of my blade!"

The door at the end of the hallway opened abruptly and General Gragor stepped through with three soldiers in tow. The group quickly made its way to the children's cell. Turning toward the dungeon guard, General Gragor laid one hand on his shoulder, with just the slightest bit of squeezing pressure. "Lower your weapon, soldier. Be proud. You have served your King with distinction and your contribution to the empire will not be forgotten."

Though a bit confused, the guard slowly lowered the sword . "Thank you, General, but I'm not exactly su…"

Before he could finish the sentence, General Gragor snatched a dagger from his side and sliced open the guard's neck. The movement was quick and precise, the cut deep and fatal. The the guard's blood was sent spitting across the room as if shot from a fire hose. In less than a second, his body fell limp to the stone floor with a heavy thud.

The children's cell door creaked open; two guards rushed inside, picking up them up. Nicky struggled to break free from the grip of the guard holding him, but the large creature's arms felt as if they had been carved out of stone. With her mind still far away, Staci made no attempt to struggle. She did not cry, she did not scream. She simply stared blankly ahead, unaware of her situation.

With the side of his face still sore, Fellow stood up and ran to his cell bars. "LISTEN TO ME, EVERYONE! WE CANNOT LET THEM HURT THESE CHILDREN! WE HAVE TO DO SOMETHING! WE CANNOT LET THEM HURT THESE CHILDREN!"

General Gragor violently shoved his boot through the bar, kicking Fellow in the chest. The blow was heavy and precise, fracturing three of his ribs which caused him to collapse yet again. Fellow immediately clutched his chest, gasping for air.

Fellow's ribs that had been magically repaired earlier were broken again. Had the situation not been so dire, he might have laughed at the idiocy of it all.

The two guards carrying the children walked to the end of the hallway and exited through the massive door.

General Gragor turned toward the remaining guard. "Lieutenant, I want every single creature down here killed immediately. No pomp or circumstance. I simply want them dead, and I want them dead now. Bring as many men as you need to get the job done. Understood?"

The soldier nodded and pulled the sword from his back as he licked his lips, anxious to carry out the orders.

General Gragor turned toward the cell of Fellow Undergotten, his eyes filled with a mixture of disdain and disgust. With a deep, heavy voice he growled, "Start with this one."

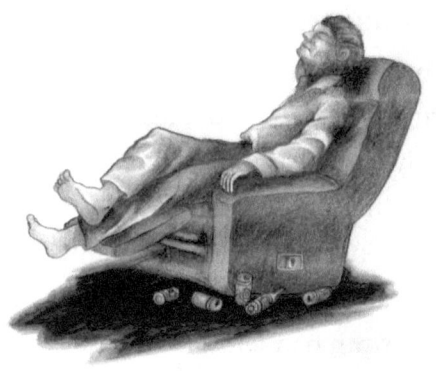

33. THE TATTLE TALE THUGS

For hours Chris Jarvis sat unmoving, comfortably reclined on an old green chair in his living room. Were it not for his occasionally blinking eyes and the soft, slow rise and fall of his chest, it was almost impossible to tell if he were still alive. On the mantle above the fireplace, a picture of his wife Megan with his two young sons stared back at him. Try as he might, he could not bring himself to look at anything else. Their faces were frozen in time, their smiles carved forever, silently judging him. Their eyes, red from the flash of the camera, cut through him and into his chest as they peered through the bones of his ribs, examining what little remained of what once had been a proud man's soul.

At one point in his life Chris Jarvis had been a good man, or at least he once believed this to be.

Chris could remember a time when the sun, the moon and the stars revolved around Megan. He had breathed her air deeply every night before drifting off to sleep. It was the milky blue of her eyes in which he had bathed and the softness of her skin that had instantly transformed the day's troubles into faint remembrances. It was the wondrously soft, beautiful and warm light that she had emitted from inside that illuminated his world. She had given his life purpose and reason. He had never met anyone quite like her and he knew that he never would again. When she passed away, her light and her warmth had left with her. Shrouded in darkness by the reality of life without her, Chris had lost his way. He had neglected his job, his family and his friends. He had brushed aside responsibilities in favor of an endless and unyielding process of grieving that encompassed him fully. When even that became too unbearable he had enlisted the aid of a bottle, drowning what little remained into its wholly numbing liquid.

Now, with both of his boys missing and possibly dead, he found himself sitting in quiet reflection of his life, not being sure that it deserved to be called such.

What would Megan think of him if she could see him now? What would she say if she could see the way he had treated Nicky or the things he had done to Tommy? What if she had found some way to do just that? What if she was staring at him right now, using the photo on the mantle across the darkened living room to watch his every move, shaking her head in disgust and wiping tears from her eyes? The idea chilled him to the core.

Inside his head he softly whispered the words, *"I'm sorry"* hoping that wherever she may be, she would hear and possibly forgive. In his heart he knew that she would not – and he honestly did not blame her.

A knock at the front door pulled Chris away from the photo and back to the world of the living. Another heavier, more insistent set of knocks splashed against his brain like a bucket of cold water, causing him to leap to his feet. He made his way to the door and opened it. Standing stiffly on his front porch was a tall, thick man in a trench coat, with dark hair and a neatly trimmed goatee. Two local sheriffs stood at the foot of the porch. Behind them, Chris noticed a row of cars parked along the street, two of which bore the markings of the local police department. The man with the goatee reached into a pocket and removed a badge, flashing it at Chris.

With a steely look on his face, he asked in a deep voice, "Christopher Jarvis?"

"Yes."

"I'm Detective Myerson. I've been working on the disappearance of your sons and a few other local children. Could I come in and ask you a few questions?"

For some reason a shiver of fear traveled up Chris' back, caught the muscles in his neck and caused his head to jerk straighter than it had been in years.

Through a set of dry lips he managed to stutter, "S...sure. Sure, come in..."

Stepping meekly aside, Chris motioned for the detective to enter. Myerson turned and gestured toward the officers behind him, letting them know that their presence was not necessary. After the detective moved past him and into the house, Chris closed the door. He followed Myerson, who walked into the living room as if he had lived in the house his entire life. Myerson stopped and took note of everything around him, cataloguing it in his brain for future reference.

Chris eyed the man intently. The detective was clearly looking for something, but he seemed unsure as to just exactly what it was.

"Do you have news on my boys?" Chris asked, breaking the uncomfortable silence.

Slowly Myerson turned to Chris. He took a deep breath and motioned for him to sit. "Actually, yes. You might want to have a seat, Mr. Jarvis."

Every muscle in Chris' body froze. His legs locked up and his back turned to solid concrete. He could inhale but found it almost impossible to exhale, which caused irregular breathing. Myerson again motioned for him to sit. Chris again brushed off the offer, indicating that he would rather stand. Out of the corner of his eye, Chris caught a brief glimpse of the photo on the mantle. He could still feel Megan's eyes looking at him from across the room, watching his reactions and judging his every move.

Content with the fact that Chris wished to remain standing, Myerson reached into his jacket and retrieved a small notepad.

Flipping it open quickly, he continued to speak. "A couple of local boys confirmed for us this morning that they had seen four of the five missing children…two of which were your sons…near a stream about a mile from here. They claim that your eldest son, Tommy, was engaged in a fight with a local boy by the name of Donald Rondage. They told us that both your son and Donald fell into the stream while wrestling and that neither ever came up."

Were it not for the fact that his muscles appeared to have been frozen, Chris Jarvis would have toppled over.

What had he done? All those years, all those mistakes, all the things he had said – and now this. His brain tried to formulate an appropriate response to everything the detective had just said but it failed. His mouth opened but little more than a small puff of hot breath escaped his lips.

"Mr. Jarvis, we have teams checking every square inch of that stream right now. If your boys are in there, we'll find them."

Chris turned away from Myerson and from the picture on the mantle. His breathing became significantly more awkward and labored. Myerson took note. The air around Chris tasted stale and vile, every breath feeling as if he inhaled a fire so old that it had existed since the dawn of time. The slightest movement of his eyes caused them to well up. The furniture, the walls, the carpet, the action figures Nicky had left strewn across the kitchen floor, everything in his home was taunting him. Everywhere he looked at harsh reminders of what he had done to his wife and his boys – of how he had failed them.

From behind him came the voice of Detective Myerson. "There's one other thing, Mr. Jarvis…"

Chris turned around just in time to see the detective pull a plastic bag with several pieces of paper out of another pocket. After holding it up in front of his face for a brief second, he tossed it onto the coffee table near Chris. Tentatively Chris reached over and picked up the bag. He cautiously examined it.

"We found those taped to the walls inside a tree fort near the stream where your sons were last seen."

Chris pulled the papers from the plastic bag, slowly riffling through them. They were drawings – Tommy's drawings – crude drawings depicting the cause of Chris's greatest shame. There, recreated and brought to life by rubbing colored pencil and crayon against paper, were images of him hitting his eldest son.

Myerson glared at Chris from across the room. His eyes burned a hole in the center of Chris' skull. "I was wondering if you wouldn't mind answering a few other questions for me, Mr. Jarvis."

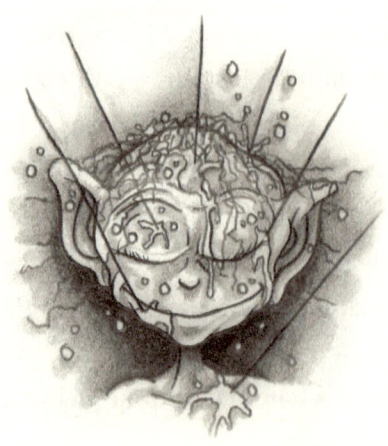

34. THE PASSING OF THE SIGHT

Zanell ran for what had seemed like forever through the nearly black, tight and crowded southern passage. Every single muscle in her legs ached and burned, protesting and begging for her to stop. It had only been an hour since she had stopped crying. She was quite simply cried out. The image of her grandfather buried in the rubble as her friends and family were slaughtered all around her was something that she would never forget and something that would bring tears for years to come. At the end of the dank corridor, she stopped to catch her breath. Above her was the hidden passageway leading into the forest. Once she left the safe walls of Tipoloo and its many passages, she would be completely exposed. From here on out she would be an easy target for the Dark Army's patrols. From the time she was little, Zanell had been told repeatedly to stay out of the red forest. She had occasionally watched friends, neighbors, and local toughs who ignored the warnings fail to return. Every single inch of her being told her that she should, even now, heed those warnings, but where else was she to go? Traveling back to Tipoloo was impossible. There was no Tipoloo to return to. This reality caused her tired eyes to once again attempt to produce tears; it would prove to be a fruitless undertaking.

In her heart Zanell knew what must be done. Her grandfather had instructed her that she needed to run and keep running until she was in the forest and that was exactly what she intended to do – what she had to do – no matter how scary the proposition. Despite her fear, she would do this because she owed it to him.

From somewhere behind her, nestled in the darkness of the southern passage, she could hear the distant voices of the King's soldiers – they were tracking her. Quickly moving toward the dirt wall, she climbed to the camouflaged hatch. Pushing it open with one hand she pulled herself up into the forest. A steady stream of rain poured through the trees above her head, blocking out the slowly darkening evening sky. For the life of her, she could not remember the last time she had felt actual, real-life rain. Every droplet on her skin brought with it a million childhood sensations long since forgotten. Lifting her hands, she let it cascade down her arms, and seep into every dry, burning pore. Trickling into her dry eyes, it moistened and healed them. Still unable to cry, she decided to let the rain do the crying for her – to cover her entire body in tears, ensuring that she would never forget this day and the things she had left behind.

The hatch on the ground beneath her feet began to move as someone pushed against it. Zanell ran. She did not know where she was going, but it really did not matter. Her muscles were sore and her heart was beating faster than it ever had in her life. Her lanky, awkward, leggy form sprinted across the forest floor with graceful speed. She flew over fallen lumber and around large rocks, darting in and out of the enormous gray trunks of trees like someone who had spent a lifetime nestled in the bosom of the forest. Somewhere behind her the voices of the King's guards, still hot on her trail, were slowly fading. In the open air, she simply moved too fast for them and the storm had made it even more difficult for the soldiers to keep pace. When she no longer heard their footsteps, Zanell slowed to a trot, glancing briefly over her shoulder. There were no guards now, only trees, heavy rain, and a thick layer of fog slowly rising from the ground to aid in her escape.

Had she not known better, she might have thought the forest itself was helping her get away.

Coming to a complete stop, she took advantage of the lull to catch her breath and slow her rapidly beating heart. She sat in the thick mud and rested her hands on her knees. Breathing deeply, she closed her eyes and felt the falling rain wash over her body. It was such a wonderful sensation. Hanging on every drop was the sweet odor of the trees. The crispness of the outside air filled her lungs, traveled to her brain and cushioned the awful memories of the day's madness like a soft pillow. The wonderful, unending silence seeped into her ears, filling them with a beautiful nothingness that she welcomed like a long lost friend.

For a brief moment, Zanell forgot everything. There was no Tipoloo or saviors from another world. No evil King or invading armies that left dead bodies scattered across the streets of the only place she had ever called home. For a second, her mother and father were alive and well, as was her grandfather. The red forest was once again her home rather than her tomb.

During this fleeting hiccup in time, Zanell understood that her life had been forever changed.

The spirit of something more than herself boiled up inside her stomach and spread over her. Something new and different instantly rooted underneath her skin, pushing out with incredible force. Ideas and thoughts that belonged not only to her but also to someone else filled each and every pore in her body. With these fantastic ideas came ethereal warmth. Zanell slowly opened her eyes. Suddenly everything looked different – softer – as if the universe had been dipped in a heavenly white cloud. In an instant, she saw everything, everywhere, always. Tommy, Donald, Pleebo, the Prince and his father, worlds she did not know existed, and situations she could never have dreamt. Suddenly she knew how everything began and she understood how it would one day end. She understood her grandfather's words, not only why he told her to run, but every single cryptic, confusing sentence he had ever uttered during the course of her young life. As improbable as it seemed to her, there was no denying that this was the sight beyond sight and it now resided in her.

She was the Elder.

A slight grin formed on her soaking wet face. Grandfather had been right all along. There was, in fact, great beauty in endings.

35. REVOLUTION

Immediately after General Gragor had left the dungeon to catch up with the soldiers carrying Nicky and Staci, the remaining Ochan flashed a sadistic grin at Fellow Undergotten. Pulling a long broad sword from a sheath strapped to his back, he slowly ran the sharp blade across the steel bars. The clank of metal upon metal echoed through the dank dungeon passageways.

"You know, I was a part of the invasion party that finally overtook Chintaran," he growled mockingly.

With his back to the cold stone of the cell wall, the pain of his broken ribs slowly cascaded across his chest, Fellow straightened up, gazing angrily toward the hideous Ochan.

The soldier smiled brightly, lifting his sword to his face and carefully examining its contours; he remembered fondly the many he had killed in the King's name.

Turning his attention once again to Fellow, he spoke softly through a wide smile. "Your people fought well, creature. You should be proud of them. Even your children. Such a feisty bunch. They showed considerable bravery when they tried to go toe to toe with trained Ochan warriors, despite being so heavily overmatched. If it had not been so much fun, I would almost be tempted to say that it was a shame that we were forced to slaughter them the way we did. Bravery, no matter how misguided, is still commendable…is it not?"

Scalding hot images of those lost in the war flashed in the deepest recesses of Fellow's mind, causing his blood to boil and his heart to race. Using the wall as a brace, he pushed himself to his feet and removed his hand from his sore chest.

Upon seeing this, the soldier's smile widened further. "Yes…yes, indeed. This is the look. This is the look I remember so fondly. Such a rare and wonderful thing is a look of defiance these days. Too many of you have become complacent with your situation. Too many of you have accepted the inevitability of your fate. You have given up. You walk into the slaughter with dreary, tired eyes. I miss the defiance you showed when we first arrived in your worlds." The Ochan unlocked the cell and slowly opened the door.

Assuming a battle-ready stance, he chuckled with giddy anticipation. "It's much more rewarding to take the life of a creature when it wants so badly to live."

In every cell throughout the dungeon, tired, hungry prisoners pressed their faces against the steel bars. Some went so far as to attempt to wedge their heads through the chilly metal in order to get a better view of the situation that had escalated between Fellow and the soldier. The stories of Staci's power, Fellow's words, and General Gragor's orders to kill had spread like wild fire among them, passing in hushed whispers from cell to cell. Hope mixed with anger and lathered in a thick urgency had spread among them. It infected them and had grown at an astonishing rate.

Fellow Undergotten felt the growing tension in the dungeon as the soldier slowly approached, anxious to kill him where he stood. It was palatable, heavy and real. Fellow had been born a builder and in his heart he would always be a builder. In the years since the war began, though, he had changed into something very different. The madness of war had morphed him. Like a shapeless lump of clay, it had twisted and molded him into something else, fired him with an intense heat and hardened him to stone. Everything he had experienced and seen, the tears he had shed, had succeeded in preparing him for this moment.

Throughout the dungeon came the heavy rhythmic sound of hands beating against the bars. The cries and howls, bordering on screams, of nearly a hundred different species from nearly a hundred different worlds rose up, bounced off of walls and shot like daggers in every direction. The uncommon sound of life in a place so accustomed to death drew the soldier's attention away from Fellow for a fraction of a second as he turned toward the ever-mounting ruckus.

That fraction of a second was all that was needed for Fellow to strike.

Ignoring the pain in his chest, he lunged forward, slamming the entire weight of his body into the soldier's heavily armored chest. The pair tumbled out of the cell and into the hall. Like a rowdy crowd at a prizefight, a mighty cheer rose arose. Pinning one of the soldier's arms to the floor, Fellow wedged it underneath his knee and sat on the Ochan's chest. With his free hand, he threw punches at the creature's exposed face, each blow landing flush, eliciting a deep, guttural grunt from the squirming soldier. The muscled Ochan was bigger and stronger, though, and with every passing moment he slowly inched himself out from underneath Fellow's body. Snaking one of his arms loose, the Ochan managed to grab a small dagger strapped to his thigh. Bridging his body, he used Fellow's momentum against him and shoved the enraged Chintaran off his chest. In the scramble, the Ochan drove the dagger into Fellow's scaly hip – violently grinding it against bone as it sliced through the moist flesh. Fellow yelped in pain, rolled away from the soldier and pulled the dagger from his side. His eyes caught a glimpse of the lever that was used to unlock the cell doors and realized that he had to reach it. Ignoring the pain shooting through the right side of his body, he crawled as quickly as he could in its direction. Every movement was a symphony of pain. His jaw clenched shut, his teeth ground together so hard that he could almost feel them crack and break against each other.

"Ignore the pain and keep moving. Ignore the pain and keep moving."

He repeated the mantra over and over in his head. The gaping wound in his side left a long trail of blood across the stone. Reaching behind him, he covered the gash as best he could, pressing hard. The warm, thick liquid of his insides seeped between the cracks of his fingers. Looking up, he saw that the lever was only a few feet away – just a few more feet.

"Ignore the pain and keep moving. Ignore the pain and keep moving."

The soldier grimaced, shaking the cobwebs from his fuzzy head. He wiped a trickle of blood from a large cut above his eye, stood and retrieved the sword. He followed the trail of blood toward the end of the hall and found Fellow Undergotten.

The wobbly-legged fish man was standing upright, leaning against the wall near the locking mechanism for the cells. His eyes were glassy, a waterfall of blood gushing from his side. On his face was an unstable, shaky, defiant and distinct smile. It was the smile of a creature that did not simply want to live, but hungered for victory. It was a smile that the Ochan soldier had not seen in years.

Fellow grabbed the locking lever, tugging it downward. One after another, in perfect synchronicity, the heavy locks on every cell popped open with a deep, echoing clank. A wave of starved, multi-colored flesh prisoners, both in front and back of the soldier, converged on his position. The enormous, moving, breathing, angry mass of snarling creatures folded in on him like the mouth of a great hungry beast.

Fellow's legs gave way to the arduous strain of trying to remain upright. He slid against the wall and fell upon the stone floor. Somewhere down the hallway he heard the Ochan guard scream briefly before his voice was muffled by the attacking horde. Fellow's mind wandered back to the home that he had built with his own two hands, to the ocean where he had watched his nieces first learn to swim, to his brother Leeko, who had been his best friend. He recalled with immeasurable sadness how it had all been taken from him. He remembered watching his house burn to the ground and how he had buried his brother with his family in the sea near the ash of the place he had once called home. He remembered these things and wept deeply in his heart.

It would be so easy.

Giving into the blurriness that overtook his vision would be effortless. It would be so simple to let the loss of blood coax him lovingly into unconsciousness and eventual death, but he knew that he could not, not yet. There was still work to do, children to rescue, and a world to save.

Fellow took a breath and held it. He pulled himself to his feet, using the locking lever as a brace. He scanned the crowded. The angry mass of creatures crammed into the dungeon, having their way with what remained of the Ochan soldier's corpse. Their various faces all had one thing in common. They looked rejuvenated, angry and ready to fight. In a different life that seemed far away, Fellow Undergotten had been that simple builder. Things had come full circle. Once more he would be a builder. He would use the rejuvenated spirits of these prisoners to build a revolution.

36. THE GREAT ESCAPE

Nicky Jarvis continued to kick, squirm and struggle against the enormous Ochan who clutched him tightly to his chest. In a last ditch effort, he had tried to bite the soldier's arm but succeeded only in chipping a tooth on the creature's thick skin. Wrapped tightly in the arms of the soldier next to him, Staci Andrews remained motionless, lost somewhere within herself, unable to cope with what had happened since she chose to follow the Jarvis boys into the woods. The soldiers lugged the children out of the dungeon and through a long winding hallway and into an elaborately decorated open chamber with a ceiling nearly twenty stories high. General Gragor was behind the soldiers, moving with surprising speed for one with such a massive frame.

After catching up to the group, General Gragor tapped one of the soldiers on the shoulder and said in his deep grave voice, "I've changed my mind. Take them to the courtyard. I want every single slave to see these two die. I want them to witness firsthand the color of their blood as it seeps from their severed heads. We need to remind these things of their position in the hierarchy of the Ochan nation."

Squirming sideways, Nicky glanced over the soldier's shoulder toward General Gragor.

The massive Ochan General glared back at him, grinning. "If you have something you feel the need to say, little one, please, share. I suppose even a mutt such as yourself deserves a chance for final words."

Nicky said nothing, choosing instead to simply scowl. Once again his tiny body flailed wildly in the soldier's arms. General Gragor's grin turned into a full smile as he chuckled – albeit underneath his breath. He was anxious to be rid of these bothersome pink creatures – anxious to put an end to what they represented.

"GENERAL! GENERAL!" The voice came from a doorway at the far end of the chamber. A fully armored soldier sprinted across the massive room and came to a sliding stop. "General, I have urgent news!"

General Gragor glanced at the children briefly, then back to the soldier. "Is it so urgent that it can't wait a few moments, Lieutenant?" He wanted to kill these meddlesome children - so much so that every muscle in his body jittered with anxious anticipation. The Prince had delayed their execution far too long as it was.

"Extremely urgent, sir, yes."

General Gragor sighed, disappointed. "Then speak…but be quick."

The young Lieutenant found it difficult to turn his eyes away from the children. The stories of their arrival had spread throughout the fortress. As he saw them now - up close – an odd mixture of interest and cautious fear overtook him. But on top of it all there was disappointment – disappointment that so many of his fellow soldiers seemed to entertain the possibility that these pathetic creatures could be the downfall of his great Ochan nation. General Gragor noted the manner in which his Lieutenant eyed the children. It served only to further his resolve toward killing them as soon as possible.

Annoyed by his Lieutenant's inattention, General Gragor grabbed him by the chest plate, violently pulling him close. "I suggest that you tell me what it is you need to tell me right this minute, soldier…before I decide that you should share the same fate as these disgusting creatures."

The seriousness in the General's voice and the expression on his face was successful. "Yes, yes, of course, sir…the regiment stationed inside the doorway to Tycaria, sir…"

"The seventh division, yes…what about them?"

"They're gone."

"What?"

"They're gone, sir."

General Gragor released his grip and stared at the helmeted head of the young soldier quizzically. "What do you mean they're gone?"

"They missed their scheduled check-in last night, so a messenger was sent and found only corpses."

Time stopped for General Gragor. He found it impossible to formulate a response. It had been years since the Tycarians had offered any sort of resistance. The seventh division was comprised of his finest battle-tested warriors. He knew, of course, that what had been left of the Tycarian army had scattered into the mountains, probably being led by their pathetic King. The groups were believed to be small in numbers and hardly capable of decimating an entire regiment, even if they had managed to combine their forces for a single, large-scale attack. There was another, more pressing question that he was unable get out of his head – Why there, and why now? He glanced at the two children that were wrapped securely in the arms of his soldiers. They were so innocent looking, so utterly pathetic and useless. What a fitting disguise for harbingers of death.

Prince Valkea might be able to ignore the coincidences cropping up on a regular basis, but he could not. Not now, not with so much on the line. The Prince had specifically ordered him to keep King Kragamel in the dark about the arrival of the children, but it was a stupid, petty order given by a juvenile Prince who had proven time and time again to be little more than a disillusioned child desperately seeking his father's approval. It was an order that General Gragor could not in good conscience keep.

Turning toward his Lieutenant, he stiffly placed his gloved hand on the young soldier's shoulder. "I need you to travel to Ocha immediately. The King needs to be informed of everything that has happened here. Take three men with you as well as whatever provisions you think necessary. Ride through the night. Do not make a single stop. Do you understand?"

"Yes, sir, of course…but, what exactly should I tell him?"

General Gragor looked at the children once more – so small, so weak - so dangerous. They were dangerous not just for what they

221

could or could not do, but more importantly for what they represented.

If the Prince was unable or unwilling to put a stop to this travesty before it went any further, he would. "Tell him that the day he so dreaded could very well be upon us."

The young Lieutenant saw General Gragor glance at the children. He also looked at them with the same disgusted fear as did his General. He understood the urgency as he headed out of the chamber the same way he had entered.

Young Nicky Jarvis listened intently to the entire conversation and stared into the eyes of the imposing General Gragor with a renewed defiance. Though he really did not understand what was happening, he saw the concern buried deep inside his enormous captor. Just understanding that the monstrous creature was as frightened of him as he was of them made the boy feel better.

Never once averting his gaze from the young boy, General Gragor broke the silence. "Take them to the courtyards. I'm putting an end to this nonsen..."

His sentence was interrupted by the sound of a collapsing door. The heavy crack of splintering wood brought forth the shattering of his control over the land of Fillagrou and shot through the castle, signaling the start of a great battle. In a single, swift motion General Gragor, pulled the sword from his back and readied himself for battle. From the corridor which led to the dungeon, a massive living tidal wave of anger, armed with the battle cries of a hundred different dialects spoken by the released prisoners, flooded the room. At the front, with a piece of fabric knotted tightly around his waist to stop the bleeding was the reborn builder turned revolutionary, Fellow Undergotten.

37. UNLEASH THE DOGS OF WAR

As he peered through a thick layer of foliage at the large group of heavily armored, very mean looking Ochan soldiers a few hundred yards away, Donald Rondage could think of only one slightly sarcastic thing to say. "All right then…so I guess we're pretty much screwed then, huh?"

Hunkered down next to him, just inside the tree line and out of sight from the soldiers, were the rest of the motley bunch. An aging King and his small band of war-weary soldiers, a local from a race that practiced non-violence, a tough guy who was just barely six inches tall, and saviors from another world who had not yet entered high school hardly seemed an intimidating force. Off in the distance and behind the Ochan soldiers, lay an enormous lake filled with dirty, murky, greenish-gray water. At one time the lake had been a smallish pond. After it was discovered to be the doorway leading to Tycaria, the nefarious King Kragamel had ordered it dug open until it was large enough for Ochan forces to pass through in massive numbers, which was exactly what had happened. Once the Ochan army had been able to move into this new world freely, it had been only a matter of time before the land of Tycaria was overrun.

Receiving no response, Donald spoke up again. "Well, what are we supposed to do now...anyone? It's a serious question. No offense to your soldiers, SLOW-amennes, but even with their help, I don't think we stand a chance of taking those dudes in a fight."

Annoyed, King Walcott quickly interjected. "Now you listen here, young man...I've had just about enough of you." He found it difficult to maintain his King-like composure and stay his tongue concerning the perennially negative Donald.

Just as he was about to raise his voice and give the pudgy boy an earful, Nestor Rockshell - the scar-faced commander of the Fighting Fifth - placed his flat paw on King Walcott's shoulder. "I would be remiss in my duties, great King, if I did not mention to you that the young boy is quite correct in his assumption. As it stands, we would offer little resistance to a well-trained Ochan regiment of that size, no matter how much it pains me to admit it."

The sensible words from one of his most honored soldiers managed to calm King Walcott's irritation. He nodded at Nestor before giving young Donald a warning look, something Donald recognized as "the stink eye". They would undoubtedly continue their discussion at a later date.

Sitting Indian style on a thick-veined, deep green leaf growing from the forest floor, Roustaf leaned toward Pleebo. "What are you thinking, Pleebs? Any ideas?"

Pleebo had none. He had no real military experience. He had never led men into battle, planned an invasion or even picked up a sword, for that matter. He was quite plainly out of his element. When they started the journey he had always assumed that things would just work themselves out somehow. Never in his wildest dreams did he imagine that others would look to him for answers to questions such as these. Timidly he glanced toward Roustaf, then at the others.

Lowering his head he gave them the only answer he could. He knew that it was the last thing they wanted to hear. "I...I don't know..."

Donald rolled his eyes, moaning. "You know...if Tommy could figure out how to shoot those lasers or whatever they were from his hands again, he could just blast them all to smithereens and be done with it."

Tommy shot Donald a nasty glance. In truth, though, Donald was right once again. Since they had started their journey, Tommy tried several times to replicate what he did in Tipoloo and failed miserably every time. He was no closer to understanding how or why it had happened in the first place, let alone learning anything about how to control it. A large part of him believed it had been a fluke, while a small part wondered if it even had happened at all. Incredible powers or no incredible powers, Tommy understood that nothing about his situation had changed. He needed to get past those guards, into that lake and to the Prince's castle. Nicky needed his help and that was really all that mattered.

Determined, Tommy glanced at Pleebo and said, "We need to get through that doorway."

Ever since Pleebo met Tommy Jarvis, he had known that something was different about the boy. He had not fully understood why he knew this, but he did. Tommy was right; they had to get past the guards at any cost. He owed it to boy to continue. He owed it to his people, his world, and his grandfather. Pleebo looked toward King Walcott and the seven soldiers with pleading eyes.

No words needed to be spoken.

A simple glance from Pleebo was returned by an acknowledging nod from King Walcott. Though each had their own personal reasons for taking part in the mission, everyone involved had understood the great importance of its success.

King Walcott stretched his neck and looked at Nestor. "Tell me, commander...do you think the Fightin' Fifth might have one great battle left in them?"

Nestor Rockshell had spent the majority of his adult life in the service of his King and country. He had buried friends and family and had witnessed brothers- at- arms laid to rest. He fought because he believed in a single solitary cause - his people – and he would fight for them until the very last breath.

A somewhat hesitant smile, slowly brimming with a necessary confidence, stretched across his battered green snout. In a deep voice he said, "For you, my King...always."

King Walcott smiled proudly. "Good...very good. You are a credit to the Tycarian people, my friend. I assure you upon my honor that I will not let them forget what you will do here today."

Rising, Nestor faced his soldiers. "Three of you will follow the tree line south, while the rest of us go north. Once in position, we'll attack from both sides and catch them off guard. Our ultimate goal is to pull their division in two directions...to create safe passage for our comrades." He turned toward King Walcott and the others. "Once we've separated the regiment, you should be able to pass through the middle, get into the water and through the doorway. We'll do our best to keep them from following, but I suggest that you continue moving once you're on the other side."

The group nodded in agreement. Within minutes Nestor and his men parted ways, making their way through the trees in opposite directions. For Owen, Tommy and the rest, time seemed to move slowly. They quickly lost sight of Nestor's men, staring off in the distance waiting for the battle to begin. Tommy dug his heels into the dirt, ready for a full on sprint. Beside him, Owen Little bit nervously at his fingernails, which were already chewed back as far as they could go. Roustaf floated off the leaf and perched on Pleebo's shoulder. With the fury of a crash of thunder in a dead night sky, Nestor's army ran from the trees on either side of the Ochan regiment, swords and shields at the ready. Moving like a well-oiled machine, the Ochans quickly rushed to meet them. Steel crashed against steel and flesh met flesh. The grunts, screams, and howls of war pierced the silence that encapsulated the travelers like a stone shattering glass. For their part, the Fifth Regiment fought brilliantly. What they lacked in speed they made up in strength and, most importantly, heart. Outnumbered by nearly five to one, the Tycarians still managed to separate the Ochan division exactly as planned.

Still hidden behind the tree line, the group realized that the opening they needed had been created. One by one, they nodded, acknowledging the break. Tommy looked past the fighting and ignored the fact that he had just seen one of Nestor's men die on the end of an Ochan soldier's blade. Instead he focused on the body of water behind the madness. Focusing on the destination rather than the journey, thinking only of his little brother, proved to be exactly what he needed to build up his courage and move across the battlefield.

He took one big, deep breath and dug the toes of his sneakers into the ground. Lowering his brow, tightening every muscle in his face, he screamed only one word, "GO!"

In a flash, Tommy shot off like a rocket. He ran full speed toward the opening in the line that the Fighting Fifth had created. Large chunks of dirt kicked up underneath his feet and spit into the air behind him. His legs pumped as his arms swung back and forth in a frantic rhythm. He was quickly closing the gap between his flying feet and the battle when he noticed that he was running alone. Sure, Tommy was relatively fast, but he knew that Pleebo was a heck of a lot faster. Why was no one else around him? He stopped so quickly that his feet skid across the grass. He turned and glanced behind him. Still at the tree line, scattering in random, wild directions were the others. Moving like a pack of predators in the trees behind them, with weapons drawn and large smiles barely visible underneath their deep gray helmets, were four Ochan soldiers. Tommy turned again toward the doorway. The opening created by the Tycarians been closed and only three of Nestor's men remained standing. Everything had fallen apart quickly and now they were trapped.

38. JAR OF FIREFLIES

Tommy's hand moved with assured swiftness over the thin sheet of paper. The dark colored crayon between his fingers was worn nearly to a nub, and with each flick of his wrist it grew smaller. To the layman, the marks left in its wake seemed to be random at best. A line here, a thicker line there, a lightly colored space just a bit off center in-between the two – random lines haphazardly scratched on parchment, nothing more. Through the eyes of Tommy Jarvis though, not a single stroke was without meaning or purpose. In his head, the picture was already there, the possibilities of every contour, angle, twist and turn already existed. He was simply bringing them to light, giving them form, and voice – making the invisible, visible.

Looking up momentarily from his drawing, he glanced at his younger brother Nicky, sitting with his back against the wall of their newly constructed tree fort. In his tiny hands, Nicky held a glass jar filled with fireflies that he had captured earlier in the afternoon. The tiny black bodies were invisible to Tommy's eye, appearing only briefly out of nowhere in quick flashes of soft yellow light, then disappearing once again into nothingness - their existence brief, yet beautiful. Nicky lifted the jar high and close to his face, smiling widely. Every flicker of a firefly's body cast a soft reflection in the wetness of his eye, giving the appearance that the light was a great energy growing from somewhere deep within the young boy.

While staring at his little brother, Tommy was still absentmindedly drawing. The face of a young girl, though only half sketched, could now be made out. Peering through a half sketched strand of hair, she stared at her creator with warm, inquisitive eyes. A slight smile seemed to be forming on the side of her mouth, almost as if she were pleading for him to smile back, though in her heart she understood that he could not – not anymore.

Tommy glanced out the crudely constructed window. Off in the distance the sun had already half-descended behind a landscape of trees. Extending from the heart of the sun itself, the sky was a hauntingly beautiful hue of orange, red, and a million variations in between. Traveling further into the air, the color faded into a soft, warm purple, which had been swallowed by a cool blue. At the blue edge, transformed into an open, endless black, sporadically lit by the freckles in the sky, were the stars. A total, all-encompassing night was quickly approaching, bringing with it the reality that both Tommy and Nicky would have to return home. Neither boy wanted to leave the safety of their fortress. Far away from the real world and its real people with their very real problems, the tree fort was a welcome change from their repetitively sad lives.

Tommy turned his attention to Nicky who was lying on his stomach, staring happily into the glass jar resting on the floor. "Nicky, we have to go soon."

Nicky glanced at his older brother with sad eyes that revealed his emotion. Tommy hated that look. He hated the way it made him feel. He hated the fact that he seemed to be the only person remaining in the universe who cared how Nicky felt.

"It'll be alright...I'll sneak you in the back door...He'll never even hear us come in."

Nicky's expression remained cheerless. Tommy could not stand the idea that any little boy had to feel the way he knew his little brother felt at that moment, ignoring the fact that he too was still a little boy.

"Don't worry...you know that I won't let anything happen to you...I promise."

Dejected, Nicky turned away from his brother, again staring into his jar of fireflies. He watched closely the rhythmic dance of light brought to life inside. Each burst reflected off the jar's glass, creating the illusion of a million more, slightly dimmer, tiny insects residing somewhere within. After a minute of losing himself in the intoxicating glow, he snatched the jar in his hands and stood up, moving toward the window, dragging his shoeless feet the entire way. Once there, he leaned out and opened the jar. Tommy stood and moved towards his little brother. "What are you doing?"

By the time he was standing beside him, Nicky had already removed the cap and turned the jar upside down. One by one, the tiny fireflies escaped from their glass cage into the night sky. The brothers followed their movements until they eventually disappeared into the deep blackness. Occasionally the glow of their tiny bodies mixed with the glow of the evening stars, becoming one and the same.

Tommy Jarvis believed that for the first time in a very long time, he had found an appropriate moment to smile.

39. FEAR OF THE UNDERDOG

Donald Rondage had tried to conceal the fear washing over his body, but his rapid breathing, not to mention the massive amounts of salty sweat dripping down his face and into his mouth, told another story. He dug his fingers deeply into the soft dirt to try to stop his shaking hands, while looking at the others to see if anyone had noticed. Perched like a minuscule red gargoyle on Pleebo's shoulder, tiny Roustaf smiled knowingly at the boy. In contrast to his usually somewhat harsh demeanor, he nodded, as if to tell Donald that it was okay to be scared. Donald shot him an embarrassed, angry glance, and quickly looked away. Before he had time to curse the little man with the transparent wings, he heard Tommy scream, "GO!" Donald looked over just in time to see Tommy leap up from his crouched position and run towards the battling Ochans and Tycarians.

Donald took a deep breath, tightened the muscles in his lower body, lifted off his knees and burst through the foliage in front of him. He had gone less than three feet before he was snagged by the collar of his shirt. The soldier pulled him back, dropping him like a sack of potatoes onto his rear. Grimacing through the pain, Donald opened his eyes and looked over his shoulder. Standing over him was an enormous, heavily armored soldier, grinning from one end of his disgusting scaled face to the other. In his massive gloved hand, the angry creature held a sword that seemed as long as Donald's body. The sunlight caught the blade, shimmering across his face like a dagger of light. Donald looked about him and saw that everyone else was also in a similarly precarious situation.

An even larger soldier had Pleebo and Roustaf backed up against a tree trunk. The gutsy little Roustaf charged at the creature while screaming at the top of his tiny lungs, but was brushed away, being considered more of a pest than an actual threat. Roustaf's little body slammed into a tree, knocking him unconscious. Pleebo moved toward his friend but was stopped by a soldier's drawn sword. Pleebo's upper lip quivered angrily as his eyes narrowed and a very un-Pleebo-like growl rumbled frighteningly through his thin lips. This was as intimidating as Pleebo would ever hope to look. The burly Ochan found it more comical than frightening. Slowly he moved his sword toward Pleebo, pointing the dangerous tip at the Fillagrou's bony chest. A sly smile crept across his face as a disgusting mixture of laughter and terrible breath shot in Pleebo's direction. The Ochan soldier lived for moments like this.

Farther down the line, another soldier connected with a stiff right hook to the side of King Walcott's face. The large bodied turtle-man stumbled awkwardly as if his thick legs had become floppy, useless noodles. His shell collided with the trunk of a thin tree, snapping it in half as his body tumbled to the ground, landing with a heavy, reverberating thump.

A slightly smaller, equally dangerous Ochan towered over a curled up and sobbing Owen Little. With his face pressed hard into the dirt and grass, Owen could not fully see the creature looming dangerously over him but he could feel his presence.

Quietly into the soil he mumbled, "Please don't kill me, please don't kill me, please don't kill me, please don't kill me." He hoped that it might somehow make a difference.

The monstrous Ochan standing above Donald lifted his sword, attempting to deliver a fatal blow. Instinctively Donald rolled his burly body to the side as he tried to crawl away. He turned when the soldier's foot collided with his chest, pinning him to the grass. Donald wrapped his arms around the creature's thick leg and tried to squirm out from underneath the massive boot. It was hopeless. The evil thing was too strong and too large. Every movement on Donald's part succeeded only in spreading the pain caused by the ridged, textured soles of the heavy boot. Once again the soldier hoisted the sword high above his head and smiled devilishly at the squirming mass of pink flesh pinned underneath him. A mocking, heavily sarcastic burp of laughter built up, gushing through the spaces between the jagged points of his yellow teeth. Donald closed his eyes tight, tears flowing like a heavy torrent of rain.

This was it. This was how it was going to end, pinned underneath the foot of a massive lizard-man, far away from anyone and everything that he knew. He wondered if his family would notice his disappearance. If they did, he wondered if they would even care. The young boy found no solace in the fact that he believed the answer to both questions would be, unfortunately, "no". He closed his eyes tightly and tried to steady his shaking body, preparing himself for the inevitable. The wet, burning sensation pouring from his eyes rapidly spread into his skull. It was an odd feeling, unlike anything Donald had ever experienced. Similar to electricity being carried along a conductive cable, the strange warmth stretched its way throughout his body, into his chest, arms and the tips of his fingers. It moved into his legs, reaching the tip of the nails on his toes. It cascaded across him like warm sunshine coming from somewhere deep inside. His entire body was alive, crackling and popping with massive, explosive amounts of energy straining to be released. Every muscle suddenly felt hot and tingly in ways that gave new definition to the words.

Though not fully aware of what he was doing, Donald tightened his grip on the leg of the soldier, lifted and pushed.

The massive bodied creature seemed to weigh no more than a small rock. Donald tossed him straight into the air as if he had been shot from a catapult. The Ochan hung against the background of the sky, arched, and fell quickly to the ground. His body slammed into the dirt nearly thirty feet away with a puff of smoke, knocking him completely unconscious and breaking several bones in the process. Donald sat and stared blankly at his arms. He wiggled his fingers slowly. His limbs quivered. He could not make sense of what he had just done.

From the corner of his eye he spotted the soldier that had knocked King Walcott unconscious. He was sprinting towards him, weapon at the ready. Once again the boy's body moved before his brain could process what was happening around him. This was action, rather than reaction. Body and mind seemed to be two beings, completely independent of each other. Propping himself up on one knee, he flung his hands into the dirt like a pair of jackhammers. The incredible strength of the movement buried his arms up to his shoulders and sent a shockwave cascading across the soil toward the charging soldier. The ground popped, rattled, and shook, as if an earthquake rumbled underneath his feet. Thick plumes of dirt and rock flew into the air, exploding underneath the soldier like a bomb. The explosion sent him flailing wildly into the air before crashing violently into a nearby tree. Donald tugged his arms from the ground, dusted the dirt and rocks off his sleeves and lifted them to his face.

Now it was his turn to smile widely.

Somewhere in-between the fighting, Tommy Jarvis was sprawled out on his hands and knees, his head buried in his sweaty palms. The moment he noticed that his group was trapped, the strange, warm feeling he had experienced in Tipoloo started to wash over him. His entire body felt as if it were on fire – a fire so hot and all-encompassing that it seemed to consume every part of him at an alarming rate. His heart, which had been pumping in double time, now pushed itself to triple time. His breaths were quick and deep, each one echoing in his chest, picking up speed like a swinging pendulum. It seemed unbearable. Tommy lifted his head and gazed at the sky. Every part of him wanted to scream – to do something – anything to release the pressure pressing against his insides like a million tiny little hands attached to a million tiny fire bombs. Beams of pure white light poured through his eyes and mouth. The beams parted the clouds like a great gust of wind, disintegrating them on contact. The release of energy provided Tommy temporary relief but the relief was fleeting. He felt it building inside him once again. It did not take long for the boy's entire body to light up with the strange, crackling energy. Even the slightest movement on his part resulted in a popping and crackling sound, much like static from a television set. The need to release again the pressure was painfully obvious to the boy. Not only did he need to be rid of it, he needed to do it quickly. Awash in the strange glow, Tommy slowly rose to his feet and lifted his hands. He pointed them at the doorway to Fillagrou. Though he could not explain why, it seemed the obvious choice.

Of his regiment, only Nestor Rockshell remained standing. His men had fought gallantly in the name of their King but each had tasted the blade of the enemy and lay dead in the blood-stained grass. Out of breath and unable to lift his blade due to a badly injured arm, he was surrounded by five Ochan soldiers. Nestor breathed in the odor of Tycaria one final time, so moist, so soft, and so very much home. He would miss this place; yet if anything, it was worth dying for. Nestor closed his eyes and defiantly raised his head, awaiting the inevitable. The Ochan soldiers closed in on his position. The soldier closest to Nestor's fallen body was given the honor of the kill.

The Ochan raised his sword, ready to strike his injured foe, but then froze. His wide eyes focused on a tidal wave of light that was moving in his direction at an alarming rate. Confused, he stepped away from Nestor. The Ochan realized that he could not out run the great wall of light and raised his shield, bracing himself for whatever impact the incredible sight would bring. All around him, his fellow soldiers followed his lead and assumed a similar defensive position.

Nestor wondered why he was not dead and slowly opened his eyes. He noticed that his executioner was hiding behind his shield. From the corner of his eye, Nestor spotted the gargantuan, rapidly approaching wall of light. Instinct a million years old instructed him to tuck his limbs into his shell and hide, which was exactly what he did without hesitation.

The ominous glowing wall slammed into the soldiers with the force of a freight train, leaving heavy scorch marks across their armor and tossing them wildly for miles in every direction. An entire regiment of well- trained, battle- tested, war-tough Ochan soldiers had been wiped out in the blink of an eye. Amazingly, the light had targeted only the Ochan soldiers, leaving Nester's protective shell unscathed. Tommy Jarvis turned his still glowing body to Pleebo and lifted his arms. The boy's fingertips crackled to life once again, humming and popping, aglow with their otherworldly light. Swiftly the light expanded and extended in every direction. A sound eerily reminiscent of a growl filled the air, shook the ground and blew apart the clouds as the radiance from his fingers blasted toward the soldiers near the tree line.

Little Roustaf, who had been knocked unconscious when the soldier swatted him away, woke just in time to see the incredible light rushing toward him.

His mouth agape, he managed to whisper only two words before it was upon him, "Oh, crap."

40. PROPHECIES AND VISIONS

Zanell's feet splashed in the muddy puddles as she walked steadily through the forest. The rain beat gently down on her head, cooling her skin and washing away years of dirt and grime from her stringy hair. Opening her mouth, she let some of it catch on the tip of her long, flat tongue. It tasted good – cool and salty – and brought with it memories of a place she had never had the opportunity to fully understand. The forest, the world and the universe seemed different to her now. Everything around her had a story and a history all its own. The minuscule and meaningless things that she might never have noticed only hours ago suddenly played a crucial part in a grand and complicated tale. Even with her new eyes filled with wonderful sight, she could never hope to fully understand the magnitude of her gift. The death of a flower, the birth of another, each was a piece in an absurdly complicated puzzle that was nowhere near its completion.

Zanell stopped in a particularly deep puddle of muddy water, pausing for a second as an image flashed in her head. Amazing sensations exploded and cascaded across her brain like a trillion stars coming to a tragically beautiful end in a brilliant chorus.

Without a doubt this was a unique feeling – warm, comforting and scary, all at the same time. It was unique, though a uniqueness for which she was slowly growing accustomed.

Pivoting on one foot, she turned and looked behind her with a steady, assured gaze. As if on cue, two Ochan soldiers seated atop a pair of massive, drooling, multi-horned creatures called Megalots, passed through a thick set of trees in the distance. They spotted Zanell and kicked at the sides of the large creatures, eliciting a deep, guttural growl from the snarling snouts of the beasts. They ran toward her as quickly as their massive bodies could manage. Not long ago such a sight would have scared the daylights out of Zanell. Her first response would have been to run in the opposite direction, to keep running until her legs gave out.

Now, though, things were different. She was different.

The creatures came to a stop just ten feet from her. Their massive hoofed feet slid across the damp soil, almost spinning out of control in the process. The creatures secured their footing, and the soldiers hopped off of their backs, heading for Zanell. The larger of the two stepped in close, his face inches from her, his breath warm on her flesh.

The soldier clacked his teeth menacingly, sporting a quizzical half grin-half frown. "Look at this one...not even running. I'm not sure if we should give her credit for bravery, laugh at her stupidity, or remove the head from her shoulders for her insolence."

From behind him the other soldier laughed so deeply that his armor clanked and rattled with each heave of his burly chest.

The first Ochan moved closer to Zanell, sniffing at her skin while licking his lips. His face was now so close that she could almost taste his rancid, acid smelling breath in her mouth. "Well...which is it, female? Are you brave or stupid...or both?"

Zanell said nothing but stared at the trees. She spotted a tiny black Muridon spider. With a little grin, she watched it crawl underneath a large leaf on the forest floor in order to escape the falling rain. Fillagrou, Ocha, the war, her grandfather, The Five to save them all, none of it meant anything to the tiny sixteen-legged, thirty-four-eyed arachnid. He was simply trying to get home to his family. He had his own battles to fight, his own tests to complete. Her world and her problems meant absolutely nothing to him and never would. Beyond a fleeting glance in her direction, the Muridon barely acknowledged her existence. Zanell found this truth to be quite funny in a bittersweet sort of way. Smiling broadly she winked at the tiny creature.

The soldier took note of the unexpected gesture.

Angrily he shoved her against a nearby tree. "Do you find something funny, female? Please share it with me. I would love to know exactly what you find so comical about your current situation." Pulling a dagger from his side he held it up to her face, gently running the sharp blade against the skin of her forehead. "I'll tell you what's funny...the way your pathetic little underground city fell...now that's funny."

242

His comment immediately garnered Zanell's attention. Turning her head slowly she gazed into his eyes.

"Ooh, what happened to your sweet smile, female? It seems to have suddenly disappeared...how strange. What is it? Did you have some family down there, friends maybe? Yes, that's it...I bet you did, didn't you? Lots of friends...lots of friends and family who are now dead."

In one long, slow movement the creature repositioned his blade underneath her small nostrils. The disgusting, dirty yellow of his teeth now showed through his broad, sarcastic smile. "Can you smell that? On the edge of my blade, can you smell that? That's the smell of your mother and your father...or maybe your sister. It's the smell of your best friend's life ending. It's the smell of destiny...both yours and mine."

Zanell's flat lips curved into a grin. While the brutish soldier saw himself as one thing, she saw him as another entirely. Try as he might to intimidate her, he could not and would not – not ever again. She saw his past, his present and his future reflected in his eyes. Her mind wandered back in time, overflowing with images of the soldier as a youth, the lost and lonely son of a father that had died in a pointless war over land. The knife resting precariously against her face, the sharpness of his teeth, the fact that he was twice her size and could easily overpower her no longer meant a thing. Hiding behind his dark helmet, thick skin and menacing eyes, she saw only a young boy that had been raised by an overbearing, domineering mother, a young man who had sought love and a feeling of belonging and a sad young man who, when unable to find what he had desired, forced himself to settle for the next closest thing in the military.

No, Zanell did not fear this creature at all but rather pitied him.

In a soft, gentle voice she whispered, "You're not going to kill me."

The soldier cackled. "Oh, I'm not, am I?"

"No, in fact you're going to take me exactly where I need to go."

"Is that what I'm going to do?"

"Yes it is."

The young Ochan's smile gradually faded as he examined the emotionless features of the young Fillagrou female, somewhat confused.

The confusion quickly turned to anger. Who did this girl think she was? Where did she get the nerve? To speak to him in such a manner was unheard of! Annoyance intertwined with rage boiled up his belly. He was quickly growing tired of the disgusting female and her strange, blank stare. With a flick of his hand he moved his dagger to her throat, fully prepared to slice it open and spray her thick, warm blood across the forest floor. His plan came to an abrupt halt when a regiment of Ochan soldiers burst through the trees behind them. Every soldier was seated atop one of at least five different types of creatures, each adorned in armor built to meet their specific dimensions. The regiment was obviously in a hurry, moving hastily through the forest with purpose.

As the group thundered past, a Lieutenant perched on top of an animal resembling a large snake with twelve tiny muscular legs growing along the length of its enormous, squirmy body, came to a stop ten feet from the soldier with his knife to Zanell's throat. "You, there! All regiments have been called back to the fortress immediately! There's been an uprising, and reinforcements are needed!"

The two soldiers confronting Zanell looked briefly at each other in shock and astonishment. There had not been an uprising worthy of even one regiment in a very long time, let alone one requiring all of them at once.

The Lieutenant tugged angrily at the reins of his multi-footed snake and turned to rejoin the group of galloping beasts that by now had passed by.

Stopping only momentarily, he turned briefly to Zanell and her tormentors. "On the off chance that she may prove useful, bring that…thing…with you," he stated gruffly.

The soldier who had her pinned against the tree reluctantly removed the blade from her neck, grumbling under his breath his dissatisfaction with the order from his superior.

Zanell smiled slightly and shrugged her shoulders as if to say, *"I told you so."*

41. THE GREAT SLAVE REVOLT

"GUARDS! GET THEM!" General Gragor bellowed at the top of his lungs, pulling his broad sword from the sheath on his back as he prepared himself for battle.

Across from him a horde of snarling, angry prisoners emerged from the dungeon corridors, spreading out across the interior of the great hall like liquid poured into a goblet. At the front, leading the charge was the injured Fellow Undergotten.

General Gragor stared directly into Fellow's eyes and nodded. The movement was barely noticeable to the others, but Fellow had recognized it immediately and smiled back in defiance, his mouth slowly filling with his own blood.

The Chintaran scum had managed quite a feat escaping from the dungeon and for this act deserved credit. General Gragor could admit this. At the same time the Ochan General promised himself that he would ensure that it was the Chintaran's very last accomplishment.

The crowd of screaming prisoners broke off in two directions in order to defend themselves against the Ochan guards who had entered the hall through the large doors lining its outer walls. Simultaneously, a large group immediately moved in the direction of General Gragor and the two guards who still held the children captive. They had no weapons – save for the occasional lantern, jimmied steel rod or loose brick that they had acquired while in the dungeon. They outnumbered the guards in the hall at least ten to one, and this was their lone advantage. As the horde descended on General Gragor, the Ochan fought them off as best he could, slicing and chopping with deadly accuracy. Despite putting down prisoners in threes, three quickly took their place. General Gragor ultimately found himself backed into a corner, away from the brunt of the fighting. It was a fantastic tactical maneuver on the part of Fellow Undergotten who had intended to get the skilled warrior as far away from the children as possible. The guards holding Nicky and Staci had to drop the children in order to unsheathe their weapons and fully defend themselves.

From inside the flailing, screaming mass of half-starved prisoners now clawing at his every limb, General Gragor noticed his soldiers' actions.

Furious, he screamed, "NO, YOU FOOLS! DO NOT LET THE CHILDREN GO!"

Avoiding the occasional swinging blade and trying his best to keep his insides from spilling onto the floor, Fellow quickly made his way through the fighting, wailing mass of bodies, and headed toward the children. Staci was lying curled upon the stone with little Nicky Jarvis hovering over her. With his hands pressed tightly over his ears, the boy tried in vain to block out the sounds of death which assaulted his senses from every angle. Fellow snatched Staci in his arms.

Turning to Nicky he barked over the noise, "FOLLOW ME!"

With Nicky close behind, Fellow carried Staci through the raucous fighting toward a door at the far end of the hall. He kicked it open with his foot and passed into another long hallway. A few feet behind the fish-man ran Nicky. Once the boy was inside, Fellow slammed his shoulder into the door and shut it behind them. His wound was throbbing underneath the thin cloth that barely held him together. For Fellow, even the slightest movement on his part resulted in a considerable amount of discomfort. Sharp stabs of pain exploded in his side, traveled up his body and exploded more violently in his head. His sight was getting more blurry by the second, his breathing labored. Standing at his side, Nicky looked at the fish-man with tears in his eyes. The boy was confused, scared and in desperate need of his help. Nicky's expression reminded Fellow that they had to keep moving.

Breathing in deeply, Fellow held his breath for a second, shut his eyes tightly and gritted his teeth. He tried to block out the pain. In his arms, Staci still seemed to be lost somewhere else. Her hands hung limply to the side, her eyes wide open, her gaze blank and distant. Fellow looked down the dark hallway and back toward Nicky, who was hiding behind his leg, the boy's tiny body trembling as if he were freezing cold.

Readjusting his grip on Staci, Fellow at last exhaled and sternly said, "Come on…we have to keep moving."

The horde of prisoners poured from the doors lining the exterior walls of the great hall. The sea of angry, defiant creatures thundered forward into the courtyard with the ferocity of a hurricane. Each had come from a different world with different beliefs and ideas – some in stark contrast to one another. None of that mattered now.

In this singular moment in time they moved as one.

The similarities now shared were too great to ignore. Nearly all had watched their families murdered, seen their friends struck down, had their homes taken from them or burned to the ground It was this shared agony that had brought them together. It was this awful history that bonded them, reconstructed them and had changed them into a single, solitary race – a race created for vengeance.

The suddenness of their attack had caught the Ochan forces off guard. Until this time the guards had been quite accustomed to complacency. For a moment, it seemed the prisoners had the advantage. Large groups tackled Ochan soldiers to the ground, stole their weapons and ran into the courtyard where they unlocked the slave cells lining its walls. With the turn of every key their numbers grew and with the growing numbers more Ochan soldiers were overpowered and struck down.

Despite the way the battle seemed to be playing out, it was only a matter of time before the Ochans regained control. Even with their advantageous numbers, even with the justness of their cause to guide them, the prisoners could not win this battle alone. The rage that had propelled them forward would not last forever. Years of teetering on the brink of starvation had left them weak. Though they had taken the fortress guards by surprise, there would be reinforcements. Eventually the starved and un-trained would tire and fall, no matter how badly the thirst for freedom.

Victory would only be found with the aid of others.

Fellow could feel his body slowing down. His stride had morphed into a shuffle, his feet dragging across the concrete. The fabric tied around his waist had ridden up, exposing his gushing wound to the open air, allowing it to bleed freely down his side. The Chintaran had lost a great deal of blood, yet with every passing second he lost more. Each step felt like an eternity of agony condensed into a solitary moment that repeated itself over and over. Time slowed, the sound of the world faded further away and all around him became quiet, as if lost in a deep, dark cavern, slowly replaced by the soft hum of a distant, non-existent breeze. The exit was only twenty, maybe thirty more feet away, but his injuries made it impossible for him to reach the rear courtyard. Despite his best efforts to remain standing, Fellow's legs collapsed underneath him and his body tumbled to the ground. Staci slipped from his arms and slammed against floor, skidding across its stone surface, stopping when she hit a wall. Fellow rolled onto his back, his lazy, wobbly head gazing at his feet. Behind him, covering the ground was a ghastly-looking trail of blood. There was so much blood that he could scarcely believe it had all come from his body.

A teary-eyed Nicky Jarvis grabbed one of Fellow's limp arms and tried in vain to coax the weary fish-man back to his feet. Fellow understood that he needed to get up – that he had to get up. Despite this knowledge, his body chose instead to defy his wishes and remain where it was. With the little bit of strength remaining in his tired, weary body, he pulled little Nicky Jarvis closer.

In a wheezy, strained, far away voice he whispered, "The door...is that way...you have to get through the door. Find a place to hide in the....rear...in the rear courtyard. Hide...hide, and don't come out."

Nicky violently shook his head, a hot torrent of tears streaming down his cheeks. Grabbing Fellow's arm one more time he tossed it over his shoulder and tried again to lift the limp-bodied fish-man to his feet.

"Go…you have…to go…now…" Fellow mumbled, his voice even further away than before. Pulling his arm away, Fellow shoved the tearful boy toward the door at the opposite end of the hall. Nicky continued to fight him the entire time.

Not more than five feet from the pair of them, the eyes of Staci Alexander blinked once as she came to her senses. Wearily the young girl lifted her face off of the cold floor, propped herself on her elbows and gazed wearily in the direction of Nicky and Fellow. The world around her that had been distant and unreal before was briskly coming into focus once again. She could recall everything that had happened in great detail after she brought Fellow back to life but it seemed unreal, as if it had happened to someone else. She found the experience comparable to watching television. She had seen and could recount in great detail everything that occurred, yet she had been unable to interact. Now, however, the image of the teary-eyed Nicky and the rapidly dying Fellow Undergotten snapped her violently, like a rubber band, back to the real world.

She had to help them and something buried deep inside convinced her that she was capable of doing exactly that.

Pulling herself to her knees, Staci felt the now familiar and odd warmness growing in her chest. Slowly it spread across her chest and into her pores. As it had before, the odd sensation made its way down her side and into her hand. It tickled the insides of her fingertips like a billion microscopic feathers underneath her skin. Lifting her fingers to her face, Staci watched with wide-eyed familiarity as they began to glow.

Yes, she could help them. She could help Fellow exactly the same way she had before. None of it made an ounce of sense, but it was there right in front of her eyes. She could heal him and make everything all right. She could help him and that was exactly what she was going to do.

Feverishly, Staci started crawling across the floor toward Fellow and Nicky. She stretched her arm in front of her as far as her joints would allow. Never for a second did her eyes deviate from the youngest Jarvis boy and her strange new friend.

She was a mere foot and a half away from them when Nicky noticed her moving in their direction, her strange glowing arm leading the way.

Just then, the look of relief that washed over his face was abruptly replaced by one of sheer terror.

Nicky's eyes looked over her shoulder; his mouth opened wide to scream but no sound escaped.

Staci was six inches from touching the top of Fellow's scaly blue head, when something grabbed her shirt and jerked her violently into the air.

As the collar of her top pulled tightly around her neck she screamed in vain, "NO!"

Her feet were dangling, kicking wildly in the air. Stretching her body forward, choking herself on her shirt, she tried again to touch Fellow Undergotten but could not reach him. Something pulled her away from him, and the further she was pulled, the more the intensity of her glowing arm dimmed. The feathers underneath her skin stopped tickling. The warmth slowly crept back into her chest, eventually fading into the nothingness from whence it came.

Only inches away – a couple of measly inches. She was only inches from saving him, but she had failed.

Angry, frustrated tears rolled down her cheeks. Staci twisted her dangling body as she attempted to see her captor. When she recognized Prince Valkea, her heart sank.

The Prince flashed a cocky smile at the squirming girl. A tiny chuckle escaped his lips. An incredible amount of annoyance bubbled up inside . With a flick of his wrist he tightened the grip on Staci's collar, strangling her with the fabric around her neck. Pulling her close, his smile disappeared, his eyes thin and tight.

In a deep, breathy voice he growled, "You cannot possibly imagine how tired I am of you, little girl."

Staci kicked her feet at him wildly. Prince Valkea tightened his grip and choked her further, instantly stopping her defiant squirming. The Prince watched her struggling to breathe, letting the moment linger before he loosened his grip just enough to keep her alive.

Turning his attention to Nicky, who was still on his hands and knees hovering over the body of Fellow Undergotten, Prince Valkea spoke plainly. "He'll be of no help to you anymore, little one."

As he maintained his grip on Staci, the Prince moved towards Nicky. The frightened child tried to get out of the way but stopped when he reached the wall. With his free hand, Prince Valkea grabbed the boy's shirt and lifted him easily into the air. He tightened his grip on the garments of both children just enough to ensure that they felt discomfort. They were in no danger of dying when he lowered them to the ground. Prince Valkea pulled them by their collars and headed toward the doorway which led to the rear courtyard. Nicky and Staci wiggled, kicked and flailed while struggling to breathe, as they were dragged across the stone like sacks of rocks.

With his face pressed against the cold floor, precious life escaping his body with every breath, Fellow Undergotten watched through blurry eyes as the children were pulled further and further away from him. Once again he tried, with every fiber of his being, to force his body to move, and once again he failed. Despite his desire, the Chintaran's body continued to ignore his brain, refusing to respond. He had failed. He had failed and the children would die because of his stupidity. He had failed when he was needed the most. He had failed for the final time. Though he did not have the strength or fluids left to produce tears, Fellow Undergotten wept deeper inside than he had ever wept before.

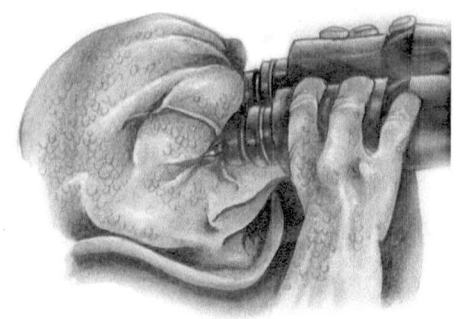

42. DISTRACTION BRINGS OPPORTUNITY

For the most part the group had been quiet since crossing the doorway from Tycaria into Fillagrou. Though they had witnessed firsthand what Tommy and Donald could do, many among them had trouble rationalizing exactly what they had seen. The astounding, slightly frightening glow from Tommy's hands had laid waste to an entire Ochan regiment in a matter of minutes. A regiment filled with the finest, best-trained, war-hardened soldiers in ninety-nine known worlds, had literally been obliterated with the snap of a boy's fingers. The idea boggled the mind. Nursing a slightly bent wing, Roustaf sat motionless on Pleebo's shoulder, the pair bringing up the rear. Feeling the need to break the uncomfortable silence, Roustaf flew across Pleebo's gray skinned shoulder, stopping when he reached his ear.

Bracing himself on the ridge of Pleebo's earlobe, he leaned the upper half of his body inside his friend's massive ear canal and whispered, "So what are you thinking, Pleebs?"

Pleebo was walking not far behind Tommy and Donald. The emotions in Pleebo's head ranged from cautious fascination to downright fear. To be so young and have so much power was an awe-inspiring combination. At the same time, forces such as the Tommy and Donald had wielded brought endless unknowns that could simply not be ignored.

"What do you mean what do I think?" Pleebo answered bluntly, his eyes never wavering.

"You know…do you think they really are the ones?"

Pleebo found his little friend's question comical. "You're kidding right? Who else do you know that can do what they did?"

"There are a whole lot of species out there that can do magic, Pleebs…trust me, I've met quite a few weirdoes in my time."

"Magic is one thing, my friend, but what that boy did today is something else altogether. If these kids aren't the ones, then I honestly don't know who are."

Roustaf slowly backed away from Pleebo's ear and sat down. He stared at the children walking in the distance with a questioning, extremely cautious look on his tiny face. Part of him wanted to fall under their spell like his friend, but the fables they represented did not belong to his people. Unlike Pleebo, his grandfather had not raised him to believe in the coming of "The Five to save them all." In fact, the concepts of prophets, saviors and destiny were mostly foreign concepts to him; but that was before the war and before he had ended up living among the castaways of the lost city of Tipoloo. The Ochan armies and this war had taken everything from him. Unlike King Walcott or Pleebo, he believed he was the very last of his race. The King's army had not only invaded his world, they had decimated it. They had destroyed everything and murdered everyone. This had been genocide at its purest and most evil. Every living thing – plant, animal, or otherwise – had been wiped from existence. Sure, he had made new friends in Tipoloo. Some he might even go so far as to call family. At the same time, though, Roustaf was painfully aware that he would never see another of his people again. To believe that these children would help him get the revenge he had dreamt about for so many years was a wonderful idea, but at the moment it was just that – an idea. After all he had seen, after everything he had lived through, Roustaf found it difficult to give himself over to the idea fully, no matter how badly he wished that he could.

Tommy Jarvis walked silently through the thick forest brush trying to keep pace with King Walcott, Owen and Nestor . Beside him, Donald was equally mum. Both boys had just done things they believed impossible – things they should not have been able to do. Scariest though, was the fact that both believed they could do it again when called upon – whether they wanted to or not. To go from being average children in an average town leading average lives to whatever it was they were doing now had boggled their minds. Donald silently admitted that a small part of him was anxious to use his powers again. Tommy simply wanted to find his brother and Staci and go home. Nothing else mattered.

Picking up his pace just a bit, Donald moved closer to Tommy.

Nudging him slightly with his shoulder, he softly whispered, "Hey, loser...don't think that just because you helped me out back there that we're friends or anything. You know...'cause we're not...at all."

Though Tommy's face showed no emotion, he laughed just a little on the inside. As much as he hated to admit it, he was starting to not dislike Donald. He was also beginning to get the impression that Donald felt the very same way. With everything that had happened Tommy began to see his oversized nemesis in a slightly different light. In a world filled with armies of lizard men, doorways to other dimensions, man-sized turtles and walls of energy shooting from the fingertips of fourteen-year olds, not totally hating Donald Rondage seemed to make perfect sense.

Without lifting his head or looking in Donald's direction Tommy muttered, "No…of course not. The thought never crossed my mind."

"Good, because I could have taken those guys, anyway. Seriously…I could have picked them up by their legs and smacked them together like Moe if I wanted to. In fact, that's exactly what I was planning on doing before you started shooting lightning bolts all over the place like a wacko."

"I know it."

"Good…as long as we've got that straight, freak."

"Ya, don't worry…we've got it straight."

The boys were quiet for a minute or two while they walked.

Donald looked around to see if anyone was watching him, then nudged Tommy once more. "Don't worry, freak… We're gonna find your bro."

Ahead of the boys walked Nestor and King Walcott, with Owen Little sandwiched between them. Nestor had tied his wounds well enough to stop his bleeding but moved with a noticeable limp.

King Walcott massaged his sore jaw and glanced at his injured friend. "You did a mighty fine job back there, soldier…mighty fine, indeed. The Fightin' Fifth has once again brought great honor to Tycaria...and to your King. I guarantee you, their sacrifice will not be forgotten, my friend."

Nestor's grin was barely noticeable. Were it not for the great sadness overwhelming him as a result of the deaths of his soldiers, the smile would have been a mile wide.

"Your words fill me with great pride, my King, and I am humbled that you offer them to me," he responded coolly.

Owen glanced at the two giant turtle men, while walking between their massive, bobbing shells. He looked behind him, his gaze settling on Tommy and Donald. He still could not fully wrap his mind around what he had seen them do earlier. This world, the prophecy, it seemed like such nonsense at first. Now, though, after he had watched Tommy shoot light beams from his hands and Donald toss a three hundred pound talking lizard twenty feet, it seemed a little less wacky. One thing bothered him, though. If Tommy and Donald could do things like that, could he do something cool as well? He was supposed to be one of The Five, right? If he were one of The Five, and The Five apparently have super powers, then it stood to reason that he had super powers. After Owen made sure that no one was paying any attention to him, he closed his eyes and thrust his arms forward quickly. Nothing happened. Gritting his teeth, he closed his eyes tighter and concentrated as hard as he could on doing something "super powered." This time he pictured beams of light shooting from his fingers, like Tommy. He imagined himself flying through the air, or shooting webs from his hands, or moving faster than a speeding bullet. Again, he thrust his hands forward comically, expecting something to happen. Again, he was left looking foolish.

King Walcott's voice came from above. "Say there, Mr. Owen...what is it exactly that you think you're doing?"

Embarrassed, Owen shoved his hands in his pockets, opening his eyes wide. Scratching at the inside of his arms, he pretended to have an itch. "Nothing...I...I wasn't doing anything. What are you doing? I wasn't doing anything other than walking...hey, that's a neat plant, what do you guys call it?"

King Walcott looked at the boy, somewhat puzzled. It was rapidly becoming a common expression when dealing with Owen.

Nestor spoke quietly. "We're here...everyone get down."

Immediately after hearing the words, the entire group crouched down. Just ahead of them where Nestor stooped the forest opened to a vast treeless field extending off into the horizon. The Prince's fortress was nestled at the base of a steep hill. The castle itself was enormous. Huge, dark, fortified walls surrounded it, not only keeping it safe from its enemies, but giving the entire complex an impenetrable feeling. The group crawled to the edge of the hill and peered down at the massive gothic structure.

Donald was the first to speak. "Great...we found it...now just how in the hell are we supposed to get in there?"

The question was of course directed at the group's honorary leader, Pleebo. Unfortunately for them, he had no idea.

Tommy noticed a large and unusual amount of movement in the courtyard near the center of the great structure. "Wait a minute...do you see that?"

"What is it, kiddo? I don't see anything," Roustaf replied.

"There, in the center...there's something going on."

Nestor pulled a pair of binoculars out of his leather satchel and focused his attention on the area that Tommy had pointed out. Throughout the entire structure, small battles were being waged between Ochan soldiers and creatures from a variety of different species.

"Keen eye, son," Nestor commented. "It would seem that the Prince has a bit of a slave revolt on his hands. This might be exactly the diversion we need."

Tommy quickly slid alongside Nestor. "Can I see those for a second?"

"Of course, lad."

Nestor handed the boy the binoculars before he spoke to the others. "If we can figure out a way in, this would be the ideal time to strike. With the Prince's guards spread out as they are, this is an opportunity we can't afford to let pass."

King Walcott nodded in agreement as did Roustaf and Pleebo. Though terribly frightened, Donald did his best to disguise his fear, smiling when he nodded. Owen gulped deeply, wishing for the five-hundredth time that he had never followed Donald and his goons into the woods.

As the rest of them discussed how they were going to get inside the fortress, Tommy was busy scanning the entire structure, looking for any indication that his little brother was or had been there. He stopped scanning when he noticed a large, ornately dressed figure ascending a winding staircase to one of the castle's towers with Nicky and Staci in tow. Not only was Nicky alive, Tommy now knew exactly where to find him. As if a switch flipped on somewhere deep inside, the beating of the young boy's heart doubled in pace. His breathing rapidly increased, his jaw clenched tightly while a renewed feeling of determination mixed with furious anger washed over his body.

Dropping the binoculars , Tommy said with determination, "We have to get in there now."

As he completed his sentence, the gray sky above rolled with a deep, bellowing thunder. Cloud cover thicker and more menacing than the one it was replacing slowly settled over the brooding sky. Its size, thickness, and foreboding color indicated beyond a shadow of a doubt that a mighty storm was brewing. Off in the distance the wind whipped and whistled, rattling the trees and shaking the soil from which they grew.

The entire world of Fillagrou prepared for the coming of this great first battle. The players found their marks. The audience settled in. The house lights dimmed.

All that remained was the drawing of the curtain.

43. THUNDEROUS BOOM

Prince Valkea passed through the massive doorway leading into his throne room, still dragging the flailing and screaming bodies of Nicky and Staci behind him. He strode angrily across the floor, depositing both of the children against a wall. Smacked against the stone, Staci fell into a violent, uncontrollable coughing fit. Staci had struggled to breathe while being dragged up the long staircase with her shirt pulled extraordinarily tight against her neck.

Ignoring her obvious discomfort, the Prince moved toward the window at the far end of the room and glanced at the vast courtyard. Below, his soldiers were engaged in various forms of armed and unarmed combat with escaped slaves and prisoners. The sound of clanging swords and pained screams filled the night air as a soft drizzle descended from the thick, dark menacing clouds. While he watched the battle play out, the first thoughts to enter Prince Valkea's mind were thoughts of his father. What would the cranky old cretin think if he could see what was going on within the fortress walls right at this moment? The young Prince could only think of one answer - disappointment – unending, unrelenting, disappointment. His failure to maintain control over even the weakest of enemies would at last confirm every concern his father had ever raised about his ability to lead.

He would be seen as weak. Worse than that, he would be seen as a failure.

Though Prince Valkea was confident that his forces would eventually overwhelm and regain control of this pathetic revolt, it would make no difference to his father. The uprising should have never happened in the first place. The damage had already been done, and disgrace had been wrought. What was done could never be undone.

The Prince turned away from the window and spoke to the children through clenched teeth, "It's quite astounding really…when you think about it. How two pathetic…useless looking creatures such as yourselves could manage to create such havoc by doing so very little is astonishing."

Nicky and Staci huddled close together, backing themselves into a corner as the Ochan Prince steadily approached. A flash of lightening cut across the sky outside, casting deep ghastly shadows across Prince Valkea's dark green face.

His voice was low and steady, filled with a rage so deep that it built to a crescendo. "You've ruined everything, you know. Everything that I have spent my life working toward, everything that I have built…the two of you have erased it from existence in a matter of days. This is quite an accomplishment from your standpoint. From mine, though, it is an unforgivable act of war."

Prince Valkea grabbed Nicky's shirt, lifting the little boy into the air violently.

In conjunction with the sudden movement his voice raised exponentially, now on the brink of a scream. "Quite unforgivable indeed…and for this most grave of indiscretions you must be punished!"

With Nicky dangling in one hand, the Prince removed the dagger from his belt with the other. Nicky tried in vain to wiggle free as Prince Valkea hurried toward the window. Staci protested as loud as she could, running toward the prince at full speed, punching him with one hand while wrapping the other around his leg, doing everything within her power to stop him. .

Prince Valkea glared at the girl and yelped, "INSOLENT WHELP!"

Kicking his leg angrily, his foot sent the young girl airborne. Sliding across the floor, she slammed into a nearby wall with considerable force.

Prince Valkea then shoved Nicky through the open window. Young Nicky Jarvis suddenly found himself dangling a good twenty stories above ground. He instantly stopped squirming; he feared the thin fabric might rip and send him tumbling to his death. Prince Valkea placed the tip of a dagger against Nicky's throat.

Hot breath snarled through the tiny nostrils on the front of his flat face as Prince Valkea screamed across the courtyard for all to hear. "HEAR ME NOW, YOU WHO DARE TO REVOLT! HEAR ME NOW AND HEED THE WORDS OF YOUR PRINCE AND MASTER! HERE IS YOUR SAVIOR! HERE IS THE CHILD THAT YOU FOOLISHLY BELIEVE WILL BRING YOU FREEDOM!"

The blade of the dagger cut slightly into Nicky's skin, eliciting the smallest amount of warm blood, which rolled down his neck, into his shirt, and onto his chest.

"WATCH THIS BOY DIE AND REMEMBER THIS MOMENT WELL! LET HIS END REMIND YOU OF YOUR PLACE IN THIS WORLD! LET HIS DEATH SOLIDIFY TO YOU WHO INDEED IS MASTER, AND WHO IS SLAVE! WATCH THIS BOY TAKE HIS FINAL BREATH AND PREPARE YOURSELF TO SHARE HIS FA..." The Prince's voice quickly trailed off as his eyes caught a glimpse of an incredible sight over the darkened horizon.

Sailing through the air at an incredible speed was an enormous rock. Not just any rock. It was a rock so large that no creature or contraption from any of the known worlds could have tossed it with such force. The rock was so large and heavy that it crashed through the wall with relative ease.

The shattering wall shook the ground, sending enormous blocks of stone flying in every direction. The massive boulder bounced across the courtyard, leaving colossal divots in the ground, crushing several Ochan guards underneath its weight. The rock came to a stop only after colliding with the castle's thick brick wall. The collision rocked the fortress back and forth from base to tower like an earthquake. Prince Valkea stumbled into his throne room. Both he and Nicky fell to the floor. The castle still vibrated while Nicky scurried to Staci. Once the shaking subsided, the Prince angrily rose to his feet, stumbling awkwardly to the window once again. He arrived just in time to see another massive boulder sail through the air, heading directly for the outer wall of his fortress. Right behind it was a third and behind that a fourth.

44. AND SO FORTH UNTO THE BREACH

Donald Rondage strained terribly as he hoisted yet another mammoth stone above his head and tossed it at the fortress at the base of the hill. To watch the young boy lift such an incredible weight and throw it with such ease was as amazing a sight as Pleebo had ever seen.

After the fourth stone smashed into the fortress wall, reducing it to little more than airborne pebbles and a cloud of dust, Nestor screamed, "Well done, child, we have our opening! Everyone aboard! We have to move quickly!"

Nestor and King Walcott positioned themselves near the edge of the cliff. Lying flat on the underside of their shells, they tucked their limbs inside the protective exterior, leaving their heads exposed.

Buried deep inside his shell, King Walcott's heart pounded. An incredible amount of fear was building inside him, mixed with the excitement over what he was about to do. The result was a feeling that was both wonderful and terrifying.

King Walcott glanced at the massive cloud of dust that had been created by Donald's tossed boulders. He then looked at Nestor and smiled. "Not since I single-handedly faced the Talax Griffin and recaptured the sacred Mud Chalice have I felt so alive, old friend!"

The look on Nestor's face was the same.

In a careful, honest voice Nestor responded, "No matter what may happen from this point out, Sire...I feel it my duty to inform you that it has been the greatest honor of my life to fight alongside you these last few days."

King Walcott paused, letting the falling rain cascade over his face, taking a moment to admire his most loyal of soldiers. "No, my dear friend, I assure you...the honor has, indeed, been mine."

Subtly the Tycarians nodded to each other. The gesture was slight, barely noticeable in the rapidly darkening sky and heavily falling rain. Despite its simplicity, both recognized and understood it completely. The admiration was mutual.

Realizing that time was running short, Nestor turned his attention back to the task at hand.

He barked at the others, "We must hurry! Take your places!"

Just as they had discussed moments ago, Donald and Owen crawled on top of Nestor's slippery shell. Lying flat, they tightly grabbed the leather belt. Pleebo and Tommy climbed on top of King Walcott and did the same. The drizzling rain had slowly progressed into a full downpour, drenching the ground around them, making everything slick and dangerous. Once the Tycarians were convinced that their passengers were securely attached to their shells, King Walcott and Nestor slowly rocked their massive bodies back and forth. Each motion moved them closer to the edge of the cliff. They soon found themselves teetering between solid ground and open air.

With his heart beating painfully against his ribs, Owen Little tightly shut his eyes. Though a part of the young boy wanted to look, a more dominant part decided that it simply was not going to happen. Fluttering just above the ground behind them, tiny Roustaf shook his head in disbelief. The plan they had put together – what they were about to do – was completely insane even at its best. Despite the fact that every movement of his wings caused incredible pain throughout the upper half of his body, he was glad he had them. Flying down to the castle was going to be an exercise in pain. If the only alternative, however, was riding down the side of a mountain on the slippery backside of a Tycarian shell, he would take the pain of flying.

With the weight of his shell moving away from the ground and over the edge of the cliff, King Walcott held his head back as the weight of his shell moved over the edge of the cliff. He screamed at the two passengers hanging loosely on his back, "HOLD ON, MY FRIENDS! HERE WE GO!"

A moment later King Walcott's body was sliding down the side of the muddy hill, picking up speed. Dirt and rock flew into the faces of Tommy and Pleebo as they lay perched atop his slippery-slick back. Spinning wildly in circles, they continued to slide at an almost ninety-degree angle, tightening their grip on King Walcott's belt strap. Occasionally the underside of his massive shell hit a lump of dirt, propelling all three of them momentarily into the air. To his right Tommy spotted Owen and Donald bouncing crazily on Nestor in much the same fashion, both boys screaming at the top of their lungs. Though the falling rain obscured his vision noticeably, Tommy saw that the cloud of debris was getting closer. The massive cloud seemed to grow significantly larger and more imposing with every second. The closer they got, the more massive it seemed. After bouncing off another particularly sturdy mound of dirt, the threesome hung in the air for several seconds before crashing to the ground yet again.

At last the cloud engulfed them. King Walcott's shell lost momentum, slowing and skidding to a halt after he had extended his rear legs, digging them into the muddy ground, using them as a brake. Both Pleebo and Tommy lurched forward, rolling off King Walcott's back into the mud. The dust around them was thick. The falling rain was heavy and the visibility was next to none. What they could not see, they could most definitely hear. The sound of chaos surrounded them – awful screaming - downright frightening chaos. The clash of steel, the tearing of flesh, the terrifying symphony of war bombarded their ears from every direction.

For Tommy, getting to the tower and finding his brother was his only goal, but finding his way through the cloudy madness was going to prove a more difficult task than he had anticipated.

"Take my hand!" Pleebo yelled as he extended his long bony arm. "In this case, I have an advantage that even you don't, lightning boy!" he said, his free hand pointing at his enormous red eyes.

Tommy grabbed his hand as Pleebo led him slowly through the dust toward the tower. Now on his feet, King Walcott followed close behind while scanning the debris cloud surrounding them for any sign of Nestor and the other two boys.

Unlike the great King Shellamennes, Nestor had allowed himself to continue skidding across the ground until he had passed through the massive dust cloud to the other side. Coming to a stop, he and the boys found themselves surrounded by the insanity of war. Battles between Ochan soldiers and prisoners were taking place throughout the courtyard. No less than a second after rolling off Nestor's back, Donald spotted a pair of Ochan soldiers advancing on their position. Nestor saw them and quickly rose to his feet, pulling the long broad sword from his side. He retrieved a dagger from his belt, tossing it gently to Donald.

In a steady serious tone he half-smiled at the young boy, "Remember this moment, lad…from this point forward …everything changes."

Donald may not have understood the meaning of the words but he was seconds away from learning.

For Owen Little, the images of tripping over his own feet while running the track in gym class, getting tossed around like a useless rag doll during flag football or any of the other thousand times he had proven his lack of athleticism, flashed in his head while he shuffled in the opposite direction. His one and only goal was to get as far away from the battle as fast as he could. Fighting had never been his thing – it was never going to be his thing – and he did not like the idea of having to make it his thing anytime soon. First and foremost on Owen's agenda was to find a hiding place, crawl into it, and stay there until this all blew over. It did not take long before his shuffling turned into a full run, which quite predictably – and almost comically – caused him to crash into something solid which caused him to fall on his face. Rubbing a throbbing welt on his head, Owen rolled onto his back and saw what he had hit. Standing above him with sword drawn, was a substantial and angry-looking Ochan soldier. The top of the creature's helmet was split open, blood slowly creeping down the side of his scowling face. Owen scurried on his rear across the muddied ground. The colossal Ochan followed, lifting his sword into the air, ready to remove the young boy's head from his

271

shoulders. The soldier grinned evilly as the trail of blood from his head seeped into his mouth, stained his razor sharp teeth and caused him to lick it with his dark green lips. Owen's heart pumped double time. His pulse pounded so loudly that he could hear it over the madness of war around him. His brain started to beat against the interior of his skull, reverberating back and forth painfully into his ears. Tears streamed down his cheeks as Owen rolled back onto his stomach, curled himself into a ball and jammed his eyes shut.

A few seconds passed, then a few more. After those came and went, a few more skipped by.

"Why was not he dead yet? He should be dead, shouldn't he"?

Confused as to why the soldier had not chopped him right down the middle into two pieces, Owen cautiously rolled onto his back one more time. The extremely large, angry soldier was still standing above him, sword still drawn. Gone, however, was the look of anger on his face. It had been replaced by a look of confusion. The soldier was staring directly at Owen, his toothy mouth hanging wide open – looking right at him – yet he looked right past him - almost as if he could not see Owen at all.

Still trying to slow the unrelenting pounding in his head, Owen cautiously backed away from the creature. He moved a few feet away, but the soldier remained still. Not only that, the creature was backing away, an expression of confusion, fear and shock etched into his ghastly maw. Owen braced himself on a nearby wall in order to stand. When he glanced at his hand he noticed that it could not be seen.

He could feel his hand as he steadied himself against the wall. His eyes, though, told a different story. Owen moved in hand in front of his face but saw nothing. He looked down at his feet which also seemed not to exist. Torso, arms, shoulder, feet, neck, head, every part of the young boy's body was now invisible.

The boy instantly thought that this was a blessing, because it meant that no one would notice that this incredible revelation had caused him to pee his pants.

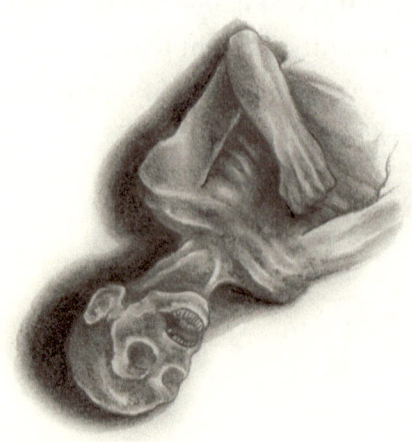

45. ASHES TO ASHES

After Pleebo and Tommy had passed though what remained of the gradually receding cloud of dust and debris, the massive shadows of the large castle tower emerged - its silhouette slicing eerily though the rainy night sky. Tommy had previously thought the that fortress looked large from a distance, but it was enormous when one stood beneath its walls. He was intimidated by its incredible size, not to mention the ghastly looking gargoyles hanging off of its sides. Tommy reminded himself to ignore such things. No matter how ominous it might look, no matter how impossible the task at hand might seem, he needed to ignore it all. His brother was up there somewhere in grave danger and he had to get to him.

Many times in his young life Tommy Jarvis had been forced to ignore fear. He discovered long ago that emotions could be stuffed down deep – pushed down so far that they could not do harm. Though still a young boy, Tommy had practiced this many times. He had become a master, a specialist - the best of the best. He had done it before and he could do it again. Despite burying so much inside him over the last few years, there was room for a bit more, and if there was not he would make it. About forty feet away Tommy spotted a half-open doorway at the foot of the tower and sprinted toward it. The falling rain smacked against his face as he ran. His feet splashed loudly in muddy puddles. His nose inhaled the tangy-crisp night air, while his mouth exhaled steely-hot determination.

From the moment the smoke had cleared, Pleebo was engrossed in the madness. Creatures of different sizes and shapes were fighting tooth and nail with Ochan soldiers for as far as he could see. Not only were they fighting, they were fighting with a ferocity and determination he had not seen since he was a child. An undeniable sense of rebellion mixed with defiant hope hung heavy and thick in the air. The scene was frightening, inspiring, and oddly beautiful in its sadness. Out of the corner of his eye he noticed Tommy running toward the castle. Pleebo turned his attention from the battles and moved briskly to catch up with the boy.

Tommy sprinted up a set of stairs while carefully avoiding the bodies of prisoners and soldiers strewn haphazardly across the floor, their dead eyes glassy and open. At the top of the stairwell he passed through a half-open doorway into an enormous chamber at the foot of the tower. His sudden appearance caught the attention of a group of Ochan soldiers who had just finished putting down a small group of rebels and were already searching for their next target. Pleebo entered the room just behind Tommy. Seeing the battle-hungry creatures, he stopped dead in his tracks.

He tapped Tommy lightly on the shoulder and quietly muttered, "If you've still got any juice left in those magic hands of yours, now would be a good time to put it to use."

The soldiers started to move toward the intruders. Their pace was slow and deliberate, their weapons drawn. The steel of their blades dripped with the blood of those they had just killed. Directly behind the advancing soldiers Tommy noticed a doorway that appeared to lead to the top of the tower. He needed to get through that door and the only thing standing in his way were four, angry, blood-thirsty lizard men.

Not allowing his brain time to think, his body simply reacted.

As if on cue, the familiar warmth began to build. Tommy was slowly becoming comfortable with the strange hot pressure, possibly even beginning to like it. Pleebo noticed the young boy's hands begin to glow, his fingertips crackled and popped. Slowly Pleebo backed away. As the group of soldiers moved within striking distance, Tommy pointed in their direction. Within seconds he fired an incredible blast of white-hot light from his skin. Humming loud enough for even those outside the castle to hear, the wall of searing bright light blasted the soldiers, violently scattering them in every direction. It was similar to fireworks exploding from one single point strewn across the sky. Their bodies slammed into the surrounding walls with such force that enormous cracks splintered the stone. To Tommy's left another group of soldiers entered the room. In a single, quick deliberate movement Tommy spun in their direction, launching another powerful blast of light. Not only did this blast send the soldiers flailing wildly into the air it also took large chunks of wall with them. Sturdy Ochan construction made of stones whose weight could be measured only in tons was reduced to a massive hole, the edges of which were little more than a fine powder that caught the breeze and floated away. The energy built up inside Tommy's body tingled across the surface of his skin, causing every hair follicle to stand at attention. The strange, haunting glow seeped through the space around his eyeballs. It lit them up from behind, shooting forward like the beams of two flashlights. Without uttering a single word Tommy moved toward the doorway

Pleebo made sure the coast was clear before he left his hiding place and entered the chamber. Cautiously he followed Tommy across the destroyed room, stepping carefully over the fallen body of an Ochan soldier that Tommy had blasted into oblivion. The creature's armor was scalding hot. A soft gray smoke rose from the super-heated metal. The head inside the helmet was charred black – barely recognizable as something that had once been a living, breathing thing. The sight sent a chill down Pleebo's spine.

Tommy stood at the doorway on the far end of the room and turned toward Pleebo. "Come on, we have to keep moving." Every time the young boy opened his mouth an eerie beam of light escaped.

This was no longer the quiet, unassuming fourteen-year-old boy Pleebo had met only days before. No doubt some of that Tommy still remained but the boy had definitely changed. He had grown - evolved. He was partially a living thing but partially something else, something Pleebo could not fully recognize, and something so far beyond him that he would never entirely understand. Yes, Tommy Jarvis had indeed changed.

For better or worse.

46. THE LAST STAND OF NESTOR ROCKSHELL

Nestor Rockshell pushed the indescribable smothering discomfort and pain as far back into his mind as he could. With Ochan soldiers attacking him from every angle, the acknowledgement of pain was a luxury he could not afford. Every movement of his body resulted in sheer agony; every thrust of his blade felt like an act of self-mutilation. The semi-circle of Ochan soldiers surrounding him outnumbered him four to one. Despite the incredible pain, despite the fact that he was faced with an insurmountable situation, his movements remained deft and sure. His was a showcase in the economy of motion, of insurmountable spirit, of the will to survive. Despite his best efforts though, it was obvious he was fighting a losing battle, There were simply too many of them coming from too many angles. Eventually he would misstep, or simply tire. Defeating four untrained, unarmed creatures would be one thing; fending off four of Ocha's best-trained and well-armed was something else entirely. From behind him, the heavy blade of a soldier cracked against his shell, splitting it open ever so slightly. Much like the flashes of lightning above, the pain shot down Nestor's back and into his already tired legs. The blinding bolt of agony caused him to crumble to the mud. From his knees he continued to ward off the advancing soldiers, screaming at the top of his lungs with every thrust of his sword.

The Ochan warriors had moved some of their forces away from the attacking prisoners who posed much less a threat in order to deal with the much larger problem that Nestor and Donald posed. For every soldier that Nestor struck down, another moved in to take its place. The cycle was unrelenting.

On the other end of the courtyard Donald stood defiantly with a large carriage hoisted into the air. The Ochan soldiers were shocked when they saw the pudgy little boy easily lift a piece of equipment that normally had required three massive beasts to move. Donald swatted huge groups of soldiers with it. Through the haze of night and the falling rain, Donald had caught a glimpse of Nestor a hundred yards away. The turtle man was down on one knee, fending off soldiers with every last ounce of energy in his body. How had they gotten so far away from each other? One minute they were fighting side by side and at the next they were separated by the length of a football field. Donald suddenly noticed a group of three soldiers moving toward him. In one quick movement he spun around, whacking the them with the rattling, wooden carriage. The force of the blow sent all three Ochans sailing into the air. Their unconscious bodies were eventually swallowed by the dark, rainy night as they disappeared from view.

The pain Nestor had been pushing to the back of his mind, forced its way into consciousness, coursed through his every limb and was eating him alive from the inside out. For the second time in as many days, he now believed his life was nearing an end. Once again he accepted his fate. All other options seemed to be exhausted. He had met his breaking point and crossed over it. He had seen this moment of realization firsthand in the faces of those who had fought beside him during the Great War. He recognized its truth, its honesty, and in the end accepted it as reality. To die in battle doing what he had been trained to do – fighting for his home, his people, a brighter future – was an honorable way to die. Unable to hold his arms up any longer, the pain in his cracked shell at last became too much to bear. Nestor dropped his weapons to his side, closed his eyes and prepared for the inevitable. Yet, just as before, the end did not come.

From somewhere behind him a deep, familiar voice bellowed the words, "FOR TYCARIA!"

Opening his eyes, Nestor saw his King, Walcott Shellamennes, charge the group of soldiers. With his weapon drawn, a furious battle- ready expression stretched across his wet, strained face. Surprisingly light on his feet, King Walcott took a protective stance near Nestor; the King was anxious to engage the Ochans in battle.

Through his blood stained teeth, King Walcott growled, "If you want him, you'll have to go through me, you foul-breathed monstrosities!"

Every muscle in King Walcott's body creaked, aching in displeasure at the demands placed upon them. Every twist, turn, crouch, and strike was both a chore and revelation for the Tycarian King. Despite the urging of his body to halt, he continued to fight.

His lungs heaved and burned inside his chest cavity. A thousand invisible tiny soldiers with tiny little swords chopped at his aching muscles. What the old King lacked in strength and speed he more than made up with experience. A precision that could only have been gained through an endless number of battles throughout the course of his life ensured that every swing of his blade was as precise a strike as it could possibly be.

One by one, each Ochan soldier surrounding him tasted the business end of his sword. Defying the very laws of logic and common sense, one by one their bodies splashed into the mud, defeated. With corpses now scattered at his feet, King Walcott dropped his hands to his knees, taking full advantage of a much-needed opportunity to breathe in deeply. Every inch of his body ached. Every muscle strained with warmth that, until now, he could only faintly recall in a faraway memory. For the first time in a very long time he felt alive.

When the challenge of his breathing had been sufficiently conquered, King Walcott turned toward Nestor and muttered in a strained, tired voice, "It would seem...my old friend...that there still remains some life...in these dusty old bones of mine...does it not?"

Nestor smiled at him and chuckled. Nestor had admired his King more than any other, since he had been a young boy. Yet never in his life had he admired him more than at this very moment. Never in his life had he been more proud to call himself a Tycarian.

King Walcott wrapped his arm around Nestor, doing his best to help him stand. But Nestor's massive body collapsed under his own weight and fell into the mud. His muscles were simply too worn, his body too heavy and drained. Wincing though the pain, Nestor attempted once more to stand. Once again he failed. King

Walcott grabbed Nestor's wrists and pulled him across the muddy ground, setting him against a wall and out of sight.

From a strap around one of his beefy thighs he removed a small dagger, placing it in Nestor's palm. "Remain here until the battle has reached its conclusion my friend."

"No...I can't just sit here...must..." Nestor insisted as he tried to stand.

"Your determination is an inspiring sight, indeed. You've brought great honor to your people. Now, though, I must ask you to do as your King demands and remain here. Worry not...I will retrieve you when we've claimed victory. The victory celebration shall be yours to share."

Again Nestor struggled to stand, "No! I can't! Must...fight!"

King Walcott gently sat him down, "Please...I ask you to remain here not just as your King...but as your friend."

Staring into the eyes of his childhood hero and after hearing King Walcott refer to him as a friend, Nestor finally relented.

A crooked smile crept across King Walcott's face. "Frustratingly hard headed...truly, it is Tycarian blood that courses through your veins."

King Walcott patted Nestor on the side of his shell and retrieved his sword from the muddy ground After taking a moment to allow both the fear and excitement of his current situation to sink in, the Tycarian King turned and headed toward the battle. After he had vanished from sight Nestor tightened his grip on the dagger. A renewed sense of pride and determination washed over him like the warm waters of a relaxing hot spring settling over his sore muscles.

After King Walcott turned the corner he spotted Donald Rondage fending off a horde of soldiers with the aid of an enormous carriage. The boy was swinging it like a club. Despite his astounding strength, Donald looked tired. His chest was heaving, his legs shaking with even the slightest of movements. The cold rain had drenched his clothes, causing him to shiver. Though the boy's face bore an expression of steely determination, King Walcott could easily discern the hidden terror. Even with his amazing power, Donald was still a boy. He was a boy caught in the middle of an incredibly frightening, extremely confusing situation. Try as he might to disguise it, he was clearly scared.

Taking a deep breath, King Walcott allowed the moisture in the air to fill his aching lungs. The dampness of the night air felt at home inside him. Memories of his home world crashed like the tide against the beach of his mind. Digging his heels in the slick mud he charged toward Donald as fast as his body could manage. He had to help the boy. When an Ochan soldier crossed his path, attempting to halt his progress, he struck him down quickly and precisely. There was no time to waste – he had to get to the boy - time was of the essence.

The downpour had made Donald's grip on the carriage flimsy at best. The wood slid through his tired fingers, pressing long, painful splinters into his tender flesh. At any moment he feared he would drop the massive contraption. Despite being stronger than all of them combined, the Ochan soldiers were well-organized. They sensed his inexperience early on. As a group they managed to back the boy against the outer fortress wall. The air of invincibility Donald first experienced when his new powers had been revealed to him diminished.

This was not a game – this was frighteningly real.

More and more, with every passing second, Donald could feel the danger around him growing to the point that it threatened to swallow him whole. The soldiers were outmaneuvering him quickly. Through the heavily falling rain his eyes caught a glimpse of something sailing toward him. Before he could make out what it was, the object tore through the muscles in his right shoulder like a hot knife through butter. Intense, unyielding pain shot through his body. His grip on the massive wooden carriage slipped. It shook the ground as it splashed into the muddy puddles. Donald screamed loudly as he stumbled and slammed into the wall. His legs gave way and he crumbled to his knees. The tears pouring from his eyes were barely noticeable as they mixed with the falling rain. In-between pained yelps, he peeked through a half-opened eye and looked at his shoulder. Sticking out of it was a two-foot long arrow. The soldiers surrounded him, licking their lips greedily and slowly advanced on their now helpless prey.

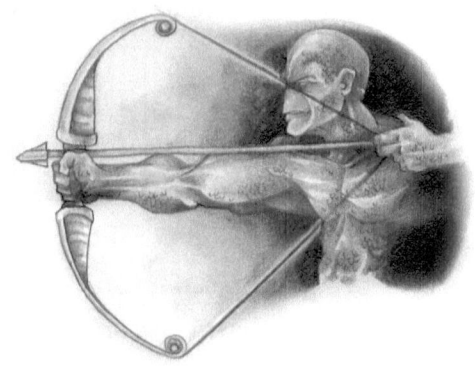

47. ANCIENT, BITTER RIVALRIES REVISITED

General Gragor pushed himself from underneath the pile of dead prisoners that had covered him like a mound of fleshy, multi-colored dirt. They might have landed a few blows and fought with more grit than he had imagined, but in the end he had beaten each and every one of them. After tossing the last of the corpses over his shoulder, he angrily pulled himself to his feet. Every inch of his body was sore and his armor felt heavier than he last remembered. The Ochan heart buried deep within his chest pounded a warrior's beat. Anger intermingled with exhilaration washed over his every inch. It was a feeling he had not had for several years. For General Gragor, this was the very meaning of life. This was living as it was meant to be and he welcomed its return. Reaching behind him he unlatched the straps of his chest plate, letting it fall to the floor. Through an open door, he saw battles being waged throughout the fortress courtyard.

These prisoners – these mongrels – where did they get the nerve?

In the back of his mind he cursed the Prince for allowing this to happen. The King would not have permitted such nonsense. The useless young Prince had made another mess, and he was now called on to clean it up. General Gragor retrieved his sword that had been left in the back of a fallen prisoner and slowly made his way toward the fighting. Stepping into the rain, his eyes were instantly drawn to a young boy swinging a carriage three hundred times his size and doing it with frightening ease. The Ochan warrior had seen many things over the course of his life, but never had he witnessed a display of strength such as this. With each twist of his body, the small boy had knocked the fortress guards senseless.

This could not be allowed to continue.

General Gragor retrieved a bow and a single arrow from a fallen soldier. Placing the arrow into position, he extended the bow forward, pulling back against the taught string. With the wind blowing buckets of heavy rain into his face, he took a deep breath and steadied his hand. His grip was firm, holding the bow for an instant before releasing the arrow. The arrow sliced through the storm, scattering droplets into eternity on a microscopic level. The arrow moved speedily through the air and despite the threatening wind pierced Donald Rondage's shoulder. General Gragor grinned maniacally and watched as the boy dropped the massive carriage and crumbled to the ground with a heavy thud. The grin instantly disappeared when he realized he had hit the boy's shoulder rather than his head. The Ochan soldiers surrounding Donald moved in for the kill. Hurriedly, General Gragor readied his sword, sprinting forward at full speed.

"YOU, THERE! HOLD YOUR POSITIONS!" he bellowed, closing the distance between him and the soldiers in a matter of seconds. "HOLD YOUR POSITIONS!"

The soldiers immediately parted, giving the higher ranking officer clear access to the injured boy. "Hold your positions. This one is mine."

Donald Rondage was curled against a wall, one finger timidly poking at the arrow sticking out of his shoulder as tears streamed down the his face. The massive form of General Gragor approached him slowly, still breathing heavily from his run. General Gragor noticed that the child looked even smaller and more pathetic than he had from a distance which made the boy's incredible show of strength all the more terrifying and dangerous.

Kneeling down, the General touched Donald's face underneath his chin and took in the contours of the boy's chubby, oval shaped head. "So powerful one moment, so pathetic the next. What a sad enigma you are, child."

When Donald at last opened his eyes, General Gragor slid his hand over the arrow sticking, twisting it slightly. The movement sent a blinding flash of pain coursing through Donald's frame and made him scream louder than he had ever screamed in his life.

"If you think for a second that I am going to allow you or any of your kind to take away everything that my people have fought for, you are sadly mistaken, young man."

While Donald continued to sob, General Gragor stood and lifted his sword. "Magic doesn't frighten me, boy, because like all who wield magic...you can bleed. In all the worlds, there is but one truth...whatever can bleed...can die."

A ravenous scowl stretched across his face as he lifted his sword higher into the air, preparing to strike down the meddlesome child of the prophecy, once and for all. A moment before he swung, a deep, heavy voice echoed throughout the courtyard . "LEAVE THE BOY ALONE, YOU BASTARD!"

General Gragor turned swiftly. Much to his surprise, standing defiantly behind him, the rain crashing forcefully off of his thick shell was none other than the King of Tycaria, Walcott Shellamennes.

48. THE INVISIBILITY GLITCH

The Ochan soldier that stood gazing menacingly at the helpless form of Owen Little found himself staring blankly at the space where the boy once sat. In utter disbelief, he extended his sword, poked at the air and found nothing. A bit further away the creature noticed something incredibly odd. Tilting his head slightly to the side he tried to make sense of it. Though the boy had disappeared, something resembling his shape was slowly coming into focus. Droplets of rain pooled on what seemed to be empty space and revealed, what seemed to be, a ghostly form reminiscent of the child.

Backed against a large wall, Owen tried to keep quiet and remained as still as possible. Not more than five to seven feet away, the massive soldier stared directly at him, yet seemed to look past him at the same time. Owen accepted the fact that he was still invisible. It did not make an ounce of sense, but then what in his life did anymore? He had seen Tommy Jarvis shoot lightning from his hands, had slid down hills on the backs of giant turtle-men and had traveled through secret doorways that led to castles in worlds that normally existed in books and terrible movies. It was completely insane - all of it. With insanity the norm, Owen realized his only choice was to accept the fact that he was indeed invisible, or get chopped to bits by a seven-foot tall lizard-man. He would find a way to come to terms with the idea of invisibility.

The soldier took a single, timid step in Owen's direction. The look of confusion slowly drifted from his face as he began working things out with the small brain crammed into his thick skull. Owen stepped slowly to his right – the soldier followed in turn. Owen stepped even more slowly to his left – the soldier did the same. Could the creature possibly see him? Was he not invisible anymore or was the ugly behemoth just making lucky guesses? What had changed? Lifting his invisible hands to his face, he noticed that they still did not exist. He still looked invisible. There was one minor difference though. He could make out the contours of his fingers.

The rain – the water – was outlining him.

Gazing back into the soldier's face, Owen noticed that the creature was smiling brightly, not to mention staring him right in the eyes. Without a moment's hesitation, Owen turned on his heel to run. He was not able to take more than a step before the soldier reached out and grabbed his invisible soaked shirt, halting his progress. The Ochan's massively muscled arm wrapped the boy up, pulling his flailing body close to his chest and chuckled through his mouth full of jagged, dangerous fangs.

Twisting Owen around, the soldier pulled him close to his face, staring at the invisible space where Owen's head should be. "I hate magic, little boy. I have always hated magic. I hate it so much that I am now going to kill you twice for using it against me."

Thick, disgusting spit from the creature's mouth splashed on Owen's face as he tried in vain to squirm his way from the vice-like grip which crushed his spine. It squeezed his insides together painfully. The soldier laughed again, an angry scowl sprouting across his soaking wet, green-skinned face.

With his free hand he lifted the blade of his sword to Owen's throat. "Your invisible skull will make quite a unique trophy, little one."

49. THE TINIEST OF HEROES

Little Roustaf had watched Pleebo and the three boys slide down the incredibly steep hill on the backs of King Walcott and Nestor before beginning his descent. The unrelenting soreness in his wings mixed with the strength of the heavy winds pushed against his tiny body. It forced him to take it slow. Under his breath he quietly cursed his wings, remembering a time in his youth when they would have worked at their peak ability every hour of every day, no matter the circumstance. The flight down to the fortress was taking much too long. Anything could have happened to his friends by now. For all he knew, they could be dead – or worse. Flying into what remained of the plume of dust and debris caused by Donald's giant boulders, Roustaf lost momentarily his sense of direction.

When the dust had cleared, Roustaf looked for Tommy and Pleebo but did not see either of them. The courtyard was enormous, significantly larger than it had looked from above. Pockets of prisoners were engaged in combat with Ochan guards as far as his eyes could see. Countless dead bodies lay half submerged in the large puddles of mud, victims of pointless aggression. The scene was one of complete and utter madness. Roustaf quickly realized that locating any of his friends was going to be more difficult than he had anticipated, if not impossible. Despite the overwhelmingly loud sounds of battle ringing in his ears, he heard a woman scream. He saw a soldier lurching over a scared, screaming female who had tried to hide underneath an ornately decorated awning. She looked alarmingly thin, covered in pink skin pulled tightly over the muscled skeleton. Two very odd looking ears grew from the sides of her head, connecting at the top almost as if she were wearing a pair of pink headphones. Roustaf instantly recognized her species, she was a Grilgamorph. Because it had been so long since he had seen a member of the Grilgamorph race, he assumed that they, like many others, had been wiped from existence at some point during the war. To see one now – even one that was barely alive was quite astounding.

The massive soldier hovering over her pulled back his sword, preparing to strike. Roustaf realized that if he did not act soon she would end up like the rest of her race and his own – gone forever. Ignoring the nagging pain in his wings, Roustaf pulled his body straight as a board, reached out his arms and cut through the air. To the average-sized being a single drop of rain was barely noticeable. It could hardly be classified as a nuisance. To one the size of Roustaf, though, each was akin to a boulder. Every single one was an ominous, heavy mass of rapidly descending water nearly a twentieth of his body weight, carrying with it the danger of knocking him to the ground and crushing him. Roustaf's eyes never left his intended target as he weaved and bobbed between the individual drops, skillfully avoiding them with the speed and accuracy of a hummingbird.

The soldier hovering over the pink woman was armed to the teeth, covered in thick armor capable of withstanding the blows of almost any enemy's blade. Roustaf was well aware that he would not be able to significantly injure the Ochan. Thinking quickly, he spotted a large splinter of wood, jagged and sharp, sticking out of the mud. Without deviating from his course, he swooped down and plucked it off the ground. Though the splinter was nearly the same length as his entire body, he managed to hoist it above his head, every muscle in his body straining. Almost too quick for the eye to see, he flew above the awning and used the splinter to slice through the rope which connected it to the castle wall. Just as the soldier was about to plunge his blade into the pink woman's chest, the thick awning fell onto his head. While the annoyed soldier struggled to cut himself free, Roustaf darted underneath the massive piece of material and flew back , lifting the corner to create an opening through which the pink woman could make an escape.

"Come on, lady! Move it!" He screamed at her, trying to get her attention as she shivered.

Even though it was just a simple piece of fabric to the average sized being, Roustaf's muscles had burned red-hot under its weight. The soldier flailed wildly under the tarp just a few feet away, screaming his frustration.

Again Roustaf attempted to get the female's attention. "You're killing me here, toots! This thing weighs a ton! Come on! Get the lead out!"

Overcome with fear, the woman spotted the space the tiny flying man had created for her. She quickly crawled toward Roustaf but the enraged soldier snatched her ankle and pulled her back. The pink woman cried out, her fingers digging hopelessly into the mud as she was dragged back. Roustaf landed on the soldier's hand and bit his knuckle. There was no denying that Roustaf was small, as were his jaw and teeth but a bite was a bite and would still be painful. With a hunk of flesh ripped from his finger, the soldier released his grip on the woman, recoiling momentarily underneath the fabric.

The pink woman crawled to her feet just as Roustaf zoomed towards her, hovering close to her face . "You better start running, lady! Call me crazy, but I don't think that awning is going to hold him for long."

The pink woman glanced at her rescuer briefly before she looked back at the amorphous shape of the soldier writhing underneath the rain-soaked fabric. Spinning in the air, Roustaf flew away from the downed awning but the pink woman ran toward the soldier. Completely confused, Roustaf bellowed. "Wait! What the heck are you doing!? When I told you to run, I didn't mean back toward him, you ditzy broad! Come on! We've got to go, and we've got to do it now!"

Ignoring his pleas, the pink woman grabbed a half-submerged axe from a nearby puddle and headed toward the Ochan. She stopped in front of his tarp-covered form, reeled back and swung wildly at what she believed to be his head. The axe sliced through the fabric and the flesh and bone underneath, finally lodging in the creature's thick skull. The lump of living matter fell into the mud. Still breathing heavily with fear and rage the pink woman stared at Roustaf. She was shocked about what she had just done. Tiny Roustaf shared her sentiment.

With his mouth hanging open, Roustaf quietly muttered, "Um…well…okay, then. I mean, running was just a suggestion. Ramming a huge axe into his head was another way to go. I guess. Either one works for me."

The pink woman glanced timidly at him, a slightly embarrassed smile just barely coming to life on her thin lips.

"Remind me to always stay on your good side, lady," Roustaf added, rolling his eyes.

It was at this moment that Roustaf noticed Owen Little. At least, for a moment it was Owen Little. Not more than a few seconds after he had seen the boy and the Ochan soldier, Owen disappeared. The boy had not run away, hid under something, or crawled into an opening in the castle wall. He had simply disappeared into thin air.

With his jaw hanging even lower, Roustaf said quietly to himself, "I really should be accustomed to this stuff at this point, but come on…you've got to be kidding me."

50. REINFORCEMENTS ARRIVE

Zanell had been riding on the back of the Ochan
Lieutenant's Megalot for such a long period of time that every
movement of the massive, heavy-footed beast sent ripples of pain
up her spine and into her neck. The creature moved with
remarkable speed in spite of its incredible girth and weight. Like a
souped up tank, though, it was not light on its feet. The Megalot ran
with a lumbering gait distinctly its own. Unable to maneuver
around obstacles, the beast simply lowered its head and smashed
them from its path. Its feet mashed whatever they stepped on, while
the gargantuan horns on its head turned trees to splinters, plowing
through the red forest with the destructive force of a miniature
hurricane. Other regiments joined the Lieutenant along the way.
The Ochan force mowing down the ancient forest en route to the
Prince's castle numbered a thousand or more. Every single soldier

was starved for battle, anxious and blood thirsty. It had been a long time since the Ochans had amassed a force this size. It had been an even longer time since the great Ochan nation had faced a legitimate threat of any kind. The soldiers were chomping at the bit for a little action. As the massive army moved through the trees like an angry storm, the rumors of a Fillagrou prophesy and the dangerous, incredible magic had passed between them. Some had responded to the information with a twinge of fear while others had been spurred on for battle. Others still had simply regarded them as what they were – rumors hardly worth the time to consider seriously.

With every passing moment, Zanell could feel that they were getting closer to their intended destination and with every passing moment the beating of her heart increased. Having the sight of the Elders was proving to be an odd but wonderful sensation. Through a thick haze of crystalline softness she could see the beginning and end of all things. The images were vast and confusing, often complicated in their simplicity. Thrust at her all at once, the information had proved to be more than her mind could handle. To see everything all the time and understand it completely was an impossible task. She scarcely believed even the gods themselves could understand every nuance of the universe when condensed into a single moment.

No more than a hundred or so feet ahead of her, Zanell watched as the first of the reinforcements left the red forest, stepping with heavy hooves onto the great plain. They would arrive at the castle walls within minutes. Somewhere above her she could hear all things not of terrestrial time and space wailing their displeasure with the problems that had been caused by beast, man, and creatures confined to the flesh. With their disturbingly dejected voices ringing loudly in her ears, she was amazed that she had not heard them before.

Zanell was filled with anxiety. Despite the knowledge of what was to come, she knew that the true essence of the moment was in the journey, rather than the destination. Sadness and joy. Love and hate. Death and life. Downfall and redemption. What lay ahead was both a beginning and consequently, an end.

51. BORN OF BROKEN MEN

Prince Valkea gazed through the window of the castle tower and across the courtyard. For the most part, his forces had corralled the prisoner uprising. Small pockets of resistance remained uncontained, but when reinforcements arrived, the prisoners would be overwhelmed and beaten, smothering their pathetic attempt at freedom.

One of the massive boulders that had crashed through the outer wall could be seen   from Prince Valkea's window. Massive cracks from the collision ran alongside the base of the tower and halfway up its side. Had the stone slammed into the castle with a bit more speed, the entire structure might have collapsed to the ground. Whatever force, magic, technology or otherwise tossed the stone, it would eventually be destroyed under the weight of Ochan reinforcements. Prince Valkea was confident. When the battle was finally won, the Prince would see that every prisoner met with a very long and painful drawn-out death. He would make sure that each one felt every agonizing second leading up to the end of their life. The castle would be rebuilt and he would ensure that word of what had happened here never reached his father. All things broken would be repaired. All incidents, no matter how real, would be concealed with lies.

This shameful disaster would be salvaged, no matter the cost.

Across from the Prince, still curled up against the wall were Staci and Nicky. Everything about the children disgusted Prince Valkea. Their pale flesh, their pink cheeks, the revolting mass of hair follicles growing from their scalps like sickening tumors; the very sight of them made his stomach churn. These two pathetic things were not saviors. No, these were freaks. They were useless lumps of flesh from another useless lump of a world and nothing more. When all was settled with the prisoners, he would make it his first priority to locate their home world and burn it to the ground. He would scorch the lands so deeply that no life would grow from its soil again. They deserved nothing less.

Turning away from the window, Prince Valkea stared at the two cowering children, looking them over from top to bottom. Every glance found yet another reason to hate them.

"I wonder…do all children from your world resemble the pair of you?" He asked, strangely calm, his eyes seeming to peer through their skin, examining what soul, if any, resided somewhere deep inside.

"What sort of life have you led? So soft you are…so fragile. No doubt it was one built on comfort…possibly kindness. I am not being the least bit dramatic when I say that an Ochan child…any Ochan child for that matter…would eat the pair of you alive."

Staci gazed at the prince, tears rolling down her cheeks and onto the cold floor. Nicky's lip quivered uncontrollably as Staci instinctively wrapped her arm around him, pulling the small boy close.

"Are you aware that one can learn everything one needs to learn about a race through its young? In every creature I've encountered during my rule, I've found this truth to be one of the few constants. There are no innocent Ochan children. There are no sad eyes and without question there are no tears. Each is well aware of the realities of the world they are destined to inhabit at a very young age. Each can recall every contour of their father's fists with excruciating detail before their third year…and most importantly each thanks their parents for this most harsh of lessons upon entering adulthood."

The Prince slowly moved closer to the children and looked into their eyes. "Like hardened steel, we are a race forged in fire and molded to a fine point. This is how strength is made. This is how power, greatness and legacy are given birth. This is a lesson you can never understand, and this is the reason you and all those like you will eventually fall."

Prince Valkea had barely finished his sentence when the door to his tower chamber exploded. Shards of wood in every shape and size flew in every direction. The largest among them knocked over chairs, while the smallest instantly filling the room with a fine dust. The force of the explosion knocked the Prince onto his rear. Turning his head, he shaded his eyes from the dangerous shrapnel. Staci let out a loud scream and pulled Nicky closer to her as she shielded him from the blast. By the time the thin layer of dust had settled Prince Valkea was already on his feet, dagger in hand. His dark heart pounded against his ribs, heightening his senses, preparing him for battle.

Glowing so brightly that he might have been confused for the sun, Tommy Jarvis strode angrily into the room. His entire body crackled with the porous energy emanating from his hands

The unbelievable sight was unlike anything that Prince Valkea had experienced in his life. He was no stranger to magic. But something about the strange glow made him believe that this was more than simple magic, that this was something else entirely – something unique, frightening, and new. His brain told him to hold his position but his body chose to step back.

Tommy's eyes left the Prince and rested upon his little brother and Staci. Terrified, Nicky and Staci kept their faces hidden, neither looking at Tommy when he had entered the room. Both look tired, their clothes a filthy mess of caked on dirt and grime. Seeing Nicky looking so haggard and scared caused the energy coursing through Tommy's body to boil hotter. Forming a fist, the strange ethereal light crept through the cracks, again swallowing the whole of his hand.

Tommy looked again at Prince Valkea.

In a voice much too deep for his body, Tommy calmly and firmly said, "Get away from my brother."

Both Nicky and Staci were awestruck by what they saw. With his jaw hanging open, Nicky pried himself from Staci's grip and turned toward the living ball of light that seemed to encase someone that resembled his older brother. Staci hesitantly moved beside the young boy, not sure of what she saw.

"Tom...Tom...Tommy?" She stuttered, her teeth chattering.

"Get them out of here," Tommy yelled.

303

The crackling of the energy surrounding his body was growing louder and scarier as his anger continued to rise.

Pleebo rushed into the room through the smoking rubble and made his way along the wall, grabbing Nicky and Staci. "Come with me, children!" Pleebo said as he attempted to pull them out of the way.

Staci waited next to Pleebo while Nicky pushed him away. Pleebo's second attempt failed when the small boy squirmed out of his grasp.

"We have to go, child!" Pleebo urged, lunging for Nicky as the boy crawled across the floor.

"Come on, Nicky!" Staci yelped, as she stood in the burnt out husk of the doorway and motioned for Nicky to follow.

Their pleas meant little to the youngest of the Jarvis boys. Unlike Staci, he simply could not bring himself to leave his brother alone with the Prince, glowing with energy or otherwise. How many times had his brother stood up for him? How many times had he taken the fall for him? How many times had Tommy suffered through the aftermath of those choices? No, he could not leave Tommy alone – not now and not ever again - not after everything that had happened.

Prince Valkea slowly controlled his emotions . He could see that the thing residing inside the glowing mass of light stalking him was a child. There were incredible powers at work here, and yet the thing underneath it all remained a simple, small boy. A disgusting, pink skinned, weak little creature and exactly like the other two. Like all boys, this one could no doubt bleed. He could be beaten – powers or otherwise. He was not prepared to hand over his Kingdom to a child.

This time when Tommy took a step forward, Prince Valkea did not take one back. "Your powers don't frighten me, boy. This...all of this...is my birthright. I will not allow it to be taken away by the likes of one such as you. Not now...not ever."

"Come closer and I will introduce you to the true strength of the Ochan nation," Prince Valkea defiantly added as he tightened his grip on the dagger.

With his body shaking with rage, Tommy lifted his glowing fist at Prince Valkea. Slowly he opened his fingers, intending to blast the awful green-skinned creature into the afterlife.

Unfortunately for Tommy it did not happen.

As quickly as the light had sprouted from his hands, it just as quickly disappeared. Without warning the crackling power dimmed, retreating back into the hands that had first given it life. As the last of it vanished into nothingness, a frustrated and confused Tommy, stared at his normal-looking hands. Of all the times the power could have chosen to become unreliable, this was the least opportune of all. He glanced at the Prince and noticed a cocky smile creeping across his dark green face.

"Just a boy," Prince Valkea chuckled. "Just a child who knows nothing of will or strength or pain. Strip away your magic and you're nothing. Before this day is done, I guarantee that you will have learned all these lessons, little one. I will be your teacher...and I assure you I will be quite thorough. Unfortunately for you, these will be the last things you will ever learn."

52. ONE LAST RESCUE

It did not take long for Roustaf to figure out exactly what was happening on the other side of the courtyard between Owen Little and the massive angry soldier who towered over him. If the rain had not given the boy away, he might have fooled the Ochan into believing he was gone. But the Ochan had figured it out and before long Owen's head would be rolling in the mud.

Roustaf faced the pink woman and said, "Looks like I'm going to have to cut our meeting a little short, beautiful."

His tiny wings fluttered, quickly becoming invisible to the naked eye. His body jutted forward as he zoomed between the pink woman's legs.

"Wait, where are you...?" was all she had time to say before he was gone.

Roustaf dove to the ground and picked up the very same wooden splinter he had used earlier, the pain in his wings all but forgotten. He was well aware that the boy's life depended on him. Once again Roustaf's tiny body sliced through the air like an arrow. Hoisting the long splinter of wood close, Roustaf let it rest against his hip like a knight preparing for a joust. As he cut through the droplets of rain, the tiny red man tightened his muscles, gritted his teeth and prepared himself for battle. There would only be one shot, one chance to get this right. If he let the opportunity slip, he had no back-up plan.

Failure would mean the boy's death.

The Ochan soldier tightened his grip on Owen as he gained control over the boy's squirming, transparent body. He lifted the blade of his sword to Owen's throat. "Your invisible skull will make for quite a unique trophy, little one."

Just as the cold, wet steel came in contact with Owen's invisible neck, the Ochan heard a tiny distinctive voice utter a tiny distinctive battle cry. Confused, he turned and faced the voice.

Roustaf closed his eyes and extended the long splinter of wood. While moving at an incredible speed, he jabbed not only the splinter but the upper half of his body into the creature's ear. The sharp piece of wood sliced through the fleshy insides like scissors through paper and was deep enough to poke the brain. The Ochan's eyes popped open; his jaw sank low, his vision blurred as the sounds of the world around him evaporated into a mist. The creature released his iron grip and Owen tumbled to the ground.

Bracing his legs on the side of the soldier's face, Roustaf pried himself loose. "Well...that was pretty much the most disgusting thing I've ever done." He calmly remarked, brushing a pile of sloppy, sticky earwax from the top of his head.

The half-alert Ochan stared at the tiny little man. Slowly his attention shifted to the cloudy sky. He patted the side of his head, making sure that it was still attached to his shoulders. Lost in a hypnotic trance, the soldier's body swayed. A soft growl squeaked from between his lips, his eyes rolled back in his head, and his body tumbled into the mud with a wet splash.

After scraping the remainder of the earwax from his scalp, Roustaf turned his attention to Owen. The boy was now completely visible, half submerged in the sopping mud, leaning back on his hands. His wide eyes were glued to the motionless body of the fallen Ochan.

Roustaf nodded and said with half a smile, "Good to see you again, kid."

Before Owen could respond, the sound of a massive explosion filled the night air, causing the ground to shimmy. Both he and Roustaf looked at the sky just in time to see an enormous cloud of smoke, cluttered with thick debris, rise into the air at the opposite end of the castle.

Surprised and slightly annoyed, Roustaf quietly sighed, "Now what?"

53. THE LAST STAND OF KING WALCOTT SHELLAMENNES

General Gragor smiled brightly when he recognized the King of Tycaria standing in the falling rain. He had thought the King was dead. The Tycarians had not fallen easily during the war. Time and time again they had proven themselves to be a strong-willed race, led by a crafty King, who had also been a competent military strategist. Not long after the Ochan army had finally managed to gain control of the region, rumors of King Shellamennes' death ran rampant, even though his body had never been recovered. General Gragor had never believed the rumors. For years he and his men had searched for proof of King Shellamennes' death without much success. Now the great lost King of Tycaria stood before him.

"King Walcott Shellamennes...the great ghost of a King finally comes out of hiding. I am both honored and humbled to be in your presence, your highness." General Gragor said sarcastically. "To what...oh great King...do I owe the pleasure?"

Never taking his eyes off of General Gragor, King Walcott answered sternly. "Back away from the boy, scoundrel."

"No, no, no...you see, you do not give me orders. You are not my King. You do not come into this place and give me orders, Tycarian...not now, not ever."

Like a flock of starving vultures, the Ochan soldiers standing nearby moved toward King Walcott. Responding to their advance, the Tycarian lifted his sword, ready to challenge them all.

"NO!" General Gragor screamed, "BACK AWAY FROM HIM, MUTTS!"

The large group of Ochan soldiers froze in their tracks, standing in thick mounds of mud. General Gragor gripped his sword tightly and slowly moved toward King Walcott "This one...is mine," he added with a growl, causing the surrounding horde of soldiers to slowly back away.

With weapons drawn, King Walcott and General Gragor approached one another. The Ochan soldiers formed a loose circle around them. Crouched against the fortress wall, Donald Rondage ignored the incredible pain in his shoulder long enough to see the stand-off gradually building to a boiling point. Despite everything he had said to King Walcott, despite the fact that he had done nothing but frustrate and annoy the old turtle-man, King Walcott was willing to put his life on the line for him. This concept confused Donald. No one - not his parents, not his brothers – no one had ever been willing to give so much for him. It did not make sense. An overwhelming feeling of shame trickled across his skin like the feet of a billion tiny spiders, creeping into every pore, swallowing the still childish soul buried deep within him. Overcome with the need to try and help King Walcott in some way, Donald pulled himself to his feet. He fell when the intense pain in his shoulder shot through his body. There was nothing he could do to help King Walcott and that fact settled heavily on his stomach. He could only watch – watch and hope.

As thunder roared overhead, their swords clashed violently. From the outset, it was painfully obvious that King Walcott was no match for General Gragor who was bigger, stronger and unlike many of the soldiers the King had ever faced. The Ochan general was equally adept with a blade but King Walcott matched his opponent stroke for stroke even though the King's stamina was waning. As swords clashed, the combatants were close. They dug their heels into the mud, pushing against each other in a bizarre test of strength.

General Gragor confidently hissed, "You move well...for one of such advancing age."

King Walcott's feet were sliding across the thick mud which pooled between his toes. He held his breath and pushed back with all the strength he could muster.

With a pained, determined grimace, the King growled angrily, "I...am not...leaving here...without...that boy!" King Walcott thrust forward, kicking thick clumps of mud with every step.

In one quick movement, King Walcott rammed the top of his shell into General Gragor's midsection. The sudden skillful ploy caused General Gragor to stumble, knocking the air from his lungs. King Walcott barreled forward at full speed, ramming the Ochan into a nearby prisoner hut. The pair crashed through the wooden wall and crumbled onto the floor with a wild, heavy thud that sent shrapnel sailing in every direction. In a flash, they were back on their feet, swinging their swords with deadly intention. Their bodies collided against the walls, as they engaged in close-quarter combat. The air was heavy with the familiar odor of the dead and dying. Over the course of the war the smell had inspired different reactions from each of them. For General Gragor it had been the smell of success – the undeniable, beautiful fragrance of victory. For King Walcott it had meant the end of his people, the death of his friends and family; it had been the painful, destructive odor of hopeless endings.

"You're tiring, King...I can see it in your eyes." General Gragor was smug and breathing heavily.

King Walcott ignored the verbal jab, despite the truth behind it. Every muscle in his aging body heaved, ached and screamed for him to stop. Despite the youthful fires in his heart, he was painfully aware that he was not going to be able to maintain this frantic pace. General Gragor grabbed a sword from the hand of a fallen soldier and viciously attacked his enemy. King Walcott moved quickly, deflecting each blow. But there has always been an undeniable truth in inevitability that all great warriors understood. King Walcott had been pushed to the limit; it was only a matter of time before he faltered, only a matter of time before his aged muscles failed, only a matter of time before the spirit to fight would no longer be enough. Unfortunately for the Tycarian King, the moment had arrived.

General Gragor's blade sliced King Walcott's leg, exposing the bone. The Tycarian fell, dropping his weapon. King Walcott rolled on his stomach, crawling along the slick ground, attempting to reach his sword. General Gragor thrust his sword into the King's back, splitting open the shell with a sickening crack.

King Walcott screamed, his thick fingers digging into the mud, while his body tensed. He gritted his teeth in an effort to withstand the indescribable pain. General Gragor stared at the withering King with mild disgust as a thick green liquid seeped from the massive gash, "Look at me whelp." The Ochan General mumbled. " Meet your end like a warrior."

Grimacing in agony, King Walcott rolled onto his back, groaning as his weight on the cracked shell increased the pain. A flash of lightning ominously lit the sky as General Gragor stood over the King, sword in hand. The light of the Fillagrou moon barely crept through the clouds, silhouetting the victorious Ochan. King Walcott involuntarily shook as the rain splashed his face, cooling the agonizing heat of his suffering. The King was overcome with the need to protect his limbs and slowly pulled his extremities inside his shell, leaving his head exposed. He would face his end with his eyes open as befitted a warrior and a King.

General Gragor glanced at his enemy with a mixture of disgust and admiration. It had been years since an opponent managed to meet him blow for blow. It had been years since he had found himself fulfilled in a way that could only be attained through battle with a worthy foe. As he watched King Walcott tremble, his admiration quickly waned. His adversary, the great King of the Tycarian people, looked quite pathetic covered in mud, his arms and legs hiding inside his shell.

Raising the sword, General Gragor growled, "You fought well, Tycarian...like all of your kind though, you've failed. In your death I can guarantee you only one thing... your countrymen will soon share your fate. I am glad you had survived all these years. It has afforded me the opportunity to personally end your life once and for all." He tightened his grip while raising his sword. "Safe journey to the afterlife, if there is such a place for the likes of you."

Before the General could drive his sword into King Walcott's skull, the Tycarian's uninjured leg shot out from its shell. A dagger was gripped tightly between his long, flat toes. Using what was left of his energy, he drove the dagger into General Gragor's chest. The blade sliced through thick ribs, puncturing the lungs. General Gragor's body stiffened as he attempted to pull himself off the blade. King Walcott wrapped his arms around the Ochan General's shoulders, pulling him deeper onto the blade. King Walcott grabbed the back of General Gragor's head and pulled him closer. He defiantly whispered through gritted teeth, "It's quite amazing…the kinds of things…we Tycarians are capable of storing…inside our shells…isn't it?"

A small grin slowly crept across General Gragor's face as the two combatants shared a moment of mutual dislike, sprinkled with pangs of admiration. This was indeed a warrior's moment; a moment that comes only once in a lifetime, a moment that will be remembered in the next world.

The crowd of Ochan soldiers had been more than content to watch the fight until their commander had been struck by the Tycarian's fatal blow. Rushing to his aid, the horde of soldiers ran toward their enemy as a thunderous boom tore through the air. An enormous explosion created a massive cloud of smoke and debris at the opposite side of the fortress. Caught in the heavy winds of the rainy night, it spread across the courtyard like a great dark blanket swallowing up things both living and dead.

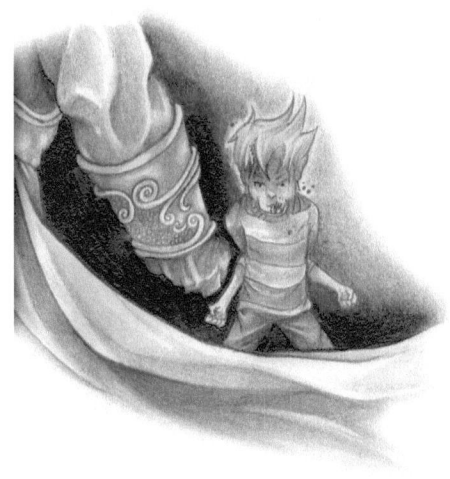

54. FORGED IN FIRE

"TOMMY, NO!" Staci screamed as loudly as her already worn and sore throat could muster.

Across the room, Prince Valkea had thrown Tommy Jarvis a good ten feet into the air. Tommy hit the corner of an enormous table, cracking the side of his head. He was unconscious when he collapsed on the cold stone floor.

Pleebo had seen Tommy brutally tossed about and had noticed the faraway look in his eyes when his head had smashed into the thick slab of wood. The normally level-headed Pleebo felt his anger rise. Pleebo's entire life had been spent drudging through the reality of a world built atop corpses. He had been a child when the war started. Try as might to rise above it and be more like his father, an unrelenting voice in the back of his mind told him that was impossible.

The finely woven fabric of our life was often stained with the blood of the past.

Life's experiences had stained Pleebo so deeply that no force born of God or flesh could ever hope to wash him clean. He could continue and ignore this fact or he could embrace the lessons learned through tragedy. Strength could be found in the most painful situations, if one was simply willing to look.

Pleebo moved with incredible speed as his long, lanky body rushed across the room, tackling the Prince to the floor with stunning force. As he sat on Prince Valkea's chest, Pleebo's thin arms swung so quickly that they became a blur. Blow after blow connected with Prince Valkea's face, shoulders and arms. Prince Valkea flailed wildly beneath his skinny, unrelenting assailant. The number of punches reached well into the double digits as the skin on Pleebo's knuckles peeled. The bones in his knuckles shattered; each punch he delivered sent a jolt of fiery, hot pain through his arms, into his shoulders and through his chest. Despite the continuous blows, Prince Valkea managed to turn on his stomach, pushing himself to his knees, shoving the manic, screaming Fillagrou off him. Before Pleebo could get back on his feet, the Prince grabbed a nearby chair, breaking it over his opponent.

"YOU DARE STRIKE ME, FILTHY SWINE!" Prince Valkea wildly screamed as he continued to hit Pleebo's squirming body with the remaining shards of shattered wood. "WHERE DO YOU GET THE RIGHT!? I'LL TEAR YOU LIMB FROM LIMB FOR THIS! I'LL OPEN YOU UP AND DECORATE THE FOREST WITH YOUR INSIDES FOR ALL TO SEE!"

The Prince tossed aside the chair, kicking Pleebo's motionless body. The fresh welts on the Ochan's face were pounding against his skull, blood freely flowing from no less than five open wounds. Prince Valkea had been driven to the brink of insanity. A disgusting froth formed on the side of his mouth as he mercilessly beat the unmoving creature lying on the floor.

While Pleebo kept Prince Valkea occupied, Staci and Nicky hurried to Tommy's side. A small trickle of blood seeped from a wound above the boy's left eye where his head had struck the table.

Grabbing Tommy's arms, Staci attempted to pull him off the floor. "Come on, Tommy! We have to get out of here!"

Nicky wedged himself underneath his brother's shoulder, doing his best to help him stand.

When Tommy had hit the table, everything went black. The cold, unending darkness had swallowed him whole and had dragged him further into nothingness. Slowly packets of sound accompanied by flashes of warmly colored lights popped into the nothingness like the implosion of stars at the other end of the galaxy. The wobbly darkness faded into something else. Gravity swept in and weighed down his body, filling him once again with the familiar heaviness of existence. Unrecognizable shapes stretched and blurred across the soft curve of his iris, patiently coming into focus, growing sharp and frightening in their clarity.

His head sat flimsily atop his wobbly neck. Tommy's gaze drifted wearily to Staci. "TOMMY! PLEASE! We have to go!" She screamed, tugging at his limp body.

Sweet Staci – all those years after his mother's death – all the times she had tried to befriend him, to help him. He should have never treated her the way he did. She had not deserved any of it.

Tommy spotted his little brother wedged underneath his arm, grimacing through his strained little boy muscles. There had been times over the last few days – more times than Tommy had cared to admit – that he doubted he would ever see Nicky again. He

317

could not go on without his brother. Any world without Nicky, quite simply, would not be a world worth living in.

Tommy was standing again, the floor planted firmly underneath his feet. He slowly reclaimed control of his legs. He noticed Pleebo lying on the floor, his dirty tunic ripped and bloodied. His pale, nearly transparent back was covered with endless bruises and cuts. Standing above him, Prince Valkea was relentlessly kicking his lifeless body. "TOMMY! MOVE! COME ON!" Staci yelled, tugging her friend toward the shattered hull of the doorway.

With a sudden burst of strength Tommy managed to wiggle free from her grasp.

He could not leave without Pleebo.

"No, we can't go yet." Tommy emphatically said. "We can't just leave him here."

As he moved away from his brother and Staci, Tommy urgently told them, "Run Find someplace to hide and stay there."

"What are you talking about? We're not leaving without you!" Staci replied, somewhat frustrated

"You have to go! I'll find you when this is over, I promise."

Staci and Nicky stared back at the boy with frightened, unbelieving eyes. Staci's jaw trembled. A waterfall of tears drenched the side of her face, sweat pooled on the tip of her nose.

Tommy glared at them though a pair of shiny-wet, soulful steel-blue eyes, "I can't just leave him here to die...I can't. You have to go though...go now. Hide, and I'll find you...I promise."

There was no time to listen to another argument. Tommy determinedly turned toward Prince Valkea and Pleebo. Behind him he heard Staci's screaming protests. Her voice slowly became softer. It faded into the background and floated away like a bottle tossed into a great vast ocean. Everything around him that was not Staci's voice became crisper and in focus. With every step, Tommy regained control over his muscles, his determination solidified with each breath. He had made the right choice – he had to help Pleebo. The situation before him was strangely familiar. Powers or not, young Tommy Jarvis had faced this before and could face it again.

In fact, one could go so far as if to say that it brought with it a notion of commonplace.

As Tommy Jarvis was well aware, commonplace could not hurt you.

55. SAME BUT DIFFERENT

Breathing heavily, his muscles straining, Prince Valkea had momentarily halted his assault on the comatose Pleebo. He also noticed that that Tommy Jarvis was heading toward him. While his rage might have subsided, the Prince still retained a repugnant air of cockiness.

Assuredly, Prince Valkea turned to the boy. "Are you still here?" He growled through heavy breaths. He chuckled as he grabbed the ornately decorated fabric hanging from his belt and used it to wipe Pleebo's splattered blood from his armor.

"I must admit, child...while reminding this Fillagrou scum of his place in the world...I had nearly forgotten all about you. I'm rather pleased that you decided not to leave without saying goodbye. It would have been such a shame to be robbed of the opportunity to properly send you on your way."

Tommy stopped ten feet away. His heartbeat had settled into a heavy, dogged thump. The space between beats had been a mathematical constant as precise as the ticking of a clock. Powerless for the time being, the tips of his fingers had ticked instead with a different sort of feeling, something more familiar – something more natural. It was a strength that had been born of a childhood spent wading neck-deep in waters children were not meant to wade. Tommy did not need the abilities of the Elders to foretell what was about to happen. He knew precisely. He knew because, in one form or another, it had happened to him many, many times before.

Darkness wore many masks, but when removed, the face underneath was generally the same. It was the remake of a movie that had not been very interesting the first time around - identical story, different actors. Even with slight tonal changes, or minuscule alterations in the performers' inflection, the basics – the script – had remained constant.

His knuckles cracked like snapping twigs as he pulled them into fists.

Prince Valkea noticed the gesture and smiled sarcastically. "How stupid of you, boy…how utterly childish. You've given into flights of fancy…into youthful, misinformed ideas of heroism. The real world doesn't work like you think it does. In the real world stupid little children meet grizzly, painful ends when they attempt to tackle situations they aren't fully prepared to handle." His smile slowly faded. The stone-serious Prince lifted his hands, motioning for Tommy to advance. "Come, then, if you must. I will be more than happy to teach you the lessons all children should learn."

Without plan, hesitation, or thought, Tommy barreled forward at full speed. His fists rose in anger. His movements were wild, untamed and sloppy. With ease Prince Valkea sidestepped the charging boy, grabbing his shirt in the process. Using Tommy's own momentum, he threw the boy face first into the wall behind him. Tommy's nose hit the stone, sending a sharp, stiff shooting pain throughout his face and into his ringing ears while the cut on his forehead opened again.

"Ignore the pain, you can take it." Tommy reminded himself.

Tommy charged at Prince Valkea and hit the Ochan in the stomach. Prince Valkea shrugged off the punches, barely feeling them. Prince Valkea shoved Tommy away, hitting him in the chest. The blow sent a shockwave of jagged, painful thunderbolts throughout Tommy's body. With his feet kicked out from underneath him, his body tumbled against the wall, landing him on his rear with his shoulders hunched over. His lungs seemed to have been punctured, weighty and useless. A heavy cough rattled against his sore ribs, violently shooting from his mouth like a handful of sharp gravel. When Tommy attempted to stand, a thousand needles poked him in the chest. He did not doubt that something had been broken, fractured or possibly both.

"Ignore the pain. This is nothing you haven't felt before."

Prince Valkea snatched a handful of the boy's hair. At an achingly slow pace, he pulled Tommy across the room, the boy's legs kicking wildly, his body thrashing from side to side. Prince Valkea tossed Tommy across the floor; spinning like a top, he crashed viciously into a set of chairs.

Prince Valkea smiled when he threw a handful of Tommy's hair onto the floor but the delicate strands caught a soft breeze and floated in the air. "Such pathetic creatures you are…every last one of you so very, very fragile," he remarked. "I will never understand why my father chose to strand me here…to force me to live among the likes of you and the rest of these mongrels. What a pointless position…useless…better left for the likes of General Gragor or one of similar breeding."

With Tommy lying motionless on the floor, Prince Valkea glanced at Nicky and Staci. Both children were seated in the center of the room, terrified by the unconscionable viciousness of what they had just seen.

Prince Valkea appeared ethereal, his mind wandering back to his youth and back to thoughts of his father. " He must be testing me…testing me to see if I'm worthy of the throne…as if my youth alone weren't test enough. No doubt he assumes I'll fail…he always has. In the back of his mind he most likely hopes for it," he whispered, obviously talking to no one but himself. "I'll have your kingdom one day, you old fool…I'll have your kingdom and I'll have your head."

Despite the fact that every inch of his body was throbbing and sore, Tommy Jarvis slowly pushed the heavy chairs off him. Disgusting, grayish-blue bruises were cropping up on his arms. While he could not see them, he could feel even more welts sprouting beneath his pants. The top of his head felt as if it had been set on fire. The cut above his eye flowed freely, a stream of warm blood cascading down his face.

"Ignore the pain. He can't hurt you."

Placing one hand on the ground to steady himself, he managed to kneel.

"This is nothing. He can't hurt you".

The leaky-warm blood splashed onto the floor, staining the fortress stone red.

"He can't hurt you. Nothing can hurt you".

Tommy took a deep breath and forced himself to stand.

In a breathy, rebellious tone he calmly said, "Ya, sure...you hate your dad...your life has sucked...so has everyone's...why don't you do us all a favor, and shut up about it."

The sound of the boy's voice brought Prince Valkea back to his immediate surroundings. He looked at the boy, uttering surprised. Though barely able to pick himself up, this creature – this child – stood defiantly before him, mocking him. Suddenly the young Prince felt naked and exposed. An unquestionably heavy, painful weight had settled deep in the pit of his stomach as if he had swallowed a mouthful of rocks. With a single sentence, this weak, powerless little child had managed to toss asunder his veneer of confidence like garbage catching the breeze. Images of his father, warnings of prophecies and visions of failure had unceremoniously invaded his brain, quickly spreading across his body, devouring him from the inside out. With the single blink of an eye, his vision had turned from crystal clear to red.

This thing, this boy, this monster – must die.

Blinded by uncontrollable rage, Prince Valkea charged at Tommy, wrapping his large hands around the boy's neck. His fingers dug into soft flesh, rapidly transforming the child's skin to a frightening shade of purple. Lifting Tommy into the air, Prince Valkea's sharp teeth ground together and sweat poured from his face as he squeezed with all his might.

Seeing Tommy in such peril forced Staci to find the courage that she needed to help her friend. Without hesitation, she charged at the Prince, slamming herself into his back as he choked the life out of Tommy. Prince Valkea shoved her away; the force from the blow knocked her to the ground, causing her to somersault across the floor

With his face soaked by salty tears, Nicky Jarvis cupped his hands tightly over his ears, shaking uncontrollably. While the Prince held Tommy in his vice-like grip, a strange sensation overcame Nicky. Less than fifteen feet away his brother was dying – being murdered right before his eyes. So many years Tommy had had suffered for him. Not once had he done anything. A steady, terrible hum was building inside Nicky's head. The maddening noise pressed against the interior of his skull, threatening to crack it open. Try as he might to make it stop, he was failing. The awful sound was not coming from outside; covering his ears did absolutely nothing. His body shook violently while a thick, crystal sheen of sweat covered him from head to toe. The boy wearily lifted his jittery, pulsing head and gazed at his brother. Tommy's face had turned a ghoulish purple-blue, his eyes were wide open. His legs had stopped kicking; his body was limp as it dangled above the floor. With a blank, very sad, yet vaguely forgiving look on his face, Tommy glanced at his little brother while his life was being taken away.

Tommy's lips softly mouthed the words, "Its okay."

The simple phrase instantly bore its way into Nicky's soul. The pressure inside the skull of the youngest Jarvis brother reached a fevered pitch. To contain it any longer would be pointless. The time had come for release.

For the first time in years, quiet little Nicky Jarvis - the boy who had lost his voice for so many years – opened his mouth. He spoke one single word. It was a word spoken so very loud that it was heard by all the worlds in all the universes.

325

56. COLD, WHITE GOODBYES

It had been less than a week since young Tommy Jarvis' mother passed away. The days since had been spent mostly alone in his bedroom. Walking through the house seemed strange with his mother gone, uncomfortable and wrong. Each day folded unnoticed into the next. At night, instead of sleeping, Tommy found himself staring blankly at the bedroom ceiling. When the sun disappeared, the world quieted down. It had never been completely silent, just quieter, and slower, like stepping from a noisy street into a library. The hushed atmosphere made it easier for Tommy to clear his mind and think about things other than his mother.

On the morning of her funeral, Chris Jarvis said very little to either of his boys. Gruffly instructing Tommy to get dressed, he seemed more than a bit annoyed with the fact that he still had to remind his children of such basic things. They were old enough and should have known better. The drive to the mortuary had been much the same. Father and sons stared blankly out the windows, their minds wandering, the luminescence created by the sunlight reflecting off the fallen snow straining their eyes. The world outside had been cold – cold, white, and achingly beautiful, reminiscent of her skin.

Thirty minutes later Tommy found himself staring at something vaguely resembling his mother, lying eerily silent in an enormous wooden coffin. Whatever this was, this painted, primed, and stretched out thing before him – was not his mother – at least, not anymore. Whoever had applied her make-up had done a terrible job. She looked clownish. The colors were totally wrong, shades she would never have chosen. The eye shadow was a pale, powdery baby blue – she hated blue.

No, this was not his mother – his mother was gone.

This had been the best guesstimate of a stranger, an art project - an approximation and nothing more. Standing on the tips of his toes, Tommy reached timidly into the coffin, letting the tip of his index finger gently touch her face. Her skin felt like ice, like chilly plastic, like a mannequin that spent the night in the freezer. It was not human and most definitely was not his mother.

His father stood stoically next to him. His younger brother, Nicky leaned against the large man's leg, the fabric gripped tightly between his fingers. The nine-year-old's thumb moved back and forth gently inside his mouth. The soft sound of his sucking echoed throughout the silent room. For years Nicky's mother had tried to convince him to stop sucking his thumb, but the boy had refused. The thumb was soothing, the thumb was safe, and the thumb was

327

constant. The thumb would always be there when he needed it and Nicky needed the thumb now more than ever.

Farther down the line stood Uncle Bill, Aunt Jenny, and Grandpa Joseph; there were also a few people Tommy had never seen before. Each waited patiently in line for the opportunity to say goodbye. Aunt Jenny glanced briefly at Tommy with teary eyes. A confused expression covered her face, when she noticed that Tommy was dry-eyed. For reasons he had not fully understood, Tommy found it impossible to cry. He had wanted to cry – to cry badly - so that the entire town drowned in his tears and was swept into sea. It simply had not happened, not today, tomorrow, and maybe never again.

No longer able to look at the shell of his mother laid out in such a disgustingly painted, strangely pristine fashion, Tommy ran down the center aisle and left through the large double-doors. No one made the slightest attempt to stop him. Even if they had, such an act would have resulted in failure. Tommy wanted nothing to do with this any longer. The air in the room had become so thick that it coagulated in his lungs, making breathing a chore. The smell of disinfectant mixed with too much cologne and perfume had caused the inside of his nose to feel itchy and sore. There was something unnatural about the whole situation, something fake, disingenuous and just plain wrong. He had to get away from it all and nothing was going to stop him.

Through the doors, down a long, dark hallway and into the lobby he sprinted past family members, neighbors and strangers, ignoring the pity and whispers.

A chilling burst of cold hit Tommy in the chest the moment that he stepped outside the mortuary. The sudden coupling of warm flesh and icy breeze sent a much needed twinge of pain throughout his body, causing every follicle of hair to stand at attention. Almost instantly, the crisp freshness of winter cleared his lungs, while gently soothing away the frustrating itch inside his nose.

The snow had fallen hard over the course of the previous night. Thick, tall drifts twisting into beautifully smooth, delicate curves pressed against the sides of houses, cars, and all things created by man and nature. Translucent icicles dancing with the reflection of the afternoon sun suspended from the branches of trees barely clinging to life.

Finally outside, finally away from his family, finally alone, Tommy could breathe again. A gentle tide of relief washed over him. Walking to the rear of the building, Tommy's feet crunched deeply into the un-shoveled snow covering the grass. No longer able to hear the whispers or the quiet sobs of the people inside, he at last stopped. He leaned against the brick wall until he could no longer stand. He sat upon the frozen ground and watched his steamy breath rise toward the sky. Swaying softly in the air for a moment, it hung like a delicate fog, eventually swallowed by the unrelenting chill, evaporating into nothing. From above, more snow fell upon the earth, slowly covering Tommy's head and shoulders. It occurred to Tommy that if were to stay there long enough, the snow would bury him alive. The idea did not frighten him one bit.

"Tommy?"

The quiet, timid voice belonged to his neighbor, Staci Alexander. She stood next to him, her hands buried in the pockets of her heavy maroon-colored winter jacket.

"Tommy...are...are you okay?" She asked, the cold making her nose redder with each passing moment.

Tommy did not respond. He had no interest in talking to her. He could not stand to hear her voice. He wanted her to leave.

He wanted her to go away and never come back. Staci had been his friend for as far back as he was able to form memories; it did not make any sense to ignore her, and yet at this moment, it was exactly what he felt that he needed to do.

Irrational annoyance rapidly grew as Tommy grumbled through cracked lips, "Go away, Staci."

"Tommy, I just wan..."

He clearly restated, "Please...please just go away."

A heavy breeze blew from the west, lifting the snow off the ground, tossing it wildly into the air, enveloping the children in a tornado of dancing white flakes. The sudden flurry covered Tommy, leaving him partially buried.

From the front of the building, Staci's mother searched for her daughter. "Staci? Staci, where are you sweetie? It's freezing out here! It's time to come inside, honey!"

Staci glanced at the pile of snow where Tommy Jarvis sat. She was not mad at him – she could not be mad at him – she simply wanted to see her friend smile again.

"Staci, come on! Get in here, young lady! You'll catch your death in this cold!" This time, her mother's voice made it an order rather than a request.

Realizing that her mother was not going to stop yelling until she came inside, Staci reluctantly turned to walk away.

Before leaving she softly whispered to the nearly buried form of her friend, "You'll always be my friend, Tommy...no matter what."

In a moment she was gone.

After the viewing had concluded and the guests all returned home, an annoyed Chris Jarvis dug his icy, shivering son from underneath the snow pile on the side of the building. He had been outside for more than forty minutes. His fingers were blue and his teeth chattered. During the car ride home, Chris admonished his eldest son for walking out on his mother's funeral. He screamed at him, letting the boy know in no uncertain terms that he was disappointed, that he would never forgive him for it. Once inside the warm safety of the house, a frustrated Chris Jarvis slapped his son on the back of the head, screaming at him to get upstairs and stay there. It was not a hard slap, yet it was not playful, either. It was a beginning, a hint of things to come.

That afternoon, while he had been buried underneath the snow, Tommy Jarvis' face froze in time. The expression was a result of his mother's passing and would be the face he would wear for the rest of his life. It would be the face he would see in the mirror every morning and the face he would take with him to bed at night. Without even realizing it, this new face would become his only face - the face he hated to love and the face he loved to hate.

57. A SINGLE WORD

Nicky Jarvis' word was so loud that the moment it had escaped from his young lips, it changed into something much more than a single, simple word. Born from years of silence, the word took shape, absorbed the particles that made up the universe around it and ultimately grew in mass. This single word ceased to be a word the moment it had passed his teeth and ventured forward into a great new world. With its newfound weight quadrupling in size every fraction of every passing second, the word expanded across the interior of the massive circular room. When it came into contact with the solidly constructed walls of Prince Valkea's fortress, it effortlessly shattered them to pieces. As if a bomb had gone off inside the tower, the solid rock was blown to bits with violent ease, ripped apart as if made of paper. Shards of wall in all shapes and sizes were thrown violently through the air, some landing as far as three miles away. A thick cloud of partially disintegrated rock rose into the sky, rapidly spreading across the land, swallowing the courtyard below.

The word took on life and folded around the dangling body of Nicky's older brother. Carefully avoiding Tommy, this destructive new life form slammed into Prince Valkea with a force unlike anything this little world had ever seen. The blow was delivered with such strength and speed that Prince Valkea's ribs shattered on impact, folded inward and crushed his vital organs. In a fraction of a second, the bones in the Ochan's arms and legs were broken in so many places that they ceased to resemble bones at all. His face collapsed into itself and the floppy mess of what remained of the Prince's body was launched into the cloud-covered sky. Spinning like a whirly-bird, it arced just below the clouds before falling back on the ground. With a disgusting wet thud, the useless mess of broken bone and disfigured flesh that once resembled the Prince of Ocha at last came to rest amidst the throes of war spread out across courtyard. When it was done, the word traveled into the dark sky where it was devoured by the thick clouds.

At last the pressure in Nicky's head was gone. His muscles slowly released the built-up tension, his diminutive body relaxing once again. A refreshing coolness rolled across his skin, seeping into his still open mouth as Nicky reopened his eyes. The roof of the tower was gone. Above him only dark clouds sobbed tears of chilling rain. The formerly impenetrable walls no longer existed. The few solid pieces that managed to survive the blast had fallen back to earth miles away or were still airborne. The floor underneath him was covered in cracks as well, extending from his knees as if his body had been the epicenter of a massive explosion. Cracks of all shapes and sizes zigzagged across every stone in every square inch of the tower. The force of a single, solitary word had violently torn the structure's foundations apart, leaving it unstable and dangerous. Every single gust of wind – even those barely moving the trees of the red forest - caused it to sway noticeably from side to side. The creaks, crackles, and pops tearing at once sturdy craftsmanship could be heard in every direction.

Across from Nicky, Staci sat motionless. The table had been tossed to the heavens like everything else in the room. The blank expression on her face was not quite shock, not quite awe. This was something else entirely, something more. A sharp pain ran up the right side of her body and back down to the tip of her toes. Crawling as quickly as she dared, Staci reached Tommy's side at the same time as Nicky. The anxious and worried friends pawed at Tommy's lifeless form, trying to reignite a spark of life.

"Tommy, no! Please, Tommy, NO!" Staci screamed as she attempted to coax him back to the world of the living. She slapped him gently while she whispered, "Wake up Tommy...please wake up Tommy, please..." She barely managed a stammer, her face steaming with salty thick tears.

Above the children the heavens roared. Flashes of lightning angrily tore across the sky. The far off, rolling crackle of thunder shook the foundations of the wobbly tower. Thick slabs of stone pulled away from its sides, splashing into the mud below.

Not far from the threesome, a woozy confused Pleebo breathed in the air of consciousness once again. Struggling to move, he lifted his weary head and saw the sobbing children. Vague memories of what had occurred after Prince Valkea's assault flashed in the back of his mind. They were only snippets – brief bursts of light, color and shape - not one among them resembling a complete story. Painfully he managed to pull himself up. For the first time he noticed that the walls around him were gone. The floor underneath him was shaky, unstable and broken. Looking out over the horizon, Pleebo realized that the entire tower was swaying dangerously in the breeze. Though he had no idea what caused the destruction, he was aware that they were no longer in a safe place

He had to get the children out and he had to do it quickly.

His movements resembled that of a marionette being manipulated by an amateur puppeteer. Pleebo's body awkwardly jerked as he stood. Every joint hurt. Every single muscle was bruised and sore in ways that gave new meaning to the word pain. Large gashes on his back were bleeding quite heavily. Precious blood poured down his legs.

Broken and wobbly, he stumbled toward the kids. "Children...we have to go...we have to go right now..."

"NO! WE CAN'T LEAVE WITHOUT TOMMY!" Staci screamed. She was angry, confused and frightened.

For the first time since awakening, Pleebo noticed the motionless body of Tommy Jarvis. Though it was impossible to tell without closer examination, it seemed as if the boy was not breathing – as if he were dead. The floor creaked and shifted underneath his feet, nearly causing him to fall on his rear. They needed to get down from the tower. It was not going to say upright much longer.

"We're not leaving him," Staci shouted. "We'll take him with us!" Pleebo yelled. "We have to go now! It isn't safe here! Everyone, grab him!"Just as Pleebo and Nicky reached for Tommy's body, Staci shoved them aside. A very familiar, very otherworldly feeling of warmth had started to spread across her chest. Suddenly she knew why she was here. She could not and would not let Tommy die. She could save him.

335

The tingly warmth rolled from her chest and into her arm, melting across the contours of her hand, pouring like wonderfully warm syrup into the tip of her fingers. With a haunting glow of bright white light emanating from her body, she turned to Pleebo with pleading eyes.

In a tired, hopeful voice she begged, "Please...I can save him."

Even as the floor beneath his feet cracked, Pleebo let Tommy slide from his arms and backed away. Common sense told him to grab the three children and run, yet every ounce of his faith told him to do the exact opposite. Despite his better judgment, he chose to let the little girl do whatever it was that she thought she could do. If this decision meant the end of his life, then so be it. Pleebo wrapped the still sobbing Nicky in his arms, pulling the boy close.

Without an ounce of hesitation, Staci softly laid her delicate palms on Tommy's chest and gazed into the his closed eyes. Tommy had come for them. He had no doubt crossed mountains and forests and faced obstacles so bizarre and dangerous that the mere thought of them would have sent the average fourteen-year old running in fear. He had come for them. Despite everything, he had come to save them.

The light from her fingertips slowly crept along Tommy's body. Wonderful memories of the time they had spent together years ago tickled in her mind's eye. Like warm butterflies, the images fluttered around her head, down her neck and into her chest. Once there, they folded themselves around her heart, molding their beautifully colored wings to meet its exact contours, enveloping the beating mass of life-giving muscle, ultimately becoming one and the same. Closing her eyes, Staci smiled. The light pouring from her fingertips not only devoured Tommy's body but spread out in every direction. It quickly moved over Pleebo and Nicky, swallowing them in its transcendent glow. From there it moved forward like a beautiful liquid poured into a container. Across the floor, down the sides of the tower and into the courtyard, its journey continued. Seeping into every corner, every doorway, every nook and cranny, it eventually encompassed the castle, lighting the structure like a magnificent star.

For miles upon miles across the land of Fillagrou, the light could be seen and felt – bringing with it the greatest gift of all – the gift of life.

Enclosed completely by the wondrous glow, Tommy Jarvis slowly opened his eyes. The world around him suddenly seemed pure, warm, and white. His body floated atop the glow as if on water. It trickled into his every crevice, healed his wounds and gently cajoled him back into the world of the living. Above him, Staci's smiling face parted the tranquil sea of light as she opened her eyes and looked at him.

For the first time in years, Tommy smiled back.

The moment shared between the two friends did not last long. The light around them began to dim, hastening its retreat into Staci's hands. As quickly as it had returned, it left. When it had diminished completely, Staci's eyes rolled back into her head and she toppled into Tommy's arms, completely and totally spent.

With the amazing light now gone, the reality of the world outside once again enveloped them. The pouring rain, the darkening night and the unsteady structure underneath their feet were things that now pushed their way to the forefront. Pleebo had only a second to come to terms with the fact that, like Tommy, his wounds as well as Nicky's, were also healed. Somehow the tiny little girl had repaired them. It made no sense, yet somehow she had done it. Briefly an image of his grandfather's words, of the prophecy and the end of the war that had taken so much from him poked its way into his head. Like the recently reanimated Tommy Jarvis, Pleebo afforded himself the briefest of smiles.

He was jarred back to reality when the floor underneath him began to give way. Like dominos, the failure of a single set of stones would cause to rest to crumble. The entire tower collapsed to the ground. The deep, awful sound of plummeting stone and mortar filled the night air. Before any of them could react to this new twist of circumstance, Pleebo and the children were falling. Gravity tugged them into a world of dirt, smoke and fractured rock. The thick, angry darkness greedily swallowed them whole.

58. ARMY OF THE DEAD

Ochan reinforcements converged on the fortress like a swarm of angry insects. In stark contrast to the lackadaisical, bored and unprepared soldiers stationed inside its walls, this was a much more impressive, appropriate show of Ochan strength. It was not simply their massive numbers but their preparedness for battle and hunger for war that chilled the spirit. Every soldier was armed to the teeth. Each was energized by the first real opportunity for battle afforded them in years. A feeling of excitement moved from soldier to soldier, growing stronger with every passing moment.

The majority of Ochans rode on a number of large, angry creatures of varying size and shape. Each one had been taken unceremoniously from their home world, tamed and forced into an existence serving the Ochan nation. Some had three legs, some four, some had long necks and some had no necks whatsoever. The beasts were as heavily armored and blood thirsty as were the soldiers seated atop. The already darkened sky grew darker still as regiments of soldiers perched on the flying creatures equally as diverse as their non-airborne counterparts swooped into the courtyard to join in the fray.

The massive force moved with incredible precision, attacking from every possible angle. Some made their way into the fortress through hidden entrances, while others chose to scale the massive walls. Many simply came in through the main entrance.

To call the sight terrifyingly impressive would be a gross understatement.

The addition of these well-trained, battle-ready soldiers had an immediate effect on the course of the slave revolt raging inside. Outnumbered twenty to one, the small chance the surviving slaves may have had was erased in an instant. In a matter of minutes, nearly all of them were wiped out. The lifeless corpses floating in puddles of water stained with blood was a dark testimony to the greatest slave revolt the war had ever seen. What had been an uprising on inspiring levels now resembled an act of genocide.

The Lieutenant had handed Zanell over to General Thrax. She sat on the General's snarling, foul-breathed Megalot and sadly watched as the prisoners were outnumbered, overrun and slaughtered.

General Thrax considered murdering the disgusting Fillagrou female after he had ordered the Lieutenant to join the battle. A part of him, though, wanted her to watch the slaves die. There would be ample time to kill her later. Better that she was taught the lesson before putting to an end her pitiful existence. .

"It would seem that this little revolt is being put down rather quickly...what a shame. My men were hoping for a bit more resistance." The aged General snarled sarcastically as he watched the battle play itself out. He wore a pair of thick glasses that also functioned like a pair of binoculars.

Zanell did not need a special lens to see what was happening. In fact, she did not even need to look at the madness. For her, what was happening below had already happened and would happen again. It was a confusing paradox of time that she did not fully understand but had come to accept. General Thrax removed his binocular glasses, smiled and sighed deeply. His soldiers were performing well. The uprising would be over sooner than he had anticipated. When word of the quick victory eventually reached the King, he would no doubt receive a royal commendation, possibly even a medal. But part of him wished that he could be in the melee, fighting alongside his Ochan comrades, his blade slicing into the flesh of the worthless sleaze. Unfortunately, those days were behind him. He was a General now. His place was to watch from a distance, giving orders for others to follow, rather than taking orders himself. This was where Ocha needed him and this was where he would remain.

A contented smile stretched across his face as he looked at Zanell. "I would have thought scum like you would have learned the futility of actions such as these at this point...ah...well, I suppose I should have expected nothing less. Intelligence is a quality so many of you lack. Trying to beat it into you kind over these past years has proven to be an impossible task."

Zanell smiled softy, teetering on the brink of laughter.

"HA! My point exactly!" The General chuckled. "Even now, as your people drown in buckets of their own bile and blood, you smile at me like a buffoon. Your idiocy would anger me, female...if it were not so very sad."

341

The sound of a massive explosion suddenly filled the air. The grin on the General's face instantly disappeared as he tried to see what had happened.

Zanell's smile widened.

The sheer size of the explosion had forced every Ochan soldier fighting in the courtyard to take notice. In near perfect synchronization, their heads turned just in time to see the walls of the tower blown apart by a massive, unbearably bright light. Gigantic blocks of stone were tossed in every direction, some of them disappearing into the clouds, while others fell back to earth, very nearly crushing those who stood in its path. A heavy cloud of smoke sprinkled with dangerous debris spread across the sky, blocking the dark cloud, covering the courtyard in a dusty grayish haze. From the cloud of scattered stone and sand fell the wildly flailing body of Prince Valkea. Without bone or internal musculature, the floppy mess of a form splashed in a puddle of muddy water. Though his face was barely recognizable, the Ochan soldiers instantly noticed the delicate royal engravings on what remained of his shattered armor, as well as the elaborate royal designs on his dirty, ripped robes. The awful blob of disgusting flesh sprawled out in front of them was their Prince. It could be no other.

Word of Prince Valkea's fate quickly spread. A deafening hush cut into the sounds of war, slowly making its way throughout the courtyard. The thin layer of dust slowly settled as the soldiers stared unbelievingly at the gnarled remains of their leader. Some who needed further confirmation cautiously approached the body. Within moments the group of soldiers surrounding the corpse numbered in the hundreds, their numbers swelling quickly. Word of the Ochan Prince's demise spread like a virus, passed from whispered hush to eager ear, filling their hearts with a very foreign feeling - dread.

"It's happening again!" A soldier screamed, pointing at the tower.

In unison the soldiers watched as a hauntingly beautiful and terrifying glow spilled over the sides of the half-broken tower like a frothy foam cresting over the top of a goblet.

"COVER!" A single voice bellowed from among the Ochan masses.

Instinctively they ducked, covering themselves with their shields. Moving with astounding speed, the light spread across the courtyard, melting over the frightened, uncertain soldiers and everything else within its path. While the light had no effect on the Ochans, its effect on the fallen slaves was pronounced. Seeping into their wounds and spreading through their bodies, it healed the injured and breathed life into those recently dead. Creeping into every hallway and through every door, the strange light found those that it deemed worthy, filling their bodies with its potent, life-giving warmth. One by one, the dead and injured alike opened their empty eyes and breathed in freshness and strength they had not experienced in years.

The light covered the fortress completely and moved across the flatlands, heading toward General Thrax and Zanell.

Removing his glasses, General Thrax stared blankly at the approaching wave of frightening brightness. The stunned General quietly muttered, "What...manner...of...magic?"

The instant the light began to fold over his body, General Thrax tugged back on the reins of the Megalot, causing the beast to recoil. The colossal creature lurched onto its hind legs, shaking its thick torso wildly, tossing Zanell into a thick patch of brush.

After the light had returned to the shaky tower, the confused Ochan soldiers peeked cautiously from underneath their shields. Patting down their bodies while searching for injuries that the fearsome glow might have caused, they realized they had not been harmed. Looking around in bewilderment, the Ochan soldiers noticed that the prisoners they had just killed were rising up from the muddy ground, their wounds healed, their bodies no longer showing signs of starvation or hardship or injuries of any kind.

"The dead...the dead...the army of the dead rise!" One frightened soldier managed to sputter as he raised his sword to defend himself against the newly reborn threat. The soldiers had no idea what was happening but their warrior instincts prepared them for combat once more.

Before the battle could begin anew, the foundation of the heavily damaged massive tower degenerated. Collapsing inward on itself, the immense structure crumbled to the ground. Soldiers and the confused reanimated slaves immediately scurried for cover. A cloud of dust and debris shot into the rainy sky like the mushroom cloud aftermath of an atomic bomb as the tower tumbled. It blocked the clouds, spread across the courtyard and shaded everything in a deep gray, concrete haze.

For a more than a minute, it was impossible to see beyond a few feet. Soldiers staggered awkwardly through the dust, partially blinded, coughing violently as it clogged their lungs. The rubble of the fallen structure stretched across the fortification. Soldiers who had not been quick enough to get out of the way were buried beneath a torrent of falling stone. The sudden, incredibly violent blast had caused a large section of the castle to become unstable as well. The sound of cracking stone and steel, mixed with the confused barks of Ochan soldiers, filled the night air, echoing into the clouds.

The first fortress constructed on Fillagrou land, a towering example of Ochan superiority and the residence of the son of the great King, lay in a shambles. For Ochan soldiers and prisoners, a sight such as this seemed impossible. To see it fall was unbelievable. This was a moment some had spent a lifetime dreaming of while others had dreaded the possibility.

Through a cloud of smoky debris, a single Ochan noticed an odd glow coming from the mountain of rubble where the tower had once stood. Others quickly noticed the hauntingly familiar glow and wondered what could possibly happen next. When the dust had settled, the cloud around the glow fluttered away, exposing it at last to the hordes of gaping onlookers. Hovering five feet above the highest slab of broken stone was a massive ball of white light, the glowing sphere blinding.

Barely visible within its center were Pleebo, Tommy, Staci and Nicky.

59. A HASTY RETREAT

Just as soon as Tommy had been awakened by Staci's healing touch, the floor beneath him gave way and gravity pulled him down into a black abyss of sound and fury. Swallowed whole by the cloudy painful darkness, the peculiarly familiar sensations crawled out from somewhere deep inside the boy so quickly that it seemed to be instinct rather than conscious thought. Instantly reaching their boiling point, the sensations frothed over the tip of his fingers. Instead of leaping wildly as had happened before, the powerful light gleamed and emanated from his pores, then immediately folded back. When it reached out, the light snatched Staci, Nicky and Pleebo, pulling their tumbling bodies back toward Tommy, encasing the four of them in a protective bubble of energy.

Shards of falling stone and wood collided with the glowing sphere as a cloud of destructive, dangerous debris rose up around them. No matter what wreckage collided with the sphere's crackling, super-heated exterior, it was either evaporated or sent bouncing in the opposite direction.

Hunched over on his hands and knees, Pleebo looked below him and saw only a wall of inconceivably bright light. The weight of his entire body was resting on pure light – as if it had form – as if it were solid. Over the past few days, Pleebo had slowly become accustomed to strange occurrences. Yet with each new one, he had found himself more astounded than the last. The experience of sitting inside what was essentially a glow was unlike anything he could have imagined – the unreal made real. Floating beneath his feet was young Tommy Jarvis. With his hands at his side, his eyes closed and his body lit up like the center of a Fillagrou sun, the boy looked almost God-like. It was only a matter of days since Pleebo had first met Tommy Jarvis. From the moment he laid eyes on the boy that afternoon in the red forest, something inside had told him that Tommy was special – that he was more than he appeared. The glowing mass of astounding crackling energy was no longer just a boy. It was something more. This thing before him now was one of The Five – the realization of his grandfather's stories. It was something special and new, something different...and something good.

It was going to save them all – this he knew.

With the dust of the collapsing structure cleared, the glowing sphere floating above the huge piles of rubble was exposed to the shocked onlookers in the courtyard. The ball of pure light and energy floated slowly over the debris of the fallen tower, past the heads of the gaping crowd and eventually touched down gently in the mud on the opposite side. The sphere disappeared gradually, the light retreating once again into Tommy's hands. The group found themselves standing firmly on solid ground. Though the glow surrounding him had dimmed, the remaining energy in Tommy's hands hummed softly. It was still there and it was ready. Slowly Tommy opened his eyes. A wall of confused and shocked Ochan soldiers stood in front of him. Behind him and to his right and left stood even more. Their swords were lowered, hanging loosely at their sides. By the looks on their faces, it was obvious that some of them would never come to terms with what they had just seen.

Nearly all of the soldiers had experienced magic on some level before. The war had introduced them to a wide variety of species, some of which practiced magic regularly and others that had simply showed a mastery over science that was often confused for magic. Though it was rarely talked about, many believed that the great King Kragamel himself had often dealt in the dark, forbidden arts. Magic on this level though – magic the likes of which they had just experienced firsthand – was unheard of.

Tommy slowly lowered his hands while an ominous glow from inside his skull lit his eyes. With slow, deliberate steps, he moved toward the Ochan soldiers. With each step forward the Ochans stepped back. With every passing second, the otherworldly energy emanating from his body grew brighter.

Pleebo pulled Nicky and Staci protectively close, keeping them together and next to Tommy. Never in his life had he imagined that he would be surrounded by so many Ochan soldiers and still be alive. Not only was he alive, his very presence seemed to terrify the soldiers. Every drop of falling rain evaporated when it came in contact with Tommy. Puddles beneath his feet transformed into grayish plumes of steam. Tommy stopped, extended his arm and slowly opened his hand, pointing his glowing palm toward the soldiers standing before him. A deep hush fell over the crowd.

With seriousness well beyond his years soaked into every word, Tommy calmly recommended, "I suggest you guys head home."

Taken aback by the confident tone in the firecracker boy's voice, the Ochans exchanged brief, confused glances. The pink-skinned creature standing before them was undoubtedly powerful, but they were the toughest of the tough – Ochan warriors born and bred. Incredible magic notwithstanding, they were not about to simply turn tail and run. The idea of considering retreat even momentarily tickled the funny bone of more than one of them. As was bound to happen, their fear quickly turned to annoyance, annoyance turned to anger and from the anger erupted peals of laughter.

Tightening the grip on his sword, the highest-ranking soldier closest to Tommy moved to within inches of the boy, a cocky swagger in his step. "Your magic doesn't frighten us, child. An Ochan warrior fears nothing…least of all a creature wielding a paltry bag of parlor tricks. Magic or not, you are outnumbered fifty to one. Heed my words, child. There will be no retreat." Lifting his sword, the Ochan extended it, pointing the tip between Tommy's glowing eyes. "I assure you, we will make your death a slow and painful one for the mere suggestion alone."

Without any warning, the glow around Tommy's face doubled in intensity and expanded to swallow half the soldier's blade, melting the solid steel to a substance that resembled dripping butter. The soldier quickly pulled his weapon out of the glow, holding the scalding tip inches from his face. Despite the smug confidence of his words just moments ago, a chill of absolute terror went through his spine. It traveled down his legs and into his feet, freezing them in place.

The glow around Tommy's body tripled in size as he whispered through the great ball of light, "I'm sorry you feel that way."

From the tree line across the flatland, General Thrax sat on his Megalot and had watched the situation unfold through his binocular glasses. In less than ten minutes he had witnessed the dead come back to life, saw the Prince's tower fall, and watched the glowing boy with his cohorts float to safety in a protective bubble. Now it was that same radiating child that stood defiantly in the face of an entire army. Though it pained his Ochan pride to admit it, the image was downright terrifying.

Whoever this child was, wherever he came from, he was clearly dangerous.

He watched one of his soldiers approach the boy and exchange words. The glow emanating from the pink-skinned child's body fluttered in lightning quick intervals, sending intense bursts into the clouds. It expanded rapidly. From the palm of the boy's hand an astoundingly large wall of light sprung to life, extending miles into the air, bathing the courtyard. The massive wall of snarling brightness advanced in every direction. Pouring over soldiers and buildings like molten steel, it hungrily gobbled everything in its path. Moving with terrifying speed, the humming whiteness pressed forward, up an over what was left of the outer fortress walls, across the flatlands, and toward the tree line. The Megalot bucked wildly and almost tossed General Thrax to the forest floor. The rapidly advancing wall of light was now less than a hundred and fifty feet away, rolling over trees and plants, and great acres of land. Instinctively the General turned away, bracing himself for impact. It dissipated mere inches from the back of his head, receding back to where it had originated.

Time passed silently, as time tends to do moments before one thinks they are about to die. His eyes closed tightly, his teeth clamped together with a vice-like grip. General Thrax held his breath and remained still as he anticipated his eventual end. The passing seconds rolled into minutes and the General wondered why he was not dead. He looked again at the fortress, trying to see exactly what had happened. The light that had encompassed his field of vision just moments earlier was gone. Not a trace of it remained. The ground around him looked the same and the trees still stood. The spooked Megalot beneath him gnawed angrily on the steel harness between its enormous, flat yellow teeth. The fortress, too, seemed to have no additional damage.

Much to his horror, the entire Ochan army that had been sent to put an end to the slave uprising was dead.

The terrifying magic seemed to have spared everything except his army.

Grotesquely spread across the courtyard and grounds remained the smoking carcasses of the heavily armored soldiers Some were charred so badly that they were barely recognizable. In the center of a circle where three hundred Ochan corpses smoldered stood the glowing boy, like a demon born from the fires of the underworld. The General had never in his life witnessed such an incredible show of destructive force. It was an insanely unreal concept better suited to the wild imagination of children and the crazy prophecies of species less evolved than his.

Never in his life had he known the true meaning of the word terror - until now.

Tugging back hard on the reins of the Megalot, General Thrax turned the creature. A group of at least a hundred and fifty

Ochan reserves sat scattered among the forest, waiting to be given the order to join the battle.

Without a moment's hesitation, General Thrax urgently barked out the one order he had yet to give during the whole of his illustrious military career. "RETREAT!"

On cue, the Megalot took off at full speed, kicking mounds of soppy mud and gray foliage with every step. The soldiers paused for a moment. They had never been given an order of retreat and reacted with a considerable amount of uncertainty. One by one, they adhered to the General's call, falling into formation, following him into the forest.

Zanell's head popped up from behind a heavily leafed bush as she watched the massive Ochan force scurry away and disappear into the dark trees. She had seen and experienced this moment in her head long before it actually happened, yet an unexpected emotion washed over her. The feeling was more than happiness, joy or pride. It was something else entirely. It was something so warm and good that no word would ever truly do it justice.

Breathing deeply she attempted to control her happiness, calming down. Silently she reminded herself that this was only the beginning. There were more moments to come - moments that would bring with them the highest of highs and the lowest of lows - moments that would make this one single victory seem like a footnote in the greater story of all things.

Try as she might to steady her emotions, she failed.

Instead, she opted to let the amazing feeling wash over her and rinse away the nastiness that had been the majority of her youth. Zanell had spent a very long time not truly knowing a feeling such as this and she was not going to let anything as frustrating as common sense ruin it.

60. THE UNLIKELY FAMILY

When the massive wall of humming, crackling energy had retreated into his body, Tommy Jarvis opened his eyes and scanned the disaster area around him. Scattered arbitrarily in every direction was row after row of burnt Ochan corpses, piled on top of each other as far as he could see. This was both terrifying and satisfying to behold. The idea that he had killed so many so easily, with little more than a flick of his wrist, sent a bolt of chilling panic to his very core. The knowledge that any one of the soldiers would have done the same to him, his brother or Staci eased a feeling of regret. He had not had a choice. It was either him or them; it was as simple as that. Tommy decided this was sound reasoning. It had to be. The alternative was something he was not prepared to face.

Behind him, a shell-shocked Pleebo released Nicky and Staci from his protective arms. The three of them silently absorbed the aftermath of Tommy's burst of explosive power. The rain that had been steadily falling since the outset of battle tapered off to a soft drizzle. The fortress reeked of burning flesh and stale Ochan blood mixed with stagnant muddy water. Soft puffs of white steam rose from the various patches of scalding Ochan corpses as they were cooled by the soft drizzle. Nicky timidly approached his older brother, his feet sinking a good three to four inches into the mud. He tenderly placed his hand on Tommy's shoulder.

In a tiny, mousy voice he whispered, "Tommy?"

The familiar sound instantly woke Tommy from his trance. The pitch, the inflection, the child-like innocence with which it had been delivered registered with memories of happier times locked somewhere deep in the back of his mind. This was a voice he had not heard in years, a voice he had forgotten just how much he missed.

"Nicky?" Tommy asked to no one in particular, believing that he had been dreaming.

Tommy spun around and faced the person who had called him. With a boyish grin covering his wet face from ear to ear and globs of sweaty, stringy hair plastered to his filthy head stood his little brother.

"Nicky? Did you...did you just...?"

Nicky chuckled. "Hi, bro."

A wide smile spread across Tommy's face. He wrapped his arms around his little brother, lifting Nicky into the air while hugging him tightly. A laugh gurgled up from inside Tommy's belly. He thought he had forgotten how to laugh. The strange new sound moved into his chest, escaping his lips with an awkward, purely sweet honesty that he had not felt in years. A little voice in the back of his head pleaded for him to retreat into the safety of his quiet, brooding façade, but it was impossible. He chose not to think. He chose, instead, to simply feel. His brother had spoken for the first time in years. If any occasion was worthy of such a reaction, this was surely it.

Giggling softly, Nicky managed to pry himself from his older brother's grasp.

Almost apologetically he muttered, "You found me...thanks for finding me."

"Of course I found you." Tommy answered as a slight, warm smile spread across his face, "You're my brother...I'll always find you."

Staci joyfully approached the overjoyed duo. The infectiousness of the grin on Tommy's face had spread to her as well. Comforting warmth filled her cheeks, making them blush a deep red as she watched the boys enjoying their moment together.

Tommy looked knowingly at Staci. She had saved his life. Though the memories of the moment were still a bit clouded, he could vaguely remember the Prince choking him. He could recall the sharp pains in his neck, struggling to make the most of every tiny snippet of air leaking into his lungs, and failing. Then there was nothing but black. Pulling him gently out of the darkness, though, coaxing him back to life with a soft voice and a tender touch was his friend Staci. Staci's smile faded briefly when she saw Tommy walking toward her. Panic overwhelmed her as she froze. But this was not fear taking hold of her, this was something entirely different. Her breathing increased and her heart thumped twice as fast.

With a soulful, thankful voice Tommy whispered only two words while staring into her wide blue eyes. "Thank you."

For reasons she could not fully understand, Tommy's words caused her already flushed face to become redder still. With a barely audible snort, she giggled and turned her head away.

To alleviate her embarrassment she quickly joked, "Ya...well...somebody had to save your butt. Let's not go making a habit of it though...okay?"

"Look at that," Pleebo interrupted as he pointed past the mounds of Ochan corpses.

Just beyond the bodies of the fallen soldiers, groups of extremely confused slaves were making their way cautiously toward them. Prisoners were streaming from around corners, behind huge chunks of debris and through the many doors within the castle walls. Their numbers swelled well into the hundreds. Each seemed to understand that the little girl had given them life, though none could quite explain how. Most had witnessed firsthand how Tommy single-handedly put an end to hundreds of Ochan soldiers. Hushed whispers of prophecies and legends had been the only viable explanation for the otherwise unexplainable occurrences.

The mass of dumbfounded, thankful creatures circled the children. Their hands patted various parts of their filthy bodies, marveling at the fact that their injuries had been healed completely. Tearful hugs were readily given as family and friends were reunited. The moment was poignant, powerful and unforgettable. A feeling, both wondrous and foreign, spread across the group like the warmth of the cresting sun in the early morning.

That feeling was hope.

A sturdy, familiar voice rose from crowd. "Step aside! Step aside, please! Make room, my friends. Make room!"

In response to the deep, burly instructions, the sea of resurrected slaves parted. As the last of them stepped aside, none other than the King of the Tycarian people, the holder of the sacred cup of Peladrov and the keeper of the great Mud Chalice, King Walcott Shellamennes, came into view.

With a grin on his tired, wrinkly face, he nodded to Tommy. "Well done, lad...well done, indeed."

Tommy smiled, happy to see that the enormous turtle man was alive. Following close behind King Walcott, trying desperately to wipe massive amounts of dirt off his shirt, was Owen Little.

In an annoyed voice, Owen mumbled, "My dad is going to kill me when he sees how dirty this thing is."

Behind Owen, Donald Rondage trudged into the the circle, stopping in front of Tommy, their faces inches apart. Staci's amazing healing powers had repaired the injury to his shoulder, leaving the boy in perfect health. Donald breathed in deeply, his eyes rolling back in his head as he over-exaggerated his annoyance.

Reluctantly he held his hand out to Tommy, "Go ahead...take it," he as he motioned for Tommy to shake his hand. "Come on, loser...I'm not going to stand here all day looking like an idiot. Shake my hand...let's get it over with."

Tommy smiled when he took hold of Donald's hand. Donald squeezed tightly, pulling him close.

Quietly he whispered, "Don't go thinking this makes us friends or anything...cause it doesn't...at all. You're still a weirdo."

Last to make their way through the ecstatic sea of slaves was the pink woman, with tiny Roustaf standing triumphantly on her shoulder. Bringing up the rear was Nestor Rockshell.

Nestor stopped near King Walcott, the two of them exchanging knowing glances.

"I'm pleased you could join us for the victory celebration, old friend," King Walcott said, patting Nestor's shell gently with his huge flat hand.

"I wouldn't miss it for the world, Sire," Nestor responded with a grin.

Pleebo moved quickly toward Roustaf, happy to see his friend alive and well.

"Pleebs! I never thought I'd be so happy to see your butt-ugly face again," the tiny red man bellowed. "Hey Pleebs...hey, wait...let me introduce you to someone." Fluttering his wings, Roustaf bowed cordially while hovering a few inches from the pink woman's face. "Pleebs, this is Tahnja...she's a Grilgamorph. Tahnja, this is Pleebs, or Pleebo, or whatever...in any case, he's one of my oldest and dearest friends."

Pleebo smiled at Roustaf, amused at the obviously lovelorn look on his friend's face. Keeping his mouth shut for the time being, he gazed at Tahnja. "Nice to meet you, Tahnja."

"A pleasure meeting you, Pleebo."

Standing together, surrounded by the cheerful, freed slaves of a hundred different species from a hundred different lands, the entire group found the moment humbling. Together they had done the impossible. They had shared moments and seen things they would never forget. The situations that had threatened to destroy them brought them closer together. Unlikely alliances had led to unlikely companions.

Unlikely companions had forged an unlikely family.

Slowly cheers rose from the ocean of slaves. The festive sound of laughter, the rhythmic clap of hands and the niceties of hopeful chatter slowly built to an excited crescendo that pushed the dark clouds away, bringing an end to the light drizzle. A fortress that had been accustomed only to cries of agony and the deafening silence attributed to the aftermath of death was filled with the joyous and hopeful sounds of freedom.

After shoving his way through the cheering hordes, Fellow Undergotten finally moved into the center of the circle. His eyes locked immediately onto Staci and Nicky. Staci spotted the fish-man from the corner of her eye and frantically tapped Nicky on the shoulder. A moment later both children were charging at him full speed, crashed into his body and grabbed whatever limb was available, hugging tightly. Their exuberance very nearly knocked Fellow into the mud.

In-between chuckles he managed to say, "Whoa, whoa, take it easy! I'm happy to see you guys too, but if you're not careful I'm going to end up with another broken leg." Putting his hands on Staci's shoulders, Fellow gazed into her soulful face. "That's twice now that you've brought me back to life, kiddo," he jokingly said , "Now, you aren't going to go holding this over my head expecting something in return, are you?"

Staci did not answer as she wrapped her arms tightly around his midsection.

For now, every living creature in the courtyard made a conscious effort not to think about the fact that the Ochan forces were by no means defeated, or that the city of Tipoloo had been destroyed, or that there would undoubtedly be repercussions for the death of Prince Valkea. There would be ample opportunity to deal with these problems later. Now was the time to simply enjoy what they had been given, no matter how fleeting it might ultimately prove to be. As a collective they would squeeze every ounce of hope and happiness that they could from this moment.

Their decision to enjoy it for all for what it was worth was not only the correct one, it was the only one.

61. SAYING GOODBYE

The trip back through the red forest was uneventful. For the first time in more years than most could remember, the entire Ochan army had been pulled from patrols. As it had been before the madness of war, the red forest was quiet. The soft breeze no longer carried with it a feeling of overwhelming dread. The million glorious shades of red contained within its foliage seemed brighter, as if the forest also appreciated the exceptional calm. For Pleebo and Zanell, the ability to walk above ground without fear proved to be an almost religious experience. Their mother had often referred to the forest as the heart of the Fillagrou people. With the arrival of the Ochan army and the onset of war, the ventricles connecting them to that heart had been cut. The forest had turned from something beautiful into something scary. Of all the terrible losses their race had suffered, this was arguably the worst .

After a couple of days' hike, King Walcott, Roustaf, Tahnja, Fellow and Nestor left the group and escorted the freed slaves home while Pleebo and, Zanell still traveled with the children. Although the vast majority of the underground city had been laid to waste, there remained sections of Tipoloo that the dark army had not discovered during their attack. There were tunnels and corridors filled with starving, anguished refugees. The freed slaves also carried much needed food and supplies that had been looted from the fortress ruins to share with the suffering masses. It was here that the process of rebuilding would begin. From their new hiding place they would formulate a plan of attack. Leading them while adding another name to his already lengthy title would be none other than the King of the Tycarian people, the holder of the sacred cup of Peladrov, the keeper of the great Mud Chalice and the leader of the New Tipoloo Rebellion, King Walcott Shellamennes. Wielding a surgical knife rather than a broad sword, the inhabitants of New Tipoloo planned to work in cells, using the element of surprise with raids, sabotage and harassment against the Ochan army, rather than fighting them on the battlefield. Despite the fact that it still seemed to be an impossible undertaking, never in the history of the war had the enemies of the Ochan nation felt so confident about their chances. They would defy the odds and they would achieve victory. The revered prophesy had not been forgotten.

"Well, Mr. Owen, I suppose this is where we part ways," King Walcott said with just a hint of sadness as he gazed at the diminutive form of Own Little. "I will miss you, my young friend. You were my original traveling companion and we've shared many incredible adventures."

While wiping a few annoying smudges from his glasses, Owen glanced at King Walcott, a look of confusion on his face, "Umm...ya, sure...I'll miss you too...I guess"

Of all the children, Owen was least likely to miss Fillagrou. In fact, he was anxious to get home. Giant turtles, lizard men with swords, invisibility, exploding castles and dead bodies – he had seen enough of it. He wanted to go home, crawl into his bed, pull the covers up to his neck and sleep for days. Getting wedgies from the Delaney brothers on his way to school now seemed like the absolute greatest thing in the world.

After patting him gently on the head with his paw, King Walcott mussed Owen's hair, adding thoughtfully, "Ahhh yes...incredible adventures, indeed, Mr. Owen...incredible adventures, indeed."

Sighing deeply, King Walcott turned to Donald Rondage, his expression changing rapidly from whimsy to serious. "As for you, young Donald..."

Donald faced the Tycarian King, his heart beating hard; he was expecting the ancient reptile to crack him in the face for all the SLOW-amennes jokes.

"You, young man..." King Walcott stated gruffly as he stood over the boy, his enormous shadow cloaking Donald in darkness, "You, my boy...fought with honor, and for it...you have earned my respect."

Extending his paw, King Walcott tipped his head slightly. Hesitantly Donald grasped the massive paw, shaking it up and down. Though he would never admit it to anyone, least of all King Walcott, Donald had grown to like the elderly turtle-man. He was going to miss him.

Nicky and Staci had wrapped their arms around Fellow Undergotten once again, squeezing as tightly as they could. Fellow patted their backs gently. Feeling his eyes water, he softly pushed the children away, wiping away a tear. He was going to miss the children greatly; it was not because of everything they had done for him and rest of the hapless souls that had been locked within Prince Valkea's fortress – no, it was much more. He was going to miss them because somewhere along the way they had become his friends.

"Are we ever going to see you again?" Nicky asked timidly.

Letting the question rest in his brain for a moment, Fellow realized that he did not have an answer. While a large part of him wanted to see the children again, another part wished they would stay away. A major battle had been won, yes – the war though – the war was far from done. In their own world, far away from the death and sadness of war, they would be safer.

"I don't know, kiddo…I'll tell you what though…no matter what happens…I'll never forget either of you. My people believe that every single thing in the universe was born of a single, solitary moment. Everything from the oceans to the trees to you and I come from the same place…that we're all connected. This means that it doesn't matter how far away we are from those we care about, we're a part of them."

Though the idea made Staci smile, she still cried.

Fellow pulled both children close, letting Staci sob into his shirt. He would miss them more than they would ever know.

"Alright! Enough with the wishy-washy, ya mooks!" Roustaf blared. "We've got to put a little hop in our get-a-long if we want to make it to the tunnels by nightfall. Everyone is gonna miss everyone, yadda, yadda, yadda, so on and so forth…does that about cover it? Good…let's get going then…I haven't cried since my pet

363

Grog died when I was a kid, and I'm not about to let you scrubs break the streak."

Everyone said their goodbyes and the two groups went their separate ways. Zanell, Pleebo and the children continued on for another day, until they at last located the tiny, barely noticeable puddle that had brought the children to Fillagrou.

Staring at the puddle disbelievingly, while shaking his head, Pleebo faced his sister, "Tell me again how you knew exactly where this thing was?"

Zanell chuckled softly, shrugged her shoulders, and smiled. During the course of the journey through the forest, she had tried repeatedly to describe to her older brother just what it was like to have the Elder's sight beyond sight, but he was not able to understand.

"Let me tell you, sis...it's not going to be easy coming to terms with the fact that you're an Elder...I mean, you're younger than me." Pleebo added jokingly. He glanced at the tiny puddle just beyond the tip of his long, flat toes and shook his head. "You guys really came here through this little thing, huh?"

Stepping beside him, Donald looked at the perfectly still water, the mid-day sunlight dancing across its surface.

"Yep, that's the one," he confirmed, mildly annoyed.

On the other side of this miniscule, nondescript, barely-there puddle was home. Donald had slowly started to resign himself to the fact that he was never going to see it again. He had come to terms with the idea that his family, his friends and everything he once knew was lost to him. Now, only minutes away from returning home, a part of him wished that he could stay, even if it meant spending the rest of his life fighting six-foot tall lizard-men with swords longer than his entire body.

Owen stepped beside Donald, gently dipping the tip of his sneaker into the puddle. "How do we know this is even going to get us home? The first thing I did after arriving here was dive back down and tried to swim back. Obviously it did not work."

"The doorway will take you home this time," Zanell assuredly told him. "It chooses to let through who it needs to let through, when they need to be let through. It's just the way it works."

"Wait a minute…that doesn't even make any sense. How do you know that?" Owen asked, annoyed by the cryptic nature of her answer.

Zanell chuckled at the innocence of his question.

After trying to think of a simple way to help Owen understand, and coming up with nothing, she responded simply, "I just do."

Before Owen could ask another question, Donald interrupted, "Alright then, that's good enough for me."

With a gentle shove, Donald pushed Owen into the puddle. Like a stone, the wiry boy sank underneath the murky waters and never resurfaced. The others stood staring at Donald, with a shockingly amused look on their faces.

"Oh come on…somebody had to do it. He would have stood here all day long blabbering on and on." Donald chimed in, while backing toward the puddle's edge.

Doing his best to maintain his veil of toughness, he lifted his hand, waving to Pleebo and Zanell. "Well, it was a blast meeting you guys, getting knocked around, punched in the face and having an arrow shot through my shoulder. I hope you understand if I don't invite you to my mom's place for Christmas dinner, though." Leaping back, he fell in with a splash.

The puddle waters settled when Donald did not return to the surface. Tommy tapped Nicky and Staci on the shoulders. "You two go next."

Staci approached the puddle first. She sat on the ground and slowly slid feet first into the water until her head was bobbing just above the surface. "Ooh, that's cold!" She shrieked through clenched, chattering teeth. Pinching her nose and closing her eyes tightly she nervously added, "See you on the other side."

After taking a deep breath, Staci slowly sank beneath the water.

Nicky went under much the same way, his tiny hand waving goodbye to no one in particular as he descended into the chilly abyss leading home. Tommy approached the puddle's edge and stopped. As much as he understood that he could not stay in Fillagrou, the world waiting for him offered very little. Here he had made a difference. He proved to be something more than he had ever thought possible. He was needed here. Once home he would again be at the mercy of his father. Home would bring only suffering, hardship, frustration and a wealth of memories that the past week had helped him to momentarily forget. At home there would be no powers – at home there would be no way out.

As if she could hear his private thoughts, Zanell told him, "You're needed there as much as you are here, Tommy...maybe even more."

Moving closely behind him, Tommy could feel her long, bony fingers resting on his shoulders.

She softly whispered into his ear. "If you only knew how special you really are, Tommy Jarvis...on any world. The gifts you have, the lives you have yet to touch...rest assured that your life is an important one, even when it may seem exactly the opposite.

There are different kinds of strength and power comes in many forms."

Zanell gently squeezed his shoulders and for some reason the gesture made Tommy feel better. There was something in her touch, something in the way her fingers moved that convinced him she did, in fact, understand what he was feeling.

"Will I ever see you again?" Tommy asked quietly, gazing down at his reflection rippling across the water.

Zanell paused for a moment as a sudden jolt of images flashed inside her head. She knew the ending to Tommy's story already. She had seen it a thousand times from a thousand different angles. She had analyzed the events leading to it and the consequences of it. She had immersed herself fully in its bittersweet nectar, allowing it to absorb into her every pore.

With a heavy head and warm heart she patted the boy's shoulder gently, whispering into his ear so softly that her words caressed the folds of his brain, easing the burden he had carried for so many years on his young back. "Indeed, you will."

When she stepped away, Tommy slowly lowered himself into the water. Floating neck deep, he looked one last time at Pleebo, Zanell and the unbelievable beauty of the alien landscape. Closing his eyes, he attempted to capture the image in his brain. He wanted to freeze this single moment in time and embed it forever, somewhere deep in his mind where he could visit it regularly, where he could call upon it when he needed it most. This place had changed him and like all things that have such a profound effect on a person, he was going to miss it.

Taking a deep breath and closing his eyes, Tommy slowly sank into the chilled water.

Pleebo's familiar voice however, brought him back to Fillagrou one last time. "Hey, Tommy..."

Opening his eyes Tommy glanced at Pleebo's rail-thin, pasty white body. Just beyond his head, the sun cut through the tree line, casting long, beautiful rays of light across the forest floor.

"To think, I was *thissssss* close to eating you guys after I met you." Pleebo joked. "Boy, my face would have been red."

Tommy chuckled while Pleebo laughed loudly at his own joke.

Once his laughter had subsided, he added with a heavy sigh, "Take care of yourself kid."

After a brief nod, Tommy again closed his eyes, took a deep breath and disappeared below the surface. Two measly pockets of air bubbled after he was fully submerged and then it was over. Pleebo and Zanell stood motionless for awhile, staring at the tiny unassuming puddle longingly, occasionally smiling and breathing deep.

Finally Pleebo broke the silence. "So what now, 'Nell?"

"I don't know."

"What do you mean you don't know? I thought you knew everything? I thought you could tell me what was happening on the surface of the sun?"

"Oh, I do…and I can…I thought maybe I'd leave it up to you, though. It would be nice if at least one of us was still able to enjoy the mystery of it all."

Pleebo thought deeply about the offer. "Alright, then. What if I were to say that I wanted to climb that tree right there and lay in the sun until nightfall?"

Zanell smiled at her brother sweetly. "I'd say it was the best idea I'd heard in a very long time."

62. THE MORE THINGS CHANGE...

The playground was quiet. Empty chain swings softly swayed back and forth in the summer breeze as the sun began its slow descent over a row of houses off in the distance. Weird little Tommy Jarvis was kicking at sporadic patches of grass sticking through the concrete of the sidewalk beneath his feet, on his way home from an hour of after-school detention. For a month and half, the trip home required a different route than it had before. Not long after returning home from Fillagrou, Tommy and Nicky had been placed in the care of a foster family on the opposite side of town until the State's case against their father came to a conclusion. Their foster parents, Mr. and Mrs. Williamson, were nice, older people, in their late fifties and early sixties respectively. They ate dinner at the dining table every night and insisted on lights out no later than nine. Edna Williamson liked to sew in her free time, while Ed enjoyed puttering around the backyard, never really getting anything of significance accomplished.

Ed and Edna – rest assured, the inherent comedy of their names was not lost on either of the Jarvis boys.

The Williamsons were normal, quiet people who led a normal, quiet life. While they seemed to have taken a liking to Nicky, his weird older brother was a nut they had yet to crack.

They were good people, though, and they were not giving up.

No concrete conclusions were ever really drawn by the authorities as to the whereabouts of the children for the week or so that they had been gone. The children had all agreed to lie, to claim they had spent the time wandering the woods together, like a weird mass-runaway cult. Only Owen Little had actually told the truth. In the end, it did not make any difference because no one had believed a word of his insane story of lizard-men, castles and underground cities dug by hand. In fact, the only thing telling the truth had accomplished for him was convincing his father that he needed therapy. He had been going twice a week ever since.

Tommy thought about Fillagrou since returning home more times than he could count. Often at night, he found himself wide-awake; memories of Pleebo or King Walcott made him grin for no apparent reason whatsoever. He missed them. He missed them a good deal and he wondered how they were doing. How was the war going? Were they alive? Were they dead? Were they hungry? The unanswered questions constantly gnawed at his brain like tiny bugs eating him from the inside. Two weeks after returning home, he had walked to the stream and dove in the water, just to see what would happen. Of course nothing did. Edna had made him dry off in the backyard that night when he returned home so that he would not drench her freshly-cleaned carpet.

Passing through the intersection of Beeker Avenue and Jefferson Street, Tommy readjusted the new backpack the Williamsons had purchased for him a week ago. It was a good backpack, sturdy construction, solid craftsmanship; the likelihood of it ripping anytime soon was small. After reaching the Neilsons' house on the corner of Cherrywood Lane, he came to an abrupt stop. The Williamsons' home was only a few blocks away – a single right turn, and he would be there in no more than ten minutes. He would no doubt be greeted by the confusing, tasty odor of whatever lavish, strange smelling meal Edna was cooking for dinner.

If he chose to turn left, the street would take him to his old home and to his father. Not a single day passed by without thoughts of his father entering his mind. When the authorities asked Tommy about the drawings they had found in his tree fort, he answered honestly. He gave the full story, with all its grisly details to a mousy, young-looking blond- haired counselor, very nearly bringing her to tears. He was not sure why he had decided to suddenly speak up. For years he had lied for his father and took the abuse; he had been alive but found little pleasure in life.

Maybe Fillagrou had changed him. Maybe he was different now – or maybe the time had just come.

When the authorities had arrived at the house to remove him and Nicky, to place them in foster care, it was a big spectacle. Neighbors watched from their porches, or hid behind the drapes in their living rooms. Gossipy chatter passed from one home to the next, into stores, businesses, and schools. Everyone knew at least a little of what had happened. Suddenly Tommy realized that everyone was looking at him differently. He had become a sideshow attraction - the poor boy everyone pitied. To this day,

Tommy hated seeing the looks on their faces but he understood that it was an unavoidable result of everything that had happened.

He could deal with it, because he had to.

Tommy had not seen Staci in weeks. Like everyone else in town, her parents had felt sorry for the Jarvis boys but wanted their daughter to have nothing to do with them. They convinced themselves that Tommy had brainwashed her, tricking her into running away. After going so long without seeing her face, Tommy realized that he missed her more than he had ever imagined he would.

As happy as he was to finally be away from his father, despite the new problems that came with it, Tommy missed his home. For every awful memory his father had burned into his soul or left clearly visible on his skin, there were equally beautiful memories of a time before his mother had died – of Christmas mornings, and bedtime stories, and laughter.

Home or the Williamsons – left or right? For little Tommy Jarvis, neither direction seemed fully appropriate.

"Hey, Tommy!" The voice came from somewhere behind, off in the distance. Tommy recognized it in an instant. Low, but squeaky, it was layered with a sticky-thick, oiliness, "Hey! Weirdo! Ya, I'm talking to you, freak! Where do you think you're going?!"

Nathan Gallagher - it had to be Nathan Gallagher. Nathan had been one of Donald Rondage's goons for years. Recently, though, he had branched out on his own.

Lowering his head, digging his chin into his chest, Tommy started walking as fast as he could, away from the voice.

"Hey, get back here, loser! Don't you walk away when I'm talking to you!"

Despite the fact that he was moving at an extremely brisk pace, Nathan must have been moving faster because his voice was quickly getting closer and louder.

Nathan came to a sliding stop in front of Tommy, the tires of his bike skidding on the sidewalk, leaving black streaks across the top of the cement. "I said…where do you think you're going, weirdo? No one told you that you could leave, so where the hell do you think you're going?"

Tommy froze as two more bicycles skidded behind him, killing any ideas that he might have had regarding retreat. He was surrounded by three foul-mouthed teenagers, hungry to pick on him for no other reason than the fact that he was different. Tommy chuckled to himself. How little things had changed.

Stepping off his bicycle, Nathan let it fall to the ground

Quickly he moved to within inches of Tommy's face, his stringy blonde hair hanging over his eyes like a big dopey dog. "You're new to this part of town, weirdo, so maybe you don't know that this is my street. If you want to walk on my street, you've got to pay the toll."

Nathan was trying his best to look intimidating, and to most other fourteen-year old children, he no doubt did. Weird little Tommy Jarvis, though, had seen it all. After abusive fathers, giant snarling beasts, and creatures four times his size wielding weapons covered in blood, a fifteen-year-old with a pimply face and braces simply was not going to have the same effect on him.

"Answer me, loser, or I'll beat your ass worse than your daddy does!" Nathan screamed, shoving Tommy hard in the chest. The blow caused Tommy to stumble, crashing into the bicycles of Nathan's goons, who instantly shoved him back toward their snarling, foul-mouthed leader. Soon Tommy was being pushed back and forth between the three laughing buffoons, his body bouncing from one angry set of hands to another like a hot potato. Out of nowhere, Nathan delivered a stiff right to Tommy's stomach. The force of the blow knocked the breath from Tommy's lungs, almost causing him to topple onto the concrete. Three months ago, Tommy would have allowed his legs to give way. Three months ago, he would have curled up on the cement and done his best to absorb the punishment.

Unfortunately for Nathan and his friends, this was not three months ago – nor was this the same weird little Tommy Jarvis.

Gritting his teeth, Tommy pulled the muscles in his legs tight. His hands curled into fists, his body lurching forward at full speed, smashing into Nathan's midsection and sending the pudgy brute on the grass. The other two goons were on him quickly, punching and kicking at whatever part of Tommy's thrashing body they could. Absorbing the blows, Tommy managed to push one of them onto his fallen bicycle. The boy let out a yelp as the pedal dug into his spine, sending a sharp pain cascading throughout his lower body. The other boy landed a stiff right to the side of Tommy's face, catching him completely off guard. One of Tommy's legs went limp, dropping him to one knee. His head was spinning. The pain in his jaw had spread to his ear but Tommy ignored the feeling and regained control.

No matter what these angry, simple-minded oafs threw at him, they were not going to hurt him. They could not hurt him, because he was not going to allow it – not anymore.

The moment the burly thug threw another punch, Tommy ducked underneath it and wrapped his arms around the boy's legs, tackling him to the ground. Like a snarling, angry dog, Tommy sat on the fallen boy's chest, dropping punches to his arms, shoulders, and face. Nathan wrapped his arms around Tommy's neck, pulling the manic boy off his teary-eyed cohort.

"Huh!? You think you're some kind of tough guy weirdo!? Huh?! Is that what you think!? I'll show you, loser! I'll show you who's tough!" Nathan screamed wildly, tightening the chokehold he had around Tommy's neck.

Tommy tried to squirm free, but Nathan's choke was deep, pressing against his throat. The burly-tough oaf had better positioning so no matter what attempts Tommy made to work his way out, he could not get free. A wet gurgle escaped Tommy's mouth, a wad of frothy spit seeping from his lips. He was having trouble breathing, and struggling seemed to only make the choke tighter.

As his vision started to blur, just as his arms began to weaken, Nathan unexpectedly released his grip. Freed from the boy's vice-like arms, Tommy's legs gave way and he tumbled onto his hands and knees, trying to fill his lungs with much-needed air. As he regained control over his breathing he glanced over his shoulder, fully expecting to see Nathan laughing at his misfortune. What he saw was not the burly bully with the blond mop-top though – well, not entirely. This was something unexpected, quite different. Nathan was sitting in the grass, leaning back on one hand, rubbing the side of his obviously sore face with other. Looming like a great dark mountain over him, hands pulled into two massive fists, was Donald Rondage.

In a deep voice Donald growled, "Get the hell out of here before I tell your new buddies how you wet your bed until you were eight, Nathan."

The comment obviously conjured up a deep embarrassment hidden somewhere inside Nathan's belly. Nathan glanced at his cohorts to see if they had heard the comment. Furious at what

Donald had just said, and more than a little frightened by the much larger brute, Nathan crawled to his feet, leaped onto his bicycle and sped away with his thugs following close behind.

"Thanks" Tommy said between coughs, pulling himself up.

"Whatever…that was as much for me as it was for you, loser. A guy's out of town for a week and suddenly every idiot thinks they run the place. I needed to remind him who's the boss, plain and simple."

Turning away, Donald walked toward his bicycle, lying a few feet away in the grass. "I know that I've told you this before, but don't go thinking that this means anything, weirdo…because it doesn't. As far as I'm concerned that handshake never happened. It's just like they say about Vegas…what happens in Fillagrou stays in Fillagrou, am I right?"

Moments later Donald was pedaling down the street in the opposite direction. Before turning the corner and heading out of sight, he yelled back once more. "You're still a weirdo, Tommy!"

63. **NEW BEGINNINGS**

"Nicholas? Nicholas, you up there, buddy?" Ed Williamson called out from the foot of the stairs.

Getting no response, he sighed deeply and reluctantly made his way up the creaky stairwell, one hand sliding across the loose railing. The stairwell needed fixing. In fact the house in general needed work – needed a lot of work. Ed found that getting the things done that needed to get done simply was not as easy as it once was. Silently he wished that Nicky had answered him. It would have saved him a trip up the stairs which would, in turn, have saved him a series of painful knee aches later in the day. Over the last few years simply making his way upstairs felt more like scaling Mount Everest. Age was a funny thing that way – the more able you become to deal with life's challenges, the fewer opportunities you are given to be a part of them.

"Nicholas? Where are you, pal?" he asked again as he reached the peak of the mountain.

Leaning on a windowsill, looking out across the Williamsons' heavily wooded backyard, sat Nicky Jarvis. For over thirty minutes Nicky had remained in this position, completely lost in thought. The outside world had ceased to exist, long ago faded into a blurry softness both real and unreal. Foremost on his young mind had been the whereabouts of his older brother. When would Tommy arrive home? His detention had been over for some time. He should be back by now. Nicky worried about his brother a lot these days. The Williamsons were treating them good for the most part. Their life here was much simpler, much slower and vastly more stress- free. Despite the drastic change in their day-to-day lives, very little had changed about Tommy's general demeanor and Nicky could not figure out why.

Behind him, the door to his bedroom opened and Mr. Williamson poked his head inside. "Hey, pal...did you not hear me calling?"

Awakened from his trance, Nicky turned to Ed, shaking his head gently. "No, sorry," he answered quietly.

"No problem, bud. Hey, do you know if your brother is home yet?"

Again Nicky shook his head no.

Ed Williamson breathed deeply, removing his hat to wipe the sweat off his head which had accumulated after working an hour or so in the yard. Neither he nor Edna had been able to break through the older Jarvis' boy's armor. Nicky seemed to be transitioning to his life with them fairly easily - as well as could be expected, anyway. Tommy, though, proved stubborn, unwilling and possibly even incapable. Edna had often reminded him that it would take time, if it ever even happened at all. The boy had been through things that most children were lucky enough to avoid. The way Chris Jarvis had treated him - the things he did to him – were moments not easily forgotten. Some lives were harder to put behind than others. To ask either child to openly accept him and his wife without hesitation was asking a lot. In his heart Ed knew this, but the fact remained that he simply wanted to help.

The couple had lost their own son Jacob to cancer at such a young age – Tommy so resembled Jacob.

"Hey, I have to head into town to pick up a replacement part for the mower...wanna tag along?" Ed offered, quickly changing the subject.

Nicky turned his head to the window again. Still no sign of Tommy. His brother had recently taken to staying out late, sometimes not getting in until long after the sun had set. Nicky wondered if Tommy was visiting the tree fort. If he was, why had he not been invited to go along?

The boys barely spoke of the fort, or the stream, or anything that had happened in Tipoloo since returning. Despite an urge to sneak out of the house, dive into the stream, and visit his friends once again, Nicky had not gone back. Tommy had made him promise not to return, telling him that it was too dangerous and that King Walcott, Pleebo, Fellow and the others could handle things just fine without him. Nicky had grudgingly promised his brother that he would stay away; despite his urges, he was going to keep that promise.

"Well pal, what do you say? We've got to get going if we want to get back before dinner. Maybe we'll spot your brother on the way...bring him home with us."

Home – it sounded so strange. This was not his home. As nice as the Williamsons had been to him, as much as they tried to

379

make him feel welcome, they were not his family, even if a part of him wished that they were.

"Sure." Nicky answered with a slight smile, "What's Edna making for dinner tonight anyway?"

"Heck if I know bud...I've been married to her for thirty-eight years now and I don't think I've eaten the same thing twice. Whatever it is, I'm sure it'll be delicious. You like Edna's cooking, don't you?"

Nicky paused for a moment, trying to come up with an appropriate response, "Umm...ya, sure...it's great...it's interesting."

Ed's voice cracked struggling to hold back his laughter, "Interesting...ya, you know what, that's the perfect word for it...interesting." After ruffling Nicky's hair he added, "Head down to the truck, bud...I'll meet you there after I wash up."

Making his way down the stairs and stepping into the crisp mid-afternoon air, Nicky reminded himself once again that these people were not his family and that this place was not his home and never would be. None of that mattered to him, though. The fact that it might be gone tomorrow was all the more reason to enjoy it while it lasted.

64. ACCEPTANCE, PUNISHMENT AND CHANGE

Chris Jarvis had barely moved since his children were taken away from him a little over a month ago. It had been some time since he had been into work. He stopped answering the phone, stopped shaving and showering, and stopped doing anything that resembled living. Every time he stepped outside, he could feel the eyes of the neighborhood on him – furrowing into his soul and judging him. Eventually he had decided that it was simply less painful to stay inside, away from the steely cold stare of prying eyes and the achingly hot sting of judgmental thoughts. The bills were piling up, the electricity had been shut off for two days and he had probably been fired from his job. None of that mattered anymore.

In fact, very little mattered to Chris these days.

He had been ordered by the State to attend classes for abusive parents, as well as attending a separate class for alcoholism.

Alcoholism. What a stupid word –so pompous, so finite – as if it could ever fully explain everything that had happened to him.

He failed to last in either class after the first meeting. This fact was probably going to result in the permanent removal of his children. They would never be allowed to come home. He would never see them again. Maybe it was better this way – certainly better for Tommy and Nicky – maybe even for him. Without Megan at his side, he had proven himself incapable of being a father.

From the mantle across the room, her photo sometimes spoke to him, *"You're no good to anyone."*

It was all she ever said. Over, and over, and over again – it was all she ever said.

The first two weeks after the boys had been taken away seemed a blur to Chris. His memories were whitewashed, smeared with a hazy, smoky film erasing the details, leaving only an uncomfortable fuzziness in its wake. There was no telling just how many bottoms of how many bottles he had reached in those fourteen days. He knew it was enough because puking his guts out three to four times a day was the routine rather than the exception. He had failed in nearly every way a person could fail and his failure had been put on display for all to see. This was shame at its most potent, a shame so bright it was displayed with a million neon lights on top of the tallest building in the world. Branded forever, with no idea of what to do next, Chris returned to the only thing he knew, and it, too, had beaten him.

At some point, the bottle had stopped working. A tolerance to its wonderful numbing agent had been built. Over the course of a day Chris went from feeling too much to feeling nothing at all. The drastic whiplash of emotions left him useless and mentally bloodied, like the victim of a car wreck. Left alone, unable to feel, or move –only to think – was Chris Jarvis' ultimate nightmare. The days faded away, morphing into a single long, unending night. Shame and regret swallowed him entirely, shrouding his reality in something deep and black, extending to a point in the distance where time lost meaning. Sprawled out across his living room floor, in the dirt and grime that had accumulated over the past month, Chris Jarvis was a broken shell of the man he used to be.

From the mantle his wife still stared at him as she had for more hours than he wished to count. Many times he wanted to flip the picture frame over, smash it against the wall, or throw it into the fire. Despite the overwhelming urge, he never did. In his heart he knew that he needed her to see him, to watch him sink deeper, to tell him what a worthless nothing he had become. He needed her to stare at him, eyes overflowing with contempt and disgust. He had let her down – let his children down – let everyone down.

"You're no good to anyone, you bum, you lowlife."

She was right, every single word.

"You're no good to anyone and you'll never be again."

She had always been his moral center, his guiding light.

"How could you do it? You're no man at all; you're a child, Chris...a child."

She had always been there to pick him up, to dust him off and convince him to move forward.

"You have to make this right, Chris."

So strong – she had always been so strong.

"Make this right, Chris...fix it. Make this better, or I swear I'll never forgive you."

God he missed her.

Awkwardly stumbling to his feet, his gangly, malnourished body resembling something out of a horror film, Chris dragged himself to the picture window on the opposite end of the room.

Breathing heavily, a disgusting sheen of sweat dripping down his filthy face, he slowly opened the blinds. The light from the afternoon sun peeked through, hitting him in the eyes, making him squint. It patiently melted over him, seeping into every pore, warming his chilled flesh. Soon the entire living room was covered in its all-encompassing glow, bringing light once again to a home that had soaked in darkness for too many years. For the first time in his life, Chris Jarvis was truly ready to be judged. For the first time in a long time, he was ready to change.

65. FRIENDSHIP

Instead of returning to the Williamsons, Tommy walked across town, making the long trek to the tree fort. The entire trip took him almost thirty minutes but he did not care. It had been weeks since he was here, and maybe not so strangely, the lonely tree fort felt more like home than the Williamsons' house ever would. By the time he arrived, the sun was beginning to set off in the distance. A beautiful mix of orange and red hues lit the sky, giving it a bizarre otherworldly feel. Were it not for the absence of two extra suns, Tommy could swear he was looking at a Fillagrou sky rather than his own. Scaling the rickety wooden ladder, he pulled himself into the fort and lay sprawled across the creaky floor, breathing deeply. The air was crisp with the slightly salty freshness that comes just before the onset of night. Outside the fort he could hear the slow, controlled chaos of the patiently moving stream. The soft rustle of the autumn leaves tumbling to the ground joined with the sound of moving water, creating a wonderfully rhythmic hum that lulled him to sleep.

The police had confiscated most of the drawings but Tommy had drawn more, taping them on the wall the last time he had been at the fort. The two new ones softly flapped in the breeze. Their corners were already beginning to curl due to the moisture in the air. Winter was approaching. Soon the snow would fall, blanketing everything in a blindingly clean white. Tommy was looking forward to winter.

Closing his eyes and clearing his mind, Tommy tried to enjoy the silence. He wanted it to soak into his skin, to slip through the tiny pockets in his muscles and meld forever with the bone underneath.

A soft, girlish voice sliced through the comfortable nothingness, waking him unexpectedly and dragging him back to reality. "Tommy?"

Sitting up, he looked around wearily, spotting Staci's head sticking awkwardly through the hole in the floor. Her hair was pulled back tightly into a ponytail, her cheeks ever so slightly red from the night chill. The moment he saw her, Tommy smiled. It was not intentional, nor for any reason in particular – it just sort of happened.

"I knew I'd find you here sooner or later," she said, pulling herself through the floor. "I've been sneaking down here every night for over a week hoping to find you. My mom would blow a major gasket if she knew where I was. You're public enemy number one around the house these days…off limits, with threat of grounding."

"And just why did you want to see me so badly?" Tommy responded with a bit of a chuckle and a sly smile.

Instantly catching on to what he was implying, Staci's face turned a shade of deep red. Embarrassed, she rolled her eyes and a soft giggle escaped her mouth. She responded simply, "Shut up, Tommy Jarvis..."

Biting her lower lip, she turned away from him, making her way to the window "I just wanted to see you is all...you're my friend, you big dork."

Tommy stood and leisurely walked toward the window. Stepping beside her, he rested his elbows on the edge. Outside the sun was still visible over the distant row of trees

"So how are things with Old Lady Williamson?" Staci asked while leaning out the window, their shoulders just inches apart.

"It's alright, I guess. Nicky likes her, I think...Mr. Williamson, too. The house has a weird smell, though."

Staci chuckled, "Weird smell?"

"Ya, you know...old people smell. Like socks filled with cottage cheese or something."

Staci's chuckle changed into laughter and Tommy followed suit.

The giggling slowly faded away, as Staci playfully bumped into him. "You're a weirdo sometimes, Tommy."

"You're the second person to tell me that today."

Turning her gaze away from the setting sun, Staci glanced at the stream below. One could watch the movement of the water, with all its tiny variations, for hours and never once see it repeat itself. Beyond the dark murky water lay a whole other world. Despite having been there, despite having seen and felt its reality firsthand, the very idea that such a thing could exist still seemed unbelievable to her.

After a long silence, she decided to say what she imagined both of them were thinking. "Do you think we'll ever see any of them again?"

Tommy paused before answering. He, too, had been staring deeply into the murky stream. He was not looking at it so much as trying to look through it – wishing for just one more glimpse into that other amazing world. "Ya...I'm positive that we will."

"How can you be so sure?"

"The prophecy. When the Elder had told us the story, he said that five would arrive and four would return. We all came back. It's not over yet."

Tommy's comment sent a flicker of fear scraping across Staci's spine like nails on a chalkboard. "Ya, but...I mean, those are just words...I mean, who knows what they mean, right?"

Tommy sensed the resistance in her voice, recognizing the twinge of fear. As if her terror was somehow palpable, it wedged itself in-between them, pushing her away. Tommy did not want her further away – quite the opposite in fact - and because of this he changed the subject. "Ya...sure...they're just words...who knows...I'm sure everything will be fine."

Playfully he bumped into Staci, trying whatever he could to bring a smile to her face . "Besides, could you imagine how much you'd get grounded if you let your weirdo neighbor drag you to another world again? You'd miss all of summer vacation."

Staci chuckled half-heartedly, deciding not to think about the subject any further.

Off in the distance, the sun had fully dropped out of sight. Only the incredible glow remained, rising up into the sky, causing the underside of the clouds to glow a hauntingly beautiful magenta. Both children stared at it with slight, soft grins. The warmth of the sun's light and the coolness of the gentle breeze massaged their skin with a temperature so perfect that they wished they could crawl inside and live there forever.

If ever there had been a perfect moment in their young lives, this was it.

Through the corner of her eye, Staci coyly glanced at Tommy. It had been so long since she had seen him smile. He had such a nice smile. Timidly her fingers walked across the edge of the windowsill like a pair of tiny legs; at last coming to a stop, her hand rested gently on top of his.

"I missed you, Tommy," she whispered, still gazing off into the clouds.

The warmth of her hand felt wonderful on his skin - soothing, and comforting, as if this was exactly where it was meant to be all along.

"I missed you too."

66. THE TYRANT KING

His body was enormous. Every limb was as thick as a tree trunk, every muscle seemed chiseled out of stone or molded from super-heated steel. His skin was tight and leathery, showing the kind of wear that could only have come from a lifetime spent treading the waters of war and power. A silver-gray beard hung from his chin, at least two feet in length, pulled into a finely manicured point by three evenly spaced gold rings. The armor adorning his bulky mass was finely decorated, carved by twenty of the finest Ochan artists over the course of three painstaking years. After completing the design, the artisans had been murdered to ensure its originality. Between his thick, scaled fingers, he held a scrap of filthy, ripped fabric that once had belonged to his son. He had sent a select group of his finest soldiers to the ruins of the Fillagrou fortress two weeks ago to retrieve the body of his only offspring.

They had returned with a mass that was barely recognizable.

Behind him, a fire large enough to be seen through all of Ocha, crackled and popped. Its dark, brownish-black smoke rose into the afternoon sky as the flames slowly ate away the remains of Prince Valkea's corpse. With every breath, the massive chest of the tyrant King heaved, stoking the flames of anger burning within his belly. For the most part, his son had been a failure – too quick to react, too weak-willed – just barely able to avoid bringing shame to the family name. His defeat and untimely death was a disgrace.

Be that as it may, worthless or not, he remained his son. Even in death, this would never change.

The one true heir to the throne had been murdered, his fortress destroyed and his corpse left in a state hardly befitting one of royal blood. If ever an act called for swift, immediate vengeance, this was it.

As sure as day turned to night, and night back to day, the great tyrant King would see to it that someone paid for the murder of his child. The blood of each and every creature involved in this heinous act would not only be spilled, but sprayed. Their deaths would be drawn out to a point so that the murderers would willingly embrace death. Their family, their friends and the friends of their friends would suffer equally. Not a single solitary creature would be spared.

From behind him, the voice of General Thrax cut the deafening silence. "I beg your pardon, Sire…shall I prepare your forces?"

The King's answer came swiftly, "No."

The seriousness in his tone caused the General to meekly back away.

"We will not leap blindly into war with creatures wielding such power. Such an act would be foolish. No, we will study them…we will learn their weaknesses and when the proper plan of attack has been made, we will descend upon them with the full might of the Ochan nation. My son's vengeance will not be found through blind rage, but I assure you General Thrax…it will be found."

Unlike his son, the tyrant King understood fully the forces that had been set in motion. Unlike his son, he believed in prophecies and acknowledged the necessity of magic. Unlike his son, he would prepare himself for every possibility. If this signaled the end of the great Ochan nation, he would not go blindly into the darkness. He would not go without a fight. If this was to be the end of all things, he would take as many of his enemies with him into death.

What sort of father would he be if he did anything less

ABOUT THE AUTHOR

Steven Novak was born and raised in Chicago, Illinois. He attended the Columbus College of Art and Design in Columbus, Ohio and currently resides in southern California with his wife of ten years.

When Steve isn't writing, he works as a freelance illustrator and endeavors to solve the mysteries of the universe. Unfortunately for him, the universe is a vast and complicated thing; he will most likely fail and decide to order pizza, instead. He has a far better grasp on the mysterious world of cheesy toppings. His work can be found at www.novakillustration.com.